KENT KNOWLTON

WOLF SUREBLADE

AMERICAN KNIGHT

WIDER PERSPECTIVES PUBLISHING ~ HAMPTON ROADS, VA ~ 2020

Wolf Sureblade
American Knight

Kent Knowlton

Cover art provided by Leila Kirkconnell
Editing services provided by Melissa Watkins Starr, she left us in 2020.

© Knowlton, Hampton Roads, Va, 2020
ISBN: 978-1-952773-28-0

Wider Perspective Publishing, HRACandWPP@outlook.com

Dedication

For Myra,

Love of my life, my beloved wife, whose contributions to her family, friends, and profession enhanced many lives over our four decades together; and, for whom this series was started before her passing several years ago.

She remains my inspiration.

Contents

Chapter 1 ~ A Boy's Story

Fourteen-year-old Caleb trembled as he sat alone in the jail cell in Summit Point, Montana, fearful of what would happen next. Whatever happened, he knew it would be bad. The deputy sheriff would soon return to send him back to the foster home—or worse. He knew stealing was bad, very bad, but he'd thought he didn't have a choice. He had spent his last few dollars on food three days ago, and, this morning, he'd been so hungry he'd stolen a couple of sandwiches from the deli case at a local curb market. When he'd been caught, he'd wished he could just sink into the pavement. As Caleb reflected on his situation, he heard the deputy sheriff's boot pounding the corridor.

The deputy sheriff had brown hair and smooth skin, and he was thin. Caleb doubted the guy had even hit thirty. The tall man opened the cell and said, "Come on. It's time for us to have a talk." Seeing no other choice, Caleb got up, followed him to his office, and took the chair next to the desk. A 2006 calendar from a local drug store hung on the wall behind the desk, and Caleb saw that no one had torn off the April page, though it was mid-May.

"What's your name?" the deputy sheriff asked.

Caleb had been questioned by the police before, so he played it tough and kept quiet. He focused his attention on a wall clock over the deputy sheriff's head. The second hand spun around for nearly a minute.

"You're not helping your situation, you know."

Still, Caleb said nothing.

"You know that if I don't return you to your home, I'll have to call the state juvenile authorities."

Caleb crossed his arms and kept quiet.

"The store owner is furious. He wants to slam you in jail."

"Better that than being in a foster home," Caleb snapped.

"So you do talk. Hi, my name is Ben, and you can call me Ben." The deputy sheriff smiled and extended his right hand to shake, but Caleb kept his arms crossed. "Are you hungry? I am."

Caleb said nothing, but Ben picked up the phone, called a Chinese restaurant, and ordered two meals. "Life is always better when you're full," he said.

"So how did you wind up in our fair town?" Ben asked, while they waited for the food.

"I hitchhiked from Nolen's Butte, caught a ride in a battered pickup with some creepy, short guy with a big nose. After I got in, I saw he had a gun, and I got scared. I thought he might try to kidnap me or something. When he stopped to get gas, I said I had to use the bathroom, which was at the back of the building. Then I ran behind the buildings along Main Street, while the man was pumped gas, and ducked into that curb market." Caleb realized he was chattering like a three-year-old and shut up.

"He may have been harmless," Ben offered, "but better safe than sorry. I suppose you know it's dangerous to hitchhike. Where were you heading?"

"Nowhere in particular."

The deliveryman arrived, and Ben paid him, opened the bag, and pulled out several containers of food, drinks, and chopsticks. He slid two containers and a drink across the table to Caleb. Then Ben started eating his meal with the chopsticks.

The smell of chicken with Chinese vegetables rose in the air, making Caleb's mouth water, but he made no move to eat until Ben had half-finished his meal. When he couldn't stand it any longer, he opened up his container and started to reach in with his fingers, but Ben stopped him by clearing his throat and passed him a plastic fork. Caleb took a bite of food and asked, "Do you hate me, too? Everybody hates me."

"No, I think you're a nice kid who has had it real bad. Why did you run away from your foster home?"

Caleb looked down and said, "I was afraid. They were going to beat me up again."

"Guys at school?"

Caleb nodded and said, "I tried to fight them, but they always ganged up on me. And I'm the one who gets in trouble."

"What about your foster parents, didn't they help you?

Caleb shrugged, staring at his hands. "No, they didn't believe me. They wouldn't do anything about it."

Did they punish you?"

"No, they just ignored me when I complained about it. They said I just made it up."

"So where did you hide?"

Surprised, Caleb looked up. "In the library. How did you know?"

"I knew another boy with the same problems." The deputy sheriff paused and smiled. "He eventually solved them."

Caleb stared at the man a long minute, and then the realization hit him. "It was you, wasn't it?"

"Yes." The deputy sheriff smiled again and said, "I'm an orphan."

Just when Caleb was beginning to relax a bit, he thought of something that made him tense up. "How do I know you aren't lying?"

"I don't have a reason to lie. I believe you aren't lying. I think you'd rather go to jail than lie."

"I never get away with lying. It just makes things worse." Caleb looked down and sighed. "Jail's better than being beat up."

"Fighting is never good. Getting beat up is never good. Running away is never good. Sometimes you don't have a choice, but you can't let people keep beating on you."

"How do I stop it?" Caleb asked.

"I can't give you a good answer to that." Ben looked Caleb directly in the eye and said, "I feel the answer you need may come sooner than you think."

"You're not going to tell me, are you?" Caleb asked, feeling bitterness and disappointment.

"The only thing I know to tell you is that you have to learn to defend yourself. You can't afford to let yourself be beat up."

Caleb started to ask how, but the deputy held up a hand and said, "You're still in big trouble. I'll have to put you in the jail cell while I try to fix this problem you have."

"And then you're going to call the juvenile authorities, aren't you?" Caleb asked, while looking at his feet.

The deputy sheriff sighed and said, "I have to." He put Caleb in the cell and left the office. Caleb spent a long hour stewing over the situation. When the deputy sheriff returned, he opened the cell. "It seems your name is Caleb," he said, as he led him back to the office.

As soon as he entered the office, Caleb noticed the front door was ajar. Another man stood in the middle of the room—a very tall, broad-shouldered man with a large knife tucked in his belt. The man looked at him with hard-set eyes. Caleb spooked and bolted out the door.

The sun shone outside, but before Caleb could get his eyes adjusted to the light, he crashed into a wall of flesh, bounced back a step, and looked up. A massive, spotted gray horse stared down at him.

Caleb looked up and saw a young, redheaded girl looking down over the horse's shoulder. "She's a Percheron. She's a real beauty, isn't she?"

"She's a monster!" Caleb yelled.

A hand on Caleb's shoulder turned him around. The big man looked down at him and said, "You'd better come back inside." Caleb followed him back into the office and sat in the chair in front of the desk. The man pulled another chair up close to Caleb and sat down.

"I've made the call to the state juvenile authorities," the deputy sheriff said. "It seems they know about you, Caleb. Someone must have it in for you. You have quite a long record of running away from foster homes. They want to send you to the juvenile center. Do you understand what that means? It means no foster homes, no running away, and no freedom. It means you could be behind walls until you're eighteen. Not just overnight."

"I'll escape," Caleb snapped, but he began to tremble and clenched his hands into fists, hoping the men didn't notice his white knuckles.

The deputy sheriff said, "I doubt it. The juvenile center is like a prison. Kids just don't escape from there. The state is sending a car down here to pick you up. It should be here within an hour, maybe sooner. The report says you're an orphan. Do you remember your real parents?"

Caleb looked down at his lap and mumbled, "No, I was a baby when they died. I cried a lot, and nobody would adopt me. Nobody will adopt me now."

"You have no family, no other relatives?"

Caleb mumbled, "No."

"Foster homes don't seem to work for you, and your prospects of being adopted are slim at best. Unfortunately, the folks at the juvenile center think they're well-equipped to handle you."

Caleb's shoulders twitched. He blurted out, "I can't go there. I'll die! I'm too small. There are gangs there. They beat up kids like me. Just let me go. I'll leave. You'll never see me again."

"I can't do that," Ben replied softly. "It would be wrong for me to turn you out like that. If it means anything to you, I don't think you should go to the juvenile center. You're a good kid. You didn't do anything to deserve this. Sure, you stole a couple of sandwiches, but feeding yourself is just basic survival. It's just not my decision." He paused a moment and said, "However, I can give you another choice, one the juvenile authorities don't like, if you'll take it."

"What's that?" Caleb asked, almost pleading.

"Go with Raven here." The deputy pointed at the large man sitting next to him. "If you leave with him, the juvenile authorities can't touch you, at least not for a while."

Caleb looked up at the big man and asked, "Who is he?"

The deputy sheriff answered, "He's called Raven. He's a friend of mine, and he's just now leaving town. I guarantee you'll do better with him than with the state."

Caleb took a closer look at the man. He had huge hands. He wore a dark green jacket and trousers with knee-high, soft, leather boots. The man's eyes spooked him; they were a flinty gray, hard set in a weathered face. He looked to be very tough and ready for a fight.

Raven said, "I can promise you that you won't be locked up. You won't go hungry, and you won't be beaten or abused. There'll be some hard work involved, but I think you can handle it. However, if you don't like it, I'll bring you back here."

"Why should I go with you?" Caleb demanded. "You're just going to cut me up with that knife. How do I know you'll bring me back here? Besides, what kind of name is Raven? It sounds like a girl's name."

"It's just what I'm called." Raven paused a moment before saying, "I can promise you the adventure of a lifetime. You'll get a chance to do things you never imagined possible. For a start, you'll learn to ride horses. What you can and will do is up to you. It seems to me to be much better than your other choice."

Caleb looked down at his feet and considered this for a long minute. For some reason, he believed the man. The hard work part scared him, but the adventure part drew him in. He had always dreamed of escaping to a different world. Ever since he had discovered adventure books in the library, he had wanted a different life. He looked at Raven and then at Ben and asked, "Why are you doing this?"

The deputy smiled. "Like I told you, you remind me of myself when I was young. I don't want you to go to the juvenile center. I think you can do better if you have a chance. If you continue the way you're headed, I think you'll have a bleak life. Living on the street or in the juvenile hall is an invitation to gang violence. Raven helped me once, and I'll bet he could help you. He didn't tell you, but the hard part is that he'll make you keep up with your schoolwork."

"Do I have a choice?"

"Yes, of course you have a choice. Raven is a fair and good man. And he'll teach you how to defend yourself against bullies. His word is gold, and he'll do right by you. In the juvenile center, who knows what'll happen to you? I think you'll do much better with him. I think you'll find it interesting and fun." Ben leaned forward, looked Caleb in the eye, and asked, "Do you want to keep running away like you're doing now?"

Caleb considered it a long minute. This had to be better than prison. He could always escape. He said, "Okay, I'll go with Raven."

"Good," Ben said. "You'd better be going because there isn't much time before the state car gets here. I'll see what I can do to placate the store manager. I'm a good friend of his son." Raven and the deputy signed some papers. Then they all stood up, and Raven said, "Let me introduce you to Amara."

Raven led Caleb outside to meet the redheaded girl, who now stood on the ground. She held the reins to four horses. Raven told Caleb, "This is Amara." Turning to her, he said, "This is Caleb." Amara nodded and said, "I prefer to be called Red."

Caleb thought Red was a year or two older than he was, and she was a little bit taller. She extended her right hand, which was small and calloused, took his hand, and shook it with an iron grip. She dressed similar to Raven, but she also sported a gray, hooded cloak with her curly, copper hair spilling out, brilliant in the morning sun.

"Why don't you like to be called Amara?" Caleb asked.

A small storm passed over her face. "Just call me Red, and we'll get along," she snapped. Then, in a calmer voice, she said, "Here, let me introduce you to Easy Rider." She passed the leads of three horses to Raven and led out a brown horse with the white legs that was saddled and loaded with large bags. "You'll ride him. He's a gelding and quite gentle."

"But I've never ridden a horse," Caleb said.

Red smirked and said, "Well, you could walk, but I wouldn't suggest doing that. We have a long way to go. Besides it's easy."

He suddenly got a cold feeling in his stomach about the whole adventure. "I don't know," he said.

"You could still stay with the deputy," Raven said. "You don't have to come with us."

Caleb had heard enough. Just the thought of the juvenile center made him shudder. He walked over to Red and whispered, "How do I get on him?"

She smiled and showed him how to get onto the horse by first mounting the horse herself. She dismounted and had Caleb place his foot in the stirrup, grab the saddle, stand up on the stirrup, and swing his other leg over the saddle all in one motion.

Red kept the reins, tied a lead to them, and then she mounted the Percheron. She turned to Caleb and said, "It's easy to sit on the horse. Don't kick or squeeze with your legs. It'll confuse him, and he might try to run away with you."

Raven tied the brown packhorse's leader to his own black horse's saddle and mounted.

Ben looked up at Raven and said, "You'd better hurry up. The state car will be here soon. I can't keep them from taking him if they show up. But before you go, I have something for Caleb." He stepped into his office and came out with a heavy coat with a deputy sheriff's badge on it. He pulled the badge off, handed the coat up to Caleb, and said, "You'll need this."

Caleb took the coat and thanked him, not wanting to appear ungrateful. He put the coat on despite it being too large and too warm.

Raven clucked his horse to a walk and turned it down a side street. Red followed on the Percheron with Caleb in tow. He found it easy to sit on the horse just like Red had said. He had only the saddle horn to hold onto, but he felt relatively safe.

They reached the edge of town, started up a large, grassy hill, and soon entered a line of trees. "Watch your head or a branch will knock you off," Red remarked looking back at Caleb. He thought, *She ought to watch out herself, sitting on the huge horse.* They continued ascending through the trees, not seeming to follow any marked path.

When they reached the top of the hill, they entered a large clearing in the woods. "We're going up there," Red said, pointing up at several mountains in the distance.

Caleb was taken aback by the immensity of the mountains, which didn't look that far away. "How long will it take to get there?"

"About a day and a half, then we go through the pass between those two peaks." She indicated two of the closer mountains. "Then it's one more day."

Caleb tried to figure the distance just in case he decided to escape. "How far is that?"

"Farther than you can walk in a week. It's all rough, up and down, switchbacks and rivers."

"Where will we stay tonight?"

"We'll camp out in the open. Camping is fun, but sometimes things don't go as expected, and you wake up with a wolf in your bedroll." Caleb almost gasped, but she grinned and winked at him, and he realized that she had played with him. "Just kidding, but you get used to sleeping outside. Besides I've never seen a wolf in these parts."

They continued past the clearing, going back into the woods and following a western course up and down hills until they descended into a forested valley. The trees were enormous and spaced well apart. The going was easy, with very little undergrowth to slow them down, the ground, almost level and soft. The horses' breathing and hoof beats were the only sounds.

They soon came to a stream, and Raven stopped to water the horses. Red pulled three packets from the Percheron's saddlebags and gave one packet to Raven, who took it, went over to a large rock, and sat down to eat. She then gave a packet to Caleb and motioned for him to follow her.

They went upstream about fifty yards, found a log to sit on, and started to eat their dried fruit, which tasted surprisingly good. It consisted of dried apples, pears, and raisins dusted with cinnamon and some other spices. "Do you like it?" Red asked. "I made it myself. Raven taught me how."

"Yeah, it's pretty good, if you're into this sort of stuff."

Red grimaced and said, "You'll eat plenty of dried fruit and vegetables in the next few months. You'll appreciate the variety soon enough."

Caleb looked in the direction of Raven and said, "He doesn't talk much does he?"

"No, but when he does, it's important. He teaches by example. Pay attention to what he does." She brought up a soft, leather water skin and offered him a drink. Caleb suddenly realized how thirsty he was. He took several big gulps before he handed it back to her, and then she took a large swallow.

Caleb asked, "Why is he called Raven?"

Red chuckled. "That's easy. He's called Raven because he's a tracker. He finds people. Ravens are good at finding things. He received the name when he became a knight."

Caleb stared at Red in disbelief. "A Knight? There are no knights. You're joking, right?"

Red crossed her arms and gave him a challenging stare. "He's a knight. You'll see."

Caleb also crossed his arms. "I don't believe you."

Red shrugged and looked darkly at him. "Look, I'm not going to waste my breath. Wait and see."

Something about her manner said not to challenge her. "Okay, have it your way. He's a knight." Then Caleb asked, "Where are we going?"

Red's eyes lit up. She said, "We're going up to the high country, to the valley where we'll camp during the summer."

Caleb asked, "What do you do there?"

"We ride a lot, take care of the horses, learn self-defense, and archery.

"I mean what do you do for fun?"

Red laughed, "When the day's work is over, I get to ride Mary a lot. There's always something fun to do. Besides, most of the work is easy."

"Just us? All summer?"

"Oh, heavens no! Most everybody will be there." She spread out her arms to indicate a lot of people. "And yes, all summer. Isn't it magnificent?"

Caleb gulped, not sure he wanted the answer, and asked, "Who's everybody?"

"Just about the whole school."

"School?"

Red looked perplexed and said, "Well, yes. It's more like a summer school."

All of a sudden, it came crashing down on him, his worst nightmare. School, the place he hated the most. It was the reason he'd run away this last time. He'd been bullied and beaten, and his lunch money had been stolen. Boys would trip him in the halls, and girls would laugh at him. There had been no help from his teachers or foster parents. Now he was going to a school he couldn't escape from. He exclaimed, "I hate school!"

"Why?"

"Because."

"Because what?"

Caleb ground his teeth. "Just because."

Red was quiet for a minute, but then she sighed and said, "You must have your reasons. I won't ask again, but I swear to you this school is like no other. This school is really good. The classwork is hard, but we have a lot of fun afterward."

Caleb asked, "What do you do there?"

"We ride a lot and take care of the horses, learn self-defense, and archery."

"I mean what do you do for fun?"

Red laughed. "When the day's work is over, we get to ride the horses for fun, play horse games, and other silly stuff. There's always something to do. Besides most of the work is fun."

Some music came through the trees. Red pulled a small fife from under her cloak, signaled back by playing a similar tune, and said, "Raven is calling us. It's time to get going." They returned to the horses, which were grazing by the stream.

Raven went over to the packhorse and retrieved something out of its saddlebags. Walking over to Red, he whispered in her ear. She nodded pulled some clothes out of one of the saddlebags, and handed them to him. Raven looked at Caleb and said, "Why don't you come with me? You need to do something."

Caleb decided it must be important, so he followed Raven downstream. When they were out of sight of the horses, Raven said, "Take off your coat."

"What?"

"Take off your coat."

"What? No."

Raven furrowed his eyebrows and repeated in a more stern voice, "Take off that coat, or I'll take it off for you."

That got Caleb's attention. He opened his eyes wide, but slipped the coat off and handed it to the Raven, who tossed it aside. "Now what?"

"Here are some clean clothes. Amara is loaning you one of her uniforms. You're going to take a bath"

Caleb yelled, "No, no way! Besides, I don't know you!"

"Before you get back to the horses, you're going to wash up, both you and your clothes. You smell like a goat."

"No!"

"Suit yourself." Raven grabbed Caleb by his belt and shoulder, lifted him, and tossed him into the stream. He landed with a large splash before coming up, struggling for breath. The shock of the freezing water seized up his muscles, and he couldn't speak.

Raven reached into his pocket, pulled out a bar of soap, and held it out to him. "I'm going back to the horses. Wash everything, especially where the sun doesn't shine. Then wash those clothes and throw them on the bank. When you're clean, get dressed and come back to the horses. We'll be waiting on you." He turned, climbed the bank, and walked upstream.

Caleb pulled his sweater off and started scrubbing it with the soap. He tossed it on a rock then started with the rest of his clothes. He managed to clean his clothes and himself while freezing in the process. He then climbed out of the stream and put on the shirt and trousers Raven had left for him. Then he slipped on the deputy's coat. He walked upstream to where Raven and Red were waiting, his sneakers squishing water.

Chapter 2 ~ A Wolf's Story

Still shivering from his forced bath in the mountain stream, Caleb reached the riders where Red held out her boots. "Here, put these on. You need them."

He said, "I've got my shoes."

"They're wet and need to dry."

Smarting from the indignity of wearing her spare uniform, he said, "But you're barefoot. I can't do that."

"Nonsense, I'm tough. I run barefoot. Do it."

Caleb gave her a dirty look, but pulled them on.

Raven spread Caleb's wet clothes over the back of the packhorse to dry. He said to Red, "It's time to teach him to ride a horse for real."

The girl held Easy Rider's reins while Caleb mounted up. He almost went over the other side of the horse, panicked, and squeezed his legs hard to keep from falling. The horse reared up, and Red dodged its hoofs as she tried to regain control. Caleb held onto the saddle horn to keep from hitting the ground as he slid out of the saddle as Red subdued her horse.

Caleb said, "You're trying to kill me!"

Red asked, "Are you ready to get back on?"

"What!"

"Are you afraid? Are you ready to get back on the horse? He spooked because you did something wrong. I'm going to teach you to ride."

Caleb took several deep breaths and said, "I'm not afraid," though he was. "Okay, what do I do?"

Red made him remount Easy Rider, and she hopped into the saddle behind him, still holding onto the horse's reins. She reached around him and taught him the basics of riding, and, in a short time, he gained enough skill to follow the other horses on his own. Red remounted Mary, and directed Caleb to go ahead of her and follow the packhorse.

They rode several more hours, and crossed several streams, taking time to tend the horses. At one break, Caleb asked Raven about using the bathroom. The man handed him a small folding shovel and instructed him on the proper way to do his business in the woods.

Caleb walked down a ravine until he found a suitable location, dug a shallow hole, and did his business. As he finished, he heard a whimpering sound from further down the ravine, and the hair stood on the back of his neck.

The plaintive sound compelled him, and he edged further down the ravine to investigate. Rounding a tree, he confronted a large wolf with its leg caught in a trap. Caleb tried to turn and run, but his legs proved too heavy to move. The wolf growled, its head low, and then it leaped towards him but yelped as it fell, dragged down by the chained trap. It lay whimpering from its injury before sitting up.

Caleb and the wolf stared at each other a long time before it lowered its eyes. It licked at the bleeding leg a couple of times and whined. Caleb shivered. He advanced towards the wolf and knelt in front of it, his arms tight at his sides. The great wolf sniffed his neck, but otherwise didn't move. He reached out and put his hands on the springs of the trap, trying not to cause further pain to the wolf. It whimpered.

He closed his eyes and said, "Please understand me." He pressed hard on the springs, allowing the trap jaws to fall open. Free, the wolf jumped with a yelp and sprinted up the slope to vanish among the trees. Caleb released the springs, letting the trap snap close.

After his heart calmed down, Caleb walked back up to the horses, packed the shovel away, and mounted Easy Rider, but he said nothing about the incident. They started up a slope, and the horses complained as they fought their way up the rocky trail. Well above the trees, Caleb had a clear view of the whole valley with its forests and open fields. The temperature had dropped, and the deputy sheriff's coat proved good armor against the biting wind. They reached a flat at the top of the slope where they rested and watered the horses. Then they crossed the gap and descended into a small valley.

They soon reached the edge of a clearing where the Raven ordered camp. As they dismounted, Caleb almost fell down, his rubbery legs refusing to support him.

Red chuckled and said, "I told you you're soft."

After the horses were unloaded and hobbled, Red laid out her bedroll and then went about collecting twigs and sticks, which she piled into a small mound, and Caleb helped without being asked. With the back edge of her knife, Red started to scrape one of the sticks until she had a palm full of hair like shavings. She put these under one edge of the mound, walked over to the pile of supplies, and pulled out a bow and a quiver of arrows, taking a small coil of string from a pocket inside her coat. She used it to string her bow.

She took two long arrows from her quiver. The heads of the arrows were the real thing—tiny, barbed flint.

Red looked at Caleb with a grin and said, "Let's go hunt dinner." After she cautioned him to be quiet and stay behind her, they walked out of the clearing. At a small meadow, she stopped, placed one arrow on the bow, brought it up, drew it to full extension, and stood still.

The arrow let loose with a sharp twap, and a rabbit exploded up into the air and fell back down, dead before it hit the ground. Before Caleb could react in surprise, the second arrow let loose from her bow, and a second rabbit jumped. This one didn't die, but hopped away.

Red dropped her bow, ran, and jumped on the wounded rabbit. She landed with her arms outstretched, her knife nailing it to the ground. She stood up, holding the bloody rabbit on the knife, and gave Caleb a wicked grin.

Pulling the knife out, she then retrieved the first rabbit, walked over to a large rock, and laid out the carcasses. She removed the arrows intact. Then she sliced each rabbit down the length of its belly, cleaned out the bloody guts, and then skinned each one.

They walked back to camp where Red used water from her water skin to clean the rabbits, their skins, and her hands.

"Is there anything you don't do?" Caleb asked.

"I don't know," she answered, holding up the skinned rabbits. "Let's cook dinner." She laid the rabbits down on a cloth, took a small packet from her saddlebag, poured some powder onto her palm, and rubbed it into the flesh of the rabbits.

She opened a small tin can and pulled a piece of charred cloth to put under the wood tender she had prepared earlier. Using a small piece of flint and the back of her knife blade, she struck a small shower of sparks, which landed on the cloth. It started a tiny glow, and by puffing on it, she lit a small flame, which she fed with the fine shavings and sticks.

She sharpened the ends of two long sticks of green wood, skewered the rabbits and propped them over the fire. Full darkness set in, and they relaxed to watch the rabbits cook.

Raven walked out of the woods with his longbow and arrows and, with a wry grin, said, "I see you had good hunting. We have company; a wolf has been shadowing us, and I think it's been wounded. We'll worry about it later for the rabbit smells tasty, and I'm hungry."

Using their fingers to pull the meat off the bones, Caleb and Red split the larger rabbit while Raven ate the smaller one, adding dried apples, raisins, and hot tea. Afterwards, Red and the Raven entertained Caleb with tunes on their fifes. Then Raven told them a long ghost story about a boy who lost himself in the woods never to be seen again and who could often be heard crying out for his friends on cold, dark nights.

~

In the morning, Caleb opened his eyes to find Red and Raven staring at him. Stiffness and soreness filled his body. "Why are you looking at me?" he asked, still sleepy.

"I was joking yesterday when I said you'd wake up with a wolf in your bedroll," Red said.

"So?"

"Well, look."

Caleb saw he had his arm draped over something furry. He jerked his arm away, and watched as the wolf scrambled to its feet and limped off into the trees.

Caleb struggled out of his bedroll and tried to get to his feet. As he made his sore legs work, he said, "It could have killed me!"

"I doubt it," Raven said. "He's injured and can't catch food, so he's come here looking for some. He didn't have the strength to leave last night, and just lay down beside you. He must like you. Besides, wolves just don't eat people."

Caleb said, "But why me?"

Raven shrugged his shoulders, "I've heard of wild wolves befriending people before. Why you? I suspect he just sees you as, well, safe."

Caleb didn't mention rescuing the wolf from the trap. They broke camp, and Caleb helped Red with the chores. They packed the saddlebags and cleaned up with Caleb noting everything Red did. They rode across the small valley and started up the slope on foot, leading the horses. During the slow climb, the packhorse balked a lot before they reached the gap in the high pass and found some level ground. There, they stopped to water the horses and ate a quick lunch.

By this time, Caleb's legs were again sore, his ears, cold, and he felt as if his lungs would explode. In the worst pain of his life, he knew complaining would be of no use, and the way down involved more walking. Red surprised him by boosting him up onto Mary, who looked back at him and snorted. The horse had warmed to him and didn't try to bite. Red also gave him warm mittens made from rabbit skins with the fur on the inside. They reached the valley floor and started across.

When they reached a stream, Raven called a stop to camp for the night. They ate fruit and dried meat, but they were unable to find rabbit. With everyone dead tired, this camp didn't have the good feeling of the previous night's camp.

~

After everyone went to sleep, Caleb dreamed that a wet tongue licked his nose and face. He jerked his hand up to fend off the wolf. The animal backed up, and he crawled out of his bedroll. He stood and started to run, looked back, and saw the wolf running behind him. He tried running harder, but the wolf kept pace with him.

With his lungs about to burst, Caleb broke through an opening in the trees. A short man with a big nose and a gun stood in front of him. He looked back one more time and saw the leaping wolf. He felt its paws on his back and slammed to the ground as the man fired the gun.

Caleb tried moving, but the wolf snarled. Then the wolf bounded forward to attack the man, who screamed before he vanished. Then the beast returned to him and licked his face. Blood soaked its side; it had taken the bullet meant for Caleb. Then Caleb's eyes jerked open to stare at the glowing remains of the campfire.

~

In the morning when Caleb awoke, the wolf lay curled up next to his bedroll. As soon as he stirred, the wolf stood up and trotted off into the brush at the edge of the woods, where it disappeared. Red and the Raven were already packing up their saddlebags, ignoring the wolf. In the chill they broke camp, saddled the horses as fast as they could, and started their ride west across the valley. After an hour, the sun arose, and the woods started to look different. The undergrowth and the ground had been cleared of dead wood.

They soon arrived at a large clearing planted with a vegetable garden. Beyond the garden, a small cabin rested with a giant of a woman standing at the doorway. Raven rode right up to the cabin, dismounted, and gave the woman a warm hug.

"It's about time you arrived. I've listened to you clump across the valley for the last hour," she said, smiling, "and you're late."

"We had a little diversion," Raven replied, pointing at Caleb. "He had a bit of trouble, so we took our time getting here."

The woman beckoned to Caleb, who had already dismounted, and he walked over to her. Her weathered face smiled at him, and, with a rugged voice, she said, "You're new to horses, Caleb. It'll get better—the soreness I mean. You'll get used to the horses soon enough. Be good to animals because one is going to save your life." She laughed, bent over, gave him a bear hug, and said, "Hello, my name is Maude."

Caleb wondered, *How did she know my name?*

Maude turned to give Red a bear hug, and she appeared to be just as crushed as Caleb had been.

"What can we do for you, Maude?" Raven asked, while unstrapping the largest load on the packhorse.

Her eyes twinkled, and she said, "Well, since you're volunteering, I could use some roof repairs. I've made some tea, and the cookies will be ready soon."

Raven puffed up his chest. "Well, we'd better get to work." He directed Red to set up the ladder. He fetched the tools, cedar shingles, and nails from the shed behind the cabin. He then ordered Caleb to help Maude with the supplies while he and Red started to work on the roof.

Caleb and the woman carried the bundles into her one-room cottage and placed them on the bed. She invited Caleb to go for a walk with her to fetch wood for the stove and asked, "You haven't been to this school before, have you?"

"No, ma'am."

She said, "They're the nicest bunch of people you'll ever meet, always helping out."

Caleb stopped, looked up at her, and said, "You went to this school?"

She threw her head back and laughed. "Nah, they just come by here once in a while to bring me my supplies. I want to talk about you."

"Me, why me?"

"You have a big future in front of you. Grab it all. Take everything they give you, and make it work for you. Raven's a great guy. Listen to him. They don't come any better."

"Who is he?" Caleb asked, somewhat miffed that he still didn't know anything about the man.

"He's a teacher." She paused and said, "And he saved my life once."

"Oh."

Maude said, "Like I said, you're destined for great things. You'll save lives if you make it through your own youth alive."

Caleb gulped and said, "How's that?"

"You aren't out of trouble yet. I feel it in my bones. Trouble will come at you from the strangest places and try to hurt you bad. You have to learn to trust your gut. It'll help you make the right decisions. Also, watch out for Amara. Protect her. She needs your help. But enough of that, things are looking up for you, and you've already made one good friend."

He looked over at the cabin and asked, "Who? Red?"

She responded by pointing up to the top of a low, grassy hill. He followed her finger to see the wolf sitting and staring at them.

Caleb asked, "Ma'am, may I tell you a secret?"

She looked down at him a moment. "When we're alone, you may call me Wah Hea Oh Te." She spit in her palm and offered it to him. He stared at it a moment, then he spit in his palm and placed it in her hand. As they shook, she gave her oath, "I would give my very life to keep your secret."

He described his encounter with the wolf and the trap, his dream, and its reappearance in the mornings.

"The wolf saves your life."

"Ma'am?"

"He'll save your life."

Unsure, Caleb asked, "I dreamed it. How did you know?"

She ignored his question. "First, you must save his life."

He looked at her blankly. "But I did."

She held up her palm facing him and said, "Not yet." Looking away, she pointed. "Let's get this wood back to the cabin."

They gathered the dried firewood from a pile into the canvas carriers the woman had brought and returned to the cabin in silence. The woman smiled, but said nothing else.

As they returned to the cabin, Raven and Red had finished the roof and put away the ladder and tools. They were inside the cabin unpacking the supplies of seeds, sugar, and tea. With the supplies put away, they sat down for some tea and large, hot cookies.

Raven brought the woman up to date on the latest news of the world. When he told her about troubles in South America, the woman took in a deep breath, "The world needs young knights. People free to fight evil. You have two in your charge right now. See well to their education."

Caleb looked at Maude with questioning eyes. Maude ignored him.

Raven promised, "I'll give them all that I have."

With tea over, they arose to get ready to leave, and again the big woman gave hugs. Going to a cabinet, she pulled out a pile of papers, folded them into an envelope, and handed it to Raven, who put it into a leather pouch.

Then they went outside, checked their horses, and reloaded the remaining supplies onto the packhorse. They mounted up and crossed the stream at a walk, heading for the trees. Maude stood at her cabin door waving after them, and when Caleb looked back one final time, she no longer remained in view.

With the packhorse largely unburdened, they made much better time, trotting at a fair clip. When they stopped for lunch, they took time to boil water for coffee and oatmeal to which Raven added pieces of dried fruit along with some ground cinnamon. The break proved pleasant, and the rest of the day promised to be much better than the bleak morning.

Caleb took the opportunity to ask Red, "Who is Maude?"

"I don't know for sure," Red replied. "She's a hermit, and she's been here for as long as I can remember. She gave me this cloak. It's spun from sheep wool blended with wolf fur."

"Can she tell the future?"

Red gave him a wide-eyed stare and said, "She told you something, didn't she? She did that to me once. I think she's crazy!"

They remounted and rode on for an hour or so when they heard a faint, deep, droning sound coming through the trees. It sounded musical.

"What's that?" Caleb asked, while looking around for the source of the sound

Red hissed at him to be quiet. After a few minutes, the sound stopped. Raven pulled the packhorse up beside him and pulled a long, tapered tube from the pack. He started blowing into the smaller end. It produced a deep, booming roar of sound. He played a five-note tune, repeating it over and over, for a minute, and then stopped to listen. About twenty seconds later, a similar tune answered. Then Raven blew one note three times.

Raven said, "Something has happened at camp. I have to go ahead. Red, you know the trail. Take over and bring Caleb to camp. Just stay safe." Raven handed the packhorse's leader to Red. Then he turned and took off up the valley at a fast canter and quickly disappeared among the trees.

"What's up, and what was that?" Caleb asked.

"I don't know, but it must be very important to call Raven from this far away," she replied. "I don't think we'll see Raven again until we get into camp. The instrument he played is a didgeridoo. Its sound carries across the open space for quite a ways."

With that, she took the packhorse's leader, tied it to Mary's saddle, and told Caleb to follow behind the packhorse. She led them in a different direction than Raven had taken. "Why aren't we following Raven?" Caleb asked.

"He's going straight to the pass. It's a steep and rough path, too dangerous for Mary or the packhorse because they're too heavily loaded. We're taking the old trail."

"What trail?" Caleb exclaimed. "I don't see a trail."

Red eyes narrowed, and she said, "The one we've been riding on all along. Can't you see it?" She seemed surprised.

"No."

"Well, open your eyes and look for it. You'll find it."

He looked around but couldn't see anything. He shrugged his shoulders and asked, "What am I looking for?"

"You're looking for a trail not a path."

"Huh?"

"You can mark a trail in such a way that you don't have to follow in a worn footpath. Most people only look in front of themselves or at their feet, not the trees or rocks around them. We try not to make paths because it hurts the land, and it can't recover. Keep your eyes open. Look around, and you'll find the trail."

They continued for most of the morning until they came to a small stream where they watered the horses and filled the water skins. Red opened some dried fruit, and they sat down to eat. "Well, did you find the trail?" she asked.

Unsure of himself, Caleb said, "I think so. I saw lines scratched on some rocks that pointed the way we were going."

"Good, anything else?"

"I once saw some orange thread hanging from a branch."

Red grinned and said, "Excellent! You have sharp eyes at least. You might make a tracker yet."

"Who is Raven?" Caleb asked, changing the subject. All of a sudden, he found himself again intensely curious about the man.

Red said, "He's a knight, a ranger, a healer, and the best tracker I know."

"Is he your father?"

"No," Red said. "You certainly are direct. He's my teacher, and I'm his squire."

Caleb started pushing his questions. "Does he have a name? Who is he?"

"I don't know his name. I'm sure he has a real name, and it might even be Raven, but he's never told me. It wouldn't be polite to ask. I'm sure the deputy sheriff knows it, and the adults at the school know, but he's just Raven to me."

"You said you're his squire?"

"Yeah, it's an old term for a person who serves a knight and is in training to become one. All of the older students are called squires. I'm his student and his aide."

"You want to become a knight?" Caleb asked.

She beamed and said, "More than anything."

Caleb looked at his feet. The whole idea of modern knights felt weird.

~

After a moment, Red said, "We need to get going."

They mounted their horses and started back on the trail, Caleb smiling to himself because he had gotten under her skin. Despite his hatred of schools, he began to think this one might be different. It might be fun. He decided to give it a chance.

After only a few minutes, the trail got steep and narrow, and Red called a halt. They dismounted and walked the path up the side of the mountain, leading the horses. "It's just too steep to ride," she said.

They continued up the slope for another hour until they reached a gap between two peaks. Crossing the gap, they mounted up and followed an open path just below the ridgeline. They soon came to another narrow gap where they dismounted. Immediately, they were challenged by two boys, twins, wearing uniforms like Red's.

"Halt! Who are you?" the first boy demanded.

Red looked him right in the eye and replied, "Two children of the forest."

"What's the password?" asked the second boy with a feral grin on his face.

Red, with a dark look on her face, answered, "You know that I don't have it yet. We're just getting here."

"Without the password, we can't let you through," the second boy said.

"You know me. Let us pass," Red demanded.

"We can't do that," the first boy said as he crossed his arms and grinned.

Red's eyes narrowed, and her face flushed. She snapped, "Let us pass, or so help me I'll gut you like the little weasels you are, skin you, roll you in habanera sauce, and slow cook you in lemon juice until you plead for mercy!"

They grinned and stepped forward to hug her.

Red asked, "So how did you two get guard duty together?"

"We got into a fight over who's a better rider," the first boy replied, with a smile.

Red turned to Caleb and said, "Typical boys. See what I have to put up with? This is Bob and Bill, my best friends. They're more trouble than a wolverine." She turned back to the twins. "This is Caleb. He's new."

They each grabbed one of Caleb's hands, shook, and gave him a hearty slap on the back. "Glad to meet you," Bob said. "We need some new faces around here."

Red asked, "So what's the news?"

"Not much, except Raven came through here earlier this morning fast as blazes," Bill said.

Red said, "We'd better get on into camp. I'll deal with you two later."

Chapter 3 ~ The High Valley

Caleb and Red descended the rocky trail into the large, green valley, and entered the thin forest. After a several hours of riding, they broke out of the trees into the first meadow.

There they met two older boys guiding two black Percherons, both bigger than Mary, that were teamed together and pulling a long, thin log. The boys waved at Red, and she stood up on her stirrups to wave back.

Caleb whistled and asked, "Does everybody have big horses? Where are they going?"

Red leaned back in her saddle and said, "Most of the squires have their own horses, and many of them are large like Mary. They're hauling logs up to the camp for the stables."

Soon they rode into camp, Caleb observing everything happening around them. A couple of older boys were cutting down a tall, dead pine tree, while others were cutting logs to length. Red waved at them all. They all wore green uniforms, similar to Red's, with patches of some sort over the heart, most of them of a horse's head.

They passed a long row of stables, open on one side, with another row of stables, still under construction with older students and adults laboring at the task.

They passed several rows of round tents, leading away from the stables to a group of big tents. There was one huge tent in the center, surrounded by about twenty banners on poles. One banner had the same black bird on a white background that Raven and Red wore on their jackets.

Red looked at him and said, "It's going to be all right; they're good guys." She led Caleb into the tent where they found several tables, at which boys and girls worked in groups on maps and notebooks.

At a small table in the center of the tent sat Raven and an older man with gray hair, a short beard, and a large, white, handlebar mustache. He wore all black with a red patch over his heart on which a golden lion reared up.

Raven waved them over. The two men stood up, and Raven said, "Let me introduce you to Sir John Fitz Osborn. We call him 'the Lion.' He's the headmaster of the school and a Knight of the British Realm."

Caleb gaped at the man and asked, "You're a real knight—with armor and swords?"

Sir John smiled, shook hands with him, and said, "Well, yes, I do have armor and a sword somewhere, and I hold the title of a British Knight but enough about me. I'm glad to meet you. Raven told me you're a hard worker and a quick study."

Raven dismissed Red to look after the horses while the Lion motioned for Caleb to sit. He waved his hand about and in a proud voice asked, "You're wondering who we are and what we're doing here?"

Caleb paused a moment and answered, "Sir, Red said this is a school."

"Indeed, it's a summer school now. For the rest of the year, we have a regular school, the Knight Riding School. Raven is one of my best teachers. He's also one of my liege knights, sworn to serve those who can't help themselves. Some of my students become knights. Others become ladies, and most go on to obtain higher education. I work to make sure all my students are successful. Raven feels that you will be an excellent student."

"But sir, I don't have any money. I can't pay for this."

"I don't expect you to pay. I have several scholarships to give out each year, and I'm considering offering you one."

Shocked, Caleb spread his arms and asked, "Why me? I'm just an orphan. Nobody cares about me." The stress of the last few days hit him, and tears started to roll out of his eyes.

The Lion took the boy's hands and brought them together in a warm clasp. "I care about you. I'm offering you the opportunity to attend our school because you listen."

The tears stopped, and Caleb gulped. "What?"

The Lion offered a handkerchief to the boy. "You pay attention and learn. Raven has already observed you learning everything you can from him and Amara. I need students who are willing to learn. I need young knights."

Surprised, Caleb asked, "You want me to be a knight?"

"Maybe, but you'll have to prove yourself worthy. I feel you'll learn a lot here, regardless of what you do, and you'll enjoy doing it."

"What if I don't make it? I mean I was in jail. You could send me back."

"You won't go back to the juvenile center or jail. We have a good lawyer. I'll see that you find a good home. It's going to be your choice, but I urge you to give us a try. At least take some time to explore the campus and meet some of the other students. Later, you can tell me what you think of this school."

Caleb said, "I can do that."

The Lion took a rolled up paper out of a tube and spread it out on the table. Raven asked, "What do you want to do? You can leave with the next supply caravan in about a week, or you can sign this document, agreeing to stay here on probation for one month with the option to join the school. It means we're obligated to take care of you for a month."

Caleb decided to try the school for a month. In as serious a voice as he could muster, he said, "I'll sign it."

Raven pointed to a line marked "witness" and then offered a pen. Caleb hesitated a second, looked at the two men, and signed the paper. Committed, he relaxed.

Raven and the Lion also signed the paper and then stood up to shake the boy's hand again.

Caleb asked, "Do I have to use my real name here?"

"No, you don't. May I inquire why?" the Lion asked.

"It's just I don't like it. The other kids laugh at it."

The Lion stroked his beard, smiled, and said, "I understand a wolf sleeps with you."

"Not because I want it to," Caleb said.

The Lion said, "Nevertheless, it accounts for something. There are naming traditions among the original inhabitants of this country. You shall be called 'The Boy Who Sleeps with Wolves' or 'Wolf' for short. It's a good, strong name, and it will serve you well."

Caleb huffed and asked, "What if I don't like it?"

The Lion smiled and replied, "Sometimes you don't have a choice, and the name chooses you." He paused a moment and said, "We also have a matter of guardianship. You must have someone who is responsible for you and makes sure you're dressed, fed, and so on. Raven will serve until a permanent guardian is assigned to you. Let's get you started."

Sir John took Wolf to the entrance of the tent and stopped the first page he saw. "You're Wart, aren't you?"

"Yes, sir, Page William Cunningham, sir"

"And you have only two other pages in your tent, Wart?"

"Yes, sir."

"Good. Here's your fourth page. Make sure he's fitted out properly. Show him around today." With that, the Lion left.

The page, who looked younger and shorter than Wolf, said, "Hi, I'm Wart."

"I'm Ca... I guess you can call me Wolf."

Wart offered his hand. "I take it you just arrived in camp?"

"Yeah, I came in with Raven."

"Cool. He's such a good teacher. He knows everything about the forest and mountains. I wish I could go out on patrol with him."

Wolf rolled his eyes and said, "All we did was ride up and down mountains."

"He must have taught you something. Did anything exciting happen?"

The question made Wolf pause. He didn't want to mention the wolf. "Nah, I just meet this queer old woman named Maude."

"Maude! That is so cool. I've heard she's a seer. She wanders around this valley, but not many people see her."

"She seems all right. She's big and hugs real hard. She also makes good cookies."

"Maybe I'll meet her someday. Hey, I'm forgetting my duty."

Wart dragged Wolf to the quartermaster's large tent where three page's uniforms, a pair of boots, a mess kit, a small notebook, and a composition book were issued to Wolf. Then Wart led Wolf to their round tent, which he called a "yurt." It contained four cots set around the sides and a small table in the center with short logs for chairs.

Wolf deposited his supplies on the empty cot and changed into his page's uniform and boots. The fresh, stiff cloth felt good. Wart showed him to the boy's latrine and all the other important places in camp. His tour ended at the stables, where some of the horses were already billeted.

There were three blasts of a horn, and Wart said, "Dinner is served." After they finished their savory stew, they laid back to enjoy the late afternoon warmth and Wolf asked, "How long have you been here?"

"This is my second summer here. I just finished up my first year at school."

Wolf took in a breath and asked, "What's school like?"

Wart sighed and answered, "It's hard. You wake up at five to take care of the horses, and then you have classes all morning and practice all afternoon. By the time you have supper, you're beat. But then you get to ride your horse. At night, you study until lights out."

Wolf looked down, "Doesn't sound like much fun."

Wart laughed and said, "Oh, we have fun. We're creative. My roommates and I play tricks on the squires and instructors."

Wolf said, "I don't have a horse."

Wart slapped him on the shoulder and said, "Don't worry. A horse will be assigned to you."

"What about here? All I've seen anybody do is work."

"Well, we work a lot. It isn't that hard, and most of it is interesting. I love it. It's just too much fun. I'm glad my parents found out about this school. It's better than that stinking academy I used to attend."

"You're rich?" asked Wolf.

Wart answered, "Yeah, but being rich isn't all it's cracked up to be. I've got more friends here than I ever had at home. Besides, it's not like I have a lot of cash. I don't need it."

Wart introduced Wolf around the camp to the other pages; however, a few of the pages got testy with him when they found out he wasn't a regular student. One of them, a tall, blond boy, got in Wolf's face and said, "So, you're a charity case. They shouldn't allow anybody here unless they can pay for it. You won't last long. As soon as they get tired of you, they'll kick you out."

Wolf felt the heat rise in his face, and he said, "I ... I'm not a charity case!"

Two other pages flanked him, and the tall page said, "You're nothing. Go away, or I'll throw you out myself."

Wart grabbed Wolf by the shoulder and pulled him away from those pages, who started laughing. Wart said, "So you've set a new record for making an enemy."

"Wart, you should know better than to mess with his kind," the tall page said before he turned and left, his two friends following.

Once they out of earshot, Wart whispered to Wolf, "That's Wayne, a real needle jerk. He thinks he's better than everybody else and God's gift to girls. He's a rich kid, and I don't think he likes it here. Stay away from him. Wayne is a pain to me. We had a bad fight, and he beat me up pretty bad."

Wolf winced and asked, "What did you do? Did you get in trouble?"

Wart chuckled and said, "Of course, I got in trouble. We both got in trouble. I got in a few good licks, but he's bigger than me. You can't hide a shiner. Listen, this is the most important thing I'm ever going to tell you: Don't rat out on anyone, and I mean anyone. Just say you tripped or something like that. You take your punishment without complaint. It's just extra work. You take self-defense courses and defend yourself the next time. It works out better."

Wolf asked, "Why are you telling me this? You want me to get hurt?"

Wart answered, "Oh heavens, no. I want you to beat the snot out of him. If anybody can, you can."

"Me?"

"Yeah, you. He won't suspect you. When you take self-defense from Whisperblade, pay attention. A bully won't pick on someone who can defend himself. You'll learn all about it."

Wolf looked down and asked, "Is everybody going to pick on me?"

"Not if you've got friends."

Wolf kicked a rock. "I've never had friends."

Wart, clamped his arm around Wolf's shoulder. "You do now!"

"Thanks," Wolf said, looking at Wart with a smile.

~

That night, Wolf met his other two tent mates, Harold and George, who asked where he came from. When he hesitated, George said, "If you're Wart's friend, you're my friend."

On his first morning in camp, Wolf slept late, along with everybody else in his tent. He awoke when Wart shook him and said, "Quick, wake up, or we'll miss breakfast!"

Wolf bolted from the cot, half asleep, pulled on his shirt, trousers, and boots and slipped his page's tunic over his head. Then he noticed wolf tracks in the tent leading to his cot and rubbed them out.

He, Wart, and their tent mates ran to the mess tent to collect their breakfast of sausage and eggs. The sun hadn't arisen over the rim of the valley, and Wolf started to shiver in the cool, dewy morning and savored the hot food.

Just as everyone finished eating, the horn sounded two blasts, and they put away their mess kits and ran to the main tent to receive their assignments.

A teacher caught up with Wolf and took him to a corner of the tent at a small table. "I need to talk with you, so I can place you in the right class."

Not knowing what to expect, Wolf said, "I almost finished eighth grade."

"We'll see." The teacher tested him in English and math. Then he assigned makeup classes for each morning.

Wolf, dismissed, took his free time to explore the camp further. At lunch, he found Wart, and they had sandwiches and tea. Afterward, Squire David had them start mapping a part of the central valley along with four other pages. They went to the quartermaster and obtained compasses, notebooks, and safety harnesses.

The party marched north for an hour to their designated area. At a large glen, they broke up into three groups, put on their safety harnesses, and climbed holly trees. Wolf discovered himself to be very nervous about heights, and Wart assured him it would get easier the more he climbed.

When they reached a couple of good branches, a dizzying height up, they made themselves comfortable and secure, and then they sketched a map of the clearing, taking compass bearings on landmarks.

Afterwards, the three groups met at a rock in the center of the glen and combined their data into a new map, taking more compass readings on as many landmarks as they could see.

Then they relaxed and ate a snack of dried fruit.

One of the boys threw a small ball on the field and yelled, "Hare and Hounds." The boys scrambled to grab sticks. Wart tossed one to Wolf and yelled, "Get the ball to our tree." Together they managed, in a few minutes, to hit and kick the ball to their tree. Wart jumped for joy, and Wolf got into the spirit and let out a war whoop.

Then Red rode up on Easy Rider and ordered them to report to the main tent. They gathered their supplies and started running back to camp, but Wolf found himself short of breath and slowed down to a walk. Wart stopped running to stay with him.

As they walked back to camp, Wolf asked Wart how he got his name.

"Wart was a nickname for King Arthur when he was just a kid and didn't know he would be king. I got it when some of the older pages discovered I liked to read stories about him. Anyway, I kind of like it."

"Do you want to become a knight?" Wolf asked.

"I haven't decided yet. It's hard. You have to work at it day and night. You aren't expected to decide until you become a squire. If you decide to, you'll be paired with a knight. Most students don't try for it, but yeah, I like the idea."

"Why haven't I heard about these knights?" Wolf asked.

"I don't know. I hadn't heard of them until my parents sent me here. They must be quiet about what they do. I see knights come and go. So I know there are more than just the teachers in this school, and they don't always wear uniforms."

They soon reached camp and the main tent. Working together on a table with their drawings, the pages made a standard size map of the glen they had just surveyed. Some of the older pages, using trigonometry, checked all the numbers and verified all landmarks.

David declared the map complete and thanked the pages. Wolf took his leave and found Raven sitting in front of his tent, writing in a notebook. Raven looked up at him and smiled, "How was your first day?"

Wolf gave the knight a description of his mapping activities.

"Did you enjoy it?" Raven asked.

"Oh yes, sir," Wolf said.

"Good, I think you'll do well here. Pay attention to all your lessons."

Raven fumbled through some papers. "I hate paperwork. It's the bane of every teacher, and there's a lot of paperwork.

"Most pages here aren't attached to a particular knight, but they work in groups for whichever knight or squire happens to need them. Every knight has a page assigned to him to act as an assistant.

"On the last day of school before summer, my page broke his arm. He's staying at home for the rest of the summer. I need a new page and want to give you a chance. It will mean extra work, hard work, but you'll have more interesting experiences. I teach wilderness survival and can use the help. Will you accept the position?"

Wolf's mouth dropped open. "You ... you want me to be your page?"

"Of course, I do. If I'm going to be responsible for you and your education, I need to see you often, and this is the best way to do it. What do you say?"

"Yes, sir, I'll do it."

"Good, we'll talk more after supper. For now, go find Amara, and the two of you report back to me."

Knowlton

Chapter 4 ~ A Lesson in Manners

Wolf set out to find Red. Nobody seemed to know her location. He searched the camp before he found her at the girls' camping area, talking to a short, stocky woman, who had long brown hair braided into a ponytail, her face weathered and lined.

The woman wore a tunic with the badge of an animal Wolf didn't recognize. Wolf approached, and Red introduced him to the woman. "Lady Knight Whisperblade, this is Page Wolf."

"So, you're The Boy Who Sleeps with Wolves. I'm so glad to meet you."

"Thank you," he replied, trying to be polite.

The lady knight grimaced and corrected him by saying, "Thank you, ma'am."

When Red explained that Wolf had not yet been instructed in formal manners, the lady knight ordered, "Give him a lesson in manners by this time tomorrow."

"Yes, my lady," Red replied with a bow.

Whisperblade turned back to Wolf and asked, "Why are you here?"

"Raven wants Red."

Lady Whisperblade said, "When addressing a knight or lady knight, you will use sir or lady before their name, even if Sir Raven doesn't insist on proper formality."

"Yes, ma'am," he replied, feeling shaken.

Red grabbed Wolf by the arm and trotted him off for Raven's tent. When they were out of earshot of the lady knight, she hissed, "You'd better learn your manners and get in her good graces. She's tougher than any wolverine. Do you know what a wolverine is? It's a member of the weasel family that's so fierce even bears won't mess with it."

~

They reached Raven's tent, where Red informed him of the encounter at the girls' camp. He thought a minute and said, "We have a lot to do to make Wolf presentable to Whisperblade and not much time." He then gave them a series of orders to carry out by tomorrow and ordered them to return with their supper for Wolf's first lesson in manners.

When they returned to Raven's tent, they ate at his small table with Red playing the part of the lady and the Raven, the part of the gentleman. They put on a good, but exaggerated, show for Wolf, who felt that some of the things he would have to do were pointless. Even so, Raven assured him of the importance of knowing the reasons and seriousness of customs and manners. The lesson well taken, Wolf learned proper table manners before the evening ended.

When they left Raven's tent, Red informed Wolf they had to separate. After dark, no girls were allowed in the boys' camp and no boys in the girls' camp. There were squires posted on sentry duty at each camp throughout the night who could carry messages. This suited Wolf fine, and he went off to find his tent.

When he arrived, he had just enough energy left in him to crawl into his bedroll. When he and his tent mates awoke to the horn blast the next morning, they all saw the wolf sleeping besides Wolf's cot. The wolf stood up and hobbled out of the tent.

By breakfast, the story had spread throughout the camp, and Wolf had become a celebrity, but he still didn't tell them the whole story about the wolf. There was a lot of speculation as to why the wolf kept appearing and why it limped, but Wolf didn't give any hints.

After the horn blew to end breakfast, everyone left to do assigned duties. Wolf reported to the quartermaster's tent. The man helped Wolf trace out on black cloth the outline of a raven. He showed him how to sew it to a white square and then stitch it to his uniform. The man gave him enough cloth with needle and thread to do his other uniforms and coat.

He also gave Wolf some good bits of advice on dealing with women, the most important of which was, "The woman is always right, even if she isn't."

"Why do all the women get such special treatment?"

The quartermaster looked down at him with furrowed eyebrows and took a deep breath. "Wolf, what's the difference between Whisperblade and Raven?"

Wolf knew that her gender was not the right answer. He finally guessed, "He's a lot larger than she is."

"Right. Most men are larger than most women are. That alone demands that women should have certain rights and privileges. We have manners in part to protect women. It teaches us all that strength is not an acceptable way to deal with women."

Wolf looked down and said, "Oh, I didn't think about that."

"Maybe you will the next time you talk to a girl. Now go on your way."

Wolf then reported to Lady Jane, an instructor and chaperon, for further lessons in etiquette. She was short woman with black hair and wore a dress patterned on the standard uniform, the only woman or girl Wolf had seen at camp who wore a dress.

Lady Jane taught him the proper way to bow and set a table and the difference between a mister and a sir. He learned when to use ma'am and sir and how to address a lady, depending on whether she was wearing a dress or trousers.

Wolf went to his tent, washed up, and put on his best uniform. He borrowed a page's formal cap and went off in search of Whisperblade. He found her in the stables wearing riding clothes and grooming Cloud, her horse. He approached to ten feet of her, stopped and turned so he faced at a right angle to her, and stood quietly. She ignored him until she had finished grooming the stallion and saw to his feeding.

Then she approached him and asked, "What is your message?"

Wolf bowed to her. "Lady Knight, I carry greetings from my master, Sir Raven, and bear invitation to dine with him in such a manner as one knight would expect to be entertained by a fellow knight. That such an adventure should be pleasant, this page is to accompany my lady at the time of your choosing."

The lady knight replied, "Inform your master that the lady knight wishes to arrive promptly at six o'clock."

"He shall be informed. He also would know what time this page should arrive to escort you."

The lady knight smiled thinly. "I'll be ready at five forty-five. You're dismissed to return to your master."

"Thank you, my lady." With a deep bow, he excused himself and retreated at a respectable pace.

~

Wolf saw that Raven's tent had been transformed. It was cleaned to a spotless condition. The table, small and simple, had been covered with a cloth with two candles in the center. He watched as Red set the table, making sure both settings were equal.

Raven stepped out from the sleeping part of his tent, dressed in a military uniform that showed off his excellent physique. Then Red took Wolf to the back chamber and straightened him out. She gave him a page's dress tunic that had the Raven's symbol embroidered on it and combed his wild hair.

She showed him the food that had been prepared—fresh salad and fruits, small cakes, cooked vegetables, and best of all, two rabbits cooked in sauce with wild onions. Red showed Wolf his duties for the evening.

When it came time for Wolf to escort the lady knight, he made his way to her tent where he encountered Page Hildegard, who bore Whisperblade's symbol. He explained that he had been sent to accompany the lady knight to dinner. Hildegard disappeared into the knight's tent, and, in about a minute, reappeared and announced, "The Lady Knight Whisperblade." Whisperblade stepped out.

She appeared magnificent in a blue dress with long sleeves and a white sash, from which hung a sheathed, long, thin, dagger, held by silver chains. Her hair had been unbraided, and it spread across her back.

Wolf, dumbstruck at the sight of the lady, finally managed to bow and say, "My lady, I'm here to accompany you to my master's tent."

"Well spoken," she replied.

Wolf held out his right arm, which she took with her left hand. Together they left the women's camp and took a meandering route to the men's camp. On the way, Whisperblade asked about his past, particularly his foster parents. She then explained that her title hadn't come lightly, but it had been earned by skill in combat, her good deeds, and her knowledge in arts and science. She explained that to be a knight, one had to be very good at what one did and had to work always for the good of others. She said, "It's not only hard to become a knight, it's a hard life with little reward."

They arrived just at six to find Red standing watch outside Raven's tent. Wolf announced, "Lady Knight Whisperblade to see Sir Knight Raven." Red bowed then disappeared into the tent. She promptly returned and announced, "Sir Knight Raven."

Raven appeared from the tent and bowed, whereupon Whisperblade curtsied. Raven then took her left hand and led her into the tent, followed by Red then Wolf.

Inside the tent, Raven let go of her hand and announced, "I propose a toast." Wolf placed wine glasses in their hands, and Red filled them with wine. "To the flag of our country."

"To the flag of our country," she repeated. They both took a sip of wine.

She raised her glass and toasted, "To our school and the children in our charge."

"To our school and the children in our charge," he repeated, and they again sipped their wine.

He then invited her to sit at the table. Wolf held the chair for her as she sat down. The Raven sat down with similar assistance from Red.

Red and Wolf then went to the back room and returned with the first course of the dinner, a salad, which they served. Wolf offered them oil and vinegar for salad dressing.

The next course consisted of hot steamed vegetables, followed by the main course of rabbit and onions. The meal finished with a spicy ginger raisin cake and a dry, white wine. Red and Wolf then cleared the table and placed on it a platter of fresh fruit for the rest of the evening. Then he and Red retreated to wait outside Raven's tent until it was time for Wolf to accompany the lady knight to her tent.

Wolf handed Sir Raven his lute, and he played some quiet after dinner tunes. The Lady Whisperblade joined in with a beautiful soprano voice. To end their recital, they sang a couple of bawdy tunes, which surprised and amused Wolf.

At the end of the evening, Wolf accompanied the lady knight back to her tent, where he bowed and bid her good night.

"Tell Sir Raven we must do this again soon."

"Yes, ma'am."

"You are excused." His earlier etiquette faults appeared to be forgiven.

When he returned to Raven's tent, Red had returned the tent to normal. She said, "Raven is asleep. I think what he would tell you is that, around people, you must give them the respect their title commands. They've earned it. It makes people feel good, and it commands respect for yourself."

"I think I see what you mean. Why don't you always use titles with Raven?"

"Raven is somewhat easy about that. It's his way. Don't ever make that mistake around other knights. You need to get some rest. We have a busy day tomorrow."

They separated to go to their tents. At his tent, Wolf's tent mates peppered him with questions about Whisperblade.

It turned out that everybody took self-defense lessons from Whisperblade, even the grownups. Wolf found out she had a reputation for perfection in fighting as well as manners.

Chapter 5 ~ Saving Wolves

When Wolf awoke in the morning, the wolf again lay curled up under his dangling arm. His tent mates were staring at him, but nobody said a thing.

He whispered, "Somebody, do something" No one moved, and the gaunt wolf limped out of the tent, its right front leg matted in dried blood. Wolf ducked outside of the tent to see the animal disappearing into the woods to the north. This time a dozen or so other pages saw the wolf as it left camp.

Wolf dressed and ran to Raven's tent where the knight and Red were already dressed in their forest clothes, checking their bows and arrows.

Wolf declared, "The wolf is here!"

"We know," Red answered. "We're going to hunt it."

"No!"

Raven said, "We have to because he's hurt and in danger of dying. He's also a danger to all the other students. You stay here and go to the stables to start your riding lessons."

Wolf pleaded, "I need to go with you."

Raven furrowed his forehead and asked, "Why?"

Wolf, not sure what he could say to keep the wolf from being shot, continued, "It's important to me."

"This is serious business," Red said with a grim look.

Wolf trembled and said, "There's nothing more serious to me. It's important. The wolf picked me. He's why you call me Wolf."

Raven bent down and said, "If you come, you must understand that life is hard. You remember I said not all lessons would be fun. Out here, my word is law, no exceptions. The safety of the students comes first. If there's any danger to them, I'll kill it."

Wolf pushed his opportunity, "Okay, but let me go. He's been in my dreams. Maude said I would save him."

"You can come with us, but not a peep," Raven said. With that, he turned on his heels and headed for the woods. Soon, Raven stopped and pointed at shallow depressions and then to a bush nearby.

Raven whispered there should be two prints in the wolf's gait, as the rear paws always stepped in the front paw prints. Wolf saw three prints because one leg was out of sync. He also noticed that the morning dew had been brushed off a few leaves, and a couple of hairs were stuck to a wet leaf.

After they'd walked for another twenty minutes, they approached a rocky slope and spotted a large hole, just a few meters up.

Raven strung his bow, and Red did likewise. He whispered, "Amara, go left, and I'll go right. We'll hold our positions while Wolf advances up to the center." Wolf nodded to Raven. The two bowmen moved to flank, and Wolf advanced toward the rocks. When he approached halfway, he realized what Raven planned—if the wolf came after him, it would be caught in a cross fire of arrows. He whispered for the wolf not to move.

The hole up between the rocks appeared large enough to enter, so Wolf climbed to it and let his eyes adjust to the darkness. The wolf was at the back of the hole, panting, its snout resting on its good leg, and the injured leg sticking out. Wolf crawled into the hole and approached it on his hands and knees, keeping calm. The wolf whimpered a little but was still. Raven appeared at the entrance of the hole, his bow no longer in hand.

"Can you help him?" Wolf asked.

"I don't know. I'll have to check him out." The knight crawled into the entrance. He did a quick exam of the animal. "I think he's been shot in the leg. It's infected, and he's very sick."

"No, he was caught in a trap, and I released him. Can you do anything to help him?" Wolf asked again.

~

Raven looked at him with a stern glare. "I thought as much. I can help him, but I don't think he'll be able to hunt well enough to survive on his own. He's very lucky his leg isn't broken. That would have been fatal by now. If any tendons or muscles are too damaged, I don't believe he'll ever be able to run long distances again. If he survives, he'll be dependent upon you. He came to you. He trusts you."

Wolf pleaded, "But I don't know how to help him."

Raven said, "I'll teach you what to do."

Wolf swore, "I'll learn. I'll do whatever it takes."

Raven turned to Red, who stood at the entrance, and ordered her to go for his medical kit and gave her a list of medications to obtain from the school veterinarian, and Red took off running back to camp.

Raven had Wolf hold the wolf while he attended the wound. He washed it with water from his water skin, and then he began a very thorough examination of the wolf. The animal whimpered in obvious pain, but it didn't move.

Red returned after twenty minutes, riding Easy Rider, and handed Raven the medical supplies. She then went about setting up a small camp with a rain poncho serving as a one-man tent.

Raven prepared a syringe from the medical kit, handed it to Wolf, and had him take a large pinch of loose skin on the animal's shoulder. Wolf gave the wolf the injection in the hollow under the pinch. After a couple of minutes, the wolf relaxed and went to sleep.

The knight went to work. Taking a razor, he shaved the wolf's leg, and then he injected a syringe of antibiotics into the leg above and below the wound. He made Wolf trim the torn skin around the wound with a tiny pair of scissors. Then Raven showed him how to sew the good skin together. Wolf applied adhesive and small strips of cloth over the stitches. Raven then wrapped the leg, and then broke one of his arrows into two pieces cutting off the head and feathers. Using the pieces as a splint, he finished wrapping the leg.

"The trick," Raven said, "is to get him to stay calm and not move. He's a wild animal and not used to people, but he trusts you. You'll have to stay with him for the next day or so until he starts to improve. One of us will stay with you for the time needed. We'll take turns. I'll stay here first, and then Amara will relieve me. You sleep in the hole with the wolf, and we'll feed the two of you."

The knight eased himself out of the hole. Red returned with a skinned rabbit, which she cut into bite-sized pieces. After an hour, the wolf aroused out of its drug-induced sleep, drank a little water, and started feeding on the pieces of rabbit. After eating, the wolf lay down with his head on Wolf's lap, and Wolf stroked his head. Soon the wolf again slept. Every time it twitched, the injured leg moved, and it yelped.

Later, when Raven checked on the wolf, he said, "The wound looks good. The wolf has a chance of living."

Wolf asked Raven, "Why did you let the wolf live?"

Raven stroked his beard before he answered, "The wolf has shown no intention of harming anybody, and the wound looked treatable. He wouldn't survive if we hadn't treated him, and that couldn't have happened if he didn't trust you. As it is, if he survives, he'll still have a hard struggle to feed himself. I don't think he can survive the winter. He may be dependent upon you. A wolf is a wild animal. They don't get along with people, and, for them, that's a good thing."

In the afternoon, Red arrived on Easy Rider, leading Midnight. She brought meat stew and fruits. The wolf awoke at the smell of the stew, but showed no interest in eating. Red took the watch, and Raven returned to camp.

Red handed a bedroll to Wolf, who laid it out next to the wolf as it slept. Red then laid out her own bedroll under the poncho tent, using a pile of pine straw as a pillow.

~

Wolf awoke in the morning and found the wolf already awake, resting its head on his chest and staring at him. He could hear Red at work outside. He called to her, and she came to the opening with several pieces of raw meat in her hand. The wolf perked up and stood on three legs.

Red laid the meat in front of the wolf and backed away. The wolf started to eat the meat. Wolf crawled out of the hole and came down the rocks to the campfire, where Red had stew and tea ready.

"Raven said we need to return to camp if the wolf is better. So how is he?"

"He's doing a lot better. I think he'll get well."

~

Back at camp, Raven dismissed Red, but he asked Wolf to stay and sit down. He said, "I need to talk to you about something important. This is about you and me, not about the wolf. When you saved the wolf from the trap, you should have told me. It's a matter of trust. Do you understand what I'm talking about?"

Wolf looked down a moment then back up at Raven and said, "I don't think so, sir."

"I have to assume that you tell me everything. Important decisions could be at stake. As an example, that trap was set by an illegal hunter, and that knowledge could have led to his arrest and saved other animals.

I don't think it does, but if the wolf had had rabies, your very life would have been at stake without prompt treatment. There is just a small window of time to vaccinate you. If you're exposed, but are not vaccinated, and the disease becomes active, there is no cure. It's always fatal."

"Oh," Wolf said, and he shivered.

"In this matter of trust, I must be able to depend on you as much as you have to depend on me."

"Yes, sir."

"As it is, you'll have to be vaccinated, and it isn't pleasant. The shots are painful and go into your stomach. We'll talk more about this matter later. The vaccinations start tomorrow. You're dismissed for the night."

The boy started to walk away, then he stopped and asked, "Sir, what about the wolf?"

Raven stared at the boy, considering his answer. He sighed and said, "I'll let you vaccinate him."

In the morning after breakfast, Wolf reported to the nurse's tent where she and Dr. Lundie, the vet, administered the vaccine and waited to check for any allergic reaction. The boy had hives for a few minutes, but he recovered and was let go.

Chapter 6 ~ Real Trouble

The next night, Wolf finished supper with Raven, and Red and helped with the almost ritual cleaning. Raven, while not the most organized of knights, insisted on cleanliness. He expected Wolf to wear a clean uniform for supper and to keep his fingernails clean.

With the day's work done, Wolf headed back to the boys' camp. Near the halfway point, Wayne stepped out from behind a tree and blocked his way, and two of Wayne's buddies appeared on each side of Wolf. Wolf looked up at the page and snapped, "What do you want?"

"I want you gone." To emphasize his point, he gave Wolf a quick shove, knocking him off balance and over the outstretched leg of one of Wayne's friends.

Wolf went down in an awkward heap, and Wayne fell on top of him, hitting him in the face twice before a blur knocked Wayne off him. Wart had come to his rescue.

Wayne's friends went to work, one on Wart and one on Wolf. Wolf saw one of them hit Wart in the small of his side, and Wart curled over, apparently in excruciating pain. They both received more blows to the face until they were saved by the intervention of two squires, who pulled the boys apart. "Who started this?" Squire David demanded. He got no answer, so taking charge of Wart and Wolf, he started marching them to the main tent. Squire Bill led the two friends of Wayne. Wayne had disappeared.

When David, Wart, and Wolf reached the main tent, Eagle, the only knight present, made them sit in chairs in the corner. When Bill arrived with the two other boys, Eagle took them to the Lion's tent. Wart and Wolf were left to sweat it out under the watchful eye of the squire, who warned them to silence.

Eventually, they were called to the Lion's tent by Eagle. Wolf entered weak in the knees, terrified of being sent away. He believed that if he was sent away for fighting, he would have to go to the juvenile center, despite what the Lion had promised. He knew fighting was forbidden, and even if he didn't throw a punch, there would be no excuse. His experience with grownups had taught him they didn't like excuses.

They were placed in front of the Lion's table, where the headmaster was writing in a journal. He made them wait until he finished writing and closed the book.

The Lion looked up at them as if considering what he should say. Finally, he asked, "You do know fighting isn't permitted at this school, or any school for that matter?" Wolf started to answer when Wart nudged him with an elbow. The Lion turned to Wart and asked, "What happened?"

"I tripped, sir."

"And I suppose you fell down on each side of your face?"

"Yes, sir."

The Lion stood up and walked around from behind his small table to stand in front of Wart. He said, "You shouldn't be so clumsy. Report to the main tent after breakfast for extra assignments. You're dismissed."

"Yes, sir." Wart looked at Wolf and shook his head, then turned and left the tent.

The Lion turned to Wolf and said, "I don't suppose you could give me a better explanation about what happened?" He gently put a hand under the boy's chin and turned his head back and forth to examine the damage that Wolf could feel becoming visible.

"I tripped, sir."

"You can tell me who did this. It will be between me and you."

"I really tripped, sir."

The Lion sighed and said, "I suppose I'll never find out what happened." He pointed back at the book on his table. "I still have to make a journal entry. I have to account for every bruise and cut you receive. It's the most difficult thing I have to do as a headmaster. You'll also report to the main tent in the morning. Later, you'll be assigned to a self-defense class conducted by Whisperblade. Do you know who she is?"

"Yes, sir."

The Lion stroked his short beard a moment. "Somehow, I don't think you do. You're dismissed."

"Yes, sir." Wolf turned and left the tent, relieved that he hadn't been kicked out.

The next morning after breakfast, Wolf reported to Raven. He couldn't hide the two bruises he had on his cheeks. Raven didn't say anything about them, but he obviously knew what had happened. Raven dismissed him from all responsibilities for the day and sent him to the main tent, where he was greeted by Squire David, who said, "You took your time getting here. That'll get you an extra hour of work."

Wolf opened his mouth to object, but thought better of it. "What do I have to do?"

"Report to the stables and muck until one o'clock."

"Muck?"

The squire's eyes opened wide but returned to normal. "Shovel horse manure."

"But that means I'll miss lunch." David stared at him.

"Sorry, I'm leaving right now." Wolf ran out of the tent and down to the stables.

When Wolf arrived, he found Wart already shoveling. He donned rubber boots, grabbed a shovel, and started to work. They started down one row while the other two boys they had fought worked the other row.

As pages passed by them with their horses, they made jokes at their expense. It made for a long morning, and Wolf hated missing lunch. To make matters worse, Wayne came by with his horse and whispered to him, "Leave." To make his point, he had his horse bump into the wheelbarrow knocking it over. Wolf had to re-shovel the manure.

With his punishment over, he reported to Raven, who gave him a packet of dried apples and informed him that he had to attend self-defense class every morning.

"Sir, why was I warned against reporting what happened?"

"Who told you that?"

There was a long pause when Wolf didn't answer.

Raven started to say something, but stopped. He furrowed his eyebrows and opened his mouth, but he still didn't talk. Finally, he said, "Wolf, the other boys and girls don't like tattletales. Your chances of finding friends would disappear if you reported it. By not talking, you gain a certain measure of power over the perpetrators. They can't claim to be better than you. You took the punishment they dished out and didn't complain. That makes you just as tough as them. You need to be tougher. Pay attention to Whisperblade—they don't come any tougher than she is." Raven added, "Make no mistake, if I hear of you bullying anybody, you'll have to answer to me and then Whisperblade."

~

The next day, Wolf ran to report to his first self-defense class held in a clearing about a half mile from the main camp. The run left him breathless, and he stopped before approaching the class. There were about ten students kneeling in a circle around two who were standing and facing each other.

Whisperblade stood next to them, barefoot and dressed in a loose-fitting shirt and trousers. The lady knight looked radically different from the last time he had seen her. She looked to be the toughest person he had ever seen. Wolf thought, *Great, now I'm in for it.*

Whisperblade waved him over, and he knelt down facing her as the other students were. "Hello, everyone. I'm your instructor in self-defense. In class, I'm referred to as Master." She indicated the two older students. "These two students are my assistants. The purpose of this class is to keep you alive when you are attacked. I teach by example and constant repetition. What you learn today, you'll practice before breakfast, before lunch, before dinner, and before bed."

She and her two assistants then went through a series of moves in perfect precision. They took a left step forward, swept their right arms to the left with forearms vertical, and then repeated with the other leg and arm. This was followed by a twist to the left, a right waist-high kick, and an extension of their left arms palm open. As they pulled their arms back, their right fists were snapped forward and back.

Whisperblade ordered the students to line up and start performing the steps. They repeated the steps many times, as she walked around, correcting the students to get their moves right. When she reached Wolf, he asked without thinking, "Master, what is the purpose of this exercise?"

She smiled at him and said, "That's an excellent question." She stopped the exercise and had the students kneel again in a circle. She then had her two assistants stand to either side, had Wolf stand in front of her, and gave them orders to kick and hit at her when she approached. She stood back a moment then launched into a flurry of action, performing the exercise at a much faster speed.

As she confronted the two assistants, their blows were blocked and deflected, but when she confronted Wolf, she blocked his punch with her right forearm, and, with her left hand, she grabbed his shirt and pulled as her right fist came up to his neck. She froze in that position, and, although he had not been hurt, Wolf felt overwhelmed.

"Those steps are precursors to defensive blocks and strikes, and the repetition of these steps lead to speed and accuracy. Are there any more questions?" There were none. "Class is over."

She stopped Wolf from leaving right away. "I just want to explain why you suffered through that demonstration. First, everyone gets their turn to be a victim; secondly, it was to impresses on your memory how powerful these skills are."

"I think I understand, Master."

Whisperblade put a hand under his chin, turning his head side to side, examining his bruises. She smiled and said, "I'll tell you a secret. Blocking is more important than punching. This course is called self-defense for a reason. Learn to block."

"Yes, Master."

"Good. I expect to see you an hour early tomorrow," she said and dismissed him.

~

The next morning he ran to make the appointment. Whisperblade stood in the field practicing steps and moves, and he came up to her and knelt down to watch. She performed a very intricate series of moves involving leaps, kicks, and punches.

When she finished, she bowed and indicated for him to stand up and bow. She had him practice his steps repeatedly, while making adjustments to his form here and there. This continued until he started to sweat. Then she let him have a drink of water and a short break.

After Wolf had refreshed himself, Whisperblade had him restart his steps, but this time she met him step for step with the moves she had been practicing earlier. Every move, block, or punch he made met an opposing punch or block. He was amazed at the efficiency of the moves and at how well he was protected.

Whisperblade then did something unusual. She had Wolf sit opposite her, cross-legged, with his arms resting on his legs and his eyes closed. "Try to think of nothing but your breathing and your heartbeat. Listen to the sound your breathing makes inside you. Just relax and listen." He did as instructed.

When he opened his eyes again, they were surrounded by a ring of students, all sitting in the same fashion with their eyes closed. Many of these students were older, including Red and another squire, Willow, a tall, strong brunette, who appeared to be a full-grown woman. Wolf could tell that today's session would be different.

Whisperblade called an end to the relaxation exercises, and they all stood up and started their self-defense exercises. After a few repetitions, she had the new students kneel while the rest of the students started a different exercise. When they were done, a few more students knelt, and the exercises got more complex. With each new exercise, more students knelt down until only four were left standing, Red, Willow, Bob, and Bill, and they performed the most demanding and complex exercise of all.

When all exercises were over, Red and Willow bowed to each other and, on cue, engaged in actual combat, trading blows and blocks. It seemed that Willow would overpower Red, but despite Willow's obvious size advantage, Red came off very well. Whisperblade called a halt, and then it was the boys' turn. They went at each other with equal ferocity.

With the practice fighting finished, Whisperblade arranged a demonstration. Six senior students held three jousting lances by each end in a large triangle around the Whisperblade. She began slowly, going through the whole routine with kicks and blows to the lances. On the repetition of the exercise, she became a whirlwind of fury, blowing through the whole routine. When finished, the three lances had been broken into pieces by well-placed kicks.

Whisperblade ordered the students, "I expect everyone to practice their routines before each meal and bedtime, and I expect to see all of you running everywhere you go." She then dismissed the students.

Knowlton

Chapter 7 ~ Horse Games

"Today's the big day," Wart announced. "We get to prove our horse riding skills and have some fun."

"What are you going to do?" Wolf asked.

Wart grinned, "I'll race my horse cross country."

"Are you any good at it?"

"I'm better than most pages. It doesn't seem to matter how old you are, if you like horses, you'll learn to ride. I'm not afraid of galloping hard anymore. It's thrilling."

Wolf thought about Red and her two horses, "What kind of rider is Red?"

"She's the best! She puts all the other boys and girls to shame. She's the only one I know who can ride standing up."

"What? How does she do that?"

Wart shrugged and said, "I don't know how, but she owns the best trained horses of any squire. They'll come to her when she calls. From what I hear, she raised Mary from a foal."

Wolf seemed surprised, "They're her horses?"

"Yeah, Easy Rider and Mary are hers, not the schools." Wart pulled Wolf close to him to whisper, "I don't know how she did it. She's like you. She has no family."

That tidbit of information stunned Wolf. "Where did she come from?"

"Nobody knows, or they're not talking. Some of us think she was left at the school as a baby, but some think she was born at the school."

Wolf realized that Red was unusual, more so than himself. "What do you think?"

"I think she is a knight's daughter, maybe Whisperblade's. They hang out together enough."

"How old is she?"

"Sixteen, I think. At least she goes to class with sixteen-year-old squires."

"She doesn't look much older than us!"

"Yeah, I know. It's weird."

Wolf stopped whispering and asked, "So when do you race?"

"Fairly late. You go before me."

Wolf frowned. "I don't have any horse skills. What am I supposed to do?"

"Just get on the horse they give you and show them that you can ride and turn. You know, the basic stuff. All the new students have to do it. It's sort of like being graded."

"I think I can do that. It sounds easy."

"You can do it easily. I know you can do it," Wart said and gave him a pat on his back."

They reached the stables and went to the bulletin board to look up their assignments. Wolf's riding test would be the first event of the morning, and he had to ride Easy Rider.

He went down the line of stables and found Red grooming Easy Rider. She had already brushed him to a fine sheen, and now she stood on a stool, braiding his mane. Mary stood next to them, looking magnificent, her mane braided into knots every three inches and her tail braided short with a large knot in the end.

Red announced, "I managed to get Easy Rider assigned to you since he's the only horse you've ridden. However, you must saddle him up and walk him out. It's part of the test, and I'm not allowed to help you. You have to show the judges you can do it yourself."

"Who are the judges?"

"Some of the knights and maybe some other adults. It really doesn't matter. All the grownups are going to be there anyway. You'd better saddle Easy and get going. I'll be there doing the same thing with Mary."

Wolf started to saddle Easy by placing the horse blanket after careful inspection of his back. He prepared the saddle and then realized that he needed to clean and shine the leather to make it presentable because he had to show off. He started by brushing the saddle and tack with a soft brush to get all the dust off. When satisfied, he used a rag to apply wax to the leather and buffed it to a shine using a large, fine-haired brush.

Wolf, ready to saddle the horse, struggled to lift the saddle and put it on the horse by himself. He managed the job by standing on a stool. He cinched the straps tight, taking care that Easy didn't hold his breath, thus keeping the straps loose. Next, came the halter and bit. Then Wolf led Easy out of the stables, just as Red led Mary out.

"You did a good job of saddling Easy," Red said. "I would have stopped you if you were doing it wrong. I think you have a good chance of making it in this school."

"Really?"

"Yes, really. Raven is a very good judge of people, and he picked you to be his page. I'm beginning to think he might be right about you."

They continued walking to the lists—the lists being a long stretch of level ground at least two hundred meters long with a series of stakes going down the center and a ribbon tied to the top of the stakes dividing the lists into two lanes. Near the middle, there were two low hills off to each side, where spectators were milling about. The adults had a row of crude split log benches to sit on.

When they were in the field with the other new pages, Red told him, "Go ahead and mount up. Don't do anything fancy, but most of all be calm. Easy knows what to do. I trained him myself." With that, she and Mary turned and walked away toward the other squires and their horses.

Once Wolf had mounted, Eagle came over and told him to line up with several other younger pages that were on their horses. He ended up being fourth in line, which suited him. It would be over soon, and he would be able to see what the routine was before he started.

He didn't have long to wait. Eagle called up the first rider and directed him into a series of basic maneuvers: turn around to the right, turn around to the left, walk forward, trot, stop, back up, trot around the pillions in a figure eight, stop, dismount, and remount. That completed the whole test. When Wolf's turn came, he had a good idea of what to do.

Eagle signaled him to start the exercise. He walked Easy Rider up to Eagle, who examined the horse and tack.

Then Eagle ordered them through the series of maneuvers. Wolf pulled off the maneuvers well, except for backing up. The knight congratulated him and directed him off the lists. As he exited the lists, Raven came up to him, congratulated him, and said, "You've learned well from Amara, but it's time for you to take lessons for real."

Wolf asked, "Red won't be teaching me?"

"She doesn't have time to teach you. Besides her duties are to me and her own lessons. You need to report to the stables in the morning after your self-defense class for riding lessons."

"Yes, sir. May I ask what's next?"

"The knights are giving riding demonstrations. You'll enjoy it, but first go fetch Midnight for me."

Wolf ran to fetch the high-spirited warhorse. He noticed the saddle sat a little loose so he cinched it up.

When Wolf reached Raven, he informed him of the loose strap.

The knight double-checked the saddle. "Good observation, it's not fun to fall off of your horse when you're at full gallop. So stand back and enjoy the rest of the day, but look after Amara. She could use some help when she rides. She'll tell you what to do."

Wolf ran to check on Red, who was giving a demonstration to the other squires on how to ride standing. Seeing she didn't need help at the moment, he returned to the lists to watch.

Raven mounted Midnight and trotted to the far end of the lists where he turned and came charging at a full gallop. Wolf saw Whisperblade galloping from the opposite end of the lists holding a sword up high. As they charged to meet at the center of the lists, she brought the sword down in a sweeping motion at just the right height to cut Raven's head off. But Raven wasn't there.

Wolf had closed his eyes in anticipation of the blood. He blinked again only to see Raven back in the saddle. The two knights had reached the opposite ends of the lists and turned to come back at each other. They charged again, and, this time, he could see Raven slip to the side of his horse as the sword came sweeping over him. Raven pulled himself back up in the saddle just as fast, and everybody cheered.

Soon the squires would be performing. While everyone waited, pages set up a series of stands in each lane of the lists. Each had an arm sticking out with a small ring suspended by a string at its end. The rings were of different sizes. Some were about three inches in diameter, some, two inches, and a few were one inch.

Wolf located Red among the other squires and ran to her. "Is there anything I can do for you, Red?"

"Yeah, wear this red scarf around your arm, and, if any squires or pages offer you any wager money, take note of whom they are and pocket the money, and for goodness sake, be careful about it, if you know what I mean."

"I think I do—no adults," Wolf replied.

"Yeah, now go fetch me a lance," she said. When he returned, she mounted Mary and took the lance from him. "When I return, be ready with a new lance, but most of all, keep track of the wagers."

"What's the game?"

"Jousting."

"Jousting? Isn't that where you knock each other off the horse, like kill each other?"

"Sort of, but only the knights get to kill each other. We don't wear armor, so we joust and race for points. The skill is in snagging the rings. If you feel brave enough, you can borrow a couple of bucks to bet on me. It's my gift to you."

With that, Red and another squire cantered their great horses to the far end of the lists where they lined up in front of a knight holding up a green flag. As soon as the knight dropped the flag, they were off at a full gallop. Wolf had never seen anything like it. The big horses kicked up huge clods of dirt, and the very ground began to shake.

The squires lowered their lances down to level, and, about halfway down the lists, they began to snag rings from the posts. Red missed the first large ring and snagged the next ring, the smallest size, and she continued to snag all the small rings. The other squire snagged a mixture of big and small rings and beat Red and Mary to the end of the lists.

Then a knight tallied the rings and marked their times. While a group of pages put new rings on the posts, Red trotted Mary up to Wolf and handed him the lance. She jumped off Mary and started massaging the horse's legs. Wolf put the lance in a stand then held up a bucket of water for the horse to drink.

"We have about ten minutes before the next run. Go check with the scorekeeper and see how I did."

As soon as Mary had her fill, Wolf ran to check with the scorekeeper, then ran back and announced, "You've won by twenty points!"

"See, it's not how big or fast you are; it's all about strategy. Since you can't possibly snag all the rings, you have to go for the big points. The next round will be harder. That's where the money will be. Squire Willow is just as good as me, and I can't afford any mistakes."

They watched the next three pairs run, and Squire Willow won her round by a larger margin then Red had won hers. She looked formidable, and by her insignia, he could tell she squired for Whisperblade.

Red mounted Mary, and, when Wolf handed her a new lance, she wheeled the giant horse around, started a canter to the far end of the lists, and arrived before Willow and her mount, giving Red time to line up and calm Mary. The horse seemed to know exactly what she needed to do.

When the green flag went up, Mary jumped to a full stride ahead of Willow and her mount. Mary reached full speed before the first ring, and Red had her lance down to snag it. Red continued to snag almost every ring and finished even with Willow.

Again, they deposited their rings with the judges. Red returned to Wolf, handed him her lance, and then dismounted. Wolf again watered the horse and ran to get the judge's decision.

When he returned, he announced, "You won by three points!" Red let out a yell.

"Now I have a chance for gold." While waiting for her next run, Red explained jousting a little more. "We do it a little differently here then they do elsewhere. Our rings are larger; there are more of them, and horse speed counts a lot, which is what makes it so hard. The faster you ride, the harder it is. You have to be a natural on the horse. David, the squire I'm up against, is very good. I've beat him only once."

"What are you going to do?"

"Ride like the wind and snag all the rings."

"All of them?"

"Every last one."

"You said it couldn't be done."

"Did I? I've been practicing, and I've developed a few tricks of my own. Maybe I'll surprise everyone."

"I'll bet on you."

"You better, or I'll make your life miserable." She grinned and winked at him.

Wolf asked, "What odds should I ask for?"

"You're not so dumb, either. Ask at least three to one."

"I'll get you five." Wolf made good on his word. Squire David seemed such a sure bet. With just a few minutes available for Wolf to take bets, he scrambled. Unfortunately, only a few squires and pages had the nerve to bet, but Wolf could remember them all. He knew he wouldn't forget Wayne. The page made a snide remark about both him and Red not being worth the money, but he bet ten dollars. Once the bets were collected, Wolf ran to attend to Red and tell her about the bets. She seemed to be pleased.

Red asked for a particularly light lance, which Wolf handed her. This time she trotted Mary to the far end of the lists with the other squire on her tail. The determination in his eyes made it obvious there would be no mistakes on his part.

This time, when the green flag rose, they were off together. They reached the first ring together and both snagged them and the ten rings after. When it came to the last ring, Red got hers, but David managed only to knock his off the hook, and it went spinning into the grass. It looked good for Red, but the other squire's horse was a head faster than Mary.

Red didn't return to the paddock but waited for the judge's call. It didn't take long before Red was declared the winner by two points, the smallest margin of the day. A cluster of pages who had bet on her were cheering and hollering for her.

There were other horse games to play and more demonstrations by the knights. The best action came near the end when Raven and Whisperblade, clad in full armor on their warhorses, faced each other in full frontal armor, carrying long lances with blunted tips.

They started on opposite ends of the lists. Red started Midnight with a hearty slap on the rump. Willow did the same for Cloud. On the first pass, the riders' lances connected with each other's shield and shattered in a shower of splinters. The entire school went wild cheering for one or the other.

The second pass went better. Whisperblade's lance shattered, and Raven drove her shield so hard with his lance that she almost lifted from the saddle. She managed to hang on and return upright. There was a hushed pause until Whisperblade lifted an arm. Then the cheering began anew. Wolf ran to Raven to see if he needed anything. He found the knight's armor to be modern Kevlar with a thin layer of stainless steel bonded to it.

"Are you all right, sir?" Wolf asked.

"I'm fine," Raven answered. He walked his horse over to Whisperblade and pointed his lance at her chest.

"Do you yield, Lady Knight?" Raven demanded.

"I do not yield," Whisperblade replied just as loudly.

"Then I offer you another lance."

"I accept." Whisperblade trotted her horse to the far end of the lists where she picked up another lance and waited for the drop of the flag. Raven went to his end of the lists and exchanged his lance for a new one. After signaling his readiness, the green flag raised, and the two knights started their charge.

They came at each other, leaning forward in their saddles, their shields pulled against their armor. As their lances connected with each other's shield, Raven's lance shattered, and the Whisperblade's drove hard into his shield.

This time Raven was dumped onto the turf. Red and Wolf were there in a flash to help him up.

Whisperblade removed her helmet, handed it to Willow, dismounted, and went to Raven and gave him a bear hug. More than a few pages snickered at the sight.

~

With the jousting finished, it was time for the racing. While the racers prepared their horses, adults and non-racers worked at removing the ribbon and posts marking the two lanes of the lists. Riders accumulated in a long line in the lists. The first to line up were the pages, Wart amidst them. The squires lined up behind the pages on a mixture of horses, including the Percherons.

When the green flag rose, a wild wave of horses moved out in a thunderous mass. The tumult of riders soon stretched into a long line. Wolf could see Wart riding among the faster horses.

The racers galloped hard, streaming for the far end of the open part of the valley where a red flag could be seen. They raised a large cloud of dust. The line of racers reached the flag and rounded it to the left. They crossed the valley from right to left, splashing through several streams before they reached the second red flag.

Rounding the flag, the horsemen started the long return to the lists. The riders encountered a shallow stream they had to ride lengthwise for quarter of a kilometer. The next obstacle was a field of brush pine through which they had to weave their horses. Finally, they rode through a stand of trees with low branches that favored the smaller horses and younger riders. The obstacles bunched the horses for the last dash to the finish line at the lists. The line of horses galloped through the lists and kept the ground shaking.

Wolf soon realized the loud din of the horses was matched by the cheering of the students. Wart placed well, finishing fourth among all the pages.

Wolf took charge of Wart's horse, walking it to cool down and then leading it to the water trough to drink while Red and Raven rode the course to check on any stragglers and to note any damage to the land that would require immediate attention.

~

Later Red and Wolf counted the bets that she had won. She gave Wolf twelve dollars to pay his winnings. He marveled that he now had more money he had had in the last year.

He asked Red with a bit of sarcasm, "Now that I'm rich, what do I do with it? I haven't seen money used at camp since I've been here."

"Bet with it next week or keep it. You'll get plenty of chances to spend when school starts back up. It's how I managed to afford Easy Rider and his saddle, and it's how I pay for his upkeep. Saddles are quite expensive unless you can get a bargain on a good used one."

"What about Mary?" he asked.

"She pays for herself. She's a working horse, and the school values her to be worth her upkeep, besides she doesn't eat that much. The school bought her saddle and pulling harness. They'll keep them when I leave, so I have to work to earn a few more dollars."

Chapter 8 ~ A Horse's Story

After breakfast, Wolf reported to the stables for his first riding lesson. There were just a couple of pages and a squire cleaning stalls and laying fresh hay. Wolf introduced himself to the squire, who set him to work shoveling manure.

Wolf worked for about a half hour before the teacher arrived. "So you're the boy who sleeps with wolves. They won't sleep with you after you muck these stables. Wolves and horses don't get along very well."

Wolf's senses went on full alert. There was something about this teacher he didn't like. He sounded a lot like his last math teacher, who'd always called on him when a difficult problem was being discussed. Then the teacher had made little comments about his lack of knowledge.

"Pull over a couple of stools so we can sit and chat." Wolf did it and they sat down. The instructor said, "I said those things to you, not to make you mad, but to judge your reaction. Your face went flush and you stiffened up. Kids who hope to have fun at your expense want to see those reactions. The reason this is important is twofold: it teaches you that you have reactions that people use to judge you, and it introduces you to the possibility that you can control your reactions. Do you understand what I'm trying to say?"

"I don't think so, sir."

"It's like this—people sense your reactions and act on them. Horses do the same. If a horse senses you're afraid of him or that you don't like him, you can be sure he'll make your life miserable. Horses and people can be alike in that way."

"Oh."

"All horses are different. Some are nice and easy going, and some are downright hateful. And that's just the tame ones. Let's see if we can find the right one for you."

"Thank you, sir." They went down the line of the stables discussing the merits of every horse, and then they walked back to look at the school horses. In the end, they chose Pinto Bean, a smaller brown and white horse with a friendly disposition.

The next order of business was a saddle. Wolf would have to share it among several pages. The instructor explained that this was normal, and he expected Wolf to return it in as good condition as he received it or someone could be hurt. Safety being first priority, Wolf would have to learn to repair his tack.

Wolf had to be fitted for a helmet, a motorcycle helmet. The teacher explained it gave him the best protection for his head for when he fell. He expected Wolf to wear it whenever he rode a horse, at least until he qualified to ride just by himself. It felt weird and geeky.

The instructor then explained that every hour of riding time required at least an hour of work to look after the horses. Horses required a lot of attention, and all riders shared in the responsibility. When he was away from camp, someone else had to be found to take care of the horse. Wolf readily accepted the responsibility. Riding lessons were to start for real tomorrow.

The instructor left for another class, and Wolf cleaned Pinto Bean's stall. After he finished, he took time to get acquainted with Pinto Bean, feeding him a fresh apple like Red had taught him and then brushing his coat clean.

Red came in and looked at Pinto Bean. She checked out his teeth and hooves, and she seemed pleased. Then she rubbed the horse's legs one by one.

She stood up, turned to Wolf, and said, "He's a good horse. I used to ride him. He knows what's expected. He may be a little long in the tooth, but that's to be expected for a school horse. They don't get too many young ones because they want experienced horses. I would say he's older than you."

"Isn't that kind of old for a horse?"

"Nah, he'll live another ten years easily. Why don't you saddle him up? I want to check out the two of you together."

Wolf went to get the horse blanket, "Are you going to teach me riding?"

Red grinned and said, "Nope, the horse is going to teach you."

Wolf frowned, knowing Red was up to something. "How is that?"

"You'll see," Red said with an innocent smile.

Wolf finished saddling the horse and putting on the tack. Red walked around the horse, checking his work. She grabbed the girth strap and eased her knee into the horse's ribs; pulling the strap tight. "There, that should do it."

"So what's this about the horse teaching me?" Wolf asked.

"Just mount up and follow me." Red turned and walked out of the stables.

Wolf hurried to comply. They rode into the meadow, and Red turned on her heels to Wolf. Pinto Bean stopped without Wolf pulling on the reins.

"How did you do that?" Wolf asked.

"It's easy. The horse followed me, not taking orders from you. You don't have the feel of riding him yet. But he didn't try to go off on his own. I want you to ride in a circle around me and follow my instructions."

Wolf clucked the horse to a walk and started him around her. "Okay, now what?"

"I want you to attempt to fall off."

"Are you trying to kill me?"

"Please trust me."

Wolf looked at Red to see if she was serious. She appeared to be, so he started leaning over and instinctively squeezed his legs. He dropped his reins and put his arms out in anticipation of hitting the ground. The horse stopped and turned to stay under him. Wolf grabbed the saddle horn and pulled himself back up.

Red approached the horse, secured the reins, and handed them back up to Wolf. "This horse is very experienced with new riders. He'll look after you. Pay attention to him, and he'll teach you a lot." Red started to walk away, but turned back and said, "Pinto Bean is all heart. Why don't you ride him awhile and become acquainted?"

Wolf took her advice and trotted Pinto Bean out into the large meadow north of the stables. The horse went right with a small pull of the reins. He gave the reins a slight pull to the left, and the horse turned left.

Wolf decided to try the fall maneuver. He started to lean over and dropped the reins. Pinto Bean slowed down and turned to keep Wolf up in the saddle. The horse quickly came to a stop. Wolf for once felt safe on a horse. It was a revelation for him.

He gave the horse a gentle kick, and they accelerated to a canter. It was easy. It was exhilarating. And it was a surprise when he ended up on the ground. When he got over the initial surprise, he remembered flying off to the side of the horse, hitting the ground, and rolling to a stop. He looked up and a large white horse appeared in his view. It looked familiar, and its rider was Whisperblade.

The lady knight dismounted and knelt down to look at him closer. She placed a hand on his chest, holding him down. "What's your name?"

"Caleb."

Whisperblade frowned. "What name do you use now?"

He paused for a moment and said, "Wolf?"

"Do you know who I am?"

"Lady Knight, Wolf, no, Whisperblade."

"Just lay down until the nurse arrives." The knight ordered her page, Hildegard, to fetch the nurse. Hildegard galloped off to carry out her orders. "So what do you think you were trying to do?"

"Ride my horse."

"You were going at a fast canter. You were leaning wrong when you turned. Did the riding instructor approve your riding that fast?"

"No, ma'am. Red told me to get to know him. I thought the horse would turn under me."

"Not while you're going that fast. I'm going to have a talk with Amara. She knows better. How do you feel?"

"I feel all right."

"Good, I don't want you to be in pain while you're mucking out stalls. Here comes the nurse. When she is done with you, report to my tent."

~

When Wolf reported to Whisperblade's tent, she said, "Have a seat." He sat in a camp chair, and the knight sat next to him. "Wolf, I've talked to the riding instructor and to Amara. Nobody told you that you could go that fast on a horse. They also didn't tell you not to. You have to realize that when there is danger, you have to go by the rules. I've decided what your punishment is."

Wolf cringed.

"You're going to muck Cloud's stall for seven days. Also, I'm going to give you a personal riding lesson each day."

"Yes, my Lady."

"And Wolf..."

"Yes, my Lady?"

"Try to obey the rules. They're there to keep you out of trouble."

"Yes, my Lady."

"You're dismissed."

Knowlton

Chapter 9 ~ Boar Hunting

A week later, after breakfast, Raven sent Red and Wolf to prepare their horses and draw supplies for Wolf's first experience on patrol. They first went to the stables where they saddled Midnight, Easy Rider, and Pinto Bean. They also saddled Raven's packhorse with a utility saddle with large saddlebags and extra tie down straps.

Wolf and Red stopped by to see the quartermaster, who gave them fresh bedrolls, rain ponchos, and water skins. They visited the mess tent where they loaded up on dried fruit, cheeses, dried meats, and fresh vegetables. Red mixed up some of her formulas of spices and herbs for cooking and then made the selection of teas and coffee.

Red and Wolf returned to Raven's tent just as he finished packing. They loaded the horses and mounted up. They rode through camp to the weapon master's tent where Raven and Red each picked out a lance. Each lance had a razor-sharp, steel point. The points were broad and not barbed, designed to slice. Heavy leather caps covered the points for safety.

The riders headed west across the valley floor and soon cleared the fields and entered the forest. They rode for a couple of hours, passing the incoming patrol led by Eagle. He relayed the news of their findings and the disposition of the outposts.

Red took the time to explain to Wolf how they managed the security of the valley. She said, "The outposts are manned by two squires each. They're posted at the three entrances to the valley. They're at the east and west mountain ridge trails and in the south at the valley's river exit. There are none in the north since there are no usable trails there.

"The purpose of the outposts is to provide control and warning of any intruders. We regularly patrol the valley, often beyond the mountain ridges into other valleys as a service to the state. The outposts are manned in twenty-four hour shifts by the two squires. Two horse patrols are always circling the valley, like we are, visiting the outposts.

"We're starting a three-day patrol and expect to cover the entire rim of the valley. We'll ride for long periods without breaks other than to rest and refresh our horses. It'll be tough on the horses and you."

"Why won't it be tough on you?" Wolf asked.

"It will; I'm just so used to it that I don't notice."

For Wolf, it would be a true test of his riding skills. Raven expected him to keep up with his studies and to learn whatever Red could teach him. Pinto Bean turned out to be a very good horse and forgiving of the errors Wolf made. On dangerous, steep trails, the horse kept his footing, giving Wolf a sense of ease.

Wolf had to keep performing his mapping. He frequently had to climb trees during rest breaks, and Red often climbed up with him and used the time to work with him on his math. Wolf had graduated from using a book of logarithms to do his calculations to using a slide rule. The slide rule enabled him to multiply and divide and to work trigonometric problems far faster and easier. He wished they'd let him use a scientific calculator as they did in normal schools.

The patrol reached the western mountain pass into the valley where they were challenged by the two squires on watch. "Halt. Who goes there?" Squire John demanded.

"Three children of the forest," Raven replied.

"What is the password?"

"Pegasus," Raven said.

"Horse feathers," Squire Mike countered.

"Well meet," concluded Raven.

Raven then took a full report from the two squires, John and Mike. Wolf listened in and heard there had been no trouble to speak of except some deer passing through during the night, possibly chased by wolves. Both squires were sure they had heard the wolves howling.

Raven searched for tracks with Red and Wolf, accompanied by the two squires of the watch. The tracks were easy enough to find, and they were cloven hoofed, but the Raven pointed out the pattern didn't fit a deer's track, the gait being too short and the impressions too deep. Raven then pointed to some of the damage the animal had caused by digging for roots. He stood up, and Wolf could tell by Raven's dark expression that something was wrong.

Red said it first. "Pig."

"Wild boar," Raven said, "a very dangerous one. You two squires are very lucky that it was chased by wolves." He then issued orders for the younger squire, John, to carry news back to camp, and John took off at a gallop.

Raven said, "Wolf, this is very dangerous. You have no weapons training, so you can go back to camp with John if you want."

Wolf's heart was pounding, but he said, "I'd rather stay."

"All right," Raven said, "but you must stay out of the way and obey all orders immediately."

Wolf nodded. Raven said, "Mike, you ride with me and Amara. We'll have to make a suitable lance for you as soon as a proper tree can be found."

Mike and Red removed their arrows and bows from the horse packs, and Red checked her broad hunting knife.

Raven pulled out three swords and gave one to Mike and one to Red, who strapped it to her back. The last weapon he pulled out was a small, but fearsome-looking, tomahawk, which he tucked in his belt. The blade on its head extended only three inches wide, but the other side of the head had a long sharp spike with a sharp inner edge. Wolf thought it looked like it could rip through the top of an automobile.

They mounted up and started down the trail into the valley until they reached the tree line where the track of the boar diverged off to the right. Raven followed the boar's trail. The boar had traveled fast, but Raven did not hurry. "It will head for water," he said. Soon, they came upon a small, dead pine tree, which, with a few chops with his war hatchet, Raven felled and stripped of its branches. He then attached a spear point to the end of the pole thus forming a deadly lance. Raven and Red then uncapped their own lances exposing the lethal points.

Again, they mounted up, and with lances pointing up, they started hunting for the boar, Wolf following close behind them. Raven followed the trail with Red twenty yards to the right and behind and Mike twenty yards to the left and behind, thus forming a triangle of armed hunters. They slowly trailed the boar until they came to a stream where the boar had been. The banks of the stream were torn up from the rooting the boar had done.

Keeping his voice low, Raven said, "Without question, this beast is big—at least 400 pounds. If left alone, it will tear up a good part of the valley and it might hurt someone. It has to be killed."

They crossed the stream and continued following the trail. They were in deep woods now, and Raven walked Midnight carefully. Wolf understood that Raven was wary of coming upon the beast unexpectedly.

Wolf looked to his right, and, even at a distance, he could see sweat running down Red's forehead. He wondered if she were scared. She used her free arm to mop her brow. Every once in a while, they came to a spot where the boar had dug a hole, rooting for a morsel. An untiring machine of destruction, the animal would rub pieces of bark off trees with its sharp tusks.

Raven, the voice of calm, said, "Mike and Amara, you're doing all right. Keep up your courage." Wolf looked around him, hoping he wouldn't see the boar come rushing toward him. They kept advancing through the trees, the knight keeping to the tracks, the squires at his flanks, and Wolf following closely.

Soon they heard the boar rooting ahead. The hunters lowered their lances to attack position. Wolf noticed that the boar seemed to sense their presence and went quiet. Everyone held their positions.

Then the boar came from their left, bursting out of the undergrowth with surprising speed.
Mike managed to prick the animal's back, cutting a long gash. The boar wailed as it passed by him, crossing behind Raven, who couldn't get his lance around fast enough. It ran by Red, who instantly gave chase, spurring Easy Rider to action as the boar disappeared into the brush.

Wolf and the others followed and broke out onto the bank of the stream. The boar had already crossed the stream into an open field, and Red had lowered her lance to the pig's height. She caught up with it at midfield and managed to stab it in the back with her weapon, but Wolf noticed she had to slow down to keep from overrunning the pig.

Wolf saw she was only twenty yards from the edge of the field when her horse slipped on loose grass, and Red went sprawling, rolled once, and managed to get to her knees. He felt like his heart was in his throat when the boar turned and charged toward her. To him, everything seemed to happen in slow motion. Red had lost her grip on the lance, but she pulled her sword from its scabbard over her shoulder. However, the boar was too close for her to plunge her sword into its back. She dived to her left as it rushed by. Red then sprang to her feet and started running for the trees. She dropped her sword, dived, rolled, and came up at the base of the lance, as Raven and Mike rode in to help her.

Red grabbed the lance with both hands, bringing the point up just as the boar reached her. The boar hit the point of the lance square in its breast. Its momentum carried it forward until a yard of the slicing point and shaft emerged out of its lower back.

The butt end of the lance dug into the ground, and the boar collapsed, face to face with Red, but it still swung its head from side to side, the deadly, sharp tusks inches from Red's nose. Amazingly, while spewing blood, the boar still tried to get to its feet, and Red kept holding onto the lance for her very life.

Raven jumped off his horse, plunged the spike of his tomahawk into the boar's head, and gave it a hard twist that finally stilled the beast.

Red was splattered with blood from the massive pig. She kept holding onto the lance with an iron hard grip, until the Raven gently pried her hands loose. He kept reassuring her, "Everything's all right. It's over."

Wolf watched as Raven led Red over to the stream and dunked her face and hands in the water to wash off most of the blood. He then took her over to Easy Rider, boosted her into the saddle, and gave her a bedroll to wrap herself in to keep warm.

Then Raven turned his attention to the boar and, using his big knife, gutted the beast. He left Red's lance still sticking through it, but retrieved his tomahawk. Wolf then helped Raven and Mike build a horse sled, which they rigged together in a few minutes from their lances. Rolling the pig onto it, they hoisted the long ends of the sled and secured them to the sides of the packhorse's saddle.

Wolf rode beside Red on the trip back to camp. Raven and Mike walked their horses for a ways while Wolf and Red rode slowly. They were met halfway back to camp by Whisperblade, Willow, Bob, and Bill, who stared wide-eyed at the boar.

Whisperblade and Willow flanked Red and Wolf, and Whisperblade started a tale. "I knew a young knight who had just earned his spurs. He was hunting for rabbit in a valley far to the north when he came to a large stream. It had some of the purest water imaginable, bone chilling cold. The salmon were swimming and jumping over the rocks. The knight put down his bow and quiver and took off his boots to wade in and catch one of the large fish.

"He snatched a jumping fish right out of the air, a huge fish. As he tried to make his way to the bank, a mother bear came wandering out of the woods leading her two cubs.

"This knight stopped in the stream and looked at the bear then at his prize fish. Thinking quickly, he tossed the fish onto the bank. The bear attacked the fish, killing it with a well-placed bite. The cubs attacked the knight's bow and boots using them as chew toys. The knight didn't run because he knew better than to turn his back on the bear.

"Finally, out of fear more than anything else, he decided to fight the bear. Still standing in the middle of the stream, he slipped his coat off and waited. When the bear finished with her fish, she turned her attention to the knight and started growling.

"The man didn't hesitate, but charged the bear while swinging his coat and yelling wildly. The startled bear stared at the man for a few moments then stood up on her hind legs. The knight feared for his life, for there is nothing as fearsome as a mother bear. But the knight kept charging at the bear, yelling and yelling. Soon they were face to face.

"The bear was huge, and the knight was desperate. He almost dropped his coat to pull his knife when the bear turned and dropped to all fours. It had apparently tired of the game. She walked away, trailing her cubs."

Whisperblade made a dramatic pause and said, "That night he returned to camp, much, much braver for having faced the bear, but alas, without his prized bow, without his boots, without his fish, and without the rabbit he had been hunting."

This and other tales soon had Red laughing so that Wolf could tell she had relaxed. More and more students arrived as they got closer to camp until it seemed the whole camp had decided to parade. Everyone wanted to see the boar.

Back at camp Mike recounted Red's exploit. Somebody penciled a drawing of the boar impaling itself on the lance, and somehow the boar looked bigger and fiercer while Red looked smaller, but she liked the drawing. The mess crew confiscated the boar, then butchered and cooked it. Dinner that evening turned out to be a big feast for all with dancing, merry-making, and song.

~

Later that night, when Red and Wolf reported to Raven's tent for the next day's orders, Raven didn't seem merry at all. He looked at Red and said, "It might have been brave to charge after the boar, but you foolishly put yourself in unnecessary danger. You didn't account for something bad happening. You had extra resources. I'm a resource, and Mike is a resource. As a team, we had time to do it right." He then looked at Wolf and added, "I hope you've learned something from this." Raven turned back to Red, softened a bit, and said, "But, since you showed the bravery and the quick thinking a knight should have, you should enjoy this day for the rest of your life." He handed her the lethal tusks from the boar's jaws. "Here, make a necklace for yourself." Then he said to both of them, "Tomorrow, early, we're going back on patrol."

Knowlton

Chapter 10 ~ On Patrol

The next morning Wolf awoke early and reported to Raven's tent. After breakfast, Red went to saddle the horses, and Wolf stayed to help Raven pack. He prepared the packhorses' bundles, arranging the supplies they had checked out the day before.

As soon as Red returned with the horses, they loaded up and went by the quartermaster's tent and the mess tent. They finished collecting their supplies and proceeded north up the valley at a trot until they entered a deep forest. Raven then slowed the pace, but didn't stop except to let the horses drink at a stream.

They reached the northern edge of the valley at lunchtime, and Raven called for a break. Red and Wolf gathered twigs for a small fire, and Red started it using the back of her knife and a piece of flint.

"How does that work?" Wolf asked.

"It's the sharp edge of the flint moving fast across the surface of the steel, producing very fine particles of iron, which burn in air, producing intense heat."

"I need a piece of flint. Where do I find one?"

"It's a special kind of rock. It sort of breaks like glass, but it's a lot tougher. I use them for my arrowheads. There's an ample supply of it near here. Ask Raven if we can make a stop, and we'll get some."

Wolf finished making coffee and tea, and they made lunch of fruit and beef jerky. Then he asked Raven about the flint.

"No more than you can carry and be quick about it," Raven replied.

Wolf and Red mounted up and rode about ten minutes to a small rock outcropping where they found shards and nodules of flint. They didn't have much time, so Red picked out some good, usable pieces for Wolf. On returning, they found Raven had already packed the coffeepot, put out the fire, cleaned the ground, and was ready to ride.

They rode east around the perimeter of the valley for the rest of the day, keeping just in the tree line. Raven found nothing of importance, but he did use the time to teach Wolf some of the secrets of tracking by practicing on deer tracks. It became obvious to Wolf that it would be a long time before he could follow a deer trail.

~

Towards late afternoon, they reached the eastern trail into the valley. There they watered their horses and began the climb into the pass. They climbed for an hour up before they reached the pass and encountered John, the squire on watch, who challenged them. "Halt, who goes there?"

"Three children of the forest," Raven replied.

"What is the pass word?"

"The oxen are slow."

"But the earth is patient."

"Give me your report," Raven demanded.

"Sir, no large animals have passed through here during the last twenty-four hours. Two knights and their squires and pages came into the valley. There has been no other traffic reported in the prior three days."

"Well done," Raven replied.

Squire Jimmy, who accompanied John, boiled water and fixed coffee for everybody. Wolf noted Raven drank his coffee plain.

Then Raven left orders for the squires, and they headed back down the trail to the valley floor. Upon reaching the first stream, Raven ordered a halt for the evening. They unloaded the horses, turned them loose, and laid out bedrolls.

Then Wolf received his first lesson in fire starting. He managed to get the steel and flint to spark easily, but he had difficulty getting the shavings to burn. The tender would barely smolder and refuse to flame up. After several tries, he mastered the technique.

Red then showed him how to use charred cloth patches to start the tinder more easily. She told Wolf that she prepared the cloth by cooking small patches in a candy tin to keep the cloth from catching fire. After cooking and cooling, the tin could be opened, revealing the charred black cloth.

Red didn't manage to kill a rabbit that night, but the fire was friendly, and the dried fruit and beef jerky were good. The sourdough bread toasted with cheese tasted great.

With dinner over, it was time for music and song. Red told Wolf to sit back and enjoy the music. She pulled out her fife and announced, "This is 'The World Turned Upside Down.'" She followed with "The King of the Fairies." When she finished, Wolf and Raven clapped their hands, and she bowed.

Raven answered her with a couple of tunes of his own. Wolf impressed, clapped again. Then Raven announced, "This is a little ditty I'm teaching Amara." He started playing "Brian Boru's March," and after one round, Red joined in. With every round of the tune, they picked up the pace. Wolf had never seen a flute up close much less a six-hole fife. He couldn't follow the movements of their fingers. Eventually, Red couldn't keep it up and started to stumble over the notes. Soon, she gave up and laughed, and Wolf and Raven laughed with her.

Raven jested to Red, "If you can't play a good tune, maybe you could sing one." She complied by singing "Walking in the Air." On the second verse, Raven joined in with his fife. The song had a very haunting melody, made more so by the wind in the trees.

Wolf suddenly wished he could be like the boy in the song, flying over the world.

Raven looked at him when the song was finished and asked, "Why do you look so sad? It's just a song about a dream."

"I know, sir, It's just I feel so trapped in this world."

Raven said, "I can't fly, but I've been to some amazing places and performed good deeds. Life tends to live up to your expectations. If you want them enough, I think adventures will come your way. For now, enjoy the adventures you're in. They'll prepare you for the ones you'll have later."

Red said to Wolf, "Please, why don't you join in the song? It's always better to sing with others." Wolf refused at first because he had never sung before, but with gentle encouragement, he tried the first verse of "Walking in the Air." He had to work on it, but the pitch of his voice was close enough to Red's, and it sounded good.

~

In the morning, Wolf found the wolf again curled up asleep next to him. He stroked the wolf's head, and it turned to lick his face. He checked out the wolf's wound. The bandage had been lost, but the stitches held, and the wound did not look infected or swollen. Then Wolf noticed Raven staring at him.

"The wolf is doing a lot better. You need to remove the stitches, or he'll pick at them until the wound becomes infected again." Raven gave him a tiny pair of scissors with which to snip out the stitches.

Speaking softly to the wolf, Wolf managed to get it to lay still long enough to cut the stitches and pull the thread out. Once he finished, the wolf arose and trotted off. It still had a noticeable limp.

Wolf started preparing the coffee, tea, fresh apples, and dried figs. While boiling the water, he realized there wasn't a break in a day's work. From the first day with Raven, he had picked up a new job or skill every day. While out on patrol, Raven expected him to keep up with his school lessons, so he'd started reading in the saddle. He wondered what would be added when he returned from patrol. He would find out soon enough.

From their camp near the eastern pass, they traveled south then southwest to the southern entrance to the valley. There they found a break in the mountains surrounding the valley where a small river exited the valley. A barely recognizable wagon trail paralleled the river, mostly hidden from view by dense undergrowth.

"This is the main way into the valley," Red said. "All our supplies come this way by wagon."

"There must be a lot of traffic on the trail," Wolf said.

"There was a lot when camp was being set up, but now it's food coming in and trash going out. That's a lot of what Mary and the other Percherons work at, pulling wagons."

"Why did we come through the mountain pass?"

"We have to conduct business in town," Red replied.

"What kind of business?"

"We have to deal with the National Forestry Service. We do some ranger work for them in return for their supporting our school."

"What kind of ranger work do you do?"

"We track and rescue lost people. We also track bad guys, illegal lumber operators and miners and such, but we also track drug growers. They're the worst."

"How is that?"

"They would just as soon kill you as talk to you."

"Whoa! What do you do with them? You don't have real weapons."

"Don't discount arrows and lances. We make these mountains so unpleasant for them that they just leave."

"How do you do that?"

"That's something the knights and older squires do. It's very dangerous work. Raven says I'm good enough to go on the next raid if we have one this summer."

Later, they took a northwesterly course to the base of the western pass into the mountains. There they camped for the night. Red and Wolf had time to hunt rabbit, and she killed three large ones. Wolf insisted that one be left for the wolf that still followed them.

~

In the morning, they climbed up to the gap in the western pass where Raven took a report from the squires on watch and gave them orders for the next day. The pass had been quiet since the wild boar incident. After descending from the pass, they spent the rest of the morning returning to the main camp. They demobilized, attended to the horses, and went to their tents for a long awaited rest.

Wolf, walking back to his tent, heard a whimpering sound coming from a copse of trees between camping areas. It sounded like a dog. He entered the copse and found a puppy tied to a small bush by its rear leg. It was in pain. Wolf bent down to untie it, but he was blindsided by a fist to the side of his head.

As soon as the lights stopped flashing, Wolf realized Wayne was astride him with knees on his arms. "Awake, I see. Why don't you save me the trouble and go back to the orphanage? That's where you fit in." To emphasize his point, he did a roundhouse punch to Wolf's cheek.

Wolf brought up a knee attempting to hit Wayne in the back. It wasn't enough. He tried again with a little more effect. Wayne just leaned down till he was face to face with Wolf. "I mean it. I'm going to make you go." Wayne spit on Wolf's cheek.

This time Wolf brought up both legs and forced them onto Wayne's back, knocking the page over Wolf's head. Wolf instantly rolled over and, from a kneeling position, fell on top of Wayne. He would have gotten in a few wild punches, but a low growling sound interrupted him.

Both boys stopped struggling and looked for the source of the sound. When Wayne saw it, his eyes went wide open, and he desperately tried to get out from under Wolf. When Wolf looked up, he saw the wolf about ten feet away, fangs bared.

"Call him off!" Wayne said.

Wolf didn't know what to do. He said, "I can't. He isn't mine."

"Do something. Get him away."

Wolf got up, but the wolf had disappeared.

"That wolf is dangerous; I'm telling."

"I'll tell about the puppy," Wolf countered. He bent down, untied the puppy, and cradled it in his arms. When he looked up, Wayne had disappeared. Wolf looked around the camp until he found the mother dog and returned the puppy to it. He feared what would happen if the knights found out what the wolf had done.

~

During his next self-defense class, Wolf tried to block one of Whisperblade's blows but was too slow for her unexpected swiftness. Her fist landed on his cheek where he already had been hit by Wayne. He gasped in pain and realized he would have a nasty bruise. Her next blow had similar results.

Whisperblade stopped the exercise and said, "You have to learn to block. Go report to the nurse and have that cheek looked after. Then report to my tent." Wolf ran to comply with her orders.

When he reported to her tent, she invited him in and told him to sit down. "I hope I didn't hurt your cheek too much."

"No more than it already had been." Wolf realized he had let slip that he had been in a fight.

The Whisperblade grimaced. "I noticed you had fallen on your cheek. You could have at least put your arm in the way."

"I couldn't move my arms."

"Interesting, I think I'm going to have to teach you some tricks to get those arms moving again. There's no excuse for being in a situation where you can't move your arms. I don't see any reason to discuss your clumsiness any further. Wolf, you need to make self-defense a deadly, serious business. You're dismissed."

"Yes, ma'am." Wolf stood and stepped for the entrance.

"Oh, Wolf."

He stopped and turned to face her. "Yes, ma'am?"

"Try and teach that gray wolf how to act among the other students."

Wolf, stunned, realized his jaw hung open. *Did she see what happened? Not likely,* he thought. *She would have stopped it.* He couldn't figure the woman out. "Yes, ma'am," he said.

Knowlton

Chapter 11 ~ Changes

Mary, the great Percheron, pulled wagons in and out of the valley and jousted in competitions, but she started to balk when it came to pulling logs. Red was the only person Mary obeyed for the heavy work.

Wolf, at first, didn't pay Mary much attention. Mary, however, took a shine to Wolf and seemed to be miffed at being ignored. Whenever she saw Wolf, Mary made a beeline to him and demanded attention, which he returned. Soon Red taught Wolf to stand on Mary's back as she led her around.

Wolf asked, "Mary is kind of fat, isn't she?"

"You noticed. Now what do you think is making her so fat?"

"Too many apples," Wolf ventured.

"Okay, that's a good guess, but no. She's going to have a baby."

"She's what?"

"You know those cute little things that drink milk and weigh about two hundred pounds."

"Wow, that's big. When?" Wolf asked.

"Any day now. She's been very cranky."

"But she likes you, and I think she's a good judge of character. That wolf likes you, too. In fact, I haven't seen an animal that doesn't like you."

~

When it came time for Wolf to take archery lessons, Red taught Wolf how to knap arrowheads from the flint shards he had collected. Red directed him to Mr. Grier the blacksmith, who also acted as the carpenter. Wolf asked the man to help him with making the arrows and a bow. The long arrows that Red favored were made from bamboo, an excellent material, but hard to work; it split if not trimmed right. The smith taught Wolf the secrets to make the arrows right.

Wolf couldn't make the bow, not a composite bow like Red's. "It is easy to replace a broken or lost arrow," Mr. Grier advised. "You can even experiment with its design. They can be traded; that's fun. But a bow is a personal thing; it becomes a part of you. You need a bow that fits you. The composite bow is very hard to build. It's made from layered horn, wood, and sinew and requires expert workmanship. I'll make you one, but you're going to have to work for it." The smith fitted Wolf with a longbow from his stock. Once outfitted, Wolf reported to the archery instructor.

To earn the composite bow, Wolf agreed to work mornings. They spit in their palms and shook hands to seal the deal. He had to tend the fire in the forge and hammer iron. He hammered everything from horseshoes, to wagon parts, to knives. The smith, using tongs, positioned the glowing iron on the anvil, and Wolf hammered.

The hot work started to build his arm muscles. As the bright, orange bars of steel were hammered, they would cool to a dull red before the smith put them back in the fire. When done with a piece, Mr. Grier quenched it in water and set it aside to start on another. Wolf needed no warning; the hot steel could deliver a nasty burn on the slightest contact.

After a week of swinging the hammer, Wolf's sore arms become hardened to the work. He enjoyed beating his frustrations out on the iron and steel. Mr. Grier amazed him with his creativity with iron, and he always dispensed little bits of advice, such as, "The quickest ways to kill yourself are by trying to work cold steel or not charging enough for your work."

For the first few days of archery lessons, Wolf didn't even shoot an arrow. Instead, he learned how to hold the bow, how to take care of it, and how to make bowstrings. He had to draw and hold the bow, then release it without hurting himself. Raven put him on an exercise routine of chin-ups and push-ups to further strengthened his arms.

With his time at the blacksmith's shop almost over, Wolf felt he had hammered new shoes for every horse in the valley. Mr. Grier gave him one last task—to hammer out a long bar of steel. Every time it extended as long as his arm, the smith put a crimp in the middle and folded the bar on the crimp. Wolf welded the two halves together by more hammering. The bar had to be reheated to a bright orange glow before repeating the process. Once the bar had been hammered out and folded several times, the smith left it at full length and quenched it in water. He put the bar aside. "Wolf, that bar will be forged further into a sword. You're all done for the week. You've been a big help. Maybe we can do more business later. Let me show you your new bow."

The composite bow had no decorations save the maker's mark. Wolf tested it, felt its heavy pull and said, "Sir, I can't pay you what this is worth."

"Nonsense, you'll make me proud when you kill your first rabbit. However, if you ever have some time, I could always use more help." Wolf resolved to pay the man back with more work. He enjoyed working the steel.

~

A winded page delivered a message to the archery master, and, after a quick read, the knight dismissed Wolf and told him Mary was in labor. Wolf ran as fast as he could to the stables where a crowd had formed around Mary's stall. He worked his way up front to find Mary lying down on a bed of straw with Red at her head and Raven and Dr. Lundie, the veterinarian, attending to Mary. When Raven saw Wolf, he waved him over and told him it would be a difficult birth and Mary needed help. He gave him a list of supplies to obtain from the quartermaster and the nurse, and Wolf ran off to get the items.

From the quartermaster, he received a length of soft nylon rope, several liters of alcohol, a towel, and a blanket. From the nurse, he obtained a number of medicines, syringes, and a surgery kit. The nurse packed the medicines in a bag and came with Wolf, saying she was not about to miss the birth.

When Wolf returned to the stable, he delivered the supplies to the vet and went to Mary's head to be with Red. The Vet went to work washing his bare arms and the rope with the alcohol. He then made a loop at the end of the rope, reached up the birth canal, and placed the loop on the foal's hooves. The vet waited while Mary went through two more sets of contractions before he said she was ready.

With the next contraction, the vet and Raven started pulling on the rope as hard as they could. It seemed like a long time before two hooves came out, followed by a large, slimy sack containing the baby horse, the size of a very large dog. The vet cut the sack from around the foal and wiped it down with a towel. It was a male. He then placed him on a sheet where Mary could tend to and lick him. The foal perked up and started breathing and coughing, and all the pages cheered. Wolf watched as the vet clamped the umbilical cord and delivered the placenta.

Red cried and hugged Mary. The foal took it all in stride. Raven had Wolf slide the foal aside while he and Red tried to get Mary onto her feet. Once Mary stood up, she took charge of the foal, and for the next hour, nobody got close to him. Mary cleaned the foal then got him to stand. She then nudged the foal to where he could nurse.

Chapter 12 ~ More Changes

Just before supper Raven, Red, Wolf, and several other pages were practicing their self-defense exercises when a page came running up and delivered a written message to Raven. He wrote a reply on the message, folded it, and returned it to the page who took off for the main tent. Raven signaled for Red to join him in his tent. Soon afterward, Red came out and told Wolf, "We're to have a formal dinner with Raven and guests."

~

When they arrived, the headmaster, the Lion was there. The table had been set for four. Raven indicated for Red to sit at one end and Wolf at the other. Raven assisted Red into her chair and signaled everyone to sit down.

A pleasant, but formal meal ensued with polite conversation, and Wolf was relieved that there was not even a hint of talk about his recent fight or his bruises. With dinner over, Raven poured grape juice into their cups. Raven, as host, made the first toast, "To the flag of our country, may it always represent freedom."

The others chorused, "Here, here," and everybody took a sip of juice.

The Lion toasted, "To the school, may it always stand for what is right."

Red toasted, "To our knights and teachers, may they ever be wise."

Everyone looked at Wolf. He paused to think and then toasted, "To the new foal, may he grow big and strong."

"Here, here," all replied.

With the toasting over, Wolf and Red cleared the table, and the Raven invited everybody to sit down. "Wolf, it has been a month since I brought you here. Have you had the adventure I promised?"

"Yes, sir."

"Have you been treated well?"

"Yes, sir."

"Very good, I'm glad to hear that. Your probationary period is now over, and it's time for you to decide what you want to do. I'm going to ask you some important questions. Do you want to leave here and go to a foster home that we can arrange?"

Wolf grimaced and answered, "No, sir."

"Do you wish to join this school, knowing what kind of school it is, knowing that you will have to be appointed a legal guardian, a foster parent, to whom you must answer?"

Wolf looked at Raven and said, "Yes, sir."

"Good. Headmaster, are you satisfied?"

"I am," he replied.

Raven pulled out the contract that Wolf had signed a month earlier. "Wolf, this is a full scholarship. You won't have to pay for school, so if you will, please sign here." He indicated the spot. Wolf signed with his real name and handed the document to Raven, who witnessed it. Raven handed it to the Lion, who signed it, and to Amara, who also witnessed it.

The Lion took the paper and poured some molten red sealing wax next to the signatures. He affixed the impression of his signet ring onto the hardening wax, making it look very official.

Raven offered his congratulations with a handshake and a slap on the shoulder, and Red gave Wolf a bear hug. The Lion congratulated him with a hearty handshake, and Red assured him he would never regret it.

After the headmaster left the tent, Raven requested that Wolf and Red sit back down. "It's time to get to some serious stuff. Amara, do you have something to say?"

"Yes, sir. Wolf, I've been watching you since we first met, and you impress me. You don't lie, cheat, or steal. You work hard without complaint, and you take care of your friends and the animals. It's time to name the foal, and I want to give that privilege to you."

"Why me?" he asked.

Red paused and a mischievous grin appeared on her face. "Because he's yours, if you will have him."

"What?" he stammered. "But I don't deserve him! I can't afford him!"

"You do, and you can. I received Mary the same way I'm offering the foal to you, with the promise that you just help someone else out later. As for affording him, he can earn his keep when he's older, working for the school. He can also earn his keep in other ways. We'll talk about it later." Red and the Raven shot glances at each other.

"I accept," Wolf answered.

Raven said, "Now on to other matters, Amara, if you please."

Red got up and left the tent.

"Wolf, there is the small matter of a legal guardian. One has already been picked out for you."

Wolf stared, unbelieving, at the knight and said, "I thought it would be you."

"Heavens no, I'm not responsible enough. I was just a temporary guardian. You can still be a page under my mentorship if you want."

"I'd like that, sir."

Red reappeared at the entrance to the tent with Whisperblade. Raven swept his arm to her and said, "Wolf, meet your new mother and sister."

Wolf's mouth dropped open. "Mother? Sister?"

"Yes," they all replied.

Wolf had nothing to say.

Red broke the silence, "Wolf, it's like this, Raven sort of saved my life and brought me to the school. Lady Whisperblade is my adoptive mother. Now she has been appointed your guardian, your foster mother. That makes you my brother."

Wolf managed to say, "But you work for Raven."

Red grinned and said, "Of course, I do. I wouldn't want to spend all my time with my mother, would I? It would be too much. Besides, I want to become a tracker, and Raven is the best there is."

"But what does this mean for me?" Wolf asked.

Whisperblade answered, "It means you have someone you can go to when all else fails. I'll always be here for you."

"Oh. Thank you, my lady."

"Good. Meet me at my tent after you finish cleaning up the mess in here."

~

Later, after the Raven dismissed him, Wolf reported to Whisperblade. He looked around the tent and saw nothing except a table and two stools. Whisperblade looked at him with kind eyes, and a smile developed on her face. "I wanted to have a talk with you about being your guardian."

"Yes, my lady."

"First, I've been appointed your legal guardian by the state. I'm your foster mother."

"Yes, my lady."

"Also any legal proceedings against you by the state have been dropped. You're no longer in any danger of going to the juvenile center."

"Thank you, my lady."

"Don't thank me; thank Raven. His recommendations set you free from the law."

"Yes, my lady."

"And stop saying that when I'm talking to you as a parent."

"Yes, uh, yes, ma'am."

"That's better. Now I want you to listen to me. I have all the duties of a parent. I'll see to it that you are fed, clothed, and sheltered. I'll listen to you and advise you, even when no else can or will. I'll be here when you hurt the most. I take this responsibility above all else. Be at peace with me and take my hand." He took her hand, and she said, "I swear to you now that, as long as I breathe, I'll be here for you. On this, I place my honor among men and women."

"Thank you," was all Wolf could manage, and he started crying. Whisperblade held him tight.

They talked late into the night until Whisperblade reminded Wolf of his exercise routine, and they ran through the steps of his routine. When she dismissed him, he had a slow, thoughtful walk back to his tent. When he arrived, the wolf sat in front of his tent, waiting. Wolf entered his tent and stared at the hangers on which his clothes were drying. He now knew what he had to do. Grabbing his old blue jeans, shirt, and sweater, he marched out of the tent to the nearest campfire and threw them into the flames. Without waiting, he went back to his tent, aware that the wolf followed him. He turned, stared at it for a minute, and said, "I think I'll call you Shadow." He ducked into his tent, and Shadow followed him.

Knowlton

Chapter 13 ~ Shadow Wolf

Wolf checked on his foal whenever he had a long break and when Mary would let him close enough to do his job. Red told him patience was a virtue when doing anything new with a horse. Red also told him that Mary would let him know when she was ready, and that would not happen soon. For the time being, Mary and the foal were kept in a separate field from the other horses.

Wolf continued to tend to Mary and the foal. After a few days, they soon were playing a game where Mary would keep between Wolf and the foal and the foal would make end runs to get at Wolf and push him in the back. The foal, which was bigger than Wolf, nudged him hard. Red told him horses had an excellent memory and a game like this could be a problem later as the foal matured. It had been a problem with Mary, but how do you break a bad habit in an oversized horse?

A week later, as Wolf cleaned and rubbed the foal, an idea hit him. He waited until he saw Red and told her, "I'm naming him Nudge."

Red smiled and said, "That's an excellent name. You need to tell Raven and then get the name registered."

"Why is that?" Wolf asked.

"There are a couple of good reasons. First, it's like getting a license for a dog; it's just necessary. Second, it will increase his value if you breed him. He's a purebred Percheron after all. Now that Mary lets you handle him, it's time to get him used to some basic things. When you're just standing around with him, pick up and hold one of his hooves as if you were cleaning it. Don't do anything else to the hoof because he's too

97

tender at this age. Talk to him. Put a blanket on his back, just to get him used to it. Brush him; he'll like that. Other than that, he stays with his mom."

Wolf thought a second then said, "So I just get him used to me."

"Yeah, but it's a delicate process. Nudge can kick and bite hard without realizing what he's doing. You have to be very careful about how you train him. You don't want him to be afraid of you or hate you."

"Or Mary could get mad at me," Wolf mused.

"Oh yeah, there's that. It's been nice knowing you," Red quipped.

Wolf turned to Red and saw her grin. "If Mary kills me, you'll have to deal with Shadow."

"Who?"

"The wolf, that's his name." This time, Wolf grinned.

Red said, "Okay, I give. You'd better tell me more about Shadow."

"I keep playing with him any time I go into the woods."

"Does Raven know?"

"Yeah, I can't hide anything from him."

"And he approves?"

"Not exactly."

Red furrowed her forehead and then asked, "What do you mean by not exactly?"

"Raven says he can't come with me at the end of summer, and there will be some very tough decisions then."

"You've got that right."

"I'll figure something out."

Red exclaimed, "That wolf is wild! It just isn't going to happen."

Wolf snorted, "I was wild just a short while ago. Remember that. Look at me now, just as civilized as I can be, even here in the mountains."

"I'm not so sure of that. I'd better check you for rabies." She felt his forehead, "Just as I suspected—crazy."

Wolf took a swipe at Red's shoulder, but she dodged the blow. He ended up chasing her across the meadow, followed by Nudge and Mary. Wolf, now a good runner, caught up with Red, but he couldn't get his hands on her. She would duck and weave while evading his grasp. Nudge enjoyed the game and galloped between them. The foal would knock one down then the other.

Mary seemed to be the only responsible party and chased Nudge away. It was her way of saying the game was over. Red and Wolf were laughing so hard it took a minute before Wolf noticed they were being watched.

Besides the handful of pages and squires watching the fun, Shadow sat above them on the hill with his head cocked to one side. Red, first on her feet, ran, and Shadow chased after her, jumping and landing square on her back, knocking her down. Before Wolf could reach her, Shadow was on top of her, licking her face.

"Shadow, sit!" Wolf commanded, and the wolf sat. "Shadow, lay down," he said, and the wolf did. Red sat up, looking stunned.

"Did you just make him sit?" Red demanded.

"He sits if he feels like it," Wolf answered.

"You win. Maybe he can be saved. I'll see what I can do to keep the two of you together. But we need to do some serious talking before we approach Raven."

"I know," Wolf replied.

That evening after supper, Red and Wolf took their leave of Raven and went to see Whisperblade. They explained the situation to her in detail, making sure to leave nothing out and answered her questions in full.

Wolf pleaded for the animal. He explained how the wolf had tried to become a part of the camp, showing no aggression toward any of the students. He argued that because of its injury he didn't think the wolf could live on its own anymore.

Whisperblade listened and then said, "There are good reasons we don't encourage pets in this school. All the animals we have here have a purpose. The horses work and help us teach. The dogs help with tracking and keeping wild animals out of the camp. The cats even have a purpose. A wolf is a wild animal and cannot be domesticated."

Wolf started to protest, but Red tapped his elbow, and he held his tongue.

Whisperblade continued, "From what I've heard of this wolf, he isn't easy going. He would have to get along with everyone, and he will never be above some people's suspicion."

Red said, "I think the wolf is a very good judge of people. He stays away from people I just wouldn't want to be around. He doesn't threaten anyone."

"How can you be sure of that?" Whisperblade asked.

"Ask him yourself. He's lying down behind you."

Whisperblade spun around, and at her feet laid the wolf. She asked, "Did you arrange this?"

"No, ma'am," Red replied.

"Ma'am, I can't explain it, but he seems to know when he's needed," Wolf said.

Whisperblade sat down and said, "I'll talk to the Lion. I can't promise anything. Raven isn't your obstacle; trust me. I'll do the best I can. They don't call me Whisperblade for nothing."

After much discussion, they came up with a plan of attack. Each partner had a job to do, and Wolf's was the hardest. He would acclimate Shadow to living with people and to camp life. He would have to help Shadow get used to a collar and leash, and Shadow would have to obey commands.

Red set about trying to get Mary to accept Shadow. Mary was still very protective of Nudge and was in no mood to get acquainted with a wolf. Red said she didn't think the wolf would survive a violent encounter between the two. The Percheron could outrun the lame wolf, and she had a kick that could kill.

Whisperblade had the job of presenting the case for Shadow, and she would advise Wolf on who to talk to and how he should go about it. She told him to talk to a knight known as Bear.

Bear, a big man, the biggest man in camp, instructed the older squires on the use of weapons in armed combat. There were rumors that he was the only person who could best Whisperblade, bare handed or with a sword.

~

The next day, Wolf found Bear and addressed him, "Sir Knight Bear."

"Sleeps with Wolves," he answered with a big smile.

"How did you know?" Wolf asked in surprise.

"I see him in you. You've come to me to ask about him."

"Yes, sir."

"What is it you seek?"

"Sir, I'm trying to—"

"Sleeps with Wolves, I think you already see the problem. I think it's time we ask the wolf what he wants."

"How will we do that?" Wolf asked. "I mean how do I talk to him?"

"We'll see. I think you'll find he understands more than you think. How do you find him?"

"He comes to me when I'm alone. He tends to stay away when other people are around, but he'll play with my tent mates. When I'm alone with him in the woods, he runs with me, but he expects me to run faster than I can. I mean, he'll run ahead, but he keeps coming back nudging me to run faster."

"Does he try to do what you want him to do?" Bear asked.

"He'll sit and stay for a short while or until I say 'okay.' He sneaks around camp sometimes and surprises me. He's always around when I go into the woods alone and follows wherever I take a journey on horseback."

"Sleeps with Wolves, he's already talking to you, but you don't understand his language yet. Maybe I can help you." They talked for a long time, after which they went to the woods where Shadow joined them.

~

Later that day, Wolf crossed paths with Wart. "So Wolf, tell me more about the foal."

"Well, Red is giving him to me for free."

Wart narrowed his eyes. "For free! Don't consider it a gift. She just saved herself a lot of money."

"What? How's that?"

Wart explained, "She doesn't have to buy a saddle and tack. I think she got you."

Wolf slumped, "No wonder she gave him to me. I can't afford a saddle."

"Well, you don't need one now, at least, but I warn you, they're expensive. I couldn't afford mine, even with my allowance. My father loaned me the money."

"What's the matter?" someone asked. Wayne and his two buddies, Ralph and Edgar, approached. "Can't afford a saddle. I knew you shouldn't be here." Wayne stepped right up to Wolf, and his buddies flanked him.

Wolf didn't back down, but the older page towered over him.

Wart, standing even shorter, put a hand on Wolf's shoulder and said, "If you mess with him, you'll also have to mess with me."

Without taking his eyes off Wolf, Wayne snapped, "Wart, this doesn't concern you. Why don't you just walk away?"

"I don't think he needs to," Harold, Wolf's muscular tent mate, said.

"You mess with Wolf you mess with me," George, his other tent mate, said.

Wayne appeared flustered. "Look, I didn't come here to mess with anybody." He gave Wolf a slight shove, turned, and strode away.

Wart mused, "You haven't seen the last of him. He'll try to find you alone."

"What can I do?" Wolf asked.

Wart smiled and said, "He's going to fight you—that's for sure. We're going to have to prepare you."

Wolf complained, "But I'm already taking self-defense."

"So is he. Self-defense isn't going to discourage him. We have to teach you to fight.

"Right," Harold said. "Tough fighting."

"We have to be secret about it," George added.

"Wolf, are you in?" Wart asked.

Wolf looked at his three tent mates, but he said nothing.

"We're all in this together, or it won't work," Wart said with a growl.

Wolf smiled and said, "I'm in."

"I'm in," repeated Harold and George.

"Good, spit on it," Wart said. He spit on his palm and held it out. The others did the same and placed their hands on top of his.

Chapter 14 ~ Night of the Wolf

Wolf spent all his spare time trying to acclimate Shadow to a collar and leash and help him lose his fear of horses. He used Pinto Bean and Easy Rider as test subjects. Up until then, Shadow had followed just out of sight whenever they were out on patrol and, as a rule, had stayed away from the horses. Wolf and Red would arrange meetings between Shadow and one of the horses in an open space where neither would feel threatened. Bear provided invaluable help in training the wolf, and the wolf took to him. They spent a lot of time playing together. One day, Bear managed to get a collar on Shadow. "How did you do that?" Wolf asked.

"The wolf knows I'm his friend. He sees a part of himself in me. Are there other people he likes?"

"He likes my tent mates," Wolf replied.

"He may be a better judge of people than you or me. Everyone emits an aura or personality, and he notices it. It's you he identifies with, and I believe he thinks of you as a puppy."

By now, Wolf had learned that what a knight said could be trusted as the truth. "How can this be? I'm older than him, and almost as large as he is."

"What you say is true, but the wolf still sees you as a puppy compared to other people. The wolf also sees that you don't have the necessary survival skills to live on your own in his world. He's trying to teach you, and you must learn from him before he'll let you teach him."

Wolf explained Bear's plan to Raven and asked permission to take a day and night's leave. Carrying only a knife, he entered the woods and was greeted by Shadow, who started running. Wolf followed at a smart pace for an hour or so until they came to a large glen, and the wolf stopped running. Wolf's lungs felt on fire. Once he stopped breathing hard, the wolf trotted back and forth in the field, sniffing the ground. Wolf got the idea, and started a search pattern like Shadow's, and found signs of rabbit. He recognized their paths.

Wolf followed a well-traveled rabbit path until it merged with another path and then another until he came to a hole in the ground, the rabbit's warren. Now Shadow nudged him to a place next to the hole, but not in front of it. Shadow circled around several times until he found another hole and started digging with vigor.

Wolf got the idea and pulled his knife. The first rabbit to leave the hole surprised him. He stabbed at the next rabbit to leave the den. He missed this animal as well as the following one. The next rabbit was slower, and he managed to come down on it, stabbing it.

He was amazed to realize he had taken a rabbit by hand. He looked up to see Shadow sitting with another dead rabbit in his jaws. The wolf looked at him a few seconds, then started tearing his rabbit apart, ripping and biting, pulling off pieces of meat.

Wolf used his knife to gut and skin his rabbit, cutting the meat into bite size pieces. Bear had warned him this would not be pretty, and he proved right. Raw rabbit left a lot to be desired, it was chewy and unappetizing. Wolf found it easiest to cut it into small pieces and just swallow. He decided he needed to learn to cook rabbit as well as Red could. After eating their fill, Shadow led Wolf to a stream where they both drank and washed up.

When Wolf had finished washing, Shadow started running again. There didn't seem to be any urgency this time, and Wolf took breaks to catch his breath. Before the day ended, they had hunted rabbit again.

On their next run, Shadow stopped and sat down. Wolf drew up short and almost bumped into Maude. "Whoa, Caleb, or should I call you Wolf?"

Wolf gaped at the woman, wondering how she happened to be here, and said, "Wolf, Ma'am."

Maude smiled at him, "What has Shadow taught you?"

"Taught me? Say, how do you know his name?

"He told me. Now what has he taught you?"

Wolf had a hard time trying to figure out if he could believe her. He said, "He's taught me to hunt rabbit."

"It's a most useful skill. He'll teach you other things if you let him."

"Ma'am?"

"He is going to teach you loyalty and responsibility."

"Oh."

"Please call me Maude."

"Ma'... Maude, I saved Shadow's life."

She beamed, "Yes, you did well. Why don't you give this old woman a big hug? I could use one."

As Wolf embraced the woman, she bent down and kissed him on his forehead.

As soon as they broke their embrace, she told him, "Wolf, it's going to get cold. You need to make a shelter. Look after Shadow."

Wolf turned to look at Shadow. The animal stood there, so he stroked the wolf's head, and got his hand licked in return. When he looked back, Maude had disappeared.

The sun started to set, and the air started to chill. Wolf, who thought he had become used to the cool nights in the high country, became aware of being very cold. He hadn't brought the heavy sheriff's coat or even a light page's jacket, and his shirt was soaked with sweat from all his running. Shadow had fur and didn't seem to mind the cold, but Wolf knew that he had to do something quick to keep from freezing.

Remembering Raven's survival class, he started cutting long, thin, flexible branches from some bushes. Stripping them of their leaves, he wove them into a small dome. He then cut more branches, leaving the leaves on and weaving them into the dome's framework until he had a thick layer of leaves. As long as he kept his legs folded, he could fit inside. He left a small opening to crawl into and made a small bundle of leaves to act as a plug for the opening. Just in time, the last of twilight left the valley.

Satisfied with his work, he crawled in. Shadow came up and crawled in, and Wolf closed the opening, curled up with Shadow, and tried to go to sleep. Eventually, he dreamed. The moon had risen, and he had no trouble following the wolf. He could feel the cold on his cheeks, but he remained warm. They were following a narrow path, zigzagging through the trees at a speed he did not believe possible. It seemed he flew among the trees, and the path seemed as wide as a highway.

He looked behind and saw a massive horse with a small, hooded rider, a skeleton, chasing him, its horse's hooves pounding, tossing up clods of earth.

When he looked ahead, the wolf had disappeared. He entered an open field and stopped to yell at the hooded rider, "Who are you? Why are you chasing me?"

The hooded figure pointed a bony finger at him and demanded, "Who are you? What have you done with him?"

"It's me! Don't you see?"

Again, the rider pointed at him and asked, "What have you done with the boy?"

He looked down at himself, and saw that he was the wolf. He looked back up at the hooded figure and saw the horse charging him, the rider clutching a lance. As the lance penetrated his breast, he saw that the rider's cloak bore the insignia of a fox.

Wolf awakened to Shadow licking his face. The sun had arisen. His shelter had been kicked to a pile of rubble, sticks, and leaves, and the bitter cold left him stiff and shivering. After stroking Shadow a few times, he stood up and started to trot towards camp.

Camp turned out to be a lot closer than he had thought. As he crested the hill, he saw Red sitting on Easy Rider, holding her lance upright, waiting for him.

Red grimaced, "You sure look the sight. Why don't you get up behind me and ride into camp?"

"I'd rather walk if you don't mind."

"When you get back, go clean yourself up and put on fresh clothes. We have a lot to do today." Red left, riding at a canter.

Wolf walked into camp and made a beeline for his tent with Shadow walking beside him. Almost every page and squire stopped to stare at him. Not until he reached his tent did he realize he had two bloody rabbit skins tucked in his belt. As he started to wash up, he saw his clothes were splattered with blood from the dead rabbits.

Tired and sore, but ready to start a new day, Wolf changed into a clean uniform and reported to Raven's tent. While brewing the coffee, he had a talk with Red. "I know what your sign will be. I mean what you will be called when you become a knight. I saw it in a dream."

"Don't tell me. I'll find out for myself when the time comes. What you saw is yours to know. Every knight has had a similar experience. If you must talk about it, talk to Bear. He's our interpreter of dreams. By the way, I hope you didn't waste those rabbits when you took their skins."

"No, I ate them."

"How did you cook them?"

"I didn't."

Red gave him a funny look. "So how was it?"

Wolf snapped, "About as good as yours."

"You're getting pretty big for that uniform aren't you?"

"It's just payback for the coffee gag."

Chapter 15 ~ Raiding

Raven came out of his tent and spoke up, "When you two clowns are finished, we have work to do. We're going out of the valley to check out some reports that have come to our attention. We'll travel light and fast."

Red and Wolf went to the stables to saddle the horses and arrange for another mare to nurse Nudge. Red set up Mary with a light pulling harness and a coil of heavy rope. When Wolf asked about it, she said, "A specific request for Mary means heavy work could be involved." After saddling the horses, they returned to Raven's tent to find him engaged in some last minute conversations with the Lion.

Raven mounted up, and they made a quick stop at the mess tent where Wolf picked up dried food and stowed it in their saddlebags. They headed west and spent the rest of the morning crossing the valley and climbing the steep slope to the pass.

At the pass, Raven took reports from the squires on watch and left messages for the next patrol. Raven did not let them waste time on niceties like coffee but started down the western trail toward the valley floor. The wide valley supported a large river and ample vegetation with many stands of very large trees that thinned out the further up the slope they went. The trail down from the pass was well hidden, but a fire road that paralleled the river appeared well traveled.

Raven led them up the river on the road at a fast pace with occasional stops to refresh the horses and read the signs. He didn't say what he was looking for, but it became clear when they came to a place where a grove of trees should have been next to the river. All that remained were stumps and cutting trash. The sight stunned Wolf. It must have once been a magnificent stand of trees.

The loggers were nowhere to be seen, and Raven went into action. The loggers had left a tree-harvesting machine and a log truck at the site for further work. The Raven set to work with Mary, Midnight, and Easy Rider, pulling the logging scraps to the machine and the truck and forming a big pile around them. Red took Mary back a ways with the other two horses, while Raven rigged the pulling rope and Wolf untied the rope at the machines. When Raven was satisfied, he struck a fire into the piles and let them burn.

Satisfied the fire would do its job, they all continued up the fire road. Raven said, "Our job is to scout this illegal logging operation to see how big it is. If we can, we'll do a little raiding and sabotage. The three of us can't do much by ourselves. We'll have to return with a bigger force. Then we'll do enough damage to stop this operation. I set the fire to flush out the loggers."

Raven turned his horse up slope, and they climbed a large hill to a plateau where they could hide the horses out of sight. They laid down at the edge of the plateau where they watched and waited. It didn't take long for three pickup trucks with about twelve people in them to race down the road, accompanied by four men on motorcycles. Raven had Wolf and Red mount up, and he rode with them upriver until they were within sight of the main logging operation.

Raven pulled a small telescope from his bag and made an inventory of equipment and men. He handed the spyglass to Red and then Wolf and said, "I think we have all the information we need. We'll return to camp to make a report."

They started the climb to the pass back to the valley, taking a different route to keep the pass hidden from any followers.

Wolf estimated that it would be dark by the time they reached the pass. He asked Red about making the pass at night, and she just shrugged.

Raven surprised them both when he called for a camp before going above the tree line. Red and Wolf unsaddled the horses and set up a shelter from the wind using their rain ponchos. Meanwhile Raven went scouting

Wolf Sureblade: American Knight

with the promise to be back soon. He ordered a small, smokeless fire for warmth and tea and the horses tied up at the ready.

After the camp had been set up Shadow walked in and sat down next to Wolf and Red, demanding attention. Mary and Easy Rider didn't seem to mind the wolf's presence, and the two students had a peaceful moment from the work of the day.

About an hour after dark, Raven returned to camp, sat down, and shared tea, jerky, and dried fruit with them. He said, "So far we haven't been followed, but I want a watch tonight. Red will take the first watch. I'll take the second, and Wolf, the third. Wolf, you look like you need the sleep." With that, he crawled into his bedroll and went to sleep. Wolf took longer to go to sleep, but he managed. Raven left the camp during Wolf's watch. At sunrise, Wolf left his post on a ridge and joined Red, who said, "We need to be ready to leave when Raven gets back. Depending on what he finds, we may move fast."

"I guess those loggers aren't very happy with what we did."

"You've got that right. Let's get busy."

They broke camp, packed everything, and saddled the horses in minutes. They just mounted when a buzzing sound could be heard becoming louder.

A dirt bike burst through the trees, its engine roaring. The rider, a rough man, glared at them with hatred in his eyes. The motorcycle came straight for the students.

Wolf and Red spurred their horses to a gallop and separated. The dirt bike followed Red, so Wolf pulled up on his horse and started stringing his bow. He wheeled about and started chasing after the biker holding the bow and two arrows in his left hand and guiding Easy Rider with his right.

Wolf could tell Red was pushing Mary hard, and the sure-footed horse was weaving between the rocks and trees, trying to shake the motorcycle off. The biker also ran hard. The rider knew his business and kept close to the horse. Red and Mary ran out of room at a rock wall. Red wheeled her to a stop with the wall behind her.

The man on the bike also stopped. He reached into his jacket, pulled out a handgun, and pointed it at Red. Wolf, without hesitation,

111

dropped the reins, raised the bow, and let loose. The arrow struck the biker through the hand, knocking the gun loose. The man screamed and turned in Wolf's direction.

Wolf and Easy Rider bore down on him, but the horse turned away from running the man over. Red followed suit, chasing the man on Mary until the horse reared up and brought her front hooves down on the man and bike. The man screamed again as the arm with the wounded hand snapped under one of the giant hooves. The other hoof had come down on the bike with a sickening metallic thud.

Wolf dismounted and, standing at a safe distance, kept his bow with the second arrow trained on the man. Red stopped Mary's attack before the horse could do more damage. The man squirmed in pain. He stretched for the gun with his good hand, but he couldn't reach it. Shadow stood over the gun with wicked, bared teeth, growling. "Call your dog off!" yelled the man.

Wolf yelled, "He's a wolf; you back off."

Red yelled, "Back off or my horse will stomp you again."

Raven's voice came from behind Wolf and said, "Do as she says. That horse can kill."

The wounded man raised his good arm in submission. Raven soon had the man kneeling, ankles bound together, and his good hand tied to the remains of the motorcycle. He attended the man's wounds without mercy. First, he splinted the man's upper arm, bandaging it to his body, and then splinted the lower arm. He said, "You shouldn't point guns at children. They have so little restraint."

The man looked up at Red, who aimed her bow at his eye, and said, "Tell her to point that thing somewhere else."

Raven replied, "I could try, but you know how teenagers are. Don't worry. Unlike the boy, she never misses. You should hope her arm doesn't give out. I'd hate to do all this doctoring for nothing."

The man yelped when, in one motion, Raven broke the point off Wolf's arrow and pulled the shaft back out of the man's hand.

"Well, that didn't hurt too much, did it?" Red asked. "Or should I have my horse dance on you some more?"

The man glowered at her, but he kept his mouth shut. Raven

finished bandaging the man and made sure the man was secure He called for a war conference and said, "You both did the right thing; you saved each other. Our problem is this, what do we do with him? I don't want to turn him loose, but I also don't think we can take him back to camp."

"What happens if we turn him loose?" Wolf asked.

"He goes to his buddies and tells them about us," Red answered.

"So what? They already know we're here," Wolf exclaimed.

"We'll even provide food and water to sustain him in his journey back to his gang," Raven said.

At noon, they reached the western pass where they found the watch increased to two knights and two squires. Coffee had been brewed, good, hot, and welcome. Raven stopped long enough to apprise the watch of the situation and of what to expect. He decided to keep patrols scouting the logging operation until the authorities could arrive in force. It would require great care because the loggers showed a willingness to use firearms.

Raven descended alone into the valley and headed for camp to report to the Lion. Red and Wolf took more time to make it back to camp to spare their horses any more hard riding.

When Red and Wolf arrived, word of their adventures had already spread throughout the camp. They were greeted with cheers, and Wolf became a hero among the other pages.

Red had three horses to look after: Easy Rider, Mary, and Midnight. Wolf helped her, but a group of young female pages kept interrupting him, asking questions. He paid attention to Easy Rider, whom he had ridden so hard. Red took care of Mary as best she could while Mary nursed Nudge.

Supper provided a better opportunity for Wolf and Red to tell their stories. They, of course, played the game of embellishing the other's narrative. Some of the squires were skeptical until Wolf showed the bloody, broken arrow.

The arrow had been one of his finer pieces of workmanship, and soon he had orders for arrows from some of the squires. Red reminded him of the trade value that good workmanship carried. He might later be able to get help with his schoolwork for the price of a few arrows.

Wolf realized for the first time how well he fit in with his peers. He was no longer an object of ridicule because of his small size or his social status. Younger pages looked up to him, and he was respected by others of his age and by some who were already squires.

Wolf and Red reported to Raven's tent and sat down to discuss their situation. Reports indicated they were being hunted by the loggers because of the damage they had done to the logging equipment.

Raven praised each of them for their quick thinking in protecting each other. And to Shadow, who lay at his feet, he said, "You've earned your keep today." He petted the wolf's head and smiled.

Then Raven dismissed Red for ten minutes so he could talk with Wolf. His first question was, "Why did you put yourself in danger, chasing after the biker?"

"I didn't think about the danger. I wanted to help Red."

"Why did you shoot the man's hand? You haven't been taught archery from a moving horse yet."

Wolf thought about this and said, "I missed. I've watched squires shooting from a horse, and, at the time, it seemed to feel right." Wolf noted that Raven didn't ask him what he had shot at when he missed.

"The wolf has won my support. But even Shadow thought with greater care than you did. You're dismissed for the night. Report to Whisperblade, and send in Amara."

Wolf went outside to find Red and asked her, "Raven doesn't let you off easy, does he?"

Red looked Wolf in the eye without her usual humor and said, "Never."

~

Whisperblade welcomed Wolf with open arms and a big hug. She told him to sit down and tell her the whole tale, and she paid careful attention to every word and asked questions. Her last question was, "What were you aiming at?"

Somehow, it seemed easier to tell her than Raven. "I was aiming at the man's heart."

"You were right in aiming at him. You couldn't know his intentions.

You may have saved Amara's life. However, your miss was good in more ways than one. Know this truth, any time a person points a weapon, he is ready to use it."

Afterward Wolf pondered her statement. *Was she talking about the man or about me?* He decided she was talking about him.

Knowlton

Chapter 16 ~ War

Wolf awoke with a start. Shadow stood over him, licking his face. As soon as he could get his arms to move, he pushed Shadow away from his face. It was still night, and no one else was awake. "Wolf," a voice whispered from outside the tent.

"Yes, I'm awake."

"You need to report to Raven's tent right away."

"Okay, okay. Let me get dressed." Wolf crawled out of his bedroll and pulled on his trousers, shirt, and boots. A single candle illuminated Raven's tent, and he entered to find Raven still in his nightshirt and trousers.

"You've done well, young pup," said a voice from behind him.

Wolf spun around to find Deputy Sheriff Ben standing there. "Hello, sir."

"Please don't call me sir. I'm not a knight. Besides, I understand you're now my brother."

It took Wolf a minute to realize the implications, "The Whisperblade is your—"

"Mother? Yes, she is," Ben answered. "It's a long story." "Perhaps another time," Raven said. "I just wanted you to understand the relationship before tomorrow's events. Go back to your tent. You need your sleep because you're going to have a big day tomorrow."

~

Wolf arose before dawn to prepare their horses. Red donned a bulletproof vest, very similar to a police vest. Wolf saddled up two horses as planned, Pinto Bean and Boomerang, a second school horse. Boomerang, a gelding, turned out to be quite a handful. Red handed a stiff and heavy bulletproof vest to Wolf. He packed his horses light, so he could ride fast. He put his bedroll, plenty of dried food, water, his bow, and all his arrows on his spare horse. He knew he wouldn't be allowed to see action, but he figured he could use the arrows for trading with the other squires.

With their horses saddled, Wolf and Red reported to the lists to be treated to the spectacle of the knights and large horses assembled. The sheriff and a handful of his deputies on horses, including Ben, milled in the crowd, the deputies armed with pistols and rifles.

There were perhaps twenty knights. Wolf knew only half of them, including Eagle, Bear, and Lady Knight Jessica. There were as many squires and four other pages, including Wart, Wayne, and Whisperblade's page Hildegard. Wolf hoped that Wayne would stay away, but he didn't expect trouble with all the other knights and squires about.

The knights were armed, and some held lances. Besides the lances, most carried a bow and arrows, and some were equipped with war hatchets and maces. The squires, if they didn't carry lances, had their bows and arrows and knives. They also carried stout ropes coiled over their shoulders.

Wolf gawked at the show of force. He had not realized there were so many arms in camp. It became quiet, and they all paid attention to the headmaster, who gave a speech about what they were going to do, how they were going to do it, and what each knight's responsibility would be. When he finished, the sheriff told them what they could do and what they could not do. The knights could not kill except to defend a student. The way the sheriff said it, it seemed he didn't mind if some of the loggers got roughed up. He then deputized the knights as temporary law officers.

A group of pages brought up refreshments of dried fruits, jerky, and juice to the mounted men and women. There were several toasts made, and a prayer was given for a safe adventure.

Wolf took the opportunity to ask Red about their brother.

She said, "He's nice though he likes to play tricks sometimes. He'll fight for you anytime, anywhere, and he's good with his fists. He's always been good to me. He takes his honor above all else, and, if he says he'll do something, he'll do it. He's a big brother, though, and he can be difficult to live with."

"So what is it with him being a sheriff's deputy and not a knight?" Wolf asked.

"He didn't want to become a knight. A lot of squires and knights go into law enforcement. They don't all become teachers like Raven. Ben just didn't want knighthood. It isn't for everybody."

After refreshments were finished, the Lion gave a signal, and all the horsemen lined up on the lists, and, two by two, they turned west to follow him and the sheriff. When the last horses were moving, the pace picked up until the column proceeded at a fast canter across the floor of the valley.

Later in the morning, Raven came up and ordered Wolf to ride forward and suggest to the Lion that a break for the horses would be in order at the next creek. Wolf spurred Pinto Bean to a full gallop, passing the column of riders to deliver his message. He understood why Raven had told him to use two horses. He continued to deliver messages up and down the line of riders. Red suggested when to change mounts. Each time he changed from one horse to the other, he had to stop, move the saddle over, and then catch up with the party. With the sun overhead, they reached the climb up to the pass, and the riding became hard. More than one horse with a heavy load of knight and arms balked at the climb. At the pass, the Lion ordered a break.

The two knights on watch reported on the advance scout's activities. They had sabotaged some of the small bridges on the fire road so they could not bear the weight of a loaded log truck. The loggers had been busy since their earlier encounter. The knights stayed out of sight as much as possible, but they knew their presence was known by the loggers, who worked with extra haste to pack up and leave.

Maps were updated, and plans were changed. Raven would lead several knights and squires on a lightning raid of mayhem to keep the loggers from gathering. The majority of the knights would drive the loggers south toward the sheriff's party. Then the sheriff's men would arrest the loggers. Wolf and the other pages would carry messages between the groups. The entire force would descend into a remote area of the valley and camp for the night so they could spring their surprise at daybreak.

With their final plans made, they split into three smaller bands to better position themselves. One party, commanded by the sheriff, traveled south toward the exit of the valley. They would meet up with forest rangers and drive north to arrest loggers trying to leave. The second band, commanded by the Lion, traveled north, their job being to push south, chasing the loggers away from their supplies and equipment. The last band, commanded by Raven, would disrupt any attempt of the loggers to organize any resistance. Since the loggers had weapons, all personnel wore body armor. The deputies would guard against any weapons the loggers might have by providing cover with their rifles.

Camp that evening would be primitive with no fire and no music. That night in camp Shadow stayed by Wolf's side, but he still avoided the horses, so Wolf put his bedroll on the opposite side of the camp and stayed to himself when possible.

When new scouting reports arrived, details of the plan of attack changed. Wolf knew that Red, in training to be a tracker, had scouted most of the evening, gathering information on loggers' positions.

At about midnight, Wolf was dispatched by the sheriff to the Lion with maps and messages. He had to ride with care in the dark and keep his head down to avoid tree limbs, trusting the horse to keep him safe. It took an hour to reach the Lion's camp, but the information seemed to be important. The Lion ordered Wolf to stand down and take a nap, but sleeping was the last thing he wanted to do. It turned out his brother was in camp. Ben came over and told him, "Plans have changed again. The loggers have gotten wind of us, and they're breaking camp and attempting to move out of the valley."

"What am I supposed to do?"

"Just sleep. You need to rest before your next ride. Nothing's going to happen before daylight, and you look dead on your feet. At least take a nap."

Wolf did take a nap and was awakened by his brother before dawn. All the knights and squires had left, and it was just the two of them.

"Where is everybody?" Wolf asked. "Why didn't you wake me?"

"There wasn't any point to it at the time. Besides, you're riding with me."

"How's that?"

"I'm scouting, and I need a messenger, so I asked for you," Ben replied. "We're going to find any stragglers we can, and you'll relay the information to the sheriff's team. Let's see your map."

Wolf produced the map, and Ben drew some new trails and X's, indicating some new locations that needed to be checked out. They then mounted up and headed for the closest location on the map. On arrival, they encountered two loggers attempting to secure a load of logs on a truck. The deputy yelled for them to stop and surrender. One man stopped and raised his hands. The other started to run around the truck.

The deputy spurred his horse on to follow the man. Wolf dismounted and brought his bow to bear on the first man, yelling for him to stand still. Confronted by a boy, the man lowered his arms and started running at him. He made it halfway before Shadow raced in from the left, snarling long and hard. Shadow positioned himself between the page and the man, crouched ready to jump. The man didn't stop but tried to run over the wolf. Shadow jumped striking the man in his chest and knocking him back. The man managed to keep standing and attempted to charge again. Shadow jumped, knocking the man down, and stood with his front paws on the man's chest.

"Call him off!" the man screamed.

"He's a wolf," Wolf snapped. "Don't move." The man froze, and Wolf kept his bow trained on him. After the deputy handcuffed the other man to the truck, he came over to Wolf and assessed the situation.

"Roll over, face down," he ordered. When the man complied, the deputy handcuffed him. "Very good job, Wolf. Let me see the map."

Ben made a couple of notes on the map and handed it back to Wolf. "Take this to the sheriff and tell him there are several other loggers up here besides these two. Be sure to stay off of the roads."

"I forgot to bring a compass," Wolf said, feeling embarrassed.

"Here, take this one." Ben handed him a folding compass. The well-built instrument had a flip up lens and sighting line, and it had a nice hand-braided leather lanyard for carrying it. "Keep it. It will serve you well."

Wolf said, "I don't deserve this!"

"Oh, yes you do. You've impressed me by how much you've changed in the last two months. Now go on your way."

Wolf headed south, following beside the trail as marked on the map. Raven and Red had taught him well, and he could parallel the trail with ease. He let Pinto Bean run as fast as he wanted, and the horse seemed to be enjoying it. In a little over an hour, he reached the sheriff at the southern end of the valley. He delivered his message and map to a happy sheriff, who ordered him to take a short rest and then pick a fresh horse.

The sheriff and his deputies were well prepared with food, and Wolf had his first hot meal in a day. After eating a breakfast of pancakes and eggs, he walked over to where the arrested loggers were kept, handcuffed to chains wrapped around the trees.

One prisoner stood out—the man with a broken arm. His arm had been set in a cast, and his hand was bandaged where Wolf's arrow had penetrated it. The man, on seeing him, announced, "That's the little twerp that shot me with an arrow. Boy, if I ever get my hands on you, I'll twist your scrawny neck."

"Can it, Jake," growled another prisoner. "I don't like threatening no kids, even if they think they're Robin Hood."

Wolf, who froze when the wounded man spoke, turned to see a short, wide man with a big bulbous nose and a wicked-looking grin with several teeth missing. It was the creepy man who had given him a ride into town the day Ben had arrested him for stealing sandwiches. The man hissed, "You had better look to your master, Raven. I've a quarrel or two to settle with him."

Wolf tried to calm himself, but felt his face turn red. He took a deep breath and let it out. "Who are you?" Wolf asked.

"I'm more interested in who you are, little man. I've heard all about you and that little girl. You're pretty dangerous with that bow. I saw those arrows, real nasty things those little points. I bet you paid a few pennies for them."

"What is it to you?" Wolf demanded, his anxiety rising a little.

"Temper, temper, little boy. I knew you had it in you. Where is that wolf dog you've got?" the man teased.

When the man mentioned Shadow, Wolf did calm down. He realized the man fed off his anger. "He's closer than you think. I can tell he doesn't like you. Look to your heels."

The man jerked his head around and saw the wolf behind him. Shadow started snarling like an angry police dog. To his credit, he didn't bite the man.

When the man looked back at him, Wolf grinned and said, "He likes his meat raw."

The man panicked, jerking against his handcuffs and said, "Get that animal away from me!"

Looking back, Wolf replied in an even voice, "Say the magic word—your name."

"Mace ... Mace, call him off."

"I'll try. Shadow, come." The wolf didn't move and continued growling, so Wolf just walked away. Shadow soon followed him.

The sheriff approached Wolf and said, "A most impressive display. You were pretty cool under pressure, but I think you've made a bad enemy."

"No, he made me his enemy," Wolf replied.

The sheriff handed Wolf the dispatch bag with the marked up map and messages and said, "This is for the Lion. Make all due haste."

Wolf mounted Boomerang and trotted north out of camp until he reached the trail and urged the horse to a full gallop. He avoided the areas marked red on the map, so he didn't run across any loggers. He did see the evidence of their work—whole groves of tall pine had been leveled. He also saw the Raven's handiwork, logging machines and trucks disabled. There were old pickup trucks and jeeps turned over, the work of Red and her fellow squires with their Percherons. They were having a good time.

Wolf continued trying to find the Lion. All the knights were on the move, pushing the loggers south towards the sheriff.

Wolf soon located the Lion and delivered his message pouch. The Lion read them and made some notes on the map. "It looks like our plans are working. We're rounding up the loggers almost without a fight. Why don't you take a break? It'll be awhile before I have dispatches ready."

Wolf walked over to Wart and Hildegard and asked. "Have you seen any action?"

"A little. Some of the squires were working over a jeep," Wart said. "It's amazing what they can think of."

"Was Red one of them?"

"You better believe it. She got Mary to pound a jeep with her front hooves and kick it with her rear hooves. They tied ropes to the axles on one side, threw them over the top, and pulled with the horses, rolling the jeep upside down. It was pretty cool. What about you?"

Wolf was miffed. He'd wanted to see the Percherons in action. "I was involved with one arrest," he said.

As the day wore on, the Lion and his knights pushed south finding more loggers and making arrests. Wolf saw more destroyed equipment, evidence of Raven's passing. By late afternoon, the Lion had advanced most of the way down the valley and called Wolf to make a ride to deliver messages to the sheriff.

Wolf rode hard, trying to catch up with anybody he could. He found Red, Willow, Bob, Bill and a few other squires on their Percherons in the process of flipping a banged up rusty pickup truck. He learned from Red that Raven had already reached the sheriff's camp, his job of creating mayhem accomplished. Wolf, remembering his obligations, rode on.

After dismounting and delivering the messages to the sheriff, Wolf went looking for Raven. He found the knight and Whisperblade tending their horses, which looked wet and rough. The two knights were drenched in sweat, dirty and tired looking. When they saw Wolf, Raven broke into a broad grin, and Whisperblade gave him a big hug.

Wolf chafed, embarrassed by the very public hug. There were just too many people around, including the prisoners. Wolf kept his head and asked the two of them to talk in private. They took the hint, and Raven pointed to a distant stand of trees and told Wolf to go and wait while they finished caring for their horses.

At the meeting point, Wolf explained to them the incident with Mace and told them he had a bad feeling about the man. "Who is this guy?" Wolf asked, "Did I do right? I hitched a ride with that creep once and ran away from him when he stopped to get gas. That was the day I met you and Red."

"Yes, you did very well," Raven replied. "Mace and his buddy are dangerous. Stay away from them. He's as close to being a real pirate as one can be nowadays. I've had dealings with him before. He's been around more than once when people have disappeared."

"Raven is right," Whisperblade said. "He and his buddy have no problem using and hurting children, despite what he said."

"We'll talk more when we're back in camp," Raven said. They all returned to the sheriff's camp just as the Lion arrived. As it turned out, there were twenty-one loggers captured. It took the rest of the afternoon and evening for the other knights and squires to make it into camp. The prisoners were secured for the night, and transportation was arranged to take them to the county court the next day. For the knights, squires, and pages, it was a time to relax and enjoy their success. No one had been hurt or injured except for a few minor scrapes and bruises. Any loggers not captured would have to turn themselves in if they wanted to survive the cold night.

~

The camp broke up at sunrise, and the knights, squires, and pages formed a long, slow line heading up the valley for the trail that would lead up to the pass. It turned out to be a somber day and a dreary ride with thick dark clouds blocking out the sun. Thunder rolled from somewhere further up in the valley. Late in the morning when they were ascending the trail into the pass, the cold, soaking rain reached them. They were drenched, despite wearing rain ponchos, and the higher they climbed towards the pass, the colder it became. Everyone's breath formed clouds of steam, more so the horses. Before they reached the pass, the rain turned to snow, and it came down thick. Even with the sheriff's coat, Wolf was unprepared for that kind of cold.

The party of riders did not hang around at the pass but pushed on down into the valley, and soon they were out of the snow and back into the rain. Wolf wondered what it would be like camping out in the rain. How would they get any rest? Up until then, he had been lucky in having shelter available whenever it rained. Remembering Red's comment about camping in the rain, he asked her what she did.

Her answer didn't encourage him. She said, "If you're wet, you aren't going to get dry or get warm until the rain stops." They toughed it out and didn't make camp before nightfall. They set up camp high above a stream where they could obtain fresh water. The pages fetched the water for everyone and the horses. The squires and knights made miniature lean-to shelters using swords, hatchets, and knives. Someone managed to light a small fire and brewed coffee for everybody. Bedrolls were laid out and a watch established.

Wolf found it hard to go to sleep, and he was surprised when he woke up late in the morning to find the warm sun shining. Red had hung up everything that needed drying on branches to take advantage of the sun and breeze.

"Wake up, sunshine," Red chided. "If you stay in that bedroll any longer, you'll turn into a mushroom. Go get some coffee."

~

Wolf was still wet when he mounted Pinto Bean, and he was in a lousy mood. The ride across the valley in bright sunshine went a long way to warming him up and restoring his spirits. When the party marched their horses into the main camp, the students cheered. Pages took control of their horses and led them to the stables while riders went to the mess tent for a hearty lunch of hot, thick, beef stew.

Chapter 17 ~ Sick of Homework

After lunch, Raven reminded Wolf that he had schoolwork to do. There would be no break just because of his adventure, but Wolf knew that already. Being several days behind, he had been assigned extra homework. It included more math than he could possibly do, and he had to write a long paper on his recent adventure.

It would be a long night before Wolf finished up with his homework. He fell asleep face down on the table and woke up after lights out sweating, sore, and weak. Shadow licked his face, but he didn't have the energy to argue with him. The next time he awoke, he was being carried by Wart, Harold, and George to the nurse's tent.

Wolf spent the next day alternating between fevers and chills, barely aware of people coming and going. He remembered seeing Whisperblade and Raven, and Shadow always seemed to be at the edge of his vision.

When he awakened, he realized Red sat at his side, petting Shadow. "Welcome to the world of the living," she said. "So you thought you could take a vacation on us. You've been sick."

"How long?" Wolf asked.

"Almost two days. Don't try to get up. Here drink this, Raven's orders." She handed him a cup with a foul-smelling, dark liquid in it.

Wolf drank and did not hear any more as a gentle warmth filled his belly, and he sank into a deep and peaceful sleep. When he awoke, Raven stood over him and said, "I see you're feeling better."

"You're mean," Wolf mumbled. He felt like he'd been beaten. Every muscle ached. "What's wrong with me?"

"You have the flu. How you got it, I'm not sure, but you probably caught it from one of the deputies or loggers. You were very sick for a while. How do you feel?"

"Terrible."

"Here, drink this. It tastes bad, but it will help you feel better." Raven gave him a cup.

"What is it?"

"It's a tea I made up from willow bark. It works like aspirin."

Wolf drank the bitter liquid, and Raven left him alone. Later, Red came into the tent. "Hi, good, you're awake. You look like you just ate a toad."

Wolf said, "I think I did."

"It must be Raven's tea. He's a good healer, but he doesn't sugarcoat anything. How do you feel now?"

"Much better," Wolf said, surprised that he did indeed feel better.

"Good, let's see if you can stand." Red took Wolf's arm around her neck and pulled him to his feet. That's when he noticed Shadow standing beside him.

"How long has Shadow been here?"

"Pretty much the whole time."

Red led Wolf on a short walk about the tent. "I took the liberty of keeping up with your homework. You'll find it in order and ready to be worked."

"Thanks, that's all I need, too much homework," Wolf said.

Red led him over to the mess tent and served him a bowl of chicken soup, the first real food he'd had in a couple of days. After he ate two bowls of soup, he felt full. Red took him back to see the nurse, who, after a quick examination, turned him loose from her care. Red then walked with him over to Raven's tent.

"You look like you're feeling much better," Raven said. "Your priority for the rest of the day and tomorrow is homework and exercise. When you start to feel bad, just drink another cup of willow tea."

"Yes, sir." Wolf winced at the thought of drinking more of Raven's tea. He went to his tent and started on his math homework, glad he could skip most of his chores for the day. He did drink plenty of regular tea and ate some of the dried mango slices Red had provided him.

After he'd worked on homework for a couple of hours, Wolf looked up and saw Whisperblade at the entrance to his tent. "I'm glad to see you're looking much better. Do you think you could do some light exercises?"

"Yes, Master," he replied, noting she wore her teaching outfit. They stepped out of the tent and went to an open area where she had him start his stretching, and then she had him perform his self-defense routines. When they were finished, she had him meditate, concentrating on the pain leftover from the illness. She dismissed him after a light workout, ordering him to come to class in the morning.

Wolf went back to his homework and received help from his tent mates, who were back from supper and glad to see him. Later that evening, he told them about his recent adventures, including his encounters with Mace and Jake.

The next day, he felt so much better, he went to the stable to check on the horses. Nudge had gained twenty pounds since Wolf had last seen him. Nudge appeared to have missed him and wouldn't leave him alone. Shadow now remained a constant companion and seemed to get along with Mary. Wolf realized he was happy. He had good teachers and good friends, both two- and four-legged.

Knowlton

Chapter 18 ~ The Big Race

Wolf arose early to prepare for the games and ran to the stables to attend to the horses and their tack. Today he would be tested on his new riding skills, and he wanted an A-plus proficiency rating. He also had a surprise for everybody.

After taking care of the horses, Wolf went to Raven's tent to prepare the coffee. There he met Red who had finishing setting the table. Raven came out of his tent, and they sat down for breakfast. Raven laid out the order of events for the day. Wolf would be demonstrating his riding skills early. Wolf asked if time could be arranged for a special demonstration, and Raven said he would see to it. Red would again be jousting and giving a demonstration of riding skills while standing on top of Mary.

After breakfast, Raven went into the back of his tent and donned his fighting outfit. The outfit consisted of a heavily padded shirt and pants. There were leather straps that Wolf had to cinch up. Wolf and Red had to carry Raven's armor and weapons to the lists, which required two trips.

Then Wolf helped Raven suit his horse Midnight in armor, including steel plating for its head, neck, and forequarters, all in addition to the saddle and tack. They led Midnight to the lists, and he and Red started to help suit up Raven's armor. First, his chain mail hauberk to protect him from any sword cuts or mace blows that managed to find a chink in his armor. Next, he donned the armor itself, first the leggings, and then the foot covers. He then put on the breast and back plates followed by the arms and gauntlets. Even though the armor had been made of modern materials, thin steel over a fiber composite, it still weighed 110 pounds, almost as much as Wolf himself.

The battles would be fought while it was still cool. Wolf saw that Raven had already worked up a sweat and noted he would need every bit of help that he and Red could give. They were to make sure he had plenty of water, keep his weapons at hand, and attend to his horse.

The rules for the joust were simple: two knights would have one attempt to unseat the other with a lance. The next test would be with swords, either on horses or on foot. After swords, other weapons were optional. They would fight until one of could fight no more.

Raven's opponent would be Bear, the one man he might not be able to defeat, Bear being the strongest man Wolf had ever seen.

With the help of a log for a step, Wolf and Red boosted Raven into the saddle. Wolf handed Raven's helmet up to him and then his shield, which had Raven's emblem on it. Meanwhile Red mounted Easy Rider and picked out a lance. She rode with Raven, side by side to the end of the lists. Bear was already waiting at the other end of the lists with his helmet on and visor lowered.

Red handed the lance to Raven. The knight nodded, which closed his visor. Red raised her right arm to signal to the flagman. After checking with the Bear's squire, the flagman raised the green flag.

Red brought her hand down solidly on Midnight's rump, and the horse sprang into action. Raven charged down the length of the lists toward Bear, lance lowered and crossing into the other lane. They met, and both lances shattered in an explosion of splinters. As they passed each other, they dropped the remains of the lances.

Both riders pulled up their horses, wheeled them about, and drew their swords. The horses trotted towards each other, and the knights started swinging their swords. There were sickening crunches as the swords hit against shields. After about ten blows against each other, they separated and dismounted. They again clashed with swords, only now with a higher degree of agility. They parried each other's blows with their swords and used their shields less.

The referee called for a break and a weapons change. Raven came over, and Wolf quickly held up a water skin while Red pulled up the visor on Raven's helmet. After he'd had his fill of water, Red toweled off his face and lowered his visor.

Raven picked up his heavy mace, turned back to the lists, and walked over to where Bear stood. He swung the mace overhead and down onto Bear's shield. It sounded as if two cars had collided. Bear's shield was dented. Bear responded by delivering a wide, swinging blow to Raven's shield, knocking a chunk off the corner.

There were several more blows to the shields before Wolf came to a realization—this contest was not about trying to hurt each other but about destroying the other's shield. It wasn't long before Raven's shield shattered. The referee called the match and declared Bear the winner by virtue of having more of his shield left.

The crowd gave a standing ovation for Bear. When Raven gave the remains of his shield to Bear as a prize, he received more applause. Red and Wolf then went to work on removing Raven's armor. They worked fast because Raven was very hot and exhausted.

This left Raven in his hauberk, and Wolf helped him out of the chain mail, padded vest, and chaps. Once he had all the hot padding off, he seemed to be in very good shape for the exertion he had performed. He dismissed Red and Wolf to go to their events.

~

Wolf didn't have much time to prepare for his event, so he fetched Pinto Bean, led him to the lists, and mounted up. He had to ride first in the skills competition, and he had a very good feeling about it.

Wolf performed the required maneuvers with Pinto Bean well enough to win praise from the judge. "I believe you're ready for advanced lessons; you should consider dressage in the future."

"What is dressage, sir?" Wolf asked.

"It's a demonstration of advanced riding skills," the knight replied.

~

Jousting came up next. He tied Pinto Bean to a hitching post and proceeded over to where Red was preparing to ride. "I can only get two to one odds," Red confided. "How am I going to make any money?"

"Why don't you run no faster than necessary? Make like Mary isn't doing very well," Wolf replied.

"That sounds like it might help, but it isn't very honest. It's too risky, and I hate not doing my best. I won't do it. I'll live with two to one odds."

Wolf knew Red didn't back down from any challenge. "I'll do what I can for you. My money is on you, Red."

"Good, help me get ready then, and see if you can talk some of those rich squires into some bets. Oh, and leave Shadow behind. You don't want to make them nervous."

"I'll do my best to keep Shadow on his best behavior. Besides, I have a surprise."

When Red mounted for her try at the rings, Wolf handed her a light lance. Once Red started walking Mary to the lists, he went to make some quick wagers for her.

Red won her first round with no problem. She didn't push Mary hard. Wolf knew she always tried to keep her horse cool during the hot part of the day.

After the first round, during a break in the action, Wolf was granted time to perform with Pinto Bean. He took Pinto Bean's saddle off and rearranged the saddle blanket to cover the horse's back completely. Then he brought the horse out onto the lists. Using a long lead and word commands, he soon had the horse trotting in a circle around him.

When the horse achieved an even trot, Wolf called out to Shadow. The wolf came running in from the shaded area where he had rested unnoticed. Shadow ran into the circle that Pinto Bean trotted and followed the horse just to the inside of its hindquarters. When Wolf gave Shadow the command, the animal jumped onto the back of the horse, landing on top of the blanket. The wolf then stood, riding nose to the wind, as if he had always done it.

The applause was immediate—even the knights stood to clap. After about ten laps around, Wolf stopped the horse, and Shadow jumped down and came over to Wolf, obviously expecting a head rub. The applause continued as Wolf walked off the lists, leading the horse with Shadow at his side.

As he passed Red, he grinned and challenged, "Let's see you top that."

She retorted, "I will, but I'll let you have your moment of fame first." Wolf knew she would try.

On the next round of jousting, Red pulled a perfect score. Not only did she capture all the rings, but Mary also won the race to the finish line.

In the final round, Red had to face Willow. It looked to be a tough match. Wolf had observed Willow, and she impressed him by how well she rode her gelding.

"It's going to be a real race to the end. There won't be any holding back for Mary," Red commented. "I have to win. I will win." Wolf had to agree with that because he had just bet his money on Red, all twelve dollars.

Red mounted up. Taking the lance from Wolf, she proceeded to the far end of the lists, reached the starting line before Willow, and had time to calm Mary. To Wolf, it seemed Mary understood what the stakes were and kept pawing the ground in anticipation.

Willow and her horse arrived at the starting point, and she carried a heavier lance than the one preferred by Red. The heavier lance had the advantage of being easier to hold steady, which was good if there was no wind to blow the rings around.

The flag dropped, and they both made a good start and went to a full gallop, hooves shaking the ground. To Wolf, it seemed they were going too fast to hold their lances steady. They lowered the weapons and aimed for the first ring, and both missed. They both then succeeded in capturing the next ring and had mixed success afterward. After the last ring, they ran their horses as fast as they could run. Mary finished a full length ahead of Willow's horse.

Red waited at the judge's station until the rings could be tallied. When the scoring was complete, Red had won by a margin of fifteen points, a large margin for a final round. She handed her lance to Wolf, stood on Mary's saddle, did a back flip, and landed with her feet on Mary's rump.

Red looked at Wolf, grinned, and said, "I guess that's a topper, isn't it?"

"Is not," Wolf challenged.

Red grimaced and then smiled and said, "Let's go settle the bets."

Afterward, Wolf had increased his cash from twelve to thirty-six dollars, the largest amount he had ever owned.

Red offered Wolf some advice. "Don't bet more than you can afford to lose. I've had bad days, and I won't always win. You'll want to save up for important things. You'll need a good saddle for Nudge eventually. You won't be able to use a school saddle on him since he's your responsibility. Now, that's something Raven won't tell you."

"How else can I make money?"

"Earn it, like I do."

"How's that?"

"I have a number of skills that are of value to others, like making arrows. I have to fit them in between my duties. I'll tell you this: school comes first. Tracking skills don't count for much without book learning."

Wolf thought about it for a second. "This isn't going to be easy, is it?"

"Nobody said it was," Red replied.

"No, not that. What I mean is, it's going to be hard, like forever."

"Yes."

"Why even try?" Wolf asked.

"Because, it's worth it. Look, it's time for the race. You'd better get ready."

"But I'm not in the race."

"Oh, yes, you are. Both Raven and I think you're ready, so I entered you," Red said, grinning.

Wolf took a swipe at Red and missed as she ducked out of the way.

"I'll help you get ready, even after that," she retorted.

~

The race was not what Wolf expected it to be. The first leg of the race felt like being in a crowded hallway with everybody bumping into everybody else. Twice he thought he would fall, but Pinto Bean had an uncanny ability to turn the right way to keep him on top. It wasn't a fast ride, but as the crowd of horses thinned out, Pinto Bean reached a comfortable gallop, and the going became more manageable for Wolf.

At the end of the first leg, he rounded the flag and headed for the streams. The second leg proved to be wet. The recent rains had swelled the streams to overflowing, and Wolf caught a mouthful of water when Pinto Bean plunged into the first stream. The stream was deep enough that the horse had to walk slowly, but it was still too shallow to swim. The other streams were equally deep, and Wolf was soaked when he reached the flag for the final turn to return to the lists.

The run back challenged Wolf because he'd ridden the course only once before. Pinto Bean made it easier because he had run the course many times over the years. The horse seemed to know the right path.

In the dash to the finish line, Pinto Bean managed a burst of speed and saved Wolf the embarrassment of being last in his class. Red caught up with them as they came to a halt. She steadied the horse while Wolf dismounted, and, together, they walked the horse to cool it off.

"That was some pretty good riding. Those lessons have paid off," Red commented.

"But I was almost dead last," Wolf complained.

Red threw an arm around Wolf's shoulder and said, "But you weren't. In fact, you were in the middle of the novice field, a very respectable showing."

"Very respectable indeed," Raven said from behind them. "Did you think, three months ago, you would be racing cross-country on a horse?"

"No, sir."

Raven smiled and said, "Who knows what you'll be doing three months from now? That, my boy, is adventure."

Knowlton

Chapter 19 ~ Day of the Wolf

The days became shorter, and the sun did not rise until after breakfast. One morning, Raven informed Wolf that he and Shadow were to report to the main tent. There he would have to prove that Shadow could safely travel to the school.

The day that Wolf feared the most had arrived. He gave Shadow a big hug, and that set the wolf on edge. Shadow, who was amenable to head rubs, did not care for such affection. The wolf paced, back and forth, like a trapped animal, although he could leave at any time.

Wolf, also felt uptight. Red pulled him aside and told him he had nothing to worry about, that Shadow knew what he had to do and would do it well.

When Wolf and Red had cleaned up from breakfast, they walked over to the main tent with Raven where they met the Lion, Bear, and Dr. Lundie, the veterinarian. After greetings, the Lion declared the test had begun. The adults all had a serious look about them, except for Bear, who gave Wolf a reassuring smile and some quick words of encouragement.

The Lion handed a collar and leash to Wolf. Then Wolf brought Shadow to heel and put the collar around his neck, and he sat perfectly still, allowing Wolf to do it.

Next Wolf had to walk Shadow around the tent, passing all the people who were working. Several pages reached out to pet him, and Wolf stopped to allow them to do so. Shadow accepted the head rubs without complaint and passed the first test.

Wolf ordered Shadow to sit and handed the leash to the Lion, who tried to get Shadow to walk with him, but Shadow refused. Wolf said, "It's okay, Shadow," and he stood up and followed the Lion. The Lion took the wolf over to a table where he uncovered a small plate with some raw meat on it. The wolf sniffed but refused to take the meat even when the Lion held it right in front of him.

Wolf went to the headmaster, asked for the meat, and handed it to Shadow, who ate it in one bite.

"I'm impressed, very impressed," the Lion said. "You may bring him to the school. He shows remarkable restraint and seems to get along with the other students. If he were a dog, I would be happy to have him. You should be proud of yourself, Wolf. I know you worked very hard to reach this point."

"Thank you, sir," Wolf said.

The Lion looked at Wolf and then at Shadow, furrowing his eyebrows. "One last question, Wolf. How well does he get along with the horses?"

Wolf smiled, "Him and Nudge play with each other. Mary tolerates his presence. He gets along with Pinto Bean great, but Midnight won't let him near, sir."

"That is to be expected from a stallion," the Lion mused, "especially one trained by Raven."

"Yes, sir."

"Dr. Lundie has some paperwork for you to take care of." Wolf, dismissed, walked over to a table with the veterinarian, and they sat down. The vet brought out some forms from a folder and proceeded to explain them to Wolf.

The first document was a permit allowing him to handle a wolf. The next document listed his responsibilities to the wolf, such as care and feeding. Next was an acknowledgment of what could happen if the wolf should bite, harm, or threaten someone. That document scared him, as it spelled out his responsibility. There would be serious, very serious, consequences for Shadow if something bad should happen.

The last form he had to sign was an application for a dog license for the wolf. The vet explained, for all practical purposes, the wolf could be treated the same as a dog. The vet then handed him a collar with the dog license and rabies vaccination tags on it. They stood up, and Dr. Lundie shook Wolf's hand and congratulated him on his and Shadow's accomplishment.

Wolf, Shadow, and Red went out of the tent into the bright morning sunlight. "Don't let this go to your head," Red warned. "You still have classes to go to."

"You do, too," Wolf responded as he started to run to his tent.

In the middle of the afternoon, when all of Wolf's classes were over, he got restless. He went riding through the forest scouting out rabbit warrens. Pinto Bean had been checked out by another page, so he rode Boomerang, a younger horse, normally ridden by more experienced pages. They came to a glen and started a back-and-forth sweep, looking for rabbit runs. The only traces he found were old and almost covered with new growth. He reflected that Shadow had probably already hunted the glen. The fact that Shadow didn't participate in the sweep almost confirmed it for Wolf.

Wolf headed for the tree line when a rider came bursting out of the trees heading straight for him. Wayne came towards him at a full gallop. With no time to turn, Boomerang reared up in defense, catching Wolf by surprise. He slid off the back of the horse, landing on his rear end. Wayne continued past him across the glen, hollering in an apparent attempt to spook Boomerang further. He also yelled over his shoulder, "Give it up!"

Boomerang almost stomped on Wolf and then started running toward the forest.

Wolf managed to get to his feet and start chasing the horse. He ran a couple hundred meters with a sore rump before he caught up with the agitated horse and found him being confronted by Shadow. Wolf spoke to the horse in a soothing quiet voice and secured the reins.

When he thought the horse would accept him, he mounted, and the horse calmed down. Wolf looked around, but he didn't see Shadow. Either his presence or Shadow's absence had helped to calm Boomerang. He would never know.

Wolf himself managed to calm down, but then he got angry. He believed Wayne had charged him deliberately. He was also angry with himself for falling off his horse. His buttocks hurt pretty badly, and he was sure he was going to limp. Trotting on Boomerang was out of the question. He started the horse on the long walk back to camp.

Wolf confided to Wart about Wayne upsetting him in the glen. "Don't say anything to anybody about it, especially to Wayne," Wart said.

Chapter 20 ~ Archery Lessons

During their breakfast meeting Raven announced, "That pirate, Mace, escaped from jail a couple of days ago along with his companion, Jake. He overpowered his guard while being transferred to the courthouse. They fled up into the forest and somehow eluded the bloodhounds. The guard will be in the hospital for quite a while."

"They must be very desperate," Red commented.

"More than that," Raven replied, "Mace has sworn to kill me."

Wolf said, "He'll probably be caught."

"The longer he's free, the harder it'll be to find him. I don't hold much hope that he'll be caught before he commits another crime," Raven said. "Several knights, including me, are going to help in the hunt. There will be no squires on this trip. We leave within the hour. I expect you two to stay out of trouble while we're gone. Pay attention to your teachers."

"Why can't I go?" Red inquired.

"These men are too desperate. They're armed and have already tried to kill one man," Raven replied.

It turned into a somber, gray day. With breakfast over and Red dispatched to prepare Midnight, Wolf went to the mess tent to obtain provisions for a week of hard riding. All the food had to be dry and suitable for eating in the saddle. Together, Red and Wolf packed Midnight's saddlebags and gathered and checked Raven's weapons and armor.

When Raven returned, he declined all the armor except the bulletproof vest. He mounted Midnight and accepted the weapons they handed up to him. This included his sword, bow and arrows, and a tomahawk. He declined a spear, the larger lance, and his mace. He already had his large knife on his belt.

Raven wheeled his horse about and cantered over to the other knights, who were ready and waiting by the big tent. Together they started east from the camp, accelerating to a gallop and disappearing into the trees, the sound of their hoof-beats fading soon afterward.

Wolf felt a big letdown at not being involved in Raven's adventure. It would be hard to concentrate in class. He asked Red, "You want to skip this afternoon and go find some rabbit?"

"You're thinking the same thing I am. I'll meet you after lunch at the stables. Bring your bow." Red turned around and started running to her self-defense class.

Wolf ran for his archery class with Shadow leading the way. When he got there, he found his regular instructor had joined the other knights on their mission, and Willow was teaching the class. She proved to be an expert marksman with the bow. She used a straight longbow, much like Raven's longbow, and claimed that she had taught Red how to shoot so well. "She would still be shooting an arrow every five minutes if I hadn't taught her rapid fire."

Wolf had always assumed Raven had taught Red. "I didn't know that," he said.

"Well, I'll teach you the same, if you want," Willow continued, "but there's a price."

"What's that?"

"Ten of your flint pointed arrows," Willow replied.

"I can give you five, if you want them now."

"They have to be in my colors, and I can wait for them."

"I'll make you six, and I have to find enough flint."

"Nine."

"Seven. I have to find feathers that are large enough."

"Eight and no less," Willow demanded.

"Agreed," Wolf replied. "It will take me four days after I find enough feathers."

"Shake on it," Willow demanded.

They both spit in their palms and shook on the deal.

"This is how you shoot rapid fire," Willow proceeded to demonstrate by taking three arrows and her bow in her left hand. She held the arrows near the feathers, pointed down. She reached for one of the arrows with her right hand, grabbed it at the end, pulled to notch it onto the string, drew the bow, aimed, and let loose. She brought her right hand forward and repeated the process twice.

Willow did this at a leisurely pace so Wolf could see how she did it. She then shot three arrows in a very rapid motion. "Practice with only two arrows. String your bow lightly for practice, or you'll wear your arms out. And for goodness sake, don't do it with anyone around because your aim will be wild at first."

True to Willow's advice, Wolf's second arrow went wild. He missed the target time after time and became frustrated. She made him slow down and work on the actual motions that his hands had to make in order to get the arrows onto the string. He had to do it without lowering the bow and without taking his eye off the target.

His arms became sore from holding the bow with no rest. Willow wouldn't let him rest for the entire lesson. "You need to do more arm exercises. Self-defense is not enough. Do push-ups and chin-ups to strengthen those arms. Also, hold then out straight as long as you can. It's time for your next class."

~

Wolf spent the rest of the morning at his various classes and was glad when the lunch horn blew. Eager to get up with Red and go rabbit hunting, Wolf quickly ate his stew. After cleaning his mess kit, he put it away, gathered his bow and arrows, and ran to the stables where Red finished preparing Easy Rider for his saddle.

Wolf hurried to get Pinto Bean prepared and saddled, and, when they were ready, they left the stables at a gallop heading north into a part of the forest he knew well.

What had been a gloomy day turned into a glorious day. The clouds parted and turned to just little puffs, and the bright sun made it just warm enough they didn't need their jackets. The wind felt good on Wolf's face. After about ten minutes, they slowed their pace so Shadow could keep up.

145

Thirty minutes later, they pulled up at a small stream to rest and refresh the horses.

As they were walking their horses to cool them down, Wolf asked Red, "What can you tell me about Willow? She seems to be too old to be a squire."

"She's too old to be a regular student. She teaches some classes at school."

"She's trying to become a knight?"

"Yes," Red said, "and she will be soon."

"Why did she start so late?"

"You'll have to ask her," Red snapped.

They came to a rock outcropping, and Wolf got excited because some of the rocks were flint, which he could use for arrowheads. He and Red both gathered suitable pieces and loaded them in their horses' saddlebags.

"This looks as good a place as any to find rabbit," Red declared. "You and Shadow go left, and I'll go right. I bet I bag a bigger rabbit than you do. Shadow's rabbit doesn't count because he's a professional."

"You're on," Wolf answered.

They split up and went their separate ways. Wolf knew to return to the last place they saw each other when he finished. At the first glen, he tied Pinto Bean to a tree, and Shadow took the lead on tracking rabbits. The wolf had a keen sense of smell, and he quickly found a rabbit run. Wolf picked up on the run, and it led to the warren. He positioned himself near the hole with his bow and two arrows. Shadow started digging at the other entrance hole. When the first rabbit emerged from the hole, it ran directly at Wolf. Wolf nailed the animal with the first arrow, but the rest of the animals escaped when Wolf fumbled the second arrow and could not draw it in time. Shadow couldn't catch a rabbit, but he provided some amusement for Wolf by chasing one back and forth for a half minute.

Wolf gutted his rabbit and, holding it by the arrow, headed back for his horse. When he reached it, he heard a distant scream from Red. Wolf dropped the rabbit and mounted his horse. He and Shadow headed at a gallop for the rock outcropping. They reached it, but Wolf found no sign of Red. Shadow headed up the path that she had taken, and Wolf followed. They soon found Easy Rider, eyes wide, walking back toward them, and Wolf grabbed the reins. Expecting something bad, he brought his horse to a trot and went in the direction that Easy Rider had come from.

It took a couple of minutes before Wolf reached the spot where Red had come off her horse. The signs were obvious. The small bushes around him had been crushed. He dismounted and stooped down to read the signs and found where leaves and dirt had been kicked about by the horse. There were footprints, Red's soft boots were easy enough to read, but there were different prints of someone larger or heavier than Red. No, two other sets of prints. Then he made his worst discovery—her bow and spots of blood on the ground, as well as strands of copper hair pulled out in a clump.

Shadow found more blood, and, after sniffing about, he headed down a path. Wolf tried to follow the best he could, but Shadow ran too fast and quickly was out of sight.

Wolf stopped when he heard a loud popping sound followed by a loud yelp from Shadow. That popping sound had come from a gun. It didn't sound anything like a big blast, but it was a gun just the same. Wolf had the presence of mind not to follow Shadow any further. Instead, he crouched down to think about the situation.

Red was in deep trouble and needed his help. There were at least two men involved. He had to help her, but how? Shadow had been hurt, probably shot. He needed more information. He eased up the path until he heard the voices of two men arguing. From there, Wolf went to the left into a copse of trees. He pulled three arrows from his quiver. Holding two in his left hand with the bow, he fitted the third to the string. He found himself sweating hard, and his hands shook.

Without a real plan, he stepped out from the trees to see what the situation was. Nothing prepared him for what he saw. Shadow lay on the ground, oozing blood. The two men were standing over Red, who wasn't moving. Her face was red on the right side with blood around her left eye. One man, who had a cast on his arm, held Red's knife as he faced the other man, who had a gun in his hand. Wolf recognized Mace and Jake.

When Wolf stepped on a twig, both men turned toward him. He realized he was out in the open, having walked too far from the trees.

147

Mace's face broke into a large grin. "So we meet again, little boy. Last time that wolf dog was very bad. Look at him now."

Wolf did not take his eyes off Mace. Instead, he raised his bow to shooting level.

"I wouldn't do that if I were you," the man snarled as he raised his gun. He didn't point it at Wolf. He aimed at Red.

Wolf let loose, and the arrow flew straight and buried itself in the man's upper arm pinning it to his chest. The gun flew out of the man's hand and landed in a bush. Mace screamed and clutched at the arrow with his free hand.

Jake reached for Red. Wolf already had his second arrow on the string of his bow. After taking an extra few seconds to aim, he let loose a second time. The arrow struck the man in his buttocks. The man yelped and dropped the knife. When he tried to pull the arrow out, he screamed in agony, started hopping around on one leg, and then tripped and fell on his face, as a growing red patch formed on his pants.

Wolf had mounted his third arrow and aimed back at Mace, who was trying to find the gun with his good hand. Wolf yelled, "Back off!"

Mace turned back to him, gun in hand, and screamed, "I'll kill you!"

He didn't get the chance because two arrows hit him, one in each thigh, and he collapsed writhing in pain.

Wolf lowered his bow and turned. Raven, Whisperblade, and Bear were bringing their horses up to a stop behind him. He dropped his bow and ran for Red.

Red moaned weakly. She had a gash above her left eye, and a huge lump and bruise forming over the left side of her head. Raven came to her side and performed a quick check on her. After a few seconds, he pronounced, "She'll be all right, but she's going to have a huge headache."

Wolf remembered Shadow and turned to look at the wolf. Bear hovered over the animal, working furiously, trying to stop the bleeding. Shadow whimpered and labored at breathing but otherwise laid still.

Whisperblade stood in front of the two ruffians with her bow trained on them. When Jake tried to grab at her ankle, she delivered a kick to his chin. His head snapped back then forward, and the man was out cold, face down on the ground. She turned her attention on Mace still writhing in pain from the three arrows embedded in his legs and arm.

Mace managed to growl, "I'm going to kill you, boy."

"Not likely," Whisperblade replied. The knight lowered her bow and pulled her long dagger from its sheath. She bent down holding the point at Mace's nose. "If you ever harm him, I'll relieve you of body parts, piece by piece. Do we have an understanding?" Mace glared at her but kept quiet. She turned and asked, "Wolf, how are you doing?"

Wolf hadn't thought about it, but he was shaking, and it dawned on him just how much danger he'd been in. He felt lightheaded, and his knees buckled.

When he came to, Red sat next to him with her arm around his shoulder. "How do you feel?" she asked. "I understand I have you and Shadow to thank for saving me. No, don't talk, you're still pretty gray."

He looked at her banged up head. "You're not looking so great yourself. Are you all right?"

"I've had better days, and worse days, for that matter. I think we're going to be in big trouble when we get back to camp."

"How's Shadow?" Wolf asked.

Red said, "He's tougher than you think. Raven and Bear are looking after him. They think he'll survive."

A red-faced Whisperblade snapped at them, "You'll be lucky to be alive after I'm done with you. I'm tempted to take you both over my knee. Maybe a ball and chain on your ankles would work." She turned and stomped away.

Several other knights had arrived and taken charge of the two criminals. Wolf and Red stood up to check out their horses, which seemed to be all right.

Wolf walked over to Shadow. Raven looked up at him and said, "He took a bullet under the skin and down the side of his rib cage, lots of blood, but he'll survive. It is hard for him to breathe, but he's a very lucky wolf. Mount up. You're going to tow him back to the vet."

Raven and Bear quickly fashioned a simple horse sled to carry Shadow and attached it to the sides of Pinto Bean's saddle. They laid Shadow onto the sled, strapped him down with some cloth strips, and sent him and Wolf back to camp.

The long trip dragged on since they could go no faster than a walk, and the bumpy ground made it hard on the wolf. Wolf dismounted and walked beside the sled, controlling the horse by voice command. The very quietness lulled Wolf into not paying much attention to their progress. He considered his actions and his future with the school. It didn't help when Pinto Bean stopped. Wolf clucked at him, but the horse stood still. Wolf reached for the reins and saw Maude blocking the path. Wolf stepped back in surprise. She just stood there with a kindly smile. She didn't seem inclined to say anything. Regaining his voice, Wolf asked, "How did you get here?"

Maude smiled broadly, "I walked."

Wolf said, "But that must have taken a day."

"Yes."

"But how?"

"I just walked."

"No, I mean how did you know I was here?"

She ignored his question and asked, "Did you save Amara?"

"Yes, I think so."

"You indeed saved her." She placed a hand on his shoulder and said, "You're a most brave boy." She dropped her hand.

"You saw it, you saw everything?"

"I did."

"Why didn't you do something?" he demanded.

"It was your time to save Red. Let me see to Shadow."

She bent down and placed a hand on Shadow's wound. When she stood back up, she said, "He'll survive. He will rest now, so take it easy on your trip."

Wolf stooped down to look at Shadow, and the wolf slept easily. "What did you do?" he asked.

"How is your horse?" asked Maude.

"Growing big, like his mother. Hey, how did you know about him?" He looked up from Shadow, but Maude had disappeared.

~

When they reached camp two hours later, the other students stared at them. It troubled Wolf, and he felt relieved when they arrived at the vet's tent. Dr. Lundie sent Wolf to fetch the nurse, and, when he returned with her, he dismissed Wolf before they closed the tent and started operating on Shadow to remove the bullet and stop the bleeding.

Wolf waited a long while. He then took care of his horse, but that did nothing to dispel the anxious feeling he had about Shadow. After an hour, the vet approached him. "He's going to survive, but I'm not sure how well he'll recover from his wound. He's going to be in a lot of pain when he awakes. You can go see him now."

Wolf walked into the tent to find Shadow asleep on a cot with a large bandage wrapped around his chest. He sat down on a chair next to the cot and looked the wolf over. Shadow was a mess: his fur was caked with blood; he had been shaved along his side and belly; and his breath was very shallow and labored.

Wolf stood and walked over to a stand and poured water into a bowl. He took a washcloth and towel, soaking the washcloth with water and squeezing most of the water out. He returned to the cot, placed the towel under Shadow, and started to sponge the blood out of his fur, being very careful to avoid getting the wound wet.

He had almost finished when Raven entered the tent. The knight pulled up a chair and sat down facing the boy. "Shadow's a very lucky wolf. But it's a safe bet he'll never be able to survive in the wild on his own. What were you two doing up in the forest?"

Wolf looked at the knight. He had to face the truth. "We were hunting rabbit."

Raven didn't smile, but he asked, "Why?"

Wolf had to think about this awhile. "It felt good to get away."

The knight stared at him with those piercing gray eyes. "Again, why?"

Wolf's face flushed. "I don't know. I didn't have a good reason."

"That's what I thought. Part of growing up is learning to make good decisions for good reasons. This is especially important when lives depend on those decisions."

Raven nodded at Shadow, but Wolf knew he meant Red. "Sir, I'm going to be punished, aren't I?"

Raven started to say something, but then he paused a couple of seconds, as if measuring his words. "Yes. No, if you mean being spanked or something like that. You're not even being expelled. We don't do that. What your punishment will be hasn't been decided. There are consequences to bad decisions. Shadow is paying for yours now."

Raven held out a small misshapen metal ball in the palm of his hand, the bullet the vet had removed from Shadow. "Take it." When Wolf took the bullet, Raven said, "Keep it as a reminder that all decisions have consequences."

Chapter 21 ~ Punishment

The next morning when Wolf arrived at Raven's tent with breakfast, Raven ordered him to report to the stable master. The man set him to work, mucking out the stalls—not just a few of them, but all of them. It would have been worse, but Red had already started doing the same thing. Their offense was leaving camp without permission or telling anyone where they were going.

They worked at it all day. Red reminded Wolf that you take the bad as well as the good with no complaints. They labored at the backbreaking work, were restricted from riding, and had to watch as all their friends got to ride. There was a lot of joking at their expense, some of it not so friendly. They managed to get some playtime in with Nudge and Mary, but they were bone weary by suppertime.

~

With his labor done for the day, Wolf went to check on Shadow and found that Bear had taken over Shadow's care. Shadow was awake, but not able to breathe very well. He wagged his tail when he saw Wolf.

Bear set about changing the bandages and checking the wound. He said, "The vet said his pectoral muscles were damaged and could not be fully repaired. Shadow will have a permanent weakness that will intensify his limp."

Wolf couldn't see any complaints coming from Shadow. He didn't even make a whimper when he stood to sniff Wolf's face.

Bear showed Wolf what to look out for if an infection were to set in. He gave him a syringe filled with antibiotics. Wolf injected the medication under a pinch of loose skin on Shadow's back. "You'll have to do that three times a day," Bear said.

Once Shadow had again lain down, Bear put his hands on the boy's shoulders, looking him in the eye and said, "Wolf."

Feeling nervous, Wolf shivered. "Yes, sir."

"Shadow's going to depend on you."

"I know, sir."

Bear sighed, "He may wander around to hunt rabbit or such, but he's always going to come back to you. Pay attention to him. He's going to have to be fed, especially when we go to school."

"Sir?"

"Yes."

"He can eat with us, I mean if necessary."

"Wolf, he has to eat fresh meat or eggs. He shouldn't have cooked meat. It is not good for him. I want you to think about that and any other responsibility that comes with the wolf."

"Yes, sir." Wolf thought a minute and said, "Sir, I won't always be able to find fresh meat."

"You may have to buy it. Meat does not come cheap. Not for Shadow, not for you."

Wolf stiffened, knowing he would be in a bind. "I think I understand, sir. It's going to cost a lot more than I have."

Bear smiled and said, "It's time for you get on the good side of the cooks."

Wolf relaxed, seeing a way out of his dilemma, "Yes, sir."

"And Wolf."

"Yes, sir."

"The Lion is a dog lover. He has one that stays at the school. He won't put up with disobedience from Shadow. He's supposed to remain wild, but that requires a delicate balance. He has demonstrated an aptitude to get along with people, but he has to get along with *all* people. Do you understand what I'm trying to say?

Wolf said, "I think so. You mean Wayne."

Bear smiled again and said, "Precisely, and all like him. Shadow would die trying to protect you. And that may very well happen if you aren't vigilant. Taking him to school is a compromise and a big risk. He won't survive in the harsh winter up here, and that's a shame. This is his home. The school is not his home. It's unknown to him. He may not be able to handle it. If he can't, he might have to go to a zoo. Just think about it."

Wolf didn't like the thought of the zoo or of Shadow pacing back and forth in a pen. "Sir, I was able to fit in here in the wild. Can't Shadow do the same thing among humans?"

"You couldn't survive this winter on your own. Remember, people are more adaptable than wolves."

"I'll have to adapt for Shadow."

"Now you see it. When you went out with Shadow, he taught you."

"I'll have to teach him."

"It is all up to you."

Wolf looked down and said, "Yes, sir."

Bear pulled Wolf's chin up and said, "I'll help you in any way I can. You do what you must, and I'll do what I must. Agreed?"

"Agreed."

~

After two more days of backbreaking work, Wolf and Red were released to attend classes. They, of course, had to catch up with all their homework. Wolf had never been so glad for homework.

After classes, Wolf sought out the blacksmith to request a favor.

The smith took a short, stout wire and bent it into a 'U' shape with hooks on each end. He heated up the bullet that Wolf gave him, until the lead had melted in the deformed copper jacket. Inserting the hooks of the wire into the lead, he let the bullet cool. Then Wolf slipped a lanyard through the loop to make a small necklace.

~

Shadow healed enough to come back to Wolf's care, and, after seven days, Wolf removed his stitches. He would have a nasty scar even when his fur grew back.

Though Red never once mentioned her bruises or the cut above her eye, she obviously hurt. When Wolf asked her why she didn't talk about it, she shrugged it off as just taking her lumps like a knight would.

She would not talk about how she had been attacked, but Wolf could piece it together from all the clues he had observed. While riding her horse, she had been surprised by the two men. One of them had hit her on the side of the head with a broken limb, and she had fallen off her horse unconscious. Then the men had then dragged her away.

Wolf found out from Bob, one of the twin squires, that a helicopter had been called in to evacuate the two criminals. Their wounds were too severe for them to be ridden out. He learned from the Raven that he would eventually have to go to court to testify. It took a long time for Whisperblade to assure him he would not be in any trouble with the law, but there would be tough questions, and he would have to face Mace again before a judge. This time, Mace would not be able to hurt him.

~

After a week, Wolf and Red were allowed to ride horses again, and things were starting to look up. Wolf found time to work on the arrows that Willow had ordered. He made them with the flint he had found, some bamboo from the blacksmith, thread and hide glue from the quartermaster, and some feathers obtained from the ground beneath a hawk's nest. First, he cut the bamboo to length, then split it to arrow size, and shaved it to a round shape using a flint tool. To keep it from splitting, he tightly wrapped thread within an inch from each end of the shaft. He used glue to bind the thread to the wood. He cut a notch in each end, one to receive the arrowhead, and one to fit on the bowstring. He trimmed the feathers to size and split the quills to provide a surface for gluing. Once the glue had hardened, he wrapped more thread around, securing the ends of the feather quills to the shaft. The he applied more glue to the new thread. Next, he dyed the feathers in Willow's colors, dark red and green.

Wolf worked hard on the arrowheads. They had to be small, sharp, and all the same size. He started the process by breaking flint nodules into shards, which he separated into different sizes and shapes. Using a process called flaking, he made light taps with a bone tool, which caused an undercutting of the edge. He worked the piece until the basic shape of the arrowhead was produced. He finished the piece by more flaking, using the tip of a small copper nail embedded in a wood handle. This final bit of flaking put on the razor sharp edge made the arrow deadly to small animals like rabbits and squirrels. Wolf secured the arrowhead in the arrow's notch with more thread and glue.

It took three days to make the eight arrows, but he worked meticulously, and it showed. Willow, true to her word, gave Wolf individual lessons, teaching him to rapid-fire three arrows into the bull's eye. Wolf just wished he could have done that the week before.

When he got up the nerve, he asked Willow, "Why are you older than the other squires?"

"You should never ask a woman her age," she answered sharply.

"That's not what I meant, I mean, I meant—" Wolf stopped.

"I know what you meant, and it's a fair question. I started squire training late when I quit college."

"But why? Why would you do that?"

Willow sighed, "Let's just say I think I'll find being a knight more satisfying than being a scientist."

"So how did you become involved in this school?"

"Raven saved my life."

Wolf replied, "I hear that a lot."

"It's what being a knight is all about, saving lives."

Wolf looked at his feet, "Oh. I never thought about it that way."

"That's why you're a page and not a squire. I think that's enough questions for today."

Knowlton

Chapter 22 ~ The Train

As summer ended, a steady stream of wagons flowed in and out of camp. The Percherons were put to work pulling them. Students packed equipment and loaded wagons. Tents were pulled down, starting with the students' tents. The Percherons were used to pull down the stables, which would be added to the bonfire the final night. Wolf learned that they would scatter the ashes before they left and hire farmers to come in and replant the glen where the camp had been so it would appear untouched next season, when the camp would move to a different glen. As they worked loading wagons, Wolf asked Red, "So where is the actual school?"

"In Virginia," she said.

Wolf was stunned. "Virginia? How can they afford to move everything to and from Virginia twice a year?"

Red shrugged. "Well, the school is rich and has several endowments, plus you wouldn't believe how high the tuition is for summer camp students."

On their last day at camp, games were held. Red lost to Willow in jousting, and Raven managed to unseat Whisperblade. Bear continued his winning streak in individual combat.
Wolf again entered the big race. This time, he placed much better, finishing close to the lead of the novice group. Red congratulated him and said, "You did better on Pinto Bean than I ever did. You're doing something right." Then she put a hand on his shoulder and said, "Hey, there's one more tradition for the last set of games. I've got to get Mary ready. Go join the crowd and watch."

The highlight of the day was a full cavalry charge. All of the knights and squires mounted their horses. Carrying lances, they trotted out of the lists, two by two, in a long column with the Lion in the lead. They continued to the far side of the glen where the double line of horses split, with one turning left and the other turning right. When the double line had separated, all stopped and turned to face the lists. Then the Lion rode to the center of the long line of horses.

On the Lion's command, the line of horses and riders started to canter back towards the lists. When the Lion dropped his lance to level, all others did the same. The horses accelerated to a full gallop, and the broad line of some eighty horses came charging into the lists. At the last moment, the line split, and the horses avoided the pages and remaining adults. As the horses thundered by, the earth shook, and everyone cheered and screamed for joy. It was a thunderous conclusion to the day's activities.

~

A vote was taken on the most improved horseman, and Wolf won by a landslide, since he was the only one joining the school who had never ridden a horse. His prize was the honor of lighting the bonfire, and he had to do it by striking flint on steel. Once he managed to light a visible flame, the pages cheered. The students spent rest of the night in front of the roaring bonfire. They told stories and sang, and anyone who could play a fife did so. There were hot dogs and marshmallows to toast as well as hot chocolate to drink. It proved a big night, and the hour was late when the party broke up and students drifted to their bedrolls.

~

The next morning, everyone had to clean up, and everything left had to be loaded onto the wagons and secured. When the reclaimed campsite met the approval of the Lion, everyone mounted up to move out. Red rode Mary, and Wolf rode Easy Rider since Pinto Bean had been claimed by one of the older pages. All the pages who didn't have horses had to ride in a wagon. Shadow trotted somewhere out of sight as he usually did. Raven rode in the front with the other knights. The wagons brought up the rear of the column.

~

By late afternoon, they reached a small village with a railroad station. The village had a small store, a few houses, and some grain silos. Pages and some squires flocked to the store to buy candy and sodas— treats they had done without for three months. Wolf was tempted to buy some, but he had to make coffee and tea for several of the knights. Supper consisted of dried fruit and jerky and didn't take long.

Soon a train rolled backwards into the village of Colt's Run. The locomotive seemed impossibly big and announced itself with repeated blasts of its horn. The train stopped with the flat cars at its middle closest to a loading ramp. The adults and older squires rolled the wagons up the ramp onto the cars by hand. Wolf noticed they seemed to know exactly what they were doing as they started to bind the wagons to the cars bed with chains. Once the wagons were secured, the horses were loaded into the boxcars between the flatcars and locomotive. Four passenger cars made up the rear of the train. The female students boarded in the front car, and the guys, in the next two. The adults had possession of the sleeper car at the very end. Shadow rode with Wolf.

It was still early in the evening when the train rolled out of the village. Wolf had never been on a train before, and the swaying motion of the car proved disconcerting.

The train wended its way through the mountains with some spectacular views down into valleys. Soon it was dark, and Wolf could no longer judge their progress. One of the squires produced a deck of cards and a game of poker started. Wolf had his eye on the game, but after watching for a few minutes, he realized the cards were worn, and they were playing for pennies. He declined to join in, but he observed that most of the squires were very good at the game.

After the card games were over, Wolf used his bedroll as a pillow and slept on the floor with Shadow. After months in camp, it proved just as comfortable. It didn't hurt his reputation that the wolf emitted a low growl and would not let anyone near him.

~

In the morning, everyone had to wait in line to use the bathrooms and freshen up. They were now traveling fast on flat land without a mountain in sight. The train stopped at a town where they picked up boxed meals of ham and egg biscuits and orange juice, and Raven produced a few pounds of raw beef for Shadow. Everyone got off the train for a short break to eat and to stretch their legs. Then Whisperblade conducted an impromptu self-defense class on the train platform for all the students.

After an hour, the locomotive blew its whistle, a head count was taken, and everyone loaded back onto the train.

After a full day and night, they crossed the Mississippi River, and were out of the Great Plains. The day was spent in crossing the Midwest and up into the Appalachian Mountains, and the train went long into the night as they stopped on sidings several times to allow long freight trains to pass.

~

As the train pulled out of the station, Raven told Wolf to follow him to the sleeping car. There, he presented Wolf with a brand new page's full dress uniform and a formal page's tunic. Wolf went into a compartment and changed. When he came out, all the knights were lined up, and each one shook his hand and congratulated him for making it through the summer.

Raven, last in line and with a broad grin, placed both hands on Wolf's shoulders and said, "Wolf, I believed in you from the moment I met you. You've exceeded all my expectations. I'm firmly convinced you can do anything you want." Wolf didn't quite know what to make of the little ceremony, but it felt good.

When Wolf got back to his car, he found all the pages putting on clean uniforms and tunics. Apparently, the uniforms had been loaded onto the train at the last stop.

At noon, the train stopped to pick up box lunches for everybody, consisting of chicken sandwiches, milk, and fruit. They had one more stop for supper, and Whisperblade made sure everyone did their exercises.

~

The next morning, the train pulled into the town of Stuart's Draft, Virginia. Everyone piled out of the train, and the long process of unloading everything began. Once the horses were off the train, they were washed and groomed, then saddled. Everybody re-boarded the train to put on their tunics and started inspecting each other's uniforms to make sure they were clean and dressed correctly.

The knights came out of the sleeper car wearing chain mail, swords girded, and shields borne. Everybody lined up in order to parade through the town. Raven told Wolf to put Shadow on one of the wagons in the back of the parade column, and George, Wolf's tent mate, volunteered to watch Shadow since he didn't have a horse to ride.

With all preparations made, everybody mounted up. The Lion was first in line, followed by the other knights on their destriers. They were followed by the squires riding the Percherons. Each squire attached to a knight carried a lance with the knight's ensign flag on it. Other squires and pages followed on their horses, and then came the wagons drawn by single horses. The pages without horses rode on top of the loaded wagons.

The parade proceeded to Main Street and then out to the Howardsville Turnpike, the horses' iron shod hooves making an incredible clopping noise on the pavement that bounced off the sides of the buildings. Spectators both young and old lined the streets. Wolf knew firsthand how impossibly big the draft horses seemed, so he understood the sight of the wide-eyed children. As they reached the end of Main Street and exited the town, a few boys followed the parade on their bicycles, but they soon dropped off and went back into town.

After about an hour of riding at a trot down the highway, they came near to Sherando and reached a driveway with a large gate and wrought iron archway. On the archway, spelled out in big letters, was KNIGHT RIDING SCHOOL. They turned down the lane and soon were in a forest again. This time, they rode on a paved road that twisted back and forth.

When the road broke out of the trees, they were in a huge field with a palace in the middle. It was had three floors with full size dormer windows on the roof and smaller windows at ground level. The bricks of the walls were set between stone masonry columns between every second window with stone turrets on each corner. Just to the right of the main palace stood another building, nearly as large, also with three floors and turrets. When they got closer, he could see it had large doors, wide enough for two horses to ride in side by side. It proved to be a stable. Red smiled and said, "This is your new home."

Chapter 23 ~ Knight Riding School

Orchards and gardens surrounded the palace. Beyond the gardens were open pastures with horses, cows, and goats. Surrounding the stables were riding fields and out buildings for support services.

The knights rode straight up to the palace and entered a tunnel at the front center that led into a courtyard. Two stone stairways flanked both sides of the tunnel and rose up to a grand porch with the main door to the palace was on the porch, and the second floor served as the main floor, while the ground level contained services and offices.

The squires turned right and headed for the stables, and the pages driving the wagons followed them. The squires stopped outside of the stables and dismounted to walk the horses to cool them down.

Finally, they walked their horses into the building, and Red showed Wolf where to find Easy Rider's stall. It wasn't huge, but it was much bigger than the one at camp. It had a clean, smooth, concrete floor covered with fresh hay, a feed trough, and a water bucket. The stall had been freshly painted, and the gate held a sign which read EASY RIDER, and in smaller letters, AMARA. Wolf tied Easy Rider up to the door of the stall, unsaddled him, removed his tack, and put a halter on his head.

Meanwhile, Red did the same for Mary. When they were finished, they led their horses out to another courtyard where there were stations for washing the horses. A long line of pages and squires waited to hose down their horses with clean, pressurized water, and there were plenty of long-handled brushes and soap to scrub the horses' hides. The horses loved it, and it proved hard to get them to move out of the wash stations so the next horse could get its chance.

After washing Easy Rider, Wolf took the horse out to the grass where he laid down and rolled back and forth on his back several times before standing up. When the horse had dried, Wolf led him into the stables, placed him into his stall, and brushed his hide. Mary got the same treatment from Red. Nudge, who had followed his mom into the stables, had to be taken out by Wolf to be hosed off before being placed back in the stall with Mary.

Wolf turned his attention to Shadow, but the animal would have none of the washing. Red commented, "You know, Shadow's going to have to learn to take a bath."

"Well, if he bothers you that much you can give him one," Wolf retorted.

"I would, but he's your responsibility."

"Will you at least help me out?"

"All the girls took a vote on it: Shadow stinks. If you don't give him a bath, we'll petition to keep him out of the palace. He's yours; you figure it out. It can't be that hard." Red continued, "Let me show you around the school. The upstairs of the stables is where the boys' rooms are. You'll be up there on the top floor."

"Where's your room?" he asked.

"Why, in the palace with all the other girls."

"That doesn't sound fair."

"It makes sense to me," Red countered.

"Of course it would. You're a girl."

"Yeah, but you won't have Whisperblade or Lady Jane checking in on you every ten minutes," she retorted.

They took the long walk to the palace and entered through the tunnel into the courtyard. It had a magnificent feel, and Wolf realized he wouldn't learn the layout in one day. Red showed him the dining area first, since it was one of the most important rooms. All meals and a lot of school and student business were conducted there. Supper would be formal, and all students had to dress in their best uniforms.

Red showed Wolf the kitchen and introduced him to the cooks. He recognized a couple of them from camp. Chef Howard, the head cook, was a burly, imposing man with a brusque attitude. When the chef had found out Shadow was a true wolf, he'd become very interested in him and offered Wolf any support he could give.

Next were the classrooms and study rooms, which occupied one wing of the palace. A quick survey of some of the classrooms confirmed they had all the modern equipment students could want. Also, class sizes were small, around fifteen students.

Red then took Wolf down to the administrative area on the ground floor. It included offices for all of the adults and services for the students such as the nurse's office, the students' store, and a bank. Wolf set up a savings account and put most of his money in it. Red placed a considerably larger amount of money into her account.

Red led Wolf to the second floor wing, which held the residential apartments of all the adults who lived at the school. In particular, she showed him the doors for Raven and Whisperblade, which bore ensigns of their shields.

The horn blew to call everyone to lunch, and the tour was over. They ran for the dining hall and got there early, so they grabbed trays and loaded up fish sandwiches, bananas, and milk. Red showed Wolf where the pages sat, and then she went to one of the squires' tables to eat.

Wart came over and sat next to Wolf. "So Wolf, how do you like the place?" he asked.

"It's huge, but what is school like? I mean the classrooms look good, but what is it like for us?"

"Well, it's not like classes at camp."

"How is that?" Wolf asked.

"It's no more study at your own pace. It's fast and hard. You'll be hopelessly behind by the second day."

"So how do you keep up?"

"You can't. You just take your lumps and study harder. I'm in a study group, and that helps. You're welcome to join."

"Thanks. When do we start?"

Wart sighed, "Classes don't start for a week. I'm going home till then."

"You don't seem to be too happy about that," Wolf commented.

"The last time I went home, I had a miserable time. My brothers and sisters gave me a hard time about being in this school. They seem to think it's some kind of school for bad boys."

"Oh."

Wart smiled and said, "I don't have any friends at home like I do here."

"I think I know what you mean. When do you go?"

"They're sending the car to pick me up today."

"I'd go with you if I could," Wolf volunteered.

"Thank you," Wart said. "I'll let you know how it goes."

After lunch, Wart went to pack for his trip. Wolf went to the stables to retrieve his saddlebags and bedroll and then climbed the stairs to the third level to his assigned room. Shadow, who had hung around the stables, climbed the stairs with him.

Wolf shared a room with his tent mates Wart, George and Harold. Each boy had a bed, a footlocker for clothes, and a small desk with a lamp. A common table stood in the center of the room. George and Harold were already unpacked and stowing their clothes.

Wolf unpacked his bags, stowed the contents in his chest, and looked at how empty the chest appeared. He hung his bow and quiver of arrows from nails on the wall above the bed. Shadow jumped onto the bed and claimed it as his own. George wished him good luck in getting his bed back.

Then a first year page appeared at the door with orders for Wolf to report to Raven's office right away. Wolf set his clothes down on the chest, hastened down the stairs to the stables, and ran toward the palace. He became aware of Shadow running beside him. Wolf had not even thought about Shadow following him, and he didn't have a leash handy. He stopped and gave Shadow the command to sit. Shadow sat down, and Wolf ordered him to stay, but as soon as Wolf started toward the palace, Shadow resumed running with him. He tried the sit command again with the same results. He tried to ditch Shadow at the door, but the wolf powered his way past him into the hallway.

Once the wolf had entered the building, he ducked into the first room he came to. Wolf followed him in and came up short. The wolf stood there, teeth bared and fur bristling, facing the biggest dog Wolf had ever seen. The Lion held the dog's leash, and the dog bowed its head down in a submissive pose.

The Lion looked at Shadow, at his dog, and then at Wolf. "That was a most impressive display of dominance. Wolf, I would like you to meet Brutus, up until now the big dog on campus. He's an Irish wolfhound. They were bred to hunt wolves. Now how is that for irony?"

Wolf grabbed Shadow's collar and managed to stammer, "I'm sorry, sir. He got away from me. I mean, I didn't mean for him to get inside."

The Lion chuckled, "Wolf, you have to plan better." He reached into the pocket of his tunic, pulled out an extra leash, and handed it to Wolf. "Here, always keep it handy."

"Thank you, sir." He clipped the leash onto the wolf's collar and ordered the animal to sit. At last, he managed to calm Shadow, somewhat.

"While he's in here, you might as well show him around. Introduce him to the staff. They'll like meeting a real wolf. Come see me after you finish whatever you're up to."

"Yes, sir." Wolf turned and walked out of the room, being led by Shadow, who acted in charge. Wolf went down the hall, found Raven's office, and knocked on the door.

Raven answered and stared at the wolf for a few seconds, and then he bid the two to come in and take a seat. The office was small with a desk, several chairs, and some filing cabinets. There were a couple of large, potted plants on the floor in the corners of the room, and Raven's weapons were hanging from hooks on the wall behind the desk. A book on a large shelf against the wall caught Wolf's attention, *Poisonous Plants of the World*. The knight indicated for Wolf to sit in one of the large chairs, and he sat in the other one. Shadow sat on the floor next to Wolf. "So why is Shadow here?"

"He insisted, sir." Wolf went on to explain the incident with the Lion and Brutus.

"Kind of a shaky start for your first day at school, don't you think?" Raven asked.

"Yes, sir."

"We'll have to work on that. You have one week to get Shadow acclimated to being here. I suggest you start right away. The reason I called for you is about your status as a foster child. We are in a different state, and a new set of papers will have to be filed. You'll have to be interviewed by state welfare workers. It will happen sometime this week. I don't know when. Whisperblade and I will work on it. You have to keep your nose clean and the same for Shadow. We'll talk more about it later."

After being dismissed, Wolf took Shadow to find the Lion. The knight's office occupied the turret on the main floor facing the stables. It was the best-looking room in the palace that Wolf had seen so far. It had a large ornate desk and chair, a separate area with six heavily-padded, leather chairs surrounding a low oval table, and windows on two walls, giving an excellent view of the palace grounds and stables. A large pad was on the floor next to the desk for the Lion's dog, but Brutus was not present. The Lion indicated for Wolf to sit in one of the chairs at the low table, and he sat next to him. Shadow walked around the room sniffing for the wolfhound and then returned to Wolf and sat down beside him.

"I asked you to come here because we need to set some ground rules for the wolf."

"Yes, sir."

"He has to stay out of your classroom when it's session. He also needs obedience training this week."

"Yes, sir."

The Lion took a long, hard look at the wolf and added, "And he has to be house trained. I don't expect you to put him in a cage. I don't have the heart to be that mean, but you need to keep him out of the palace unless he's on a leash."

"Yes, sir. What about his meals, sir?"

"That seems to be between you and the cook," the Lion replied. He stood up, and Wolf did the same. "Obedience class starts at six thirty in the morning in the inner courtyard."

"We'll be there, sir."

"Good afternoon, Wolf, and welcome to school."

Wolf and Shadow left the office and made their way to the kitchen. There the chef took some time to admire Shadow and discuss his diet. He gave Wolf some fresh cuttings of meat wrapped in paper.

They headed back to the stables and went to Nudge and Mary's stall. Wolf started to rub Nudge's nose and feed him a carrot.

"May I pet him?"

Wolf jerked around and found himself facing one of the older girl pages. "You're Margaret, aren't you?"

"Yes."

Wolf didn't say anything, but just stared at the girl. "May I pet him?" she asked again.

"What?"

"May I pet your wolf?"

He looked down at Shadow. The wolf already nuzzled Margaret. "I think he would like it."

Margaret squatted down and started rubbing noses with Shadow. The wolf wagged his tail. Margaret gave head rubs. She stood back up, "He's so cool. He's fun, and I cried when that vile man shot him. Perhaps we'll meet again."

~

She turned and walked away. Shadow had never been described as fun. Wolf couldn't figure the girl out.

Wolf climbed the stairs to his room, gave Shadow his meal of raw meat, and finished straightening his area. Then he went downstairs and found a hostler, who gave him a blank board and some paint to make a sign for Nudge. He painted the sign green and in large red letters wrote NUDGE and below that in smaller letters, WOLF. He hung it below Mary's sign. He stood back to admire his handy work and felt a sense of pride and wonder. Just three months ago, he had run away and stolen for food. Now he had become a part of something big. He had a mother, a sister, a school he liked, a horse, and a wolf, sort of. He didn't know who was master when it came to Shadow. He went outside with a genuine smile on his face.

171

Knowlton

Chapter 24 ~ The Other Page

When Wolf reported to Raven's office before lunch, another boy stood there. He was tall, kind of skinny, and had a mop of blond hair on his head and a serious look on his face.

Raven performed introductions. "Wolf, I'd like you to meet James, my regular page. He's the one who broke his arm just before you arrived in camp and had to be taken out of camp by helicopter. James, Wolf is my new page. He had a bit of a rough time before coming here."

They shook hands. Wolf said, "Glad to meet you," not feeling glad at all.

"Same here," James replied.

"Why don't we have a seat?" Raven said. "I think a little more than introductions are in order. James, Wolf is not your replacement so much as an understudy. You're going to pass on to being a squire soon, and I'll need a new page. I need you to teach him the ropes of the palace. Teach him the secret stuff that only pages know. Wolf pay attention. James is one of the best pages I've have had to work for me. I'll see the two of you this time tomorrow."

Taking the hint, they left and headed to the dining hall for lunch with Wolf leading Shadow on his leash. As they walked, James asked, "Is he really a wolf?"

"One hundred percent," Wolf said. "His name is Shadow. He's kind of shy until he gets to know you. How did you break your arm? What was it like to ride a helicopter out of camp?"

James took a long breath and then slumped his shoulders. "I don't remember the helicopter ride much. They gave me painkillers, and I think I slept most of the way. The accident was stupid. I tried to stand on my horse like Red does, and I fell and landed on my arm."

Wolf turned Shadow loose to wander the fields around the palace while he and James went to eat lunch. Wolf learned that James was three years older than he was and had been Raven's page for two years. James proved quite smart, and the other pages greeted him and seemed to have real respect for him.

Wolf learned that Red had been Raven's squire for at least three years, but she had not been his page. This made Red at least a year older than he had suspected. This was another mystery he could put on his list.

After lunch, they took a tour of the hidden side of the palace. The palace had a huge basement to match. The ground level held the annex to the kitchen with its huge refrigerators and storerooms. A utility elevator opened next to the kitchen for moving supplies to the different levels, an old style elevator that used a rotating lever to operate and had a gate that opened up and down instead of sideways. Wolf noted that the dial indicating the floor had the digits 3, 2, 1, G, B1 and B2. James took Wolf down to the basement, B1, where the laundry and heating plant were, along with more storerooms. Wolf asked James what was down in B2.

"I can't say. Pages aren't allowed to go down there."

Wolf looked at the older page and asked, "Don't you want to find out?"

"Well, yes. We all do, but it would get us into trouble."

"I've been in too much trouble as it is. I'll talk to Red," Wolf mused. He wondered if he could handle just a little bit more trouble.

Next, James took Wolf to the third floor, but most of the floor was restricted because the girls' rooms were there. They climbed a staircase to the attic where a collection of trunks and suitcases belonging to the various knights, the other adults, and students were stored.

The attic consisted of an extensive and open space with dormer windows to match the ones on the floors below. The view in any direction proved magnificent; they could see the hills beyond the trees and some low mountains in the distance. At regular intervals in the attic, there were ladders to the roof hatches.

That was all the time they had for exploring before they had to go to their afternoon classes. Just because school hadn't formally started didn't mean there were no classes. Wolf departed to get his self-defense outfit and report to class. Whisperblade always changed the location of her class, often to a field far from the palace, and Wolf always had to run to arrive on time.

After self-defense, archery, and staff practice, it came time for horse riding, and James showed up with his mount, Duke, a large, black gelding with a large, white star on his forehead. James turned out to be an excellent rider, and the horse seemed to be very responsive to subtle commands. It was easy to see why he thought he could ride standing up. James didn't try to show off; he just paid attention to the horse master. Wolf could tell that his arm was still sore or weak because of the way he favored it.

Wolf gave James plenty of space and didn't ask the questions he wanted to ask about Raven or the school. He figured James would talk when he was ready.

Wolf did ask James about Wayne. James said, "What a pain—he's the most stuck up person I know. Stay away from him."

"I can't seem to do that because he's made me his special target. I'm afraid Shadow will threaten him or worse. I think he would cause Shadow to do that on purpose."

James put a hand on Wolf's shoulder and said, "You can't let that happen."

Wolf looked down, "Wart wants me to beat the snot out of him."

"Not a good idea."

"I know. I'll get into more trouble," Wolf said. "I'll do anything to keep Shadow safe."

"I'll help you if I can. Wayne won't mess with me."

"Why's that?"

"I beat the snot out of him." James paused a minute, then he smiled and added, "Besides, when he becomes a squire, he can't touch you. I mean it would look very bad for him if he got into a fight with you."

When they had some free time, James continued to give Wolf mini tours of some of the hidden and secret places of the school. The palace had lots of hidden rooms and passageways. The largest room in the palace was the grand ballroom. Adjacent to the ballroom stood a formal dining room with a very long dining table, set with several fancy candelabras. James informed Wolf that pages were expected to serve dinner to guests using perfect manners. These rooms were used when parents or other very important people were present at the school.

The stable had equally interesting places. Wolf learned that there were two levels of basements at the stable, but it had no elevator to lift supplies and such. All lifting was done with muscle power using ropes and pulleys, if necessary, often using the horses to supply the power. Above the pages' floor rested an attic loft. The roof had guard turrets at the four corners, similar to the turrets over the palace. These turrets were not manned and thus became a popular place for secret activities of the pages and squires. They were just too tempting a meeting place to be ignored by the students. James let Wolf know that squires had first priority on the roof for romantic dates. How the girl squires got up there remained a mystery to Wolf, one he didn't care to explore. Girls were just plain too much trouble.

Chapter 25 ~ Mrs. Parker

The next morning Wolf woke up with the five o'clock horn, dressed, and ran down to the stable to check on the horses under his care, seeing to their feed and water. He also shoveled the manure into a wheelbarrow and disposed of it outside. Then he ran to the palace for breakfast with Shadow tagging along. At the door to the dining hall, Wolf put the leash on Shadow and entered. He collected his breakfast and went to the pages' table where he sat down with George and Harold and a few other close friends. Shadow scooted under the table and lay down.

After breakfast, Wolf walked Shadow to the inner courtyard where the Lion and Bear were waiting. Bear gave Wolf a long leash, and the obedience lessons began. Brutus, already used to the long leash, wore it, but Shadow seemed to hate it. Bear reassured Wolf that it would work out.

The first lesson Shadow learned was to sit and stay, which he already did very well, for the most part. The hard part was getting him to stay while Wolf walked away. This skill took up the whole lesson. When the lesson ended, Bear ordered Wolf to practice off and on for the rest of the day and come back at six-thirty in the evening.

The rest of the day was filled with mandatory self-defense lessons, riding lessons, caring for the horses, and lessons from Raven on medicinal plants. Wolf still had his eye on the book about poisonous plants, but he was afraid to ask about it. Wolf found out the forests around the school were teeming with interesting plants and animals.

~

Wolf settled into a routine until the day Raven ordered him to report with him to the Lion's office. Wolf had Shadow with him when he and the Raven entered the office and saw a stern-looking lady, Whisperblade, and the Lion.

The Lion looked at Shadow and asked, "Are you sure you want him in here?"

Wolf looked at the woman sitting in the chair, bowed, and said, "I think so, sir."

"Take a chair." The Lion indicated a chair next to the woman. Shadow sat down between Wolf and the woman. "You've been called here to determine your status as a foster child. This is Mrs. Parker. She's with the state child protective agency. She's here to interview you." He turned to the lady and said, "This is Caleb. We call him Wolf."

Mrs. Parker queried, "Wolf?"

"Yes, ma'am," Wolf answered. "It's my nickname. I like it, and everybody calls me that."

"So, Wolf, how do you like it here at this school?"

"I like it a lot. This is the first school I've ever been in that I've liked."

"And how is that?"

"Well, in the last school I was beaten and my lunch money taken. Here, they're teaching me self-defense, and I've learned to hunt for food."

Mrs. Parker asked, "You have to hunt for your food?"

"No, ma'am. But I could if I ever needed to."

"And they let you use guns?"

"Oh, no, ma'am. I use bow and arrow. I make my own arrows. I'm getting good at it."

"What about your schoolwork?"

"I've been studying algebra and composition. I've learned a lot at camp."

"What do you do with your time?" she asked.

"I'm pretty busy most of the time, between self-defense and taking care of my horses, I don't seem to stop until after supper. The classrooms look cool. I can't wait."

"It seems like you'll have a pretty busy schedule. Why don't you tell me about your horses?"

"Well, there's Pinto Bean. He's a school horse. He's kind of small, but he's all heart. Then there's Nudge. He's mine. He's just two months old, but he's already big. You see, he's a Percheron, and he'll get big like those Budweiser Clydesdale horses. I also help with taking care of all the other school horses."

"I see you have a dog," she said and reached down to pet it. "What's his name?"

"Shadow, ma'am, but he isn't a dog. He's a wolf."

Mrs. Parker jerked her hand back, and her eyes opened wide.

"I saved his life, ma'am. I'm licensed to handle him, and he's had all his shots. He's why I'm called Wolf. It's short for The Boy Who Sleeps with Wolves."

"He sleeps with you?"

Wolf thought quickly. "Yes, ma'am, well not in bed together."

"Well, he seems nice enough. Could you please step outside and close the door?"

Wolf led Shadow out of the room and closed the door. He knew better than to eavesdrop, so he paced up and down the hallway, upset with himself over the interview. Mrs. Parker had asked him simple questions, and he had revealed so much so easily. The muffled voices coming from behind the door were quiet and calm. Fifteen minutes later, the door opened, and he was summoned in.

After he sat down, Mrs. Parker said, "An understanding has been reached, if not an agreement."

Wolf jumped up and almost yelled, "I won't leave this school. I won't abandon Shadow or Nudge! Red needs me!"

"Who's Red?" Mrs. Parker asked.

"She's my sister," Wolf answered.

"You have a sister?"

"Yes, ma'am."

"If I may," broke in Whisperblade.

Mrs. Parker looked sharply at her. "Yes, please do."

"Amara, or Red, as she likes to be called, is my daughter by adoption and will be Wolf's sister if his adoption becomes final."

Mrs. Parker stared at the woman as if taking her measure for combat. She held up her hand to stop Whisperblade from saying anything further. She turned to Wolf and asked, "Do you want this woman to adopt you?"

Wolf said, "Oh, yes, ma'am."

"Well, in that case, I want some time to consider this situation further. I find this school to be most irregular. But you seem to thrive here. I don't have anything to do with your adoption situation, but I could, if it becomes necessary. My word counts." The she looked at Wolf and said, "If that animal hurts you or anybody else, I'll reconsider your case. Do you understand me, Wolf?"

"Yes, ma'am."

"Good. For now, you can stay here. Your papers for the wolf are good. I don't like it. Your schooling seems adequate, but I have my eye on you." She turned to the Lion and said, "If I find the boy being harmed in any way, I'll take him."

"Agreed," the Lion said. "But, you'll find that he's thrived here when he failed elsewhere. As to this school being irregular, you'll find that's what sets us apart from ordinary schools, and a lot of parents who once attended now send their children here."

"I'll be checking on him often," Mrs. Parker said, and she stood up and shook everybody's hand. She turned on her heel and left the room, heading down the hall in the wrong direction. Raven motioned for Wolf to chase her down and escort her to her car.

Wolf handed Shadow's leash to Raven and caught up with Mrs. Parker all the way down at the end of the hall. "May I escort you to your car, ma'am?"

"I do seem to have lost my way." Wolf held out his right arm, and she took it with her left hand. As Wolf escorted her down the hall, towards the front door, she asked him, "Who are these people?"

Wolf thought about it for a minute before answering, "You mean other than teachers?"

"Precisely."

"Some of them are sort of knights. They save people. They saved me."

"How is that?"

"I was caught stealing food and was going to be sent to juvenile detention. I wouldn't have done well there."

"What if you run away from here?" she asked as they arrived at her car.

"Why would I? I love it here. This is where my friends are," Wolf replied.

"Well, we'll meet again. You do have good manners."

"Thank you, ma'am."

Mrs. Parker got into her car and drove off.

Knowlton

Chapter 26 ~ The School of Hard Knocks

On the last free day before classes started, Wart returned and told Wolf, "I've got good news. I've got permission to bring you home with me during Thanksgiving vacation."

"I thought it wasn't much fun at home," Wolf replied.

"It'll be a whole lot better with you there."

"What about Shadow? I can't leave him here."

"I told my parents that you have a dog, and they're all right with that."

"But he's not a dog," Wolf exclaimed, "and I'm not allowed to pretend he is one. Besides, it wouldn't be right."

"I'll think of something, I'll make it right with my parents," Wart promised.

~

Wolf, excited about the first day of classes, jumped out of bed with the sounding of the wake-up horn at five o'clock in the morning. He and his roommates dressed and headed down to the stables, where they met the girl pages, and everybody started to work mucking and cleaning the stalls, laying fresh hay, and feeding and watering the horses. Once the stables met the approval of Henry, the senior squire, everybody washed their face and hands and ran to the dinner hall for breakfast.

The first breakfast of the school year was formal, and everybody had to stand and wait for the Lion to enter and offer a short blessing for the food and the students. With Shadow next to the table eating his meat from the bowl on the floor, Wolf despite his efforts to be quiet became the center of attention at his table. His fame had spread among the new students.

Breakfast ended when the horn for the seven o'clock class sounded. Wolf had English composition as his first class. Shadow seemed to be miffed when he couldn't follow Wolf into the classroom, but he settled down to sit by the door and sniff all the students who entered. In class, Wolf had to write a short composition on his summer activities. That was right up his alley, he thought, so he wrote: *I ran away, was arrested, then released, saved a wolf's life, was saved by the same wolf, became the legal guardian of the wolf, learned to ride a horse, became a horse owner, hunted rabbit, saved my sister twice, shot a man and shot another man twice. Most importantly, I now have a family and friends.*

Wolf turned in his paper before any other students. When the teacher read his paper, her eyes opened wide. "Wolf this is the shortest paper any one has ever turned in." There were a few chuckles from the students. "But, it has more in it. Is all of this true?"

"Yes, ma'am."

"Then you have had a most extraordinary summer. Why didn't you include any details?"

"Ma'am, I've been writing it all in a journal. There's just too much happening in each adventure for a short paper."

"I await every word. I expect five pages by tomorrow, and work on your grammar skills." Again, there were chuckles. "That goes for everybody." The class sounded off in a lot of groans.

Wolf's next class was math, and he dreaded it. It involved algebra, which he hadn't been exposed to. The basic concept the teacher tried to teach involved substituting letters for numbers. Wolf could not see why this had to be done or what it meant. By the end of the class, he had become confused. After math class, Wolf took Shadow, who had waited outside the classroom door, and turned him loose to roam the fields.

Wolf went to his history class and found the ins and outs of history to be fascinating. The final class before lunch was science, and it began with biology, the study of living things. Wolf could tell this would be interesting, but very hard. Raven taught it.

Lunch came after his fourth class. Wolf retrieved Shadow from outside the palace and led him to the dining hall. Lunch had no formalities except a blessing. Shadow did not eat three times a day and just laid on the floor next to Wolf's chair.

After lunch, Whisperblade taught the self-defense class. Whisperblade, who had been easy since they had left camp, turned brutal. Exercise routines were run until Wolf couldn't lift his arms. Then she made everybody do push-ups until the horn blew for archery class. Then the next class of the day consisted of staff fighting. The staffs were no more than long broom handles. The students had to pair off. One would strike, and the other would block, first high, then in the middle, then low. Then they would switch the direction of attack from right to left. After five minutes, the striker and blocker would switch opponents. Wolf learned that staff fighting could hurt fingers, and he had several sore knuckles before the lesson finished.

The remainder of the afternoon thankfully involved horses. Pinto Bean had been claimed by another page, so by an earlier agreement with Red, Wolf rode Easy Rider. But trotting around the field was all they did, for several of the new pages had never ridden a horse before.

Wolf took one new page named William under his wing by helping him to saddle his horse, Bones. William had a hard time because the horse had a particularly mischievous streak, but that could not be helped. The horse had been supplied by the boy's parents. Bones resisted being saddled and held his breath so his girth strap could not be tightened. Wolf put his knee into the horse's rib cage, forcing the horse to exhale, so the strap could be tightened. Wolf also taught William how to get on Bones' good side by feeding him pieces of apple when they first meet each day and when the horse behaved well.

Wolf gave William a fifteen-minute lesson before the regular lesson started. He did this the same way he learned to ride, by first mounting the horse then pulling the younger boy up into the saddle. He reached around him, grabbed the reins, and showed him the basic maneuvers while riding around the paddock.

The new riding instructor and horse master, Mr. Hart, who complimented him on helping William. After the lessons were finished and the horses were cooled down, washed and groomed, they mucked the stalls and spread new hay.

Everyone took showers, and, Shadow, surprised Wolf by joining him in the shower, and Wolf was able to bathe him. Afterwards, Shadow gave everybody standing around him another shower by shaking his thick fur. Dressed in their finest uniforms, everyone ran to the palace, grabbed trays, and filled them with fried chicken. The cooks insisted on serving green beans and Brussels sprouts, an unpopular choice. Everyone stood in front of their chairs until the knights and teachers entered.

The Lion stood at the center of the head table and said, "Squires, pages, welcome to a new year at the Knight Riding School. Most of you are returning, and you understand how this school works. To those of you who are new, I hope it will be a pleasant experience. We'll do all we can to make your time here productive and of benefit to you. You're here because you want to be here. You've already enjoyed your first day of classes." That earned a round of chuckles from the students. "It will get better. If you need help, seek it out. The teachers and older students are here to help." After a pause he said, "Bless this food we are about to share. Bless our students. Bless our country. Amen." The Lion sat down, and dinner began.

Wolf uncovered his bowl of raw meat cuttings and placed it on the floor for Shadow, who inhaled it. All the nearby new pages started peppering Wolf with questions about Shadow.

After supper, the pages retreated to their study rooms or the library to form study groups. Wolf turned Shadow loose outside to take care of his business.

Wolf and Wart walked into the library to go to their study room. As soon as Wolf opened the door, Wayne grabbed his tunic, pulled him in, and slammed him into a wall, while another boy grabbed Wart and pulled him in. The door closed behind them, and the fighting began in earnest.

Wolf got over his initial shock and started blocking the blows Wayne rained down on him, but he couldn't gain an opportunity to strike back.

Wart had been pinned, face down, bent over the table by two other boys. Wolf saw them pin one of his arms behind his back. Wart didn't make a sound but concentrated on kicking their legs.

One of Wolf's blocks met open air, so he leaned forward and butted his head into Wayne's belly, wrapping his arms around his waist. The older page let out an oomph sound as he banged into the wall, but he managed to stay upright. He brought his elbow down on Wolf's back. Wolf let go and collapsed to his knees. Wayne pushed Wolf over onto his side and then kicked him in the ribs.

~

As quickly as the fight started, Wayne and his buddies disappeared out the door. A few seconds later, Harold and George arrived. Wolf and Wart were both in excruciating pain. George helped Wolf to a sitting position. Harold closed the door and helped Wart, who cradled his arm, grimacing silently.

When Wolf could stand, they exited the study room, and made a beeline for the stables. They managed to make it to their room without being challenged by any squires. Once the door closed, Harold and George helped Wart and Wolf remove their shirts.

Wolf was heavily bruised on his back and the side of his rib cage. The bruises would not show while wearing a shirt, but would be visible when he took a shower. Wart turned out to be worse off. He could hardly lift his arm. He would have to see the school nurse, and that meant questions would be asked.

Once they had their stories straight, Wolf escorted Wart down to the squire's floor and went to the squire on duty who turned out to be David, the most senior squire at school. He took one look at the two and ordered them to follow him to the palace. As they made the trip, Wolf started shaking with dread about facing Whisperblade, Raven, and the Lion. They went to the squire on watch who made a call to the nurse. They didn't have to wait long before she arrived. She dismissed David and escorted Wolf and Wart to the infirmary. There they were confronted by Whisperblade.

The Nurse took Wart into the exam room. Wolf had to sit in a chair. Whisperblade glared at him while maintaining silence. When Wart emerged, he had his arm in a sling and held a small bottle of anti-inflammatory pills. Whisperblade ordered him to the Lion's office.

187

Wolf entered the exam room. There he had to strip his shirt off, and the bruises were plain to see.

The nurse sucked in her breath and asked Wolf how he got the bruises.

"I fell down, ma'am."

"These bruises are not consistent with a fall. How did you receive them?"

"I fell down, ma'am."

The nurse wrote the excuse on Wolf's chart, and then put it down. "You know you can tell me privately. I won't tell anyone."

Wolf offered no further explanation. The nurse sighed, then wrapped his chest with a bandage and wrote an excuse slip to forgo all physical duties and classes. He went back out to Whisperblade, who escorted him to the Lion's office.

There Wart waited silently, standing in front of the Lion's desk. Wolf went to stand by him. Whisperblade sat in one of the wingback chairs off to the side. The Lion arrived and stood behind his desk. He cleared his throat and asked, "What happened?"

"I fell down," chorused Wolf and Wart.

The Lion glared at them a long minute, "I heard there was a disturbance in the library earlier." He let them digest that information a minute. "What do you know of that?"

"I haven't heard anything about it, sir," Wart said.

The Lion didn't even bother to ask Wolf. "You'll find out what your punishment is in the morning. Wart, you're dismissed. Take care of that arm."

"Yes, sir." Wart turned and walked out very quickly.

"Wolf, I have to answer to Wart's mother about why her son was injured while in my care. As far as you're concerned, you're a ward of the school and the foster child of Whisperblade. I hate having to answer to her. You're dismissed."

Wolf turned, looked at Whisperblade, and shuddered. She had stood up, and he had never seen her so angry before.

"Come with me," she said and stalked out. Wolf had to hurry to keep up with her, his ribs hurting with each trotting step. They went downstairs to her office where she closed the door. She didn't sit but walked around him a couple of times. She turned to look at him close up, face to face. "It's the very first day of school, and I don't know what to do with you. Trouble follows you like a shadow. Like Shadow. Where is that wolf? No, don't answer that. That animal's very life depends on you staying out of trouble. Your status in this school depends on you staying out of trouble. But you know that already, don't you? I'll never abandon you, but I can't stop Mrs. Parker from taking you. What about Wart? He's suffering because of you. His injury could have been very serious. He could have lost the use of his arm.

"I can't help you if you don't tell me what happened. I've never liked this code of silence. You had better find a solution to your falling down problem and quick. It may have been tolerated in summer camp, but it won't be here." She paused and added, "From now on, you'll attend every self-defense class that doesn't occur during your regular scholastic classes. No excuses. You'll practice until you can defend yourself and those around you. Defend those who cannot defend themselves, do you understand?"

Wolf nodded.

"You're dismissed."

Wolf hastened out of the office and headed back toward the stables. Halfway there, he inhaled deeply and felt a sharp pain in his side. He remembered the nurse's excuse and pulled it out of his pocket. He looked at it a minute, then tore it up. It wasn't worth the paper it had been written on, not when it came to Whisperblade.

Chapter 27 ~ Wolf Fights Back

Wolf and his roommates spent a late afternoon in one of the turrets on the roof of the stables. It was a good place to hang out before dark. It had a magnificent view with a vista over the tops of the trees.

While they were there, they heard a vehicle driving up to the palace. It was just an ordinary Chevy, and an older one at that. They looked out from over the walls of the turret. A man got out from the driver's side, and a boy from the passenger's side. It was Wayne. The man, apparently his father, grabbed Wayne's shoulder and led him into the palace. Wayne kept trying to shrug off his father's hand.

Wart whispered into Wolf's ear, "He's not rich."

It took a few seconds for the implications of that observation to set in. Wayne was faking being rich. Wolf looked at Wart and said, "He wasn't very happy about being led into the palace."

"He doesn't get along with his father," Harold said.

Wart scrunched up his forehead and said, "It's probably worse than that. I bet he's in big trouble about the fight in the library."

"But nobody said anything," George said.

"They didn't have to," Wolf countered. "Whisperblade had it all figured out when she assigned me to all those self-defense classes. The Lion seemed to have been aware of the fight before anybody else. What about you, Wart? Did you get into trouble with your parents?"

Wart looked down. "If I get in another fight, my parents said I could be pulled for a year."

Wolf stared at Wart, who looked gloomy, and said, "It's all my fault. I got you in this mess."

Wart popped Wolf on the shoulder. "Get over it. You're here, and we're in this together."

"Besides," George said, "we said we were going to teach you to fight. I say we get to it right away."

"Where?" Harold asked. "We can't be doing this out in the open."

"The shed behind the blacksmith's building is almost empty," Wart suggested. "But there's one thing I insist on." He waited until everyone stared at him. "Nobody says anything about what we saw with Wayne and his father."

"Why?" Wolf asked.

Wart said, "It'll just make it all worse. Don't embarrass him. He doesn't need that, and we gain nothing from it."

"But they tried to twist your arm off!" Wolf exclaimed.

"If we try to take revenge, it'll never stop. We've got to do better."

Wolf said, "It'll never stop like this."

"At least not as long as he thinks he can pound one of us when we're alone."

"You're the smallest of us, Wart. He'll try to find you by yourself."

"I think in a single fight I can keep myself from being beaten up. I'm pretty good at defending myself in class."

Wolf shrugged and asked, "So what do we do?"

Wart smiled and asked, "Are you ready for some pain?"

Wolf and his roommates spent the next week practicing fight moves in the blacksmith's shed. They worked late, so they wouldn't be caught by the adults. They practiced holds and deflections, so they wouldn't have to hit. It was what Whisperblade taught with a little twist—there would be no stepping back to bow and no civilities. This would be for real.

After one of these practice sessions, Wayne's current girlfriend, Margaret, wandered into the stables. Wolf had been feeding carrots to Nudge and Mary. "May I feed them?" she asked.

Wolf looked around before handing a couple of carrots to Margaret. "Sure, but I think they've had enough."

Margaret fed the carrots to Nudge and Mary. "What was that look for? You expect somebody else?"

Wolf answered, "I hope not."

"If you're looking for Wayne, I dumped him."

"I wasn't looking for him."

Margaret smiled and said, "You're a terrible liar, Wolf. You know that."

"Yeah, I know."

"If you want to fool somebody, why don't you tell the truth, and make it sound like a lie?"

"Why would I do that?"

"After they believe the truth to be a lie, you can just tell them what you want them to hear."

Wolf had to think about it a moment. He didn't see how it would work, so he asked, "You actually get away with that?"

"Yes, a couple of times." She looked at him, then added, "Of course, it will only work a couple of times."

"I'll remember that."

"You'll forget it."

"Okay, I'll forget it."

"See it works on me already," Margaret giggled.

Over her shoulder, Wolf saw Wayne storming into the stables. As soon as he recognized both Wolf and Margaret, he let out a flurry of curses, all directed at Margaret. Her face turned pale as he came closer, and Wolf, at first, was paralyzed by Wayne's fury. But as Wayne raised his fist to strike Margaret, Wolf jumped into action. He pushed Wayne back hard. As soon as Wayne regained his balance, he started to direct blows at Wolf.

Wolf blocked every one of them, a drill Whisperblade had pounded into him endlessly. Wolf knew there would be big trouble, but it was too late. He took an opportunity to push Wayne hard again, catching the older page by surprise. Wolf, beyond angry, kept pushing harder and harder until Wayne was backed out of an open door. Wayne, unable to regain his balance, tripped into a water trough.

A small crowd of pages and squires had surrounded them and blocked any adults from seeing the fight. Most of the pages were laughing at Wayne. Squire David placed a strong grip on Wolf's arm, stopping any possible blows. "I think that is enough philosophical differences for the day. Wolf, make yourself scarce."

Wolf didn't need to be told a second time. When he turned to run, he saw James with his arm around Margaret's shoulder. James gave Wolf a thumbs up sign, and Margaret smiled at him. As he made his way to the stairs, he heard David suggesting to the other pages that Wayne had tripped into the water trough through his own clumsiness. Wolf retreated to his room and pretended to study his algebra book.

Fifteen minutes later, Whisperblade entered Wolf's room. He jumped to attention. The knight was red in the face. "There has been a disturbance downstairs in the stables. Do you know anything about it?"

"Yes, ma'am," Wolf responded quickly.

She blinked in apparent disbelief. "What do you know about it?"

"There was a philosophical difference of opinion."

"And?"

"I provided some advice."

"And what was that?"

"I suggested a cooling down period."

She asked, "Where did you learn to say that?"

"From Red."

"Humph." She stared at Wolf an uncomfortably long time. "I really don't know what to think or who to believe. Nobody has been reported as hurt. I ought to assign you extra work. What did I tell you last time?"

Wolf said, "To defend others."

Her expression changed, softening up some, and she asked, "Did you?"

"Yes, ma'am, I did."

Whisperblade opened her mouth then shut it tight. Turning around sharply, she left the room.

Wolf shuddered, knowing he wasn't going to get off free. This time it was worth the punishment. Wayne couldn't push him around.

Wart, Harold, and George entered with big smiles on their faces. "I heard it was great. What did you do?"

"I just pushed him," Wolf said.

"Into the water trough," George said. "I saw it. It was really great. Wolf was a charging bull."

"I missed it," Harold said. "How did it start?"

"I had been talking to Margaret—"

Wart interrupted. "No wonder, Wayne's girl! When did you start that?"

"I didn't start it. She came in and started talking to me. Wayne followed and started cursing at her. I believe he was going to hit her. That's when I got between them."

Harold said, "I hope you cleaned his clock."

Wolf shrugged his shoulders and said, "I didn't even hit him. I believe he was too mad to think straight."

"That's a new fighting technique—get them mad at you," Harold observed.

Wart asked, "So, what about Margaret? Are you two—"

"No! I think she had come in to see James."

"They all deserve each other," Harold concluded. "At least they'll all be squires soon."

"Then they won't be a problem," George said.

Wart looked around at the others, walked over to the door, glanced out, and then closed it. In a quiet voice, he said, "I've heard that the squires take care of their own problems. They don't tolerate fighting. You never hear of squires being punished, do you? I don't know how they do it."

"They must be pretty strict among themselves," Harold said.

Wolf said, "It isn't going to be fun, being a squire."

"Yeah," agreed Wart, Harold, and George.

There was a knock at the door. Wart shouted that the door was open. David stepped into the room, "I see you're having another secret meeting. Who are you planning to fight this time?"

Wolf was stunned. He looked directly at David and said, "I hope I never have to fight again. I'm tired of it; I'm tired of being beaten. I'm tired of being punished, and, if I thought I could make it right, I would."

The squire fumed a minute and said, "I just got back from talking with the Lion. No, make that listening to the Lion. He's hopping mad. I've been assigned to oversee your punishments from now on."

Wolf shuddered again. This didn't sound good.

"James confessed to pushing Wayne. You seem to have gotten a free pass this time. But we know better. I'm keeping a close eye on you," David said and swept his arm around. "All of you." He turned around and stormed out, slamming the door behind him.

Chapter 28 ~ Tough Questions

A week later at supper, before the Lion gave the blessing, he stated, "Some of you are at the wrong tables." About twenty pages stepped away from their tables and moved to the other side of the room, to the squires' tables. James, Margaret, and Wayne were among them. The Lion gave his blessing, and the meal commenced.

~

The next day a squire interrupted Wolf's math class with a note for Wolf to report to Raven's office and with Shadow. Taking Shadow by the leash, Wolf ran to the office and knocked on the door. Raven answered and invited him in. Mrs. Parker stood there, so Wolf bowed to her, and she took a seat. Raven indicated for Wolf to sit in the other chair.

Raven said, "Mrs. Parker is here to interview you." He patted a stack of folders on his desk and added, "She has reviewed all the records we have concerning you and wishes to talk to you alone." With that, Raven left the office.

"I read that you have had a most interesting time at the school."

"Yes, ma'am."

"You know that you can't legally sign a contract because you're a minor."

"I signed them because I wanted to. I wanted to be with this school. I knew it wasn't up to me."

"Good. If I decide you would be better someplace else, then you'll understand."

Wolf asked, "Doesn't what I want count?"

"Hmm, it depends. Why did you run away the last time?"

"I kept being beat up."

"By your foster parents?"

"No, at school!" Wolf started to get exasperated.

"Nobody did anything about it?"

"They didn't believe me, and I got beat up worse for telling. I've told you all this already."

"I'm sorry. What about here?"

"No, never."

"But you've been treated for bruises."

"Only in self-defense classes. I've also given a few. It happens. Nobody hates me."

"Hm." Mrs. Parker stood and stepped behind Raven's desk and sat down. She opened the top folder and flipped to a tabbed page. "Tell me about Wayne."

Wolf was stunned. *What does that folder say about me and Wayne? She probably knows everything.* "He's an older page and just became a squire."

Mrs. Parker looked at him. "You know that isn't what I asked. Tell me about your encounters with him."

Wolf paused. He knew he was about to lie. "I was clumsy and fell down."

"That isn't what this says."

"I've had some philosophical differences of opinion with him, nothing serious."

"It sounds like fighting. What are you not telling me?"

Wolf was desperate; this wasn't going good. Without thinking, he stood up, reached over, and placed his shaking hand flat on top of the page Mrs. Parker had in front of her. "What do you think of snitches? I told you what happened in the old school. Would I have the friends I do now if I were one? I value my friends above all. Wayne no longer scares me."

The woman looked at him with an open mouth. The spell was broken when Wolf removed his hand from the folder and sat down. Mrs.

Parker closed the folder. "Oh, I see. What about your encounter with the escaped prisoners? You actually shot them?"

"Yes, they were pointing a gun and a knife at Red. I had to save her."

"You're only fourteen years old. Were you trying to kill someone?"

"I had to save my sister. I didn't think about killing."

"You were lucky you weren't killed."

"I'm not the lucky one; I knew what I had to do to save Red. Besides, I got her into this mess."

"How is that?"

"It was my idea to disobey orders," he said and fingered the bullet hanging at his neck. "I made a bad decision, and Shadow paid the price. He was shot trying to save Red."

"And you still want to stay here?"

Wolf said, "More than ever."

Mrs. Parker paused a moment and asked, "Why should I let you stay here?"

Wolf relaxed and smiled again. "Because I now have a family I love."

"In most any other situation, I would snatch you out and place you somewhere else. There are plenty of foster parents available. What have you learned at this school?"

"Do you mean in class?" Wolf replied.

"No, I don't," Mrs. Parker answered. "I mean what have you learned on your own?"

Wolf breathed in deeply, slowly let it out, and then inhaled once more. "I've learned it's good to have friends. I've learned you have to work hard to get what you want, like riding horses or saving Shadow. I've learned you have to work together to do anything worthwhile, and it's good to ask for help, if you need it."

"My, that is a lot. It sounds like you don't have any time to play."

"We do. We play games like soccer and field hockey. We tell stories and sing and play music," Wolf said, leaving out any mention of card games.

"You don't have any iPods, no radios?"

"A few students do. I don't. I have a fife and can play a few tunes on it. Shadow hates it."

"Do you want an iPod?"

Wolf thought about this for a minute. "I don't care for the boys who have them. They seem to do nothing but listen to their music. It's not my thing. I don't want one. Besides, they're useless while out camping. We sing an awful lot. I like that."

"Do you have a girlfriend?" Mrs. Parker asked, changing the subject.

Wolf jumped out of the chair and snapped, "No. Are you crazy? Do I look like I have a girlfriend? Having Red as a sister is bad enough."

"I guess you are a little young. That will be all for today. Please send Mr. Raven back in."

Wolf stood up, bowed to Mrs. Parker, and left with Shadow to find Raven, who had gone to Whisperblade's office. After Raven left, Whisperblade told Wolf to sit down.

Her office, like Raven's, was small, but it was much simpler. She had her long, curved sword and long, dress dagger hanging on the wall behind her desk. Her desk was clean and had a flower vase with a red rose and yellow rose in it. Her bookcase held only a few books but many pictures. Some were of pages he didn't know; some were of groups of pages, and some were of her with other knights. Her walls had some very simple artwork mounted. The two guest chairs, which were well-cushioned wingbacks, with gold and green striped cloth, were the only things not plain in the office.

It was in one of these chairs that Wolf sat down and sank back into. It seemed as if the weight of the world sat on his shoulders. Whisperblade looked at him a minute before interrupting his thoughts. "I don't suppose you want to talk about it?"

He blurted out, "It's like she is trying to trap me so she can take me away. She asked the same questions again."

"She might just be trying to do that. Perhaps we can avoid the trap. Have you been telling her the truth?"

"Yes, ma'am. Should I?" Wolf looked down and said, "I didn't with Wayne. I told her we had a difference of opinion. I also told her I wasn't a snitch."

"Oh yes, you should tell the truth. You should answer all her questions honestly. You didn't exactly lie, and we aren't snitches either. We can't say more than we know. She's trying to find a reason to take you. We know that, and we're working to prevent it. You need to be yourself. You're a good boy, and you're doing excellent work."

"Thank you," he said, still feeling glum.

Whisperblade stood up, and, stepping from behind her desk, she sat down in the chair next to him. "When I said I was in the process of adopting you, you were surprised."

"Yes, ma'am."

"I was planning to tell you once I knew for sure it was possible. Well, I'm now sure that it is. What I need to know is, do you really want this?"

Wolf looked up at her and said, "Yes, Mother."

"Then you should know a few things about me. I'm not married, but I have been in the past. I have five other children, including Amara, all by adoption. Before teaching at this school, I was in the military." She asked, "Do you have any questions?"

Wolf said, "Yes, ma'am. What's your name, and were you married to Raven?"

She stared at him with wide-open eyes. "Very good questions, surprising questions. Is that what the current gossip is about? My given name is Aurora, and I sign it Aurora Walker Whisperblade. No, I wasn't married to Raven, but we've been close friends for a very long time. You should keep this information to yourself. Certain mysteries are good for the school. I've kept you from classes long enough."

Wolf stood, bowed to Whisperblade, and, taking Shadow's leash, he left for his next class. In the last five minutes, he'd learned more about Whisperblade than he had in the past five months.

Chapter 29 ~ Thanksgiving

As the days became shorter and cooler, Wolf was issued a page's coat. The outdoor activities caused him to work up plenty of sweat. He did need his new coat for riding, and, as winter approached, he knew his sheriff's coat would be invaluable. He had outgrown his first set of page's uniforms, and Whisperblade directed him to draw new ones from the quartermaster.

Wart had received permission from his parents to bring Wolf and Shadow home for the Thanksgiving break. When the time came, Wolf packed his clean uniforms into the saddlebags that Whisperblade had loaned him. Wearing his best uniform and new coat, he led Shadow to the limousine where he joined Wart in the rear seat.

It took a little convincing to get Shadow to enter the car. Wolf realized that Shadow had never been in a vehicle before, except the train, and that had taken some persuasion. The driver, a very patient man, stayed out of the way until Shadow had sniffed out the car on the outside and entered the back door with Wolf and Wart. Once inside, Shadow made a quick tour of the interior of the car before sitting on the floor next to Wolf. When the car started to move, Shadow sat up in the seat and stared out the windows.

During the long trip, there were stops to let Shadow relieve himself. There was a small refrigerator with sandwiches and drinks for the boys. They gave Shadow water in a bowl the driver provided.

It was late afternoon when they arrived in Leesburg. Wart's home was in an outlying neighborhood, and Wolf noted that the houses were large with huge yards and brick walls separating them. When the limo pulled into the driveway, the sun had just started to set.

The limo stopped at the front door of the house. The driver got out and opened the car door for the boys and Shadow, and then he retrieved their luggage from the trunk. Wart thanked the driver, and then opened the door to his house and invited Wolf and Shadow in.

Nobody was there to greet them, and Wart suggested they go outside to the garden. Walking through the house, Wolf was impressed by how big and neat it appeared. Wart's family clearly had wealth. They went outside through the back door, and Wart led them past a row of bushes into a garden. At the center of the garden stood a large pavilion with a domed roof supported by large columns, where Wart's family sat around a large, circular table centered in the pavilion.

As soon as Wart's mother saw them, she stood and came over to greet them. She bent down to give Wart a big hug and, standing back, looked at Wolf and Shadow. "So you're named Wolf, and you have a wolf. Is he friendly? What's his name?" she asked.

"Shadow, ma'am. He's more cautious than friendly, but he won't bite or attack you. He just takes his time being friendly," Wolf replied.

The woman held out her hand and shook Wolf's hand. "Welcome, I'm Mrs. Cunningham. Let me introduce you to the rest of the family." She led them to the pavilion and introduced Wolf to her husband and Wart's two brothers, John and David, and his three sisters, Elizabeth, Mary, and Hanna.

Hanna was much younger than Wart. She walked right up to Shadow, who sat beside Wolf, and reached up to pet him. Her mother let out an audible gasp, but Shadow sniffed at the girl, and then licked her face. Hanna giggled, "Can I play with him?"

Wolf looked at Hanna's mother then at her father, who shook his head, and then he told the girl, "He's had a long trip and is very tired. Ask your mother again later."

"You must be starving," the mother said. "Let's eat."

Shadow lay beside Wolf's chair during dinner. After a few minutes, Mr. Cunningham asked Wolf if Shadow would like some dog food.

"No, sir," he replied. "Shadow won't eat it."

"What does he eat?" Mrs. Cunningham asked.

Wolf thought about his answer a moment before replying. "Fresh meat is his natural diet. He won't eat cooked food."

"You mean raw?"

"Yes, ma'am."

"I think maybe the wolf knows what he needs to eat," Mr. Cunningham said. "I'll see to getting some fresh meat for him."

"Thank you, sir," Wolf responded.

Mr. Cunningham continued. "So how did you come to have him?"

"I saved him from a trap, and he sort of adopted me."

"Oh, really?"

"Yes, sir. He followed me through the mountains and started sleeping next to me. That's why I'm called 'The Boy Who Sleeps with Wolves.'"

Mr. Cunningham looked thoughtful for a minute and said, "And the grownups are all right with that?"

"Yes, sir. I'm licensed to care for him."

"That's a big responsibility."

"Yes, sir. He's a lot of work. I've had to train him to have manners around people."

"Well, you've done very well from what I see."

"Thank you, sir."

"He does seem to be well-mannered," Mrs. Cunningham said. "Is he house-trained?"

"Yes, ma'am."

Mrs. Cunningham looked at the wolf and said, "Then he is allowed in our house. Now, let's see, what about you?"

Without thinking, Wolf said, "I'm house-trained, ma'am." That brought a round of laughter from the brothers and sisters.

"What I mean is you need some clothes other than that uniform. You need some real clothes. I'll see if some of John's old clothes will fit you for tomorrow. We're going to go out to buy you some real clothes."

Wolf' said, "You don't have to do that."

"Nonsense, I insist on it."

It was dark and starting to get too cold, so everybody retreated into the house. Mrs. Cunningham took Wolf up to Wart's bedroom, set him up with the spare bed, and put a blanket down on the floor for Shadow. She told him to take Shadow out the back door into the garden when he needed to do his business, she would leave it unlocked.

~

In the morning, Wolf and Wart got up early and dressed in their uniforms, and with Shadow, they went out to the garden where they started their exercises. When they were finished, they went back in, took showers and dressed in regular clothes. Then they had breakfast with everybody else.

Mrs. Cunningham was up and cooking breakfast. The boys ate ravenously. When she asked what she could feed Shadow, Wolf suggested raw eggs. Shadow ate six of them before she said, "Enough is enough."

Wolf explained, "Shadow can eat a very large meal because in the wild it's necessary to eat what you can, when you can."

With breakfast over, all the boys went outside to play ball with Shadow. "So Will, how is reform school," David asked in a sarcastic tone.

John asked, "Have they hammered that wild streak out of you?"

Wart turned red in the face, and Wolf could see that he was embarrassed. Wart's hands clenched into fists as he faced David.

Wolf, thinking quickly, jumped between Wart and David. "I don't think you want to make him angry."

"And why is that?"

"He's pretty good with his fists, and besides, I am, too."

"Whoa, nobody's trying to fight." David held his hands up in submission. "We're just kidding our little brother. We'd never let anybody hurt him."

"Well then, why don't you act like big brothers? Wart didn't want to come home at first."

"Okay, just calm down. It's just those uniforms are so geeky. Truce?"

"If it's okay with Wart," Wolf said.

Wart unclenched his fists. David held out his right hand and said, "Truce?"

"Spit on it," Wart demanded.

David spit in his palm and held it back out. Wart matched him and they shook.

David turned to Wolf and said, "Nobody beats up on Will. That's my job. You look out for him."

"I think he can do it himself pretty well. He's already very good in self-defense."

"You'll look out for him?"

"He's my best friend, my first friend. We fight together."

"Spit on it," David demanded.

"Both Wolf and David spit and shook.

"You're all right, Wolf."

They started playing ball for real. When they were finished, Wart's mother announced that it was time to go shopping. Her big concern had been what to do with Shadow in the meantime. Mr. Cunningham settled the question when he offered to watch the wolf.

Mrs. Cunningham drove Wolf and Wart to Leesburg Corner Premium Outlets, and they were both fitted for a set of casual clothes in addition to a more formal coat and tie outfit at the Jos. A. Bank store. It was the first coat and tie Wolf had ever worn. He had to admit to himself that he looked pretty good. She also bought backpacks for both of them.

Wart's mother then dragged the boys to the Rooster's Men's Grooming Center for haircuts. They both objected, but she would have none of it. Wolf's hair was too long and wild. The boys were given very short cuts. She said she wanted them to last because they wouldn't see a proper barber again for quite a while.

Next on her agenda was lunch. They went to Giovanni's Pizza on East Market Street, where the three of them split a large pepperoni pizza. Wolf ate half of it, and Mrs. Cunningham commented, "Eat as much as you can when you can," throwing Wolf's words back at him. She added, "So this is how you're like the wolf?" This left Wart smirking.

After lunch, they went to Baskin-Robbins, and the boys ordered banana splits. It was the best ice cream Wolf had ever had, far better than the ice cream they served at school.

The last stop for the day was the grocery store, where Mrs. Cunningham picked up ten pounds of meat for Shadow.

When they got home, they found Wart's father asleep in his chair with Shadow curled up on the floor at his feet. Hanna, her head on top of the wolf, was fast asleep. Mrs. Cunningham surveyed the scene and shook her head. She walked into the kitchen to put the meat into the refrigerator.

The boys changed clothes, went outside, and started their midday exercises. When they had finished their stretching, they started a sparring match. As they finished, they found they had an audience of Wart's older brothers and sisters. Shadow came outside with Hanna walking beside him, holding the fur of his back.

John moved to separate the two of them, and Shadow pricked his ears and emitted a low growl. Wolf moved in and took charge of Shadow, putting a calming arm around his neck. It didn't take long for everybody else to realize that the wolf had adopted the little girl as his own. She looked so small next to Shadow.

Mrs. Cunningham, who had been watching from the window, came out and demanded to know what was going on. Everyone started to speak at once, and she ordered them to be quiet. She looked straight at Wolf and asked him to explain.

"He was trying to protect her. He treats her as a pup. He does the same thing with me sometimes."

Mrs. Cunningham snapped, "My daughter is not going to become a wolf pup, and I won't have my other children being threatened by him." She turned to Shadow and asked, "Do you understand me?"

The wolf pinned his ears back, ducked, and turned his head in complete submission. Wolf responded, "He understands very well. You won't have any trouble from him, ma'am."

"There had better not be. Are we clear?"

"Yes, ma'am. I've been made aware of the consequences if there's any trouble."

Mr. Cunningham came outside and asked his wife, "What's going on?"

Mrs. Cunningham pointed at Shadow and snapped, "He's trying to turn my daughter into a wolf, and you let it happen!"

The kids all erupted into shouting at each other. John and Elizabeth had one argument going while David and Mary were having another. Wolf and Shadow sneaked off to the garden pavilion where he sat down, buried his head in his hands, and started to cry.

He heard Wart say to his parents, "If you send him back to school, I'll go with him. He's an orphan, and I'm his best friend. Shadow is very protective. He almost died trying to save Wolf and his sister, Red. That bullet hanging around Wolf's neck was intended for Red, but Shadow took it trying to save her. He's that kind of wolf."

Then Wolf heard Mrs. Cunningham say, "Ask Wolf to come here, please."

Wolf tried to leave through a gate in the fence, but Shadow would have none of it. He pulled hard on his leash and wouldn't let Wolf leave. Wart caught Wolf by the arm, hauled him back into the yard, and said, "Mother wants to talk to you."

"She's just going to send me back, and they'll take Shadow away."

"I don't think so. You should talk to her first. If you run away, what do you think will happen when they catch you?"

"They'll take Shadow away," Wolf replied. "Or worse."

"Think about it. What do you have to lose?"

"Okay, I get your point. I'll come."

They walked back to the pavilion where Wart took charge of Shadow. Wolf followed Mr. and Mrs. Cunningham into the house, and Mrs. Cunningham invited him to sit down in the den.

"I hear that Shadow saved your life," she said.

"Not mine, my sister's."

"But you're an orphan."

"I'm being adopted."

"By whom?"

"Whisperblade."

Mrs. Cunningham smiled and said, "I know her well. She's still a knight isn't she?"

"Yes ma'am. She teaches self-defense and meditation."

"As she has always done. You'll have to tell me more about her later. Now about the wolf. Is he tame?"

"No, ma'am, but he acts like an overprotective dog. He's loyal to me and my friends. He plays well with people he's familiar with, and he won't bite."

"I want you to tell me more about his saving your sister's life, but that can wait until after supper." Mrs. Cunningham left the room.

Mr. Cunningham said, "I think you'll go far in life. You've been busy enough already. I like Shadow and will help you with him as much as I can. I think Mrs. Cunningham will come around. Just remember Hanna is her pride and joy. Thanksgiving dinner is tomorrow, and you won't be kicked out on Shadow's account. Let's go outside and enjoy the good weather."

Outside, a pickup game of soccer had started among the children. Wolf and Mr. Cunningham joined in and soon found out Shadow had a knack for stealing the ball and playing with it his own way.

~

The next morning, Mrs. Cunningham asked Wolf if he could cook, since everyone helped in making the Thanksgiving dinner. Wolf told her that he had cooked rabbit over a campfire and Red had taught him how to mix up spices and herbs to season the meat.

She considered this a minute then said, "You need to learn more than boiling water and burning meat." She instructed Wolf on the process of making gravy. It turned out to be a long morning of cooking. She gave Wolf several more cooking chores before the morning was done. Wart was responsible for making the pecan pie. He started from scratch, shelling the pecans and making the pie shell from fresh dough.

Shadow laid down in the corner of the kitchen as everyone went about cooking chores. Finally, Mrs. Cunningham gave Wolf several pounds of chopped meat to feed Shadow, who ate it from a bowl.

Wolf had proven his knowledge of spices to the point where he was allowed to tweak Mrs. Cunningham's recipe for gravy. When she asked how he came to know so much about spices, he told her that spices were necessary to make dried fruit and cooked rabbit tastier. He said he'd had several opportunities to experiment with the different flavors, and the chefs at school were happy to let him experiment. After the gravy had been prepared, he and Wart were given the chore of setting the dinner table. They had to place each setting just right. Mrs. Cunningham inspected their work to make sure it met her standards.

After all preparations were made, the boys went upstairs to clean up and get dressed. Wolf put on his new clothes and necktie. When they came downstairs, they helped carry the food from the kitchen to the table. Wolf indicated for Shadow to lie in the corner, which he did. Everyone sat down at the long table. The father said grace and then started carving the turkey. After the turkey was served, the yams, beans, squash, stuffing, gravy and other dishes were passed around the table. It was a marvelous feast.

The topic of conversation was about Wolf and the fact he had never had a big Thanksgiving feast before. He went on to talk about cooking rabbit with Red and Shadow. He told them about his experience of eating rabbit raw. The younger children stared at him with wide eyes. Mrs. Cunningham winced then commented that Wolf needed some serious cooking lessons, as did Red for that matter, doubly so. She instructed Wolf to invite Red and Whisperblade for Christmas. Then Mrs. Cunningham suggested Wolf talk about his horse.

Wolf said, "His name is Nudge, and he's a full blooded Percheron. It's a type of draft horse, but he's still a baby. He weighs more than five hundred pounds, and when he grows up, he may reach two thousand pounds. He plays soccer with Shadow, and he can run like the wind, but he's too young to ride. Mostly he stays with his mom."

"It sounds wonderful," Mrs. Cunningham commented.

"It is until you have to muck out the stall. I have to do triple the work to take care of Nudge, Mary, and Easy Rider. That's Red's other horse, and I have to do the work in order to ride him."

"It sounds like a lot of responsibility, Wolf."

"I guess so. It isn't bad," Wolf replied. "I just wish I could enjoy it more."

"Maybe you don't see the forest for the trees," Mr. Cunningham said.

Wolf took a sip of tea and said, "Sir?"

"It's an old expression. Maybe the purpose of life is not to work to find time to rest but to enjoy the life in everything you do."

"I don't think I understand."

Mr. Cunningham cut another slice of turkey and asked, "Did you enjoy helping with the cooking?"

"Oh, yes, sir."

"So the meal is not just sitting down to eat. It is a whole series of things that make up a meal. Having a horse is the same. Mucking the stall makes your horse happy. If you learn to enjoy work, you'll be much happier."

Wolf said, "Yes, sir."

"It's why we all help in cooking big meals." He paused and said, "Now for the part of the meal I enjoy the most—dessert."

Mr. Cunningham then passed around dessert plates loaded with slices of pecan pie topped with vanilla ice cream. It was a grand finish to a grand feast. Wolf stood and thanked the family for the meal, saying it was the best he had ever eaten, and he believed it. He offered to help with the cleanup, and he and Wart were given the job of carrying dishes from the table to the kitchen where the older children washed and put them away.

For the rest of the day, the family went outside to the garden pavilion, where Wolf and Wart told them about some of their adventures during summer camp, including the raid on the loggers and the time when Shadow had been shot. Hanna announced that she wanted to go to the school when she was old enough.

~

The next day, the parents piled all the children and Shadow into the limousine for a trip to Cavallo Farm. Mr. Cunningham rented horses for everybody, except for Hanna, who would ride with him. He asked Wart and Wolf to help pick out the best horses for riding. They walked into the corral and started with the friendliest horses, rejecting the ones who were too aggressive in snatching the apples they held out. Soon they had eight horses picked out, and with the father's and the other boys' help, saddled them.

The whole family turned out to be good riders, and Wolf could tell they rode frequently. It explained Wart's excellent riding ability. They rode the trails between the farmers' fields until about noon, when they stopped in a meadow on a hill for a picnic lunch. During lunch, Mrs. Cunningham surprised Wolf by giving Shadow a large piece of raw beef. Shadow accepted it from her, though he normally didn't accept food from anybody but Wolf unless Wolf told him it was okay.

After they had finished eating, Wart and Wolf gave a demonstration of self-defense skills. Wart's older brothers and sisters expressed a keen interest and asked about taking lessons, and their parents seemed to be agreeable to the idea.

Then the kids started a game of tag. Shadow played along and ran circles around them. When David and Wolf collided and fell down in a pile, everybody laughed. Shadow nosed into the fray, licking Wolf's face. Wolf in turn tried to push him away.

Shadow suddenly stood up ridged, his ears rotated forward. He started to growl. Wolf stopped laughing when Shadow started to growl fiercely, baring his teeth, with his hackles up. He saw that Shadow stared at Hanna now fifty yards away. She had wandered away from her mother, collecting late-blooming flowers.

Wolf reached for Shadow's collar, but Shadow launched into a dead run before he could stop him.

Mrs. Cunningham shrieked and started running for Hanna.

Wolf scrambled to his feet, yelling for Shadow to stop. Quickly, everybody started yelling and running.

Shadow, being much faster than Mrs. Cunningham, reached the girl first, but he ran past her and snatched a snake behind its head. The wolf ran a few steps further, whipped the snake around, and bit down hard until he had broken the snake's spine, and it went limp.

The wolf, still holding the snake, turned back to Hanna, who now was in her mother's arms. Everybody else had arrived, and they were staring at Shadow and the snake hanging from his jaws. It was a rattlesnake. The raw power with which Shadow had dealt with the snake surprised even Wolf.

Shadow dropped the dead snake, then pawed at it, as if making sure it no longer posed a threat. "That was scary," Mr. Cunningham said. "I think maybe Shadow has earned his keep for today."

Mrs. Cunningham hugged Hanna, who was crying and said, "I want to go home, now."

Mr. Cunningham took Hanna until her mother could mount up and passed the girl up so she could ride with her mother's arms around her. Everybody mounted up, and they took the shortest path back to the stables.

After taking care of the horses, all piled into the limousine for the trip home. As soon as they had settled in the car, Mrs. Cunningham called

Shadow and patted the seat next to her. The wolf came over and rested his head on the seat while she stroked his fur. "You've given me something to be thankful for today. I think you can come back for Christmas."

"Yippee!" Hanna yelled.

~

      Too soon, it came time for Wart and Wolf to return to school. Sunday morning, they packed their clothes into their new backpacks and went downstairs for breakfast. After eating, Mrs. Cunningham gave Wolf a big hug and handed him a sealed envelope addressed to Whisperblade. The entire family went outside to see the boys and the wolf off. They said their last goodbyes through the open window, and the car pulled out of the driveway.

Chapter 30 ~ Wolf's Day in Court

Wolf ran to Whisperblade's office to deliver Mrs. Cunningham's letter. She read the letter twice then put it down, looked up at Wolf and said, "You and Shadow must have made a pretty strong impression on your trip. It seems you two are invited to return for Christmas as well as Amara and myself. I'll ask Amara if she wants to accept this invitation. I certainly intend to. I'll make the arrangements. I'll see you bright and early in the morning for we have to see how much you have forgotten this week."

~

Wolf felt clumsy in self-defense, agitated during meditation, and out of breath when running. It was going to be one hellish week, and he knew why—he had not worked out as hard as he normally did. He resolved not to slack up again, but he wondered if it was possible to keep the exercises up forever. He asked Red about it, and she laughed and told him he could never keep in shape. The teachers were going to make it harder and harder. They were not going to let him have a break.

Mr. Cunningham's words came back to him about enjoying the work involved instead of waiting for a finished job. This started to make his head hurt, and he gave up trying to figure out if he was happy or not.

The next day, he asked Raven how he got by with all the endless work. Raven told him, "You just have to think about what you are trying to do and why. Then you have to consider the pain you're going through. Think about it and concentrate on the pain in minute detail, and you'll find it lessens, and maybe it even goes away. You might think about that the next time you hurt while running."

"Yes, sir."

After trying it, Wolf noticed that he didn't mind his exercise as much.

~

One afternoon, Raven informed him that they had to go back to his home state about the mess involving Mace and Jake. They were to testify in open court. Raven told Wolf that it would be hard and intense. He also told him it would probably be quick, and he would help prepare for the probable questions that would be asked.

On the day of the trip, Wolf found out that Red and Whisperblade were going as well. Wolf dressed in his new casual outfit and packed his coat and tie outfit into his backpack. Red dressed in her best tunic because she didn't have casual clothes. Whisperblade dressed in trousers and a woman's tunic. Raven dressed in a business suit, and this was the first time Wolf had seen the Raven in anything other than a uniform.

An empty school car waited for them at the front of the palace. Bear took charge of Shadow and promised to check on the horses for the students.

They left the school and began the hour-long trip to the airport. Tickets were already waiting for them at the check-in counter. They passed through security since none of them carried their knives or swords. The airplane taxied to the end of the runway, and, while they were waiting to take off, Raven asked Wolf if he had ever been in an airplane. Wolf answered that he hadn't, so Raven informed him that he was in for a thrill.

When the plane started to move, it rolled slowly at first, and then it turned onto the end of the runway. The jet engines started to roar as the plane sped down the runway, and Wolf found himself pressed into the back of the seat. He looked at Red, who sat next to him. She had stiffened and grabbed the arms of her seat with her fingers turning white.

When the plane left the ground, it seemed to go straight up, and the ground dropped away. In a few minutes, the airplane reached cruising altitude and leveled off, and the engines became quieter. Wolf looked at Red, who had finally relaxed a bit, and asked, "What's the matter?"

"I don't know what happened. I just felt tight," Red replied.

"You had a panic attack," Whisperblade said. "It happens sometimes."

"But I've flown before," Red protested.

"It just happens."

"But Wolf didn't have one," Red challenged.

"He did. He just didn't show it as much," Raven said.

Red elbowed Wolf in the side and said, "If you tell anybody about this, I'll put you on a spit and cook you. Understand?"

"Yeah, I understand," Wolf mumbled.

"Good."

After they disembarked, Raven hailed a taxi, and they rode into the city. Reaching the hotel, Raven checked them into their rooms, a double suite with two separate bedrooms, each having one king-sized bed. Raven informed Wolf that he had to sleep on the couch.

The next morning, they ate breakfast in the hotel restaurant, after which Wolf and Raven went back to their room, while Red and Whisperblade went out to do "girl things." Raven took their time together to prepare Wolf on the type of questions he would be asked and on how to act in court. Raven explained that there would be lawyers who would ask tricky questions. Once Wolf sat in the witness chair, no one could help him. Members of their group couldn't be in the courtroom at the same time.

About two hours before lunchtime, Red and Whisperblade returned from their trip, and Red had on a new outfit. She still wore trousers, but they were fine dress trousers. She had on a nice long-sleeved shirt. She looked like she could be a business worker. The most remarkable part of her transformation was her hair. It was brilliant. She had been to a salon and had her hair styled and spread across her back. The natural curl had been relaxed, and her hair now had a gentle wave. Red looked anything but comfortable.

Wolf told Red she looked very good, for a girl, and received a punch on his shoulder. Whisperblade grimaced and said something about dressing them up but not being able to tame them. Raven just chuckled.

~

The next morning, they rode a taxi to the courthouse, and there they found the correct courtroom and reported in. They were told to wait outside in the hallway. Raven was the first one called to testify. He was in for a good half hour, and, when he came out of the room, he remained quiet and discouraged any questions by holding a finger to his lips. The bailiff came out and invited Whisperblade in. She was in only about fifteen minutes before she came out. The bailiff ordered Red into the courtroom, and the door closed. Red testified for over an hour before she emerged, and she appeared shaken and pale.

The bailiff announced that the court had been recessed for lunch and would resume at two in the afternoon. The four of them went across the street to a café, where Raven ordered sandwiches for everybody, and after a moment's thought, ordered coffee for all.

"What happened in there? Wolf asked Red.

"I can't tell you until it's all over. It wasn't fun."

"The lawyers will ask you an awful lot of questions, and they won't be friendly," Whisperblade said.

~

When they arrived back at the courtroom, the bailiff stood waiting for them. He called Wolf's name and took him inside. He led Wolf down the aisle, past the bar, to the witness stand. There Wolf turned to face the court and saw Mace and Jake sitting behind a table. Mace had a sneer on his lips and stared at him as though he could cut him down.

The judge was on his right sitting higher than anyone else. On the other side of the judge, the jury sat in two rows. In the audience, only a handful of seats were occupied, which surprised Wolf. The bailiff stood in front of him and told him to swear to tell the truth, the whole truth, and nothing but the truth. The bailiff ordered him to sit down. The judge asked him to state his name and he said, "Wolf."

The judge looked at him a second before the lawyer for Mace objected.

"Noted," the judge said. "Wolf, what is your real name?"

"Sir, I'm an orphan, and I'm being adopted, so I'll be able to pick my own name, and I choose Wolf."

"I'll grant you your request," ordered the judge.

"I strongly object," the lawyer said, jumping up.

"Overruled," the judge said, warning against any more outbursts. "The Court recognizes the witness's name as Wolf. Wolf, that man over there is the prosecutor, and he's going to ask you questions. When he's finished, the defense lawyer will ask questions. Do you understand how this works?"

"I think so, sir."

"Good," the judge said. He turned to the prosecutor and said, "You may proceed."

The prosecutor said, "Wolf, please tell the court what you do for a living. Do you work, or are you a student?"

"I'm a student, sir."

"Do you know the defendant?"

Wolf glanced over at Mace, and the man glared at him. To Wolf, he looked insane with wild eyes. "Yes, sir." Mace sneered and muttered something under his breath. Wolf thought he heard, "...get you."

"Would you please describe how you know him?"

Wolf went into a long description of his first meeting with Mace as a hitchhiker, then his second meeting at the illegal logging operation. Frequently, the prosecutor interrupted his narrative to ask him questions about insignificant details. It took almost an hour to tell the whole story.

Mace kept muttering, trying to rattle Wolf, and the whole time, he kept up his fierce glare. Wolf just concentrated on the prosecutor. Finally, the judge rapped his gavel and warned the defense counsel to keep his client quiet. Eventually, after some urging, Mace quieted down. The judge motioned for the prosecutor to continue.

"It seems you've led an adventurous life, Wolf. Did you meet the defendant again?"

"Yes, sir." Wolf described the events that led to him shooting Mace and Jake, including Shadow being shot. The prosecutor interrupted him more frequently to ask about details of the event.

"So you were afraid for your life."

Wolf thought a moment, "No, sir."

"How so?"

"He was pointing the gun at Red. I had to save her. She's my sister."

"I see. Why did you think she needed help?"

"She was just lying there, and he pointed his gun at her. He had already shot Shadow. I couldn't let him shoot her."

Mace jumped up and yelled, "The boy's lying! That's all he's done. Lies, lies!"

The judge rapped his gavel and said, "There will be order in this court! Sit down and be quiet." When Mace sat down, the judge motioned for the prosecutor to continue.

"Tell me more about Shadow. I understand he's a real wolf."

"Yes, sir. He's a wild wolf, and he's in my care. I'm licensed to handle him. I saved his life, and he seems to have adopted me."

"How's that?"

"I can't explain it very well, but he has taught me how to hunt rabbit. He looks out for me."

"So you two take care of each other."

"Yes, sir."

"It sounds to me that you're a very responsible boy."

"Objection," the defense lawyer yelled while standing up. "The prosecution is drawing conclusions."

"Sustained," the judge said.

"That's all I have for now. I reserve the right to re-cross later," the prosecutor concluded.

"The defense may cross examine the witness," the judge said.

The defense lawyer stood and walked out from behind his table to the center of the courtroom facing the boy. "How old are you?"

"Fourteen, sir."

"That's pretty young. Perhaps you're too young to be carrying such a dangerous weapon as what you used to try to kill the defendant."

"Objection, Your Honor," the prosecutor exclaimed, "counsel is drawing conclusions."

"Sustained, strike from the record. Counsels, approach the bench." The lawyers went before the judge. Wolf heard the judge tell them, "I'll warn you both. The boy will speak for himself. Ask questions, and let him answer."

Wolf glanced over at Mace, who kept quiet but glared at him.

The lawyer started his cross-examination again. This time he was more careful with his words. "How did you come to be enrolled in this school?"

"I ran away from my last foster parents. I had been beaten in school by the other students, and I was taken in by Raven and became a foster child of Whisperblade."

"Have you run away before?"

"Yes, sir."

"Do you consider that responsible?"

"No, sir."

"Is shooting someone a responsible act?"

"Sir?"

"When you shot my client, was that a responsible act?"

"I saved my sister."

"That's not what I asked. Was shooting my client a responsible act?"

That gave Wolf pause. He stared at the lawyer and said, "Yes, it was, sir. When a person points a weapon, he's ready to use it, and he pointed his gun at my sister. I was the only one who could stop him. It was my responsibility."

"You said you were not afraid for your life?"

"Yes, sir."

"But you were willing to take another person's life?"

"Objection!" yelled the prosecutor.

"Sustained," said the Judge. "I will warn the defense to be very careful. Where are you going with this line of questions?"

"I'm about to get to the point, Your Honor." The lawyer then asked, "Was what my client was doing responsible?"

"Sir?"

"Was what my client doing any different than what you were doing?"

"Yes, sir. Mace was responsible for trying to kill Red. I was responsible for trying to stop him. If I had done nothing, Red would now be dead. I don't know if being responsible is a good or bad thing, but I know it isn't right to let someone be murdered. Saving lives is good."

The defense lawyer paused, and then he asked, "Are you saying you were ready to kill my client?"

"Yes, sir."

The lawyer looked at the jury then told the judge, "That is all that I have for the witness at this time."

Mace continued glaring.

The prosecutor stood up and said, "Request to re-cross."

"Granted."

"Wolf, if you hadn't shot Mace, what do you think would have happened?"

"He probably would have killed Amara. He had already bashed her head in."

"You lie! You little worm!" Mace yelled, as he jumped to his feet and pounded the table with clenched hands. Then the little man scrambled over the table and across the courtroom before the bailiff could capture him. He reached for Wolf's throat. To block him, Wolf drove the heel of his palm into his chin. Mace's head snapped back, and he went down, tackled by the bailiff.

The bailiff slapped handcuffs on the stunned man, and Mace recovered just enough to yell, "I'm going to kill you," before the bailiff hauled him out of the courtroom.

The judge kept rapping his gavel until the room grew quiet. "The jury will ignore that outburst."

Wolf snorted in disbelief. He would never forget it. The judge gave him a stern look and asked, "Are you hurt?"

Wolf looked at the palm of his hand, which still stung from the blow he had delivered, and said, "No, sir."

"Are you willing to continue? We can recess until you have a chance to calm down."

"I think I can go on, sir. I'd rather get it over with."

"Prosecution?"

"That's all I have, Your Honor," the prosecutor said with a slight hint of a smile.

"Defense?" The lawyer sat at his table looking half-stunned. "Your Honor, I move for a mistrial."

"Your motion is denied. Do you wish to continue?"

The defense lawyer kept looking down at the table and mumbled, "No, Your Honor."

"The witness is excused."

The bailiff escorted Wolf out of the courtroom.

He entered the hallway, and the rest of his party greeted him. "You were in there for two hours," Red said. "What happened?"

"You can tell, Wolf, it's all over," Raven said.

Wolf gave the complete story as they left the court building. They went across the street to the restaurant for a long snack.

When Wolf finished telling his story, Whisperblade grimaced. "Now you know why you're doing so much self-defense. You attract trouble. It is in your very nature. You'll make a good knight if you decide to be one. Don't fret, if I ever meet Mace again, I'll be the last person he ever sees."

~

The following morning after breakfast, Raven received a message. He read it twice and announced, "Well, it seems we're free from going back to court. The trial is now going to the jury, who will decide whether Mace and Jake are guilty or not. That means we're free for the rest of the day. I'm going to arrange return tickets to school." He left to call the ticket agent.

Whisperblade said, "That also means you and Amara are free to go about town by yourselves, with certain restrictions. You must stay together, and you must return here for supper." She gave them a little money for lunch and personal spending.

With money in their pockets, Wolf and Red were out the door of the hotel. They had a lively discussion as to what they should do with the money. It wasn't a lot and would require careful planning. First, they went window-shopping. They went into a music store and each bought penny whistles, but they cost a lot more than expected, and it cut into their agreed budget.

They went to the museum where the fee for students was cheap. Wolf wanted to find out more about knights, and, in particular, modern day knights. Red wandered into the Egyptian area of the museum while Wolf talked to one of the interpreters of the medieval exhibit. He did learn that there were no modern knights other than honorary titles granted for contributions for the good of the country.

"You mean there are no real knights anymore?" Wolf asked the interpreter.

"Not that I know of," the lady answered.

Wolf started to object but asked, "What happened to them?"

"Well, they died out."

"They died!"

"They didn't die so to speak. They weren't necessary as cities became bigger, and, as the rule of law became better, there was less need for acting knights."

"What did knights do?"

"They enforced the laws of the lord they served. They were heavy handed in how they did it. They also fought the king's wars, sort of like cavalry."

"How did it all start?"

"Do you know what the word *knight* means?" the lady asked.

"No, ma'am."

"It's an old word for *boy*. A rich landowner would hire very young men to make sure there was no trouble on their lands. They kept the peasants who worked the land in line. Back then, the landowner was the law, but landowners owed their lands to the nobility, whom they served."

"That doesn't sound very noble."

"Knights were paid with small grants of land. They had to raise their own money to pay for their horses and weapons. If a knight served his master well, he would be paid more and could become more famous. It was a step to becoming noblemen themselves."

"So how did knights become so romantic?"

"The church became involved. They didn't like the heavy hand that knights wielded and all the pointless fighting. So they drafted a set of rules to put a check on knights, a code of chivalry. The church also started several orders of knights who were fighter priests."

It was way past noon, and Wolf excused himself, went to the museum shop, and bought a book on knights. He located Red, and together, they went out to find a place to eat. They found a street café, sat down at an empty table, and, when the waitress came and gave them a menu, they found that their money would not cover the cost of a meal. They quickly excused themselves and left. They did have enough money to buy hot dogs from a street vendor.

After eating the hot dogs, they went to a small street park and practiced meditation and self-defense. Their self-defense drew a small crowd. When they realized so many people were watching them, they stopped.

The crowd scattered to go their separate ways, but a policeman approached them and asked, "What are your names? Where are you from?"

"Wolf, sir, and this is my sister, Red. We're students of the Knight Riding School."

The police officer asked them, "What are your real names? Show me some identification."

Wolf looked down and said, "Caleb, sir, but I don't use it anymore. I'm just called Wolf."

"This seems pretty fishy for me. Just show me some identification."

Wolf kept looking down and said, "I don't have any."

"Sir," Red said. "He's being adopted by my mother. He prefers Wolf. That's what his real name will be when the adoption is final. We're staying at the City Hotel, and here is our room key." She produced the key, and the officer grabbed it.

He examined it and said, "I'll just have to verify this. Let's take a walk. I still don't like your story. If you're lying, it's straight to the police station."

When they arrived at the hotel, they went to their room. The policeman knocked on the door, and when Whisperblade answered, he introduced himself. She had a complete look of surprise and invited the officer in. They talked a few minutes until the police officer had satisfied himself that the kids were hers. After he left, Whisperblade gave them an angry stare.

Whisperblade walked around them twice. "Sit," she said, pointing at the couch. They complied quickly. "Didn't I say something about not getting in trouble? No, don't answer that. You knew better. A public display of self-defense without an adult is sure to bring unwanted attention. Did the two of you stay together?"

"Yes, ma'am, except in the museum," Wolf answered.

The knight took in a deep breath and said, "That's not what I told you to do. You know the importance of working together."

"Yes, ma'am," they both said.

"There's a lesson in this. You must always think about what you're doing. Leaving each other alone in the museum was the worst thing you did. You each had a responsibility to the other. This is not the first time. Just look at what happened the last time you separated. You both almost got yourselves killed. That's why we're here now."

Raven entered the hotel room and asked, "What's going on now?"

"Just another lesson in responsibility," Whisperblade snapped. Raven gave them a long look, but said nothing.

That night after dinner, they went to the theater to see the Shakespeare's "Henry V." Wolf enjoyed the play, even though he had trouble understanding some of the words. He still understood the main plot and found the Band of Brothers speech very moving.

Chapter 31 ~ Christmas

Life at school for the next two weeks had settled into a routine. Wolf concentrated on studying his lessons and taking care of the horses and Shadow. The weather turned very cold, and riding horses on the weekend trips became a real chore, but Wolf noticed that the horses and the wolf didn't seem to care that it was cold. When he complained, Raven reminded him that it would get a lot colder and they had to compete in the horse games when it was freezing.

So it came as a relief to Wolf when it was time for Christmas break. Wart and Wolf packed their saddlebags and, together, they washed and groomed Shadow. When they were ready, they went over to the palace to meet Whisperblade and Red and ate breakfast while they waited for the limousine to arrive. This time Wolf prepared for feeding Shadow, bringing fresh meat in a sealed bag.

~

When they arrived at Wart's home, the whole Cunningham family greeted them. After dinner, Little Hanna immediately laid down with Shadow, and her mom didn't say a word about it. Then Whisperblade told them a story about her military experience and a soldier who had given her a hard time, one who was known not to like women in the military. "When he questioned my order for an assignment, I looked at him a moment and then took him over to a stack of ammunition boxes and stood on one so I could look him straight in the eye. 'You don't like me do you?' With a steely-eyed stare, he replied, 'No, ma'am.'

"I asked, 'Why don't you like me?' But the soldier didn't answer. I said, 'It's not because I'm a woman, is it?' Still there was no answer, so I said, 'It's not because I'm a superior officer, is it? I know why you don't like me.'

"The man looked perplexed and said, 'Ma'am?' I said, 'You don't like me, because I'm shorter than you.'"

It took the women and girls a full minute to stop laughing, but Wolf couldn't see what was so funny.

Mrs. Cunningham leaned toward Whisperblade and Red and said, "The three of us are going to have a ladies' day of fun and relaxation."

"I look forward to it," Whisperblade said

"What do we do?" Wolf asked.

"I leave that up to you and Mr. Cunningham," Mrs. Cunningham answered.

~

The next morning the women left in the limousine. Mr. Cunningham took Wolf, Wart, and Wart's brothers, John and David, to a paintball park, but Shadow was left in the care of Wart's older sisters, Elizabeth and Mary. Their plans were to take him on leash for a walk to the local park. Wolf left them the license documents so there would be no questions about his legitimacy.

The paintball park had an open field with obstacles and a large wooded area with plenty of natural places to hide. Mr. Cunningham rented paint ball guns and facemasks for everybody. Wart and Wolf were wearing their oldest uniforms, and the brothers and father wore play clothes. Jackets for the cold weather were not necessary, because, as Wart said, "We're going to work up a sweat."

Mr. Cunningham went to play with a bunch of his friends. The boys formed two teams with Wart and Wolf on one team and John and David on the other team. Wolf and Wart used blue paint balls, and the brothers, red paint balls. They separated and entered the woods where Wart and Wolf took off running. After they had gone a half kilometer, they stopped to work out their strategy. Wolf favored staying together as they hunted for the brothers. Wart wanted to separate but stay within sight of each other, using the hand signals Raven had taught them. "If we're in sight of each other, we're still working as a team," Wart said. Wolf agreed with Wart's idea, and they split up. It took a half hour before they found John and David.

Wolf saw them first and hid behind a tree before he was spotted. He signaled Wart, and together they began stalking the brothers. Wart fired first, drawing their attention. While the brothers were occupied with hiding behind a log and defending themselves, Wolf managed to sneak up behind them.

The boys were lying down behind the log right next to each other, exposed from the rear. Wolf stood up behind a tree about twenty feet behind them, and when Wart paused to reload his gun, Wolf stepped out and in rapid fire shot several paint balls that hit the brothers in the back. They turned around, and Wolf shot them several more times. It had been too easy. The brothers admitted defeat, and they all headed back to base to refresh their guns and themselves. The rest of the morning, they played in various combinations of partners, and several other boys joined in their games.

They broke for lunch, and Mr. Cunningham treated the boys to the hot dogs and hamburgers at the park's clubhouse. That afternoon, there were too many people to play in such small teams. They watched more experienced boys play on the open field, using the obstacles for protection. They had rapid-fire guns, and they displayed extraordinary teamwork. Wolf paid careful attention to the action. The main lesson he took away was the winners were usually the ones who attacked first and most aggressively.

Late that afternoon, when men returned to the house, the women were already there. When they entered through the back door, Mrs. Cunningham gasped at their condition and pointed to the laundry room. There were bathrobes in the laundry room, and they all changed and went upstairs to shower and put on clean clothes.

When they returned downstairs and entered the living room, Wolf's jaw dropped.

Red sat in a large wingback chair in a new green dress with her legs together and her hands in her lap. She had on gold ball earrings. Not looking very happy, she said, "Go ahead and say it."

"You look beautiful. When did you get your ears pierced?"

"I knew it. The first thing you'd notice would be my ears."

"Actually, it was the dress," Wolf said.

Wart had a big grin, and Red looked at him fiercely and asked, "What do you find so funny, Wart?"

He said, "The fearsome Red in a dress. Mom said she passed out when they pierced her ears. Wait until all the other pages hear about it."

"I'll boil you in oil if they do," Red growled.

"Enough of that," Mrs. Cunningham warned. "It's about time for supper. I think we've all had a busy day, and we'll all feel better with full bellies."

On their way to the kitchen, Wolf noticed that Hanna was wearing clip-on earrings that looked just like Red's earrings.

~

Two days later, it was Christmas and time to give gifts. Wolf gave Red a necklace with a single pearl on a delicate gold. "It's beautiful!" Red exclaimed.

"I saw you admiring it in a storefront," Wolf said.

Red gave Wolf a large hunting knife to replace the small utility knife the school had issued him.

Whisperblade gave them both new riding boots. The Cunninghams gave them new, wide-brimmed felt hats to keep the sun and rain off their faces. They were waterproof, soft, and pliable for packing, and were a dark-green that went well with the school uniform. Whisperblade, Wolf, and Red gave Mr. and Mrs. Cunningham a large basket of fruit and assorted nuts.

They spent the afternoon cooking the Christmas feast. Wolf again had to make the gravy, this time on his own. Mrs. Cunningham gave Red and Whisperblade extensive lessons on cooking vegetables and preparing fruit for the table. They also had to learn the finer points of cooking a turkey.

They all stood behind their chairs while Mr. Cunningham offered a prayer for the guests and for everybody's wellbeing. Everybody sat down, and Mr. Cunningham served the turkey as the plates were passed around. Then the rest of the food dishes were passed around.

The conversation around the table came to the subject of the food at the school. "I wish you could come and cook at the school," Red said to Mrs. Cunningham.

Wolf mentioned the wild boar Red had killed and told how it had been cooked and served. This started a flurry of questions from Wart's brothers and sisters: "How big was it? How did you kill it? Was it bloody? Weren't you afraid? How did it taste?" The questions continued until Mrs. Cunningham told the children to give Red a break so she could eat.

When dinner was finished, everybody assisted in clearing the table and putting away the food. Mrs. Cunningham presented Shadow with a bowl of fresh beef, and everyone retreated to the living room. The boys had to bring in extra chairs so everyone would be able to sit down. Mrs. Cunningham said, "Wart and Wolf, start us a fire in the fireplace."

As they enjoyed the fire's warmth, Whisperblade brought up the subject of Mrs. Cunningham's time at school. "She and Lady Jane were always in trouble. They kept skipping out of self-defense. I dare say I made them run ten laps every day."

"We weren't that bad," Mrs. Cunningham said. "They just blamed us for everything that happened."

"How you two became ladies, I'll never know," Whisperblade said. "You were guilty of most everything that happened. There was that incident with the Lion's socks."

"The laundry machine ate them," Mrs. Cunningham retorted.

Whisperblade's eyes narrowed and she asked, "How about the day Cloud turned dark gray."

"It must have been a thunderstorm," Mrs. Cunningham said and giggled.

Whisperblade snapped, "Not funny, it took a week to wash him clean."

Mrs. Cunningham asked, "How is Cloud? He is the sweetest horse."

"He's doing well, but you're not going to change the subject. What about the blue mashed potatoes?"

"They were pretty cool."

"Whose idea was that?"

Mrs. Cunningham raised her hand and said, "Guilty."

"I see that your cooking has improved considerably."

"At least I graduated near the top of the class."

"Yes, you did at that, and you learned your self-defense ... eventually," admitted Whisperblade.

The Cunningham children were all open-mouthed at the revelations about their mother.

Whisperblade continued, "Wart has a lot of potential. He pays attention and generally makes good decisions. In that respect, you've done very well."

"Thank you."

Whisperblade looked at the Cunningham children and said, "Your mother could have been a knight if she'd chosen that path. Of course, if she had, she probably wouldn't have met your father."

"You," Mrs. Cunningham said, "almost got married. We could all tell. You came back from that mission up north, and you couldn't concentrate on meditation. You never did tell us what happened."

"That's none of your business," snapped Whisperblade.

"What did he look like?" Mrs. Cunningham asked.

Whisperblade's face flushed and she maintained an icy silence.

Mrs. Cunningham turned to more mundane things, such as the boys' grades and the troubles they were having in class, and Whisperblade rejoined the conversation.

Red had worn a new skirt for the feast, and she still looked uncomfortable.

For Wolf, wearing good clothes didn't seem so bad, but there was a distinct comfort in wearing the school uniforms. At least, he didn't have to worry if he wore the right clothes for the occasion.

~

The rest of the Christmas vacation consisted of various shopping trips, going to musical concerts, and attending Shakespeare's *Romeo and Juliet*. The play was quite an eye opening experience for Wolf. He had not been prepared for how emotions could turn into violence so quickly.

He had a long conversation with Whisperblade about it. She took her time before she said, "When you form attachments to others, it hurts when they're harmed in some way. Hurt turns into anger, and anger leads to violence. It's a basic human emotional response to danger. It protects us and our loved ones."

"But they were in love."

"Love makes fools of us all. How old do you think they were?"

"Eighteen?"

Whisperblade looked at him with sad eyes and said, "Juliet was about thirteen or fourteen. That's about the age when girls start thinking of love. Boys do soon after. As children turn into adults, their minds change as well as their bodies, but not necessary at the same rate. Imagine a man having a temper tantrum."

"So all the killing is like having a temper tantrum?"

"Young adults have more deadly toys than children, but they have no more self-restraint."

Wolf smiled in sudden realization and said, "They don't think about what they're doing."

"Precisely. They aren't responsible enough. Their fathers give them weapons and turn them loose to fight their wars, avenge their grudges."

"But you teach squires to use weapons."

"We teach them, but we don't turn them loose. They have to prove themselves first."

"You have to become a knight?"

"Yes, very good."

"Have you ever used a weapon against a person?"

"Not in anger, not like in Romeo and Juliet."

This was not the answer Wolf had expected. Did it mean she had used a weapon against a person? She had admitted that she had been in the military. Wolf got the feeling he would not get an answer to his next question, but he asked, "Have you ever killed anyone?"

Whisperblade looked at him a long while, her face turning red. She finally, softly said, "Yes." Then she turned around and left the room. Whisperblade didn't talk to Wolf for the rest of the night.

~

The next day, everybody awoke at six o'clock and did their self-defense exercises in the garden even though it was freezing. The whole Cunningham family joined in the exercises, and Mrs. Cunningham insisted on doing it outside. Wolf guessed she had been talking to Whisperblade. At least their breakfast was hot and filling. Then it came time to say goodbyes and load up into the limousine.

The trip to the school was interrupted when Whisperblade asked the driver to stop at a jewelry store. She went in while everybody else waited in the car. When she returned she gave a small box to Red and invited her to open it.

When she did, her eyes went wide open. Wolf saw it contained pearl earrings to match the necklace he had given her. Whisperblade said, "I've been negligent in keeping you properly attired. Hopefully, soon you'll have an opportunity to wear your pearls. The winter ball will soon be here, and it's about time you attend as a guest as opposed to being a squire."

Chapter 32 ~ Winter Ball

Snow fell after the start of the New Year. It got cold, and then it got colder. Shadow didn't seem to mind the snow. He liked to frolic in it with anyone who would play with him.

Nudge turned out to be a different matter. He would only go out with Mary and looked for any opportunity to escape back into the stable. Mary didn't seem to mind the snow, nor did Easy Rider or Pinto Bean. Wolf had to ride every day, just as he did when the weather was better. The school had a strong emphasis on the safety of the horses and the students. There was no trick riding, no galloping, nothing that would lead to the horses slipping or tripping. They used the riding barn all day long to exercise the horses. Most of the horses needed to be shod with new shoes. When it came to the horses, there was always some work to do.

All the first year pages were getting lessons in manners. They all had to learn to bow, and if necessary, the girls learned to curtsy when wearing a dress. They were taught how to serve dinner at the table and how to escort and announce guests. Lady Jane was the principle teacher for these lessons, and she expected perfection. Wolf began to wonder if she could be more fearsome than Whisperblade. She never said anything bad and always had a pleasant smile. But she always gave more work to do, and she never slowed down. She expected a lot, and all the students ran to keep up with her.

Finally, Lady Jane announced why they were getting all the lessons. There would be a Grand Ball for the grownups, including all the parents who would be visiting for the occasion. Most of the older squires would also be attending. It didn't surprise Wolf when Raven announced that Amara would be introduced at the ball. Red protested that she wouldn't go as a guest because she was too young, but Raven insisted that she was old enough.

~

All the students had to help in preparation for the ball. They had to write and send invitations, arrange the dining tables, and assign seating as the invites responded. The pages were expected to serve dinner to the guests and to keep their glasses full. At this dinner, unlike at the Cunningham's, there would not be food sitting on the table. The pages would pour the guest's drinks, ladle the soup, and provide appetizers and salads. They would then serve the main course and finish up with desserts. Since the pages had multiple jobs to perform, they had to practice at lunch and supper by serving the adults at the head table in the dining room.

The week before the ball, the pages were issued new uniform tunics on which they had to sew the appropriate ensign over the left breast. Wolf made a black raven cutout, which he positioned and sewed into place.

~

Wolf went to his room to dress in his new uniform and tunic before the ball. When he returned to the palace, it was time to start introducing the attendees formally. The pages escorted teachers, knights, and guests into the ballroom and gave the squires cards, which the squires then read to announce their names. The first person introduced was the Lion. Wolf had the honor of escorting Raven, and Wart escorted Whisperblade. After all the knights were introduced, the teachers were next.

Wart had the honor of escorting his parents. After all the guests had been introduced, the selected squires, who attended as guests or escorts of single guests, were introduced.

This was when Wolf presented Red. When Wolf saw Red out in the hallway, she was dressed in her new green dress with her hair braided, and she wore her pearl earrings and necklace. He introduced her as "Lady

Squire Amara." There were audible gasps from the other squires and pages, and Wolf figured they had never seen her in a dress before. Red blushed, but she walked into the crowd on the ballroom floor, where at least three male squires greeted her.

Wolf had to go to the dining room and find the tables he would wait on. Just in time, the crowd in the ballroom started to enter the dining room, and pages directed them to their tables. Wolf soon had a table full of guests, all standing behind their chairs waiting for the blessing to be given. The Lion blessed the food about to be served, the health of the guests, and the success of the school and its students. Then Wolf took the opportunity to seat the ladies sitting at his table.

Once the guests had been seated, he started ladling a thin soup into their bowls. Then Wolf returned to the prep room to get a cart loaded with salads. He never made it because his foot hooked on something, and he went flying. Wolf landed with his arms outstretched, the large bowl sloshing the remaining soup over his tunic and across the hardwood floor.

Squire Henry helped Wolf up. As soon as he got his bearings, he looked to see what had tripped him. The chair at the corner of the table he had rounded was empty, but he saw Page Ralph, one of Wayne's friends, standing nearby with a big grin on his face. Wolf would have pounded Ralph, except the squire held him. Squire Henry pulled him into the food preparation room and whispered into his ear, "Stay out of it, not in front of the guests. You're not in trouble now, but you will be if you move toward him." The squire held Wolf tightly against the wall until he relaxed.

"Look at me! What am I going to do? I'm a mess."

Henry said, "Ditch the tunic. I'll get you another."

Wolf pulled the tunic off and ran for a salad cart. He was able to serve as the diners were finishing their soup. It was a simple matter to pick up a soup bowl and place a salad plate for each diner. He then had to refill any water or tea glasses that were low. A senior squire came around and poured wine for all guests who wanted some.

Back in the food prep room, Henry handed Wolf a fresh tunic, which he quickly donned. He was about to re-enter the dining hall when Henry put a hand on his shoulder. "I don't know what's going on, but keep it to yourself until the ball is over and everyone has left. There are some very important people out there. Any trouble you get into now is trouble for us. Just remember, this is a big night for everybody."

Wolf went back to the tables he was responsible for and took the time to ask the diners what their choice of their main dish would be. Their choices were chicken with rice and green beans or a steak with potatoes and spinach. Two guests at his table wanted a mixture of items on their dishes. Wolf hurried to the prep room to load his cart and to carry the dishes from the cart to the table, removing the salad plates as he went along. As he served the main course, another squire started serving more wine.

Then he had a break and could stand back and observe. One of the guests, a Mr. Morris, beckoned him over to ask him his name.

"Page Wolf, sir"

"That is an unusual name isn't it?"

"Yes, sir. I was given it by the Lion when I started this school."

"Why is that?"

"I have a real wolf as a companion, sir"

"He is a companion? That is an unusual term for a pet isn't it?"

"He isn't a pet. He's wild, but he seems to have adopted me, and I'm licensed to take care of him."

"Is he here, at the school?"

"Yes, sir. He's in the kitchen being looked after by the master chef who provides his food."

"The kitchen? Can I meet this wolf? Does he have a name?"

"Yes, sir. His name is Shadow."

"I would like to meet him after dinner if that's possible."

"Yes, sir."

It came time to start removing the empty plates from the main course. After that, Wolf started delivering ice cream and fruit bowls as an after dinner treat. Another page came by with a cart and gave the diners a choice of cakes and pies. A second roving page refilled coffee cups and water and tea glasses.

With dinner over, speeches were given by the Lion and the Chairman of the Board of Visitors. Wolf had never heard of him nor did he know what the Board of Visitors was, but he figured he was very important to the school. When the speeches were over, which were mercifully short, the guests started getting up to go back into the ballroom. Wolf helped the ladies with their chairs.

Mr. Morris stayed back and had Wolf escort him to the kitchen. When they arrived, Shadow sat on a small rug laid out in the corner of the kitchen away from any food. His area had been marked off with a strip of tape on the floor. When Shadow saw Wolf, he stood up, but he did not cross the tape. Wolf produced a leash, clipped it onto Shadow's collar, and walked him out into the hallway with Mr. Morris following. Shadow was on his best behavior, and, after sniffing Mr. Morris' hand, he returned to Wolf and sat down.

Mr. Morris said, "I'm impressed. He's a magnificent animal and very well behaved."

"Thank you, sir."

"I see he has a limp."

"Yes, sir. It's from where he was caught in a trap. He almost died from the infection. Luckily, we were able to treat it in time. I helped save him, and he adopted me."

"I had heard about this wolf, and now that I see him, I can understand your commitment to his wellbeing. I had better explain myself. I am a member of the Board of Visitors, and I was asked to check the two of you out. The Board of Visitors is an independent group, people not directly associated with the school, but our recommendations carry a lot of weight in deciding the policies of the school."

"How do I figure into this?"

"You don't actually. Our concern is with the wolf."

"He stays with me, sir."

"Oh and how is that? Those are strong words."

"Sorry, sir. I didn't mean it to sound like that. He and I belong together. He's my responsibility. He needs me. If he goes then I go."

"I see. You feel that strongly about him?"

"Yes, sir." Wolf pulled out the bullet that he had hanging around his neck. "He almost died trying to save Red and me. I won't abandon him. He can't survive on his own."

Mr. Morris looked at the bullet a minute then handed it back to Wolf. "I'll let you know how I vote on the matter. Remember I have to look out for the school as a whole. I've taken too much of your time. You have a ball to attend to."

Wolf left Shadow in the care of the chef and went to the ballroom where people were already dancing. A string quartet provided the music. Raven, in his military uniform, danced with Red, but at the first break in the music, he let a squire take over. Raven then went to Whisperblade for the next dance. She had dressed in a blue dress with a white belt from which hung her long dagger. Only Whisperblade could look so fearsome while wearing a dress.

Wolf had to carry trays of cookies or other tidbits of food. When the pages were unoccupied, they gathered in one corner of the ballroom. Most all of the squires were dancing or in their own corner of the room. Red seemed to have no problem finding dancing partners. She seemed to enjoy herself. When the ball ended, Wolf had to start escorting guests to the front door where the squires would return their cars. It was very late that night before Wolf and Shadow got to bed.

~

The next morning, Wolf sought out Wart, who had gone to the stables to muck stalls. "Why can't Wayne leave us alone?"

Wart stopped shoveling and said, "Whatever made you think he'd leave us alone? He enjoys torturing us."

"Why can't anything go right for me?"

Wart whacked Wolf on the shoulder and said, "You idiot."

Wolf jumped back, "Ow. What was that for?"

"What are you doing now?"

Wolf looked at the shovel he had picked up. "Shoveling horse manure."

"And what were you doing a year ago?"

"I was going to another school and getting beat up."

Wart leaned against the handle of his shovel grinning, "What's the difference?"

Wolf started to say something bad about manure when it hit him. "Horses."

"Think about it. There's nothing so worthwhile as just messing around with horses."

Wolf swatted at a fly. "Yeah, I guess you're right."

"Wayne is small potatoes. He tried to make you look bad, but he failed. I saw what happened."

"I was lucky the squire held me back. I would have pounded Ralph. He just grinned at me."

"I guess you didn't see Wayne. He was laughing from across the room."

Wolf said, "I'll kill him."

"No! You can't. It's what he wants. If you get kicked out, he wins. Besides I'll be kicked out, too."

"What? How's that?"

Wart smiled broadly and said, "We fight together. You said it."

Chapter 33 ~ Snow Days

Early the next weekend, Shadow awoke Wolf by licking his face and nudging him in the ribs. Wolf rolled out of bed onto the floor with a thud and woke up. The noise he made when he hit the floor, which sounded pretty much like a curse, woke up his roommates. They all grumbled, but they got up and dressed to go downstairs and take care of their horses.

As they were mucking the stalls, David, the senior squire, came downstairs and announced that, except for caring for their horses, they were free for the rest of the day. A loud cheer of joy erupted from the pages. When they finished mucking Wolf, with his roommates, ran back upstairs and dived into their beds for a few extra hours of sleep.

~

Wolf awoke to the shock of a heavy rabbit hitting him in the face, which coincided with a dream he kept having about being naked in the snow. Wolf jumped up in his bed with a yelp. Shadow backed up, and Wolf's roommates all popped up in their beds.

"What the heck is going on?" George shouted.

Wolf finally overcame his shock and surveyed the situation. He said, "Shadow wants to go hunting."

"Can I come?" Harold asked.

"Me, too," George said.

"Why don't we all go?" Wart suggested.

Wolf looked at his roommates, who had excitement on their faces. "If Shadow will take us," he answered.

Wolf took time to gut and skin the rabbit Shadow had brought them. He washed it in the sink, rolled it in a large sheet of paper, and placed it in the refrigerator in the hallway. They all put on their coats and armed themselves with their bows and arrows and knives. Then they went to the squire on watch and asked permission to go hunting.

"You may," he said, "but you know the rules. Stay together, and don't leave school lands."

They hurried to saddle their horses and rode out of the stable into a cold blast of wind, but it was nice and sunny outside. They crossed the meadows behind the palace, Shadow leading the way. When they entered the trail into the forest, the wind reduced considerably, and the cold became more tolerable as the skies became overcast.

After a half hour, they reached a promising meadow. Shadow started his back and forth hunting pattern and quickly found a rabbit run. When Wolf saw the pattern, he dismounted and, taking his bow, followed Shadow, with the others following him.

It wasn't long before they found the rabbit warren. Wolf motioned for the other boys to circle the warren while he positioned himself behind the main entrance, bow at the ready. Shadow started digging at a hidden hole he had found. Soon enough, a rabbit ran out the main entrance, and Wolf nailed it from the rear. The next two rabbits escaped. The fourth rabbit George managed to shoot. It wasn't a clean kill, but Wart shot it, killing it. Harold didn't get a rabbit. Wolf nailed the last rabbit to emerge, diving on it with his knife. They gutted the rabbits but left them un-skinned to carry back to the stables.

When they mounted up, Wolf surveyed the ground they had just hunted. A remarkable amount of blood had been scattered over the snow. He realized that the blood would be around until the snow thawed out, or the increasing snowfall covered it up. It wasn't pretty.

It had started to snow in earnest, and it was rapidly getting colder. What had been a simple half hour ride became an hour's ride back to the palace. Even with their coats, they were chilled numb. With the wind in their face, they had a hard time seeing. Soon they were depending on the horses to follow the path back.

The snow was wet, and Wolf's gloves were soaked through. His fingers started to hurt from the cold. The flakes were large, and he had to squint to keep them out of his eyes. Sometimes a flake would hit his eyeball, and he had to close his eyes from the pain. It just made the cold worse.

Wolf's trousers soaked through, and his legs got colder. Though he was used to cold nights in the mountains, this was worse. The last time he had ridden in wet snow, he'd had a poncho to keep dry, and the wind had been at his back. He knew the others behind him were also cold. What had seemed to be a simple hunt had turned into a dangerous undertaking.

Wolf could hear Shadow ahead, whining now and again, more to keep them going, Wolf figured, than in complaint. Pinto Bean kept plodding along without complaint, probably because he was heading home to the stables.

When the pages arrived at the stables, a squire took one look at them and sent a page to the palace for help. Several squires escorted the pages up the stairs and took them to the showers. They helped the boys out of their clothes, which had been soaked with melted snow, and into the hot showers. Once the boys were feeling better, they put on bathrobes, and Raven, Whisperblade, and Bear arrived with pots of hot coffee and hot apple cider. When they returned to their room, they dressed and crawled into their beds under extra blankets. Raven gave them a lecture on the dangers of rapidly changing weather. Bear lectured them about making shelter as necessary to prevent freezing.

Whisperblade demanded to know whose idea it had been to go hunting. As a group, they all said, "Shadow's."

Knowing what would happen next, Wolf said, "It was my responsibility. I suggested hunting when Shadow woke me. I'm the leader, and I failed to protect everybody."

Whisperblade smiled, but it wasn't a reassuring smile. "You're right. You were responsible. I want you in my office at two o'clock tomorrow." She strode out of the room and disappeared down the hallway.

~

Promptly at two the next day, Wolf knocked on Whisperblade's door, and she motioned for him to come in and close the door. Wolf shook but not from the cold.

"Sit down," Whisperblade said, motioning to one of the wingback chairs. She made him sit while she wrote a long document. When she finished, she handed it to him to read. It was an account of the day's adventure.

"This is a report I have to submit to Mrs. Parker. I have to justify why you should stay here. It isn't easy writing these reports." She paused a few seconds, looking at him, before she spoke again. "You're not in trouble. You asked for permission, and you stayed within the bounds of the permission you were given. The orders you had to follow should have been more specific.

"When you saw the overcast skies, you should have inquired as to the weather forecast. That's responsibility. You had three other lives in your hands. When you take on a leadership position, you have to go the extra step of considering the consequences of any choice you make. You can make good decisions. I've seen you do it. I understand you have some rabbits to skin."

Wolf, dismissed, left to go to the stables. That evening when he and a number of his friends were sharing cooked rabbit, his portion tasted somewhat bitter. It would be awhile before he hunted rabbit again.

~

At breakfast the next morning, Bear announced that because of the heavy snow there would be no riding. The pages gave a round of cheers because they had not looked forward to another freezing day. The squires, who knew what was going to happen, groaned.

Bear continued, "What we're going to do is have a little war. We're going to divide you up into two teams. And you're going to have a battle in the palace.

"You can use your staffs, your bows, and wooden practice knives. The arrows will be padded and coated with chalk, as will be the staffs and knives. Blue chalk for team Palace and red chalk for team Stable. If you are marked with chalk, you're dead and out of competition. The knights will be the judges and will pick the teams and appoint the leaders. With each skirmish, a new leader will be chosen. Raven and Whisperblade will now pick the teams."

Once the teams were chosen, they were separated, and Team Stable retreated out to the stables. There they were issued protective facemasks and lightweight arrows with large padded tips coated with red chalk, and they were given red strips of cloth to tie around their arms to identify their team. Wart was chosen as the first leader.

"How do we get to the palace?" Wolf asked. "They'll see us right away."

Raven said, "It's a little known fact, but there's a tunnel running underground to carry heating steam to the stables."

Wart set several pages to look for the tunnel, and then he assigned a small squad to attack the palace from the front as a diversion.

It was a simple and elegant plan. While the attack team of ten pages headed across the open ground to the side of the palace, Wolf, Wart, and everybody else went down the pipe tunnel. It took about ten minutes to find the tunnel, hidden in the second basement of the stables, protected by a locked door. There was some groaning until George produced a big screwdriver and hammer. They started to work on the padlock, but it was too tough. Wart suggested pulling the pins on the door hinges. Sure enough, with a few taps of the hammer and screwdriver, the pins came out, and the door opened.

Wolf and the rest of the pages made their way down the pipe tunnel, which had several sharp bends and was uncomfortably hot. They reached the end of the tunnel and found another door, also locked.

On this door, they were on the wrong side and could not get to the hinge pins. Wolf asked Raven if he could break the lock. Raven allowed that the rules of the game did not forbid it. Wolf set about driving the screwdriver into the doorjamb at the lock, using the hammer until a gap formed. Using his practice knife, he pushed the exposed lock bolt into the lock and the door opened.

The pages poured into the basement from the tunnel. It was dark in the room until someone found the light switch. When the light came on, everybody came to a halt. There on a small table in the middle of the room sat a skull and crossbones, not a Jolly Roger flag, but a real skull and real bones.

Wolf felt like he had been shocked by a bolt of lightning. They were in the second basement, the forbidden basement. He wondered whom the skull belonged to, a knight perhaps. It looked very old.

Raven stepped out of the pipe tunnel and didn't seem surprised at all. He walked over to the table, picked up the skull, and, looking into the empty eye sockets, said, "I wondered where you'd disappeared to. Pages, I want you to meet Oscar. He's part of the skeleton we use in our biology classes. He disappears from the classroom every so often. I've been looking for him for a while."

Whether from the heat from the tunnel or the shock of seeing Oscar, several of the pages looked unnaturally pale. Wolf didn't feel so good himself. Finally, he said, "Let's get out of here." There was agreement, and they started to file out into a hallway.

Raven followed, carrying the skull and bones. "Welcome to the palace dungeon. This is where we keep supplies, old relics, and bad pages. We have lost only three in the last hundred years." There were groans at the bad joke.

Wolf noted that the school had to be at least a hundred years old.

Raven took them to a stairway that led up. When they reached the ground floor, he told the pages they were on their own.

Wart peered out of the doorway, and, seeing no one there, he led his team out into the hallway. He had his team going down the hallway checking each room, looking for their opponents. They weren't having any luck finding the enemy, so they started up the next set of stairs to the main floor. The hallway at the top of the steps appeared to be clear, so Wart led the pages out of the stairway.

As soon as the whole group had gathered in the hallway, somebody yelled, "Fire!" Several doors opened, and pages popped out firing their bows. It turned into a disaster. Team Stable returned fire, but the enemy protected themselves behind the doors.

Wart headed into the first open door that didn't have a defender shooting at them. He lead Wolf and several other attackers, and they found themselves cut off from the hallway when the door slammed shut. They were surrounded by twice as many defenders. They didn't have time to reload their bows. They were attacked by staffs, and they didn't have time to unstrap their own staffs. Their knives were useless against the staffs. It turned into a slaughter. The rest of the team in the hallway was picked off by the archers in the doorways.

Finally, Bear stopped the exercise. The knights conducted a short critique in the closest classroom. They told the pages that attacking through the tunnel was a good idea, but to be fair, the defenders were also told about it. The big mistakes Wart had made were attacking a well-defended position and letting his force be separated. In attacking a well-defended position, they'd lost any advantage in numbers. And to allow your forces to be separated meant that the defenders could attack them with overwhelming odds.

There were several more skirmishes during the day, and the leaders of each team rotated out. Regardless of how they attacked the palace, Team Stable ended up being killed or captured.

"What are we doing wrong?" asked Wart. "They always know what we're going to do."

"Someone is ratting us out," George said.

Wolf said, "But, who? It can't be anyone on our team. One of the older pages, maybe."

"Or a squire," Harold said. "And I think I know who." Everybody looked at him.

"Let me guess, Wayne," Wolf said.

"I haven't seen him, but I've seen Ralph, and he kept coming and going upstairs."

"We're definitely being ratted out, and I think I know how to stop it," Wart said.

"We can't beat him up," Wolf said.

"Well, we don't have to tell him what we're going to do," Harold said.

"But we have to make plans with everybody, and he'll know," Wolf said.

"What I propose is we make our plans like we always do," Harold said. "I suggest a little change."

Harold told them his plan, and they raided a classroom before making their way back to the stables. George announced his plan for the attack, while Wolf, Wart, and Harold passed out a small note to each team member.

Once the plans for the attack were made, the pages stormed out of the stables, and, as a mass, they ran around the backside of the palace heading for the truck entrance to the courtyard. When they got there, they just continued running around to the far side of the palace. Then they bypassed the large side entrance, continued around to the front of the palace, and ran right up the steps to the main entrance.

Once they had entered the palace, they met no opposition. They ran down the hallway to the corner turret and the Lion's office. As they passed each doorway, they found defenders at windows facing into the courtyard. With a window cracked open they had a perfect shot into the courtyard. Team Stable picked off the defenders one room at a time.

Wolf and the lead squad of Team Stable entered the Lion's office. He sat at his desk smiling. George entered the office and, pointing his staff at the Lion, declared, "In the name of Team Stable, I declare you my prisoner."

"I surrender," the Lion answered, throwing up his arms.

During the debriefing, it was brought out that Team Palace believed the attackers were coming into the courtyard where there were multiple entrances into the palace. That had been the plan that George had announced. There was rumbling among the pages, and it was obvious Team Palace had found out Team Stable's plans.

George revealed that secret plans had been distributed to supersede his announced intentions. George did not reveal who he thought the rat had been or even that he suspected there was one. The lesson seemed obvious—secrets need to remain secret.

They played the game for several weekends during the winter. Everybody had at least one chance to be a leader, and not all battles were fought in the palace. A lot were fought outside; some were in the stables; and some were in the gardens, the practice yards, and even the forest. There were no more security breaches after the pages discovered the importance of good plans. When he became the leader, Wolf fought his battle in the gardens and orchards. His team won, but he was shot and killed while climbing over a garden wall.

Chapter 34 ~ Saving Grace

When the weather started to get warmer, the usual outdoor activities resumed, and Wolf worked on his riding skills and training the horses. Wolf's self-defense and staff fighting classes kept getting more and more intense. He took several hard hits in self-defense and had the wind knocked out of him when he took a hard kick to the stomach. Once he could start breathing again, he threw up his breakfast, which earned him a trip to the nurse. While there, the nurse gave him a quick check up and told him that he had grown three inches since he had joined the school.

Staff fighting was hard on the hands, and smashed fingers were a frequent occurrence. His instructor told him that as he improved with the staff there would be less smashed fingers. Red helped him in the evenings by showing him some of the finer points of trying to whack a person with a broom handle. She even showed him how to break the handle off the broom head quickly, thus making an instant staff.

Raven announced that he had to make a trip to Richmond to attend to school business. It wouldn't be more than a day, and he asked if Wolf wanted to come along. It wasn't unusual for pages or squires to travel with their knights.

Wolf, ready for a break from classes, jumped at the offer. Raven told Wolf to wear his best school uniform and pack a change of clothes. Wolf arose at three in the morning, dressed, and waited at the front of the palace until Raven drove around in an old pickup truck. It was one used to haul feed and hay to the school from town and was very decrepit.

Wolf climbed into the cab and Raven started driving. As soon as they were hidden from the palace by the trees, Raven pulled to a stop and asked, "Would you like to drive?"

"But, sir, I'm only fourteen."

"Then it's time that you learn the basics. If you can ride a horse, you can drive a truck. It's a skill you need to learn and learn early."

"This is crazy. I can't even reach the pedals."

"You'll manage. The first lesson is the clutch. It's the connection between the engine and the transmission."

The Raven brought Wolf's palms together and slightly twisting one wrist caused the other hand to twist. "The clutch is like your palms. As you release the clutch pedal, the clutch plates approach each other. When they start to touch each other, the plate on the engine, which is spinning, will start to make the transmission plate spin. You have to ease them together. Once the transmission and wheels are turning, you can release the pedal."

Raven proceeded to demonstrate with the truck. Then it came Wolf's turn in the driver's seat. After a few tries where he stalled the engine, he managed to get the truck to move. Then he had to learn was to use the brakes. Soon an hour had passed, and it came time to get on the road with Raven driving.

They drove for the rest of the morning, stopping after daybreak for breakfast to gas up the truck and put a quart of oil in the engine. Raven pulled into a parking garage, and they walked to Riverfront Plaza East, where they took an elevator to the fifteenth floor and entered the law office of Rosencrantz and Guildenstern.

The receptionist looked up at them, and her face lit up with a big smile. "Raven! It's so nice to see you again. What brings you this way?"

"School business, Miss Harper. Is Mr. Rosencrantz in today?"

"Yes, sir. He's expecting you. Please walk in." She pointed to an open door.

"Wait here, Wolf."

Wolf waited until Raven came out of the office with Mr. Rosencrantz, who came over and offered his hand. "I'm so glad to meet you. We've been following your progress with great interest."

"Does everybody know about me?" Wolf asked. "I'm just an orphan."

"The school is our biggest client. We handle all its legal matters, including your problems. We took care of that nasty business involving the supermarket in the mountains, and we're working on your adoption."

"Is that why I'm here?"

"Yes and no," Raven replied. "They just wanted to meet you, and I thought you could use a break from the school routine."

"Thank you, I think."

"Let's grab a bite to eat," Mr. Rosencrantz said. "I'm hungry. Are you coming, Miss Harper?"

"I would love to."

They bought Joe's Wood Fired Pizza from a truck outside and took their lunch to a table in the breezeway of the office building. After lunch, Mr. Rosencrantz and Miss Harper returned to the office. Raven took Wolf to a park a few blocks away to exercise. They met a few office workers doing the same thing, and they tried the exercises the office workers were doing. After an hour, Raven said it was time to return to the office building.

They were walking the first block back when they crossed an access alleyway. They hadn't cleared the alley when Raven stopped and stared down it, looking at something Wolf couldn't see. After a few seconds, he leaned down to whisper in Wolf's ear, "Stay well behind me. See if you can make yourself a staff." With no explanation, Raven started running down the alley.

Wolf, still surprised, tried to catch up with Raven while looking for a long stick. Up ahead, he saw Raven crash into a standing man who faced into a corner. He saw another man who stooped down, repeatedly hitting a third person. Raven slammed the first man into a wall, and, when the man bent over, Raven reached around and grabbed the back of his head, pulling it down as he brought his knee up into the man's face. The man went down like a sack of potatoes.

Wolf found a stick the size of a bat, not a staff, but it would work. Raven turned his attention to the second man who started to stand up. Raven gave a side kick into the man's belly, and he fell backwards while doubling up. Wolf saw out the side of his eye the first man trying to get up

253

to his knees. The man reached into his coat and pulled out a handgun. Wolf yelled and swung the stick over his head and down onto the man's wrist. There was an audible crunch, and the gun popped out of the man's hand. Raven delivered a kick to the man's face, knocking him out.

Wolf turned his attention to the person the second man had been punching, who appeared to be a boy, tall and skinny, with ill cut blond hair. He wore nasty denim trousers and a jacket. Wolf tried to see if he was alive. His face was smeared with blood, but he was breathing. Raven knelt down, pulled out a handkerchief, and started to clean his face. After a minute, the boy started to move and groaned a little. Raven asked, "What's your name?" All he got in reply was more groaning.

He asked again, and the boy mumbled, "Grace."

She was a girl. Wolf and the Raven helped her sit up. Raven asked her if she knew where she was. She seemed confused by the question. Raven gently picked her up and started carrying her to the entrance of the alley.

"What about them?" Wolf asked pointing back at the men lying in the corner.

"Leave them," Raven said. "We can't do anything about them. She's more important." They left the alley and started walking up the street toward the law office, ignoring all the stares they received from pedestrians. They soon reached the office building and went to the elevator. People in the lobby gave them a wide berth, and they had the elevator to themselves.

Once the door to the elevator had shut, Wolf blurted out, "She needs to go to the hospital."

"That's the last place she needs to be. If her injuries are too bad, we'll take her to another hospital besides the local one. Whoever did this will be looking for her. We can't have her in the same emergency room." After they reached their floor, they went to the law office and entered.

Miss Harper stood up and gasped. Then she called for Mr. Rosencrantz. Raven laid the girl on the couch and started a physical exam. There were no broken bones, but she was badly bruised, and there were several cuts on her face, around the eyes. Miss Harper brought out a first aid kit and some washcloths and towels. After Raven finished explaining what had happened, Mr. Rosencrantz made a couple of phone calls.

Raven cleaned the girl's face with the washcloths and towels. Then using some hydrogen peroxide solution, he started to flush the cuts that were located around the eyes, the cheekbones and her chin, being careful to keep the peroxide out of her eyes. Her eyes started to swell shut. The cleaning solution revived her, and she started to fight Raven while Miss Harper gently soothed her and told her she as safe.

Finally, she calmed down and tried to sit up. Wolf helped her into a sitting position. Then she bolted for the door, but she had lost her sense of balance and fell. She would have been hurt if Raven hadn't caught her. She collapsed in his arms crying. He sat her down on the couch, and Miss Harper sat beside her.

Mr. Rosencrantz told them, "A doctor should be here any minute, but she's going to take her to a hospital."

"No hospitals!" the girl exclaimed.

"Do you know where you are?" Raven asked.

She looked around a minute and said, "I'm not supposed to be here, am I?"

"You're right where you need to be," Raven answered. "How old are you?"

"Nineteen."

"Try again."

She didn't respond, and Raven didn't ask again. Instead, he asked, "What's your name?"

The girl asked, "What's yours?"

"I'm called Raven."

"That's a girl's name."

Raven smiled and said, "It could be. It's what I'm called. Now I've told you my name. What's yours?"

"Grace ... just Grace."

Raven extended his right hand and said, "Grace Just Grace, it's a pleasure to meet you."

Grace took his hand. "You ... beat up those two men didn't you?"

"Yes."

"They'll kill you if they find you. They're gang members."

"I'm sure of it, but they'll have to get in line behind everyone else who wants to kill me."

The doctor entered the office from the hallway, took one look at Grace, and exclaimed, "Oh, my!" She pulled Miss Harper and Raven away from the girl and said, "Girl, you need to be in a hospital."

"No hospitals! They'll kill me if they find me."

The doctor looked at Mr. Rosencrantz. He shook his head slightly. "I don't like it, but I'll see what I can do for you." She started a physical exam of the girl. When she finished, she looked at the men and said, "She doesn't appear to have any internal injuries, but she's going to take a long time to fully recover from this beating. I hope they catch the bastards who did this."

The doctor opened her case and started to prepare a syringe. "This is a pain killer," she said.

"No drugs," Grace said.

"Why not?"

"I can't have any."

The doctor seemed to accept this. "It's going to hurt real bad without any pain killer." She put away the syringe, but started preparing another one. "I'm still going to give you antibiotics so you won't get an infection that could make you very sick."

"I can take it."

"This is going to sting." She gave the shot in her arm, and the girl tensed up tight. "Are you sure you don't want any pain killer?"

"I'm sure."

The doctor opened the sterile kit and donned gloves. First, she cleaned the girl's face with an antiseptic. Grace winced, but she didn't make a sound. The doctor then opened a package containing a fine needle and started working on the worst cuts around the girl's eyes. For the lesser cuts, she used small adhesive strips to hold the cuts closed. Then she applied sterile adhesive bandages to the wounds.

When she finished, she pulled her gloves off and said, "She's going to need more work from a plastic surgeon before tomorrow to keep the scarring to a minimum. Whoever did this should be strung up. It was done deliberately to ruin her looks. I can give you the names of a couple of good facial surgeons." She scribbled the names on a notepad on Miss Harper's desk, tore the page out, and handed it to Raven.

"Thank you, doctor," Raven said. "She'll see one in the morning. We need to keep this quiet. She has reason to fear for her life."

"I understand, so this is between us. I've done business with Mr. Rosencrantz before. This one's on me."

"Thank you," Mr. Rosencrantz said.

"Just keep her out of trouble, and take her to the surgeon early tomorrow morning at the latest."

"That I most certainly will," Raven said, as the doctor took her leave.

"What's this keeping me out of trouble? I can take care of myself," Grace said.

"You've done a smash up job of it, too," Raven said. "You need help, and I can give it to you."

"I don't need your help."

"I'll have to turn you over to the law if no other solution to your problem can be found," Mr. Rosencrantz said. "If you go with Raven, I can possibly make your problems go away."

"Trust them. I did," Wolf said.

"What's your name?" Grace asked. "Are you two related?"

"Wolf, and no, we're not related. I'm just his student."

"Wolf! Why should I believe you? Wolf's a weird name, worse than Raven. Did he give it to you?"

"No, but I have a real wolf."

"Is it a real wild, vicious wolf?"

"He's real, and he's wild, but he isn't vicious. He sleeps with me."

"You don't sleep with a wolf! Can I see him?"

"Sure, he's at the school."

Her expression went sour. "I don't go to school."

"It's a shame. We have horses."

Grace asked, "Can I see the horses?"

"You can ride them," Raven said.

She looked down and said, "I don't know how to ride a horse."

"We'll teach you."

"How far is this school?"

"A half day's drive from here," Wolf said.

"I'd like to see the horses."

"We'll see if that is possible," Mr. Rosencrantz said. "Meanwhile, why don't you go with Raven and Wolf to find a room for the night? I have to make a number of phone calls to arrange things. We need to see what we can do about your cuts in the morning."

The three of them left the office and crossed the street to a hotel where Raven booked a room with double beds. He sent Wolf to the truck to fetch their bags. When Wolf returned, he found Raven alone; Grace was in the bathroom. Raven told her to toss her bloody clothes out the door so they could be washed. "I'm going to get us a table at the restaurant downstairs. Wolf, let her use one of your uniforms," Raven said, so Wolf took one out of his bag and passed it through the door to her.

When Grace came out, Wolf saw his uniform fit her, except for being too short in the arms and legs. She started for the door, but he held up a hand to stop her and said, "I thought you might want something to eat before you leave."

They found Raven at the hotel restaurant and ate from the buffet. Grace ate more than Wolf could. When she couldn't eat any more, she excused herself to use the bathroom. Wolf figured she'd try to escape back onto the street, so he waited outside the restrooms.

"Before you leave can we talk?"

"How did you know I was leaving?"

Wolf grinned and said, "I would if I were you."

"Well, I wasn't leaving," Grace snapped.

Wolf and Grace walked into the lobby and sat down in a quiet corner where Wolf explained, "I'm an orphan, and I was in jail. Raven saved me from juvenile detention. I think it was a good thing I went with him."

"It smells like a trap. He just wants me to be a slave for him, just like the others. He looks like he could kill me if he wanted to."

"He saved your life for real. I was there. That means he's obligated to look out for you. You should at least give him the chance."

"What if I don't like him?"

"Then you can leave."

Grace was quiet for a moment and then said, "Tell me about the horses."

Wolf told her about Nudge, who was too young to be ridden. Next, he told her about Shadow and wolves in general. Before he knew it, it had turned late, so he suggested talking back up to the room. She agreed, and they went upstairs to the room where they found Raven at the desk working on various papers. When it came time to sleep, Grace had one bed. Raven had the other, and Wolf slept on the couch.

In the morning, they walked several blocks to a plastic surgeon's office. The doctor was waiting for Grace. Wolf and Raven watched as he used local painkillers to make the work tolerable for Grace. He worked fast and made the smallest stitches. For most of the wounds, he used glue and surgical tape, to reduce the scarring.

When he finished, he bandaged Grace's wounds, and they went back to the lawyer's office, where Miss Harper gave Grace a scarf to wear over her head and face. Mr. Rosencrantz told them, "Two gang members have been admitted to the hospital with serious internal injuries and broken bones. They aren't talking about how they were injured. As soon as they're well enough to be released, they'll be going to jail because of outstanding warrants against them. You wouldn't know anything about that would you?"

Raven shrugged his shoulders and mumbled, "They must have tripped and fallen down."

Wolf smirked at Raven's explanation.

"Just be careful about where you walk. I don't want to be bailing you out of jail for accidentally tripping a citizen of our fair city," warned Mr. Rosencrantz.

Raven finished his business with Mr. Rosencrantz, and they left to go to the garage. When Grace saw the old truck, she said, "That's a piece of junk."

"It was the only vehicle available yesterday," Raven explained.

"He was teaching me to drive," Wolf offered.

It took four hours to return to the school, and it was a quiet trip. Grace had a few questions for Wolf about Shadow and about the horses, but she seemed to be absorbed in her own thoughts. When Wolf asked her how she came to live on the street, she refused to answer. They stopped once to service the truck and once to eat a late lunch. When they turned off the highway under the arched, wrought iron sign of the riding school, Grace looked around and asked where the school was.

"You'll see it soon enough," Wolf said, and, after a couple of minutes of driving on the twisting road, they broke out from the trees into the large field forming the grounds of the school.

Grace pointed at the palace and asked, "Who lives there?"

"You do, if you decide to stay," Raven said.

She pointed to the other equally impressive building. "What is that?"

"The stables. That's where I live," Wolf replied.

They parked at front of the palace. Raven ordered Wolf to escort Grace to the headmaster's office.

Wolf extended a hand to Grace. "Shall we go inside and meet the Lion?"

Chapter 35 ~ The Scarecrow

The Lion extended a warm welcome to Grace, Wolf, and Raven, and they talked about the school for a few minutes. Then the Lion called for another page and had him go and ask Lady Jane to come to their meeting. When Lady Jane arrived, he said, "Grace, since you have no guardian, I'm placing you in Lady Jane's care. She attended this school as a student, so she might be able to help you."

Grace said, "I don't like foster parents."

Lady Jane didn't skip a beat. "I had foster parents."

Before Grace could reply, the Lion announced, "It's settled then. Now, as to the important matter of your status as a student, I'll offer you a month without conditions to see if you want to stay here."

"But I don't deserve this. Why are you doing this? Do you just pick up kids off of the street?"

"Raven brought you to me. That's all the recommendation I need. I have a few discretionary scholarships each year. Wolf is one of them. Talk to him. If you don't stay, I'll place you in a good foster home."

"Why should I stay here?"

"I think I can answer that," Raven said. "You're now invisible to the gangs back in the city."

The Lion said, "You'll be expected to study and to carry your fair share of caring for the horses like any other student. Even I have to care for my horses."

"And you'll teach me to ride horses?"

The Lion said, "Our teachers will. You'll learn all about horses."

Lady Jane said, "Grace, of all the things we teach at this school, we'll teach you to defend yourself. You should never have to fear anyone again."

"Please accept the hospitality of the school for a month," continued the Lion. "After a month perhaps, we can agree on what you'll do. You won't be turned loose to live on the street again."

"Why are you doing this for me? I'm not worth it."

"You're worth it, as much as any other student," the Lion said. He swung his arm around, indicating the whole school. "I'm doing it because I've obligated my life to saving lives. You're no less than anyone else is. I'm too old to go around battling street gangs like Raven does, but I can still save you."

Grace agreed to stay for a month, so Wolf offered to escort her for a quick tour of the palace and stables. The Lion also told him to pick up some proper uniforms for Grace to wear in place of the ill-fitting one he had loaned to her.

Wolf took her to the quartermaster's office, and she was fitted. After she had changed in a fitting room, they went to the stables to see the horses and to meet Shadow. Grace froze when she saw the wolf. Shadow sniffed at her for a minute. Finally, Shadow started licking her hand, and Wolf told her she had passed her first test with animals. Wolf introduced her to Nudge and his mother Mary.

"I can't believe how big Mary is," Grace said. "I've seen police horses in the city, but they're nowhere near this big." Wolf showed her how to hold out apples in her flat palms for the horses.

Then Wolf took Grace for a quick tour of the palace. In the dining hall, they had sandwiches, and Shadow had fresh meat. He showed her where some of the other offices were, particularly Lady Jane's office.

With the tour over, Wolf took Grace to find Lady Jane. In the hallway, they met Whisperblade, who stopped them and examined Grace's face for a moment. Whisperblade said, "You'll attend my self-defense class at six o'clock in the morning in the south pasture."

Wolf saw Grace was about to object, but Whisperblade cut her off with, "No buts about this, you'll attend. Your life depends upon it." Whisperblade turned and walked away.

"Who's that?" Grace asked.

"She is Whisperblade, my mother."

"I thought you were an orphan."

"I am. She's adopting me."

"I feel sorry for you."

"Thanks," Wolf said.

They eventually found Lady Jane back in her office. She took charge of Grace while Wolf went to the stables. He had a lot of homework to make up.

~

The next morning, Whisperblade paired Wolf with Grace in the self-defense class. Grace's face was still swollen, bruised, and bandaged from the surgery she'd had the day before. She participated in the meditation exercise and then tried the basic self-defense exercises. She seemed to understand what to do and seemed to be doing well.

Grace delivered two punches at Wolf's chest, which he easily blocked. She followed with two more rapid punches to his belly, and the second escaped his block, a hard punch, not the light tap that Wolf expected. Wolf doubled over and came right back up only to receive another punch into the chest.

Whisperblade stopped the exercise and said, "Pull your punches. This is a defense exercise."

When they restarted, Wolf delivered two punches, which Grace blocked. She then returned a hard punch to his shoulder. Wolf knew it would leave a nasty bruise.

Grace seemed to realize what she had done and started pulling her punches.

After the lesson finished, Whisperblade pulled Wolf aside and said, "She seemed pretty rough on you."

"Yes, Master. It's like she was fighting for real, for her life."

"She is. Grace is a street fighter and doesn't know any other way of fighting. She doesn't trust anyone yet. You're going to have to give her that trust."

"I don't know how to do that."

"Yes, you do. Amara taught you." Then Whisperblade said, "Grace is in a lot of pain. Whoever cut her face also took away her identity.

Imagine looking in a mirror and not recognizing yourself. That's hard on a girl."

~

The next day, Wolf and Grace, with Shadow on a leash, entered the dining hall and got their breakfast, and Wolf picked up a bowl of raw meat for Shadow. When they were standing at their table, Wolf realized the room was quiet. Wolf looked around and saw everyone staring at Grace. She started to shake nervously. Wolf whispered into her ear, and she burst out laughing. The noise picked up as the students started talking again. After the Lion gave the blessing, Wolf introduced Grace to all his roommates and friends. Wart asked Wolf, "What did you whisper to her?"

"Imagine everybody bald."

"That's a good one," Harold said.

Despite the pleasantries, Grace remained very quiet during the meal. Afterward, Grace asked Wolf about his roommates. "Are they all right? I mean, do you trust them?"

"I never trusted anybody until I came to this school. I trust them. These are the best friends I could have."

~

Wolf didn't see Grace for the rest of the day until after dinner. He was mucking Pinto Bean's stall and shoveling the manure into the wheelbarrow when she showed up. Surprised, he barely missed hitting her with the shovel. "Sorry, I didn't see you standing there."

"It's my fault. I snuck up on you. Do they always make you work this hard? It stinks in here."

"If you want to ride horses, you have to be willing to take care of them. They have as much right to be comfortable as we do. This is Pinto Bean. Would you like to ride him?"

"Can I?"

"Just as soon as I finish shoveling."

Grace grabbed an extra shovel to help him with the chore. When they were done, Wolf led Pinto Bean and Easy Rider out of their stalls and started to saddle them up. Grace kept asking questions about horses and their tack. She seemed surprised to learn that Red owned two horses and that only about half the horses belonged to the school. The rest belonged to the students and knights.

Once Pinto Bean had been prepared, Wolf boosted Grace into the saddle, and then he mounted Easy Rider. He took Pinto Bean's reins and led him out of the stables into the cool evening air. Once they were outside, Wolf had the two horses walk around the field for a while. He tried to explain what she needed to do to control the horse. Talking through the instruction didn't work, so he dismounted Easy Rider and mounted Pinto Bean behind Grace. He reached his arms around her to hold onto the reins. Grace froze solid as soon as his arms touched her sides.

"What's the matter?" Wolf asked.

"I can't ... Don't put your arms around me."

Wolf dismounted and, still holding the reins, walked the horses back into the stables.

Once back, Wolf helped Grace out of the saddle, and the two of them unsaddled both horses. "Thank you," Grace said.

"For what?"

"For trying to teach me to ride."

"I didn't do a very good job of it."

"You tried. Can we do it again later?"

"I guess so, but you'll still have to take real lessons."

"How old are you?"

"Fourteen, almost fifteen," Wolf answered. "You're not even eighteen yet, are you?"

"No." Grace's face reddened. She turned and left the stables. Wolf didn't see her again until the next morning.

~

In self-defense class, Grace was again paired with Wolf, and she attacked hard and relentlessly. Wolf could barely block her wild kicks and punches. He thought he was doing well until she landed a kick to his ribs, and he collapsed to the ground out of breath.

Whisperblade attended to him immediately. He regained his breath, and Whisperblade had him sit up. When he looked at Grace, she was crying. Whisperblade said, "Page Grace, it was an accident. Accidents happen. I need for you to calm down."

When Grace stopped crying, Whisperblade commanded her, "Escort Page Wolf to the nurse, and, while you're there, have her check on your stitches." She grabbed Grace's right hand and placed the girl's arm over Wolf's shoulder and sent them walking towards the palace.

"I'm so sorry. Does it still hurt?"

"Some, it's hurting a little to breathe. Why did you kick so hard?"

"I don't know." Grace started crying again.

"Don't worry about it. We all make mistakes. Besides, it's not that bad. You should have seen some of the bruises I've received."

They arrived at the nurse's office, and Grace started to leave, but the nurse ordered her to stay. The nurse did a quick exam on Wolf and told him he would have a huge bruise, but nothing else was wrong. She told him he could leave.

Wolf excused from physical training for the rest of the day and took the opportunity to work with Shadow and Nudge. Just before lunch, Grace found him at the stables washing Nudge. "I'm sorry about this morning. I forgot I was supposed to be learning exercises, not street fighting. I don't know what happened to me."

"I let my guard down. I was concentrating on getting the exercise right. I didn't expect you to go weird on me. You're a good fighter. Did somebody teach you that?"

"A guy named Jacky taught me some punches and kicks, but I learned by trying to keep from being beat up by the others, or worse. I learned real good until Jacky got drunk and beat me to a pulp. I got over him real quick, but I had to stay with the gang."

"Didn't you try to get help from anybody, the police?"

"They wanted to put me with another foster parent. The last time I was in foster care it didn't go very well, so I managed to escape."

"I'm sorry. It makes my story look like nothing. You were out on the street a long time, weren't you? Is that why you cut your hair?"

"To look like a boy," Grace said, finishing his question. "Yeah, but it didn't work very well."

"Well, I'm sorry about asking your age yesterday. I've been told several times that you don't ask a lady her age. It was rude of me."

"I'm no lady."

"It doesn't matter. You should be treated like one. Lady Jane has been teaching us how." Wolf turned Nudge loose in the pasture to be with Mary and the other foals. Nudge then rolled in the dust, spoiling the washing he had received. Grace giggled, the first time Wolf had seen her laugh on her own.

"So much for washing your horse," she said.

"He would come right back for another washing if I let him. Horses love it. Wait until I tell you what Shadow does when he washes."

~

Over the next couple of weeks Grace's face changed colors as the bruising and swelling decreased. The nurse removed the stitches as the cuts healed. Lady Jane showed Grace how to use cosmetics to reduce the redness of the scars. Then she trimmed Grace's already short hair so she would look more feminine and less like a street kid. Wolf thought the transformation worked miracles.

Once Grace became more comfortable on a horse, she was assigned to a riding class. Wolf noticed that Grace was not very sociable, and he didn't see her much during his free time. Mostly she would come to the stables to help Wolf when he cleaned stalls or repaired tack. Wolf asked Red to help her, but she said the best way was for Grace to learn from her mistakes. She did promise to look out for her somewhat.

Red told Wolf that Squire Margaret had explained to Grace how the school worked and how to get along with the other girls, but Grace still didn't socialize with the other students very well. She just hung around with Wolf and his friends.

When Wolf asked Whisperblade about why Grace remained so distant from others, she replied that Grace didn't have a normal childhood, and she didn't get to play with anyone. Whisperblade said Grace was in a lot of pain in her mind and her heart as well as from the pain of the beatings she'd received, and it would take a long time for her to recover.

267

Whisperblade also said Grace needed a friend, someone who would listen to her when she was ready to talk, and Wolf appeared to be that person. She warned Wolf never to talk to others about whatever Grace told him.

Wolf noticed that Grace paid careful attention to her self-defense lessons and didn't go wild on him again. She worked hard at her practice sessions, and he observed her meditating by herself even when not in class.

Soon after Grace started at the school, Ernie, one of Wayne's classmates, started teasing Wolf about hanging out with "the scarecrow." Wolf's ears turned red, and he came close to hitting Ernie. He hated name-calling. He knew the name referred to Grace's bone-skinny appearance and scars. Wolf hadn't really thought about it before. He had just thought of her as slim.

Wolf asked Grace, "Do you know what you're being called?"

"Yeah, the scarecrow."

"Doesn't it bother you?"

"Yeah, but what can I do? I've been called worse. I'd like to pulverize whoever came up with it."

Wolf suspected who had started it, but kept quiet because he didn't want Grace to get in trouble. "They kind of frown on fighting. Do you know the rule?"

"No, but I can guess. Whatever you do, you get punished somehow."

"No, well, yes. You don't snitch. You tell the adults you fell down or something like that. Then you take your punishment. It will probably be extra chores or homework. You get more schoolwork than you can do anyway. Everybody gets too much work. They say it challenges you to do better."

"I get it. You don't rat on your enemy, and you get to work harder."

"They're very fair about it, and everybody gets the same punishment. Don't worry, none of the adults will hit or hurt you. Watch out for some of the rich kids. A couple of them, especially Wayne, can be cruel. He hates me, and I suppose he already hates you. Wart isn't like that. He's my best friend. He's my first friend."

"I kind of like it when they call me the scarecrow. It's a lot better than some of the things people use to call me. People can be cruel."

"Keep up with self-defense. Everybody respects that."

"Can we go riding later?"

"Sure. We could go hunting rabbit with Shadow. You'll like it."

Later that afternoon, Wolf asked Raven, and Grace asked Lady Jane, for permission to go hunting. They saddled Pinto Bean and Nellie, a mare assigned to Grace, and headed out on a wooded path to a meadow. Shadow followed at some distance and seemed to be looking for something.

They reached the meadow, dismounted, and hobbled the horses. Wolf strung his bow and placed his knife in his belt. He started walking back and forth across the meadow with Grace following behind. When he found a rabbit run, he motioned for Grace to be quiet, and they slowly walked down the trail. Wolf spotted the faintest of motion from a rabbit. He raised his bow with an arrow in the notch, and another in his left hand, which gripped the bow. He stood still for a long minute making sure of his shot, trying to see if any other rabbits were about.

Finally, he let loose and nailed the rabbit to the ground. The rabbit did not die right away so Wolf dropped his bow, ran to it, and grabbed it behind the neck. He used his knife to cut its throat for a quick kill. He turned to Grace and saw she was quietly crying.

"I had to finish it off. To let it suffer would have been cruel."

"I didn't know it would be so violent, so bloody."

Wolf said, "It's how it's done." He laid out the rabbit, sliced its belly open and cleaned out the internals. Grace threw up. He washed the rabbit with water from his water skin and removed the arrow.

~

Once Grace had recovered, they walked back to the horses, where Wolf wrapped the rabbit in a clean cloth and hung it from his saddle. Then they mounted their horses and quietly headed back to the stables.

As they were taking care of the horses, Grace turned to Wolf and said, "I know hunting rabbit is what it is, but I've seen too much blood, not just my own. I don't know if I could kill a helpless animal.

"I think I understand. I don't mind blood, but I can see why some people would," Wolf said.

"Have you ever wanted to kill somebody?" Grace asked.

"I almost did, twice."

"That's not what I asked. Did you want to kill?"

"No, being a knight is about saving lives. That's what Raven does."

"And all the swordplay these knights do—isn't it about killing?"

Wolf said, "He didn't kill those two who were beating you to a pulp."

"I would have killed them!" Grace said. She turned and stalked off, leaving Wolf to stare after her.

Chapter 36 ~ Congratulations

On a warm late spring day, Wolf received a summons from class to the Lion's office. He knew the Lion was a good man and a knight, and, as the headmaster of the school, he took an active interest in Shadow's wellbeing. But to be summoned out of class was never good. When he entered the Lion's office, in addition to the Lion, there stood Whisperblade, Raven, and Mrs. Parker. Wolf bowed then extended his hand to greet Mrs. Parker. The Lion invited everybody to sit at the coffee table.

"I understand you had an adventure in the city," Mrs. Parker said. She pointed to a folder on the low table. "It says here you were again placed in danger. A man pulled a gun intending to use it."

"I knew what I had to do. I had a staff and I knocked the gun away. I think I broke his wrist."

"You were very brave."

"I didn't think about that. We saved Grace's life. That's what was important."

"Nevertheless, you knew what to do. Risking one's life to save another is a noble thing, but it's a hard lesson at such a young age." Mrs. Parker picked up the folder and opened it to a tabbed page. "I see you have, hmm, had a few more philosophical differences of opinion. Would you care to explain?"

Wolf began to see where this conversation would go and said, "I was discussing my friend's honor."

"It seems he could do that on his own."

"She is new to this school and not familiar with the differences of opinion that might occur. I stepped in to suggest a compromise, but it wasn't accepted."

"Is this the same girl you rescued?"

"Yes, ma'am. She became my responsibility when I helped rescue her. I helped bring her here. I have to bear a part of the burden for her safety. She's a good friend, and I won't abandon her."

"My, those are very strong words on your part. Wolf, I would have been proud to have had you as one of my children. Reviewing your records, I find that you must have learned something important here. There's nothing about saving lives in your lesson plans. I must have a long conversation with Raven about it. His teaching methods are most unusual. Not many people teach by example any more.

"After a full review of your records, I find you're very well cared for. Your education is excellent, and I think Miss Whisperblade will do you well as a mother. I'm approving your status as a foster child and recommending that your adoption by Miss Whisperblade be approved." Mrs. Parker handed a folder to Whisperblade and said, "Those are the approvals for foster status." She handed another folder to the Whisperblade, but looked straight at Wolf and, "That's my recommendation for your adoption. Congratulations, your status as a foster child to Miss Whisperblade is official."

Wolf let out a breath of air and said, "Thank you, ma'am."

Whisperblade said, "Thank you, Mrs. Parker. I'll do everything in my power to ensure that Wolf will become a good man. I've raised several sons and daughters, and he's one of the best sons I've had. I expect he'll go on to do great things. Raven and I have worked as a team for a long time."

The Lion said, "I take a great personal interest in Wolf. When I brought him into this school, I pledged myself to provide him with a family. I'll live up to that pledge as long as I live."

"I pledge," Raven said, "to see to his education in all its many aspects."

The Lion stood up and everybody else followed. He extended his hand to Wolf, but then pulled him into a hug. "Congratulations, Wolf. However, I think I'm holding you from your classes. If you'll excuse us, I have other matters to discuss with Mrs. Parker."

Dismissed, Wolf left the office along with Raven and his official mother, Whisperblade. "What does this mean for me? She was like a different person."

Raven answered, "It is not much of a change for you. You still have the same duties you had before."

"And we have the same duties to you," Whisperblade added. "I don't know what has changed with Mrs. Parker. Don't you have a class you're supposed to be attending?"

Wolf ran to his next class. Despite what the knights had said, he felt a nervous energy. He felt glad about his foster status, but he also wondered what he had gotten himself into. He remembered he had once thought about running away. His world suddenly seemed so different. He still had unanswered questions about the school, and he began to wonder if it would always be so.

~

He received a big answer and a big shock the next morning when he went to his history class. The teacher had not arrived when he entered the room. When a teacher did come in, it turned out to be Mrs. Parker. She wore a school uniform with a skirt instead of trousers. "Good morning students, I'm Mrs. Parker, your substitute for this week." She wrote her name on the blackboard, turned around, and surveyed the pages. "I believe I've met one of you already. Wolf and I have had several conversations, and I'm most impressed with him and the school."

There was some mumbling in the classroom, and Wolf turned red from embarrassment. "I expect you all to be apt students." There were groans from all the pages. Mrs. Parker didn't give the pages any more time to contemplate their fate but launched into her lesson plan, a long discussion about the differences between the French and American revolutions.

At the end of class, Mrs. Parker asked Wolf to stay for a minute. "I just wanted to explain why I'm here and to answer any questions you might have. I'm trained as a teacher. I worked in the foster program, but I wasn't happy. You showed me what a good school could do, and I became interested in becoming a part of it."

"How does this affect me?" Wolf asked. "I mean my adoption."

"For the best, I hope. I left my old job on very good terms, and my recommendations will be followed. I believe you have nothing to fear from the state, and the adoption process should continue."

"Are you a tough teacher?"

"Very." She then smiled and said, "Well, I at least expect a lot from you. You seemed to enjoy the lesson."

"Yes, ma'am." Wolf thought about it and then said, "Yes, teacher."

"I'll be staying at the school on weekdays, so I'd appreciate it if you would find time to show me around."

"I'd be happy to."

"Good, now you need to go to your next class."

~

Word traveled fast around the school that Wolf would be adopted by Whisperblade. It was a unique position to be in. Wolf couldn't put his finger on it, but he knew he was being treated differently by most of the students.

Wolf stood in the bathroom when Squire Wayne walked in. The squire looked around, walked up to Wolf, and said, "There's no one around to help you now. You can't hide behind your mother's skirt." Wayne took a low swing into Wolf's belly. Unable to block it quick enough, Wolf doubled over, fell back, and hit the wall with his head.

Wolf awoke in the nurse's office. He looked into the faces of the nurse and Whisperblade. When he tried to sit up, his mother held him down. "You had a nasty fall. It seems you slipped."

"How?"

"The floor was very wet."

"Oh," Wolf thought a second. He didn't even remember falling. "I didn't see it."

"You've got to pay more attention to everything around you. But I shouldn't have to tell you that."

The nurse gave Wolf a quick exam and pronounced him fit.

Wolf felt the back of his head, he had a bump, and it hurt. He sat up and, reassuring his mother that he felt all right, begged permission to go to class.

The nurse restricted him from any physical activity for the rest of the day, and, for once, Whisperblade agreed with her.

After leaving the nurse, he finally remembered what had happened. He realized Wayne had covered his tracks well by putting water on the floor.

Wolf met Wart in the library for their study group. It took only two minutes for Wart to figure out something bad had happened, and he said, "Out with it Wolf."

"What? Nothing's going on."

"I knew it!" Wart exclaimed, pointing at Wolf, "You've been in a fight."

"It wasn't a fight."

"What was it then, a picnic?"

Wolf sighed. "Wayne sucker punched me in the bathroom."

Wart snapped to his feet and said, "You know better!"

"Yeah, I just wasn't expecting him to hit, since he's a squire."

Wart furrowed his forehead and said, "Wolf, listen to me, a rule like that isn't going to stop Wayne."

Wolf shrugged his shoulders. "I suppose you're right."

Wart put his hands on his hips. "You know I'm right."

Wolf looked down. "Yeah, you're right."

"Get smart. We'll take care of Wayne later. He's declared war, so we'll give him what he asked for. Now let's study."

The rest of the day seemed uneventful, at least until the evening when one of the school dogs gave birth to puppies. Any birth at the school became a cause for wonder and celebration, so when the golden retriever named Betsy had a litter of puppies, the pages and some squires gathered around. Red showed up, and, when she saw the first puppy born, she sent one of the younger pages to fetch the vet. Everyone wondered what was wrong, but Red didn't say until the vet arrived. The puppies as they had emerged looked healthy enough, and Betsy took care of them.

Dr. Lundie arrived and started examining one of the puppies. "Is Wolf here?" he asked. When Wolf stepped forward, the vet said, "Congratulations you're an uncle."

"W-What!" Wolf managed to get out.

"Shadow has been an active boy. These puppies are half wolf."

There was some muttering from the assembled students. Red slapped Wolf on the back and said, "I knew that wolf would be trouble." As if on cue, Shadow nudged his way into the group. He growled slightly, and the pages backed up.

"Shadow just wants them to have plenty of room," the vet said. "You all have something to do, don't you?" The pages took their cue and separated to do their chores. "Wolf, you can stay behind."

There were five puppies, and Shadow took an interest in their wellbeing. After checking each puppy, he sat down nearby and kept an eye on them.

The vet said, "We seem to have a real problem—what to do with the puppies. Typically, you get the first choice of the litter."

Wolf exclaimed, "What am I going to do with a puppy? I already have too many animals."

"I don't know, but you have time to think about it. Mom will be nursing for a while. Perhaps you could give it to someone."

As soon as the Dr. Lundie made the suggestion, Wolf knew what he wanted to do. But he would have to wait until the time was right.

The Lion showed up and mused, "I see we're having a population explosion among the dogs here at the school. We have to do something to nip this in the bud. I don't know what to do yet, but we'll see that all the puppies are taken care of. I don't see that Shadow's status should change, but we'll have to do something. The state probably frowns upon wolf-dog mixes."

"You aren't going to neuter Shadow are you? It's not fair. He doesn't have any other wolves around."

"No, I'm not going to do that. Don't worry; we'll talk more about him later." The Lion returned to the palace.

Wolf had a lot to think about. Meanwhile, he did his best to make the puppies comfortable and keep them out of the way in the stable. He propped up a couple of boards to fence them in and placed out the finest straw he could find.

Despite what the vet had said, Wolf believed he would have no choice in where any of the puppies went. He had to make a case for what he wanted, so he went upstairs to his room, sat at his desk, and took out a pen and a sheet of paper. Then he started working on his arguments. Shadow did not join him for the night, and that was a rarity. Once he had his list made, he placed it aside and took up his other homework until time for lights out.

Knowlton

Chapter 37 ~ Pledge

It turned out Wolf did indeed have the pick of the litter, and the other four puppies would be adopted by knights. The puppies had to be adopted at just the right age, young enough that they could bond to their new owners. It was critical with wolves or wolf-dog mixes.

Bear helped Wolf select the best puppy for his purpose, and it turned out to be the runt of the litter, a small female with wolf markings. When the puppy was fourteen days old, Wolf took charge of it and started feeding it with a baby bottle. He didn't have much time because he didn't want the puppy to bond to him. He had enough responsibility handling Shadow.

Wolf carried the puppy tucked into his tunic for a good part of the day. When it came time for riding lessons Wolf saddled Pinto Bean then went over to help Grace with Nellie. Once Nellie's saddle was secured, he hung a cloth bag from it.

"What is that for?" asked Grace.

Wolf pulled the puppy from his tunic and held it out to Grace. "It's for her. She needs someone to take care of her."

Grace reached out gently to hold the puppy and clutched it to her breast. She held it for a long minute, rubbing noses with it. Wolf just watched her. The puppy nipped at Grace's nose and yelped. Wolf saw that Grace had tears and said, "You're crying. What's the matter?"

"I'm not crying. She's so cute."

"She's half wolf. She won't always be cute. Here, feed her with this." He handed her the baby bottle with the special formula in it. "Dr. Lundie will help you make more."

She leaned over and kissed Wolf on the cheek. "I can't take her. They don't allow pets."

"She's not a pet, and you're her guardian. You get to look out for her until she grows up and they decide what to do with her."

"I'll take care of her."

~

Grace handed the puppy to Wolf so she could mount her horse. He handed the puppy up to her, and she placed it into the bag and slung it across her shoulder.

"You have to name her."

Grace tilted her head and, without much thought, said, "I'll call her Lady Gray."

Wolf thought about it a second and said, "That's a good name. I like it, but why?"

"So she can be something I can never be." Grace turned her horse around and walked it out to her riding lesson.

"Now you've made her cry," Red said, walking up behind Wolf, leading Mary.

"You don't understand anything," Wolf snapped. He mounted Pinto Bean and trotted out to his lesson.

~

That evening, Wolf and his roommates met up in one of the turrets on top of the stables. They were just trying to enjoy the view, but Wolf didn't talk much. Wart said, "Hey Rabbit Breath, you're being awfully quiet."

Wolf glared at Wart and said, "It's Grace, she has a pretty raw deal. She gets in more trouble than I do."

"That's hard to do."

"No, I mean no one is nice to her. She doesn't have any friends."

Wart suggested, "She's too old to be a page."

"Willow was much older when she came here and started as a page," George said.

"Yeah, but she's like a big sister to the other girls," Harold observed. "I don't think Grace can be that. She's geeky-looking. I wish she was younger, and then she would be more like my sister. I can deal with her."

"I think you're missing the point," Wart interjected. "She doesn't even know what a friend is. She's always trying to protect herself. The only one who gets close to her is you, Wolf."

"I think she likes her puppy more than she likes me," Wolf said. "You're right about always protecting herself. She can be sharp-tempered. She's worse than Red."

"They would be a good pair for sisters," George said, laughing.

"She needs friends she can count on, and she isn't finding one among the other girl pages. I want you to help me with her."

"Well, if the Wolf wants help, we're going to give him help," Wart said.

"Agreed," Harold and George said.

~

At school, a couple of days later, Wolf, Harold, and George heard a commotion and ran to find out what was going on. When they rounded the corner in the hallway, they came to a large group of girls surrounding two fighters wrestling on the floor. Grace was one of the fighters.

Wolf, seeing no adults or squires around, grabbed Grace by her arms and jerked her off the other girl. The other girls, including the one Grace had been fighting, quickly moved out of the hallway.

Wolf let go of Grace. She turned and started to hit him when Squires David and Willow came running around the corner. David jerked Wolf away from Grace. Willow stopped in front of the girl.

"What is going on?" demanded David.

Wolf remained quiet, as did Grace, George, and Harold.

Willow asked Grace, "Did he hit you?"

Grace said, "No, he didn't hit me. He stopped me from hitting someone else."

Willow said, "Just what's going on here. I'd better get the truth."

Grace said, "Wolf pulled me off another girl."

"You admit you were in a fight?"

"Yes. Wolf stopped it."

"Why should I believe you? What were you fighting about?"

"It was stupid. I got mad."

"What's stupid?"

"They all gang up on me. They kept making fun of my face."

"I believe you, and it isn't right, but I'll tell you this, fighting is going to make it worse. You're going to have to find out what you need to do to get by peacefully. It isn't easy being a girl, and girls can be worse than boys."

"What do I do?"

"The only thing I can suggest is to do your best to make friends. If you go around making enemies of everyone who looks at you wrong, they'll eventually beat you down."

Squire David said, "Both of you are going to spread manure for two hours a day for a week. If anything else happens, I'll haul you before the Lion. Do I make myself clear?"

"Yes," Wolf and Grace answered. Dismissed, they ran down the hallway to leave the building.

Wolf felt very agitated. It wasn't good that Grace would fight girls much younger than herself. He knew from experience that the fighting wouldn't stop, and he didn't know what to do for her.

~

Lady Gray grew quickly and was weaned from the bottle after two weeks' time. Unlike Shadow, she could eat dry dog food as well as raw meat. Now that the puppy was a little larger, Grace carried her around more instead of leaving it in her room. Wolf noticed that Lady Gray proved to be an icebreaker for Grace with some of the squires and pages. He also found that Grace could relate to some of the squires, including Margaret.

However, some of the pages kept teasing Grace about her scars and her skinny appearance. This resulted in several more fights. Squire David assigned punishments harshly, setting the fighters to mucking stalls and hauling manure out to the pastures. The school had trucks to haul the manure, but there was always an excuse for pages to do it with wheelbarrows.

Grace worked her punishments without complaint. She saved that for when she was alone with Wolf. "Why am I always the one getting punishment?"

Wolf wanted to tell her that she stood out like a sore thumb, that she looked different, acted different, and that she always took exception when some of the other pages poked fun at her. Instead, he said, "One page gets you in trouble and you both get punishment, then someone else does it and you both get again. You're the only one being punished every time. It used to happen to me."

"Oh? What did you do?"

"I got some good friends to hang out with. Now it just doesn't seem to matter. I get in enough trouble on my own."

"Yeah, you have a reputation for trouble. The only friends I ever had turned on me."

Wolf looked up at her and said, "I won't."

"I don't believe you."

Wolf thought for a moment then said, "Be at peace with me and take my hands."

She reached out to hold his hands.

"I swear to you now that I will be your friend. I'll keep your secrets. I'll stand by you when I can, and I won't abandon you. On this, I place my honor among men and women."

She remained quiet for a moment. Then she said, "I believe you," and let go of his hands.

Knowlton

Chapter 38 ~ Willow: A Knight's Story

Spring was a time of excitement at the school. There were more field trips on the horses, for which the pages had to participate in all aspects of planning. It was not pleasant to be in the middle of the forest without a mess kit or a bedroll. The worst mistake was to forget a jacket or coat for the cold nights. The knights had little sympathy if they thought the page knew better.

The training was serious, and the results were often fun. There were always games to be played—field hockey was one of the best, being fast, and all could play. The squires frequently accompanied the pages on these excursions and paired off with the pages to teach camping skills. They also gave demonstrations of fighting skills. The best shows were provided by Willow, who would spar with several squires at once. The results were predictable; Willow would win. Bob and Bill, the twins, were her best competition.

Willow fought with an intensity that sent shudders down Wolf's back. He asked Red, "What is up with Willow?"

"Willow's getting ready for her big test, her Ordeal of Knighthood. She has to be ready for anything."

Wolf wanted to know everything. "What is the Ordeal? What's going to happen?"

"I think I'll wait and let you see it for yourself. You need to see it first. It will happen soon, just before our final exams."

Wolf was miffed, and no one else would explain it to him. Raven held the same opinion as Red.

Wolf had occasionally gone to Willow for advice on archery, but she had become unapproachable and distant. When she didn't fight, she meditated and did very little else.

The day of the big test came, and everybody assembled in the ballroom, the biggest room in the palace. The pages and squires had to sit on the floor, and the adults sat in chairs around the edge of the room. A side door opened, and Willow walked into the room and advanced to the center where the Lion stood and started the proceedings by announcing that the purpose of the day would be to test Willow's knowledge as part of her Ordeal of Knighthood. The Lion then sat in one of the chairs next to the wall.

Prof. Bonham started with a series of questions about advanced math. The questions were way above Wolf's understanding and were hard, even for Willow. When the professor satisfied himself with her knowledge, he sat down, and then another teacher approached her and started asking questions about law. This continued for about a half hour before he seemed satisfied and sat down. The next subject was history, followed by art and music.

The examinations went on for six hours. Pages and squires came and went. Only Willow stayed the entire time. She answered every question to the satisfaction of her teachers. When there were no more teachers or questions, a big cheer came from the squires, while the knights and teachers clapped politely. Wolf felt nervous. While he knew it to be a good school, he had not realized how much was taught in the classes.

As the crowd dispersed, Wolf asked Red, "Is she a knight now?"

"No. She hasn't even started her Ordeal. That begins tonight when she stands vigil, and, in the morning, she begins her real Ordeal. She must not make a sound from now until the Ordeal is over."

~

In the morning, the school gathered near the lists, where ten knights lined up, waiting for Willow, dressed in white cotton fighting outfits. As Willow approached the first knight, he took a swing at her with his fist and connected with the arm she raised to defend her head. She returned a blow to the side of the knight's head, causing him to fall down.

The second knight hit her in the stomach, knocking the wind out of her. She doubled over and then quickly stood up. He tried a roundhouse kick to her ribs, but she deflected the blow and returned a hit with the heel of her palm to his forehead, causing the knight to stagger.

The third knight attacked with a series of punches, and Willow blocked them. Then she attacked. She continued fighting the knights. After facing eight knights, she had delivered as much pain as she had received. Some of the knights were hurt. One held his arm; another limped; and a third remained on his knees doubled over, having vomited. Willow's cotton outfit was stained with blood, mostly hers.

Then Whisperblade stood before her holding her long, curved sword. Willow's sheathed sword had been stuck in the dirt in front of Whisperblade. There was no time for her to grab and draw her sword as Whisperblade's sword came swinging around at her head. Willow ducked and fell backwards as the sword came swishing over her. Whisperblade came after her and kept swinging, as Willow kept jumping backwards. It was a very uneven match, or so Wolf thought. Whisperblade chased Willow around in a large circle until suddenly Willow turned and stood her ground. She delivered a powerful kick to Whisperblade's sword hand, breaking her grip. The sword flew into an awkward spin, landing about thirty feet away. Whisperblade ran to grab it, and, when she turned back, Willow had her sword out of its sheath and at the knight's throat. Whisperblade dropped her sword, nodded her head, and then stepped back.

Raven stepped in front of Willow and handed her a dagger. She took the dagger and dropped her sword. He pulled out his massive hunting knife and started stabbing as he bore down on her. She blocked his blows with her dagger. Next, he tried an overhead stab. She grabbed his wrist and fell backwards onto the ground, pulling the Raven off balance and above her. She placed her feet into his belly and kicked him over her. He landed hard on his back, and before he could recover, she jumped on top of him with her knife at his throat. Raven dropped his knife and yielded.

The fighting was over. Willow had passed her Ordeal. Whisperblade placed a hand on her shoulder, and she stood up. Willow shuddered a moment then started to cry as Whisperblade led her into the palace. Everybody else returned to the palace to eat lunch.

~

Nobody saw Willow for the rest of the afternoon. Just before supper, a summons came to go to the ballroom where chairs had been set up in rows on two opposite sides of the room facing each other. At one end of the room stood a small platform.

Once everybody had been seated, the doors at the end of the room opened, and the knights marched in two by two. They were all in their best uniforms and tunics. They had their swords girded on and carried their shields. Once they were in the room, they sat in the two innermost rows facing each other.

The Lion came through the door. He walked the length of the room to the platform, stepped up on it, and sat down. The door opened one final time, and the Lion stood as a signal for everybody to stand up. Whisperblade walked in followed by Willow. Willow had dressed in a new uniform and tunic with no ensign over the left breast. They marched to the platform where Whisperblade stepped to one side, and Willow stood in front of the Lion.

"Willow you are here for the final Ordeal of Knighthood. It is a grave obligation you take upon yourself. Do you wish to proceed?"

"I do."

"Who sponsors this woman into knighthood?"

"I do," Whisperblade answered.

"Is she well trained? Is she worthy to be a knight? Will she uphold her duty?"

"I have trained her well. She is worthy, and she will uphold her duty," answered Whisperblade.

Willow knelt, and the Lion pronounced the oath, "Do you Willow swear to uphold the laws of your country? Do you swear to do good for mankind? Do you swear that all worthy people shall have your attention? Do you swear you will support and defend the helpless to the extent of your life?"

Willow answered, "I swear these to be my duties as a knight, even to the extent of my life."

The Lion stepped off the platform to stand directly in front of her. He drew his sword and held it in front of himself, point up. "By my right as a liege knight, I confer upon you the title, the rights, and the responsibilities of knighthood." He brought the flat of his blade down on her left shoulder, raised it and placed it on her right shoulder, then returned it to her left shoulder. He withdrew and sheathed his sword. He reached down, took her right hand with his, and said, "Arise, Lady Knight Willow, as a knight of the Order of the Hatchet." He motioned for her to turn around, and when she did, there were cheers from the assembled gathering.

When the cheering ended, Willow turned back to face the Lion. He reached over and picked up a sheathed sword from a stand. He presented it to her still in the sheath. She accepted the sword and slowly withdrew it from the sheath. She held it point up, turned around, and extended it above her head, and everybody cheered. She turned back to face the Lion, sheathing her sword. Raven and Eagle knelt on each side of her and strapped spurs to her feet. Lady Jane came forward bearing a shield covered with a cotton cloth, and Whisperblade moved to stand next to her. Together, they pulled the cloth off the shield, revealing a dark red field with a green willow tree. This would to be Willow's ensign as a knight, and she would always be identified by it.

Willow mounted the shield on her left arm, then taking up her sword, started to walk out of the room. All the other knights pulled their swords and raised them in a salute, forming a tunnel under which she had to walk. When she had left, the knights sheathed their swords and followed her out, the Lion last.

The room was abuzz with talk. To Wolf, the ceremony seemed too short. He had expected it to be more like a big, long church ceremony, and he asked Red about it.

"They like to keep things short and sweet. She earned her knighthood, so there's no point torturing her and everybody else with a lot of useless ceremony. Tomorrow is David's turn. You'll get to see it all over again. Let's go eat."

They went to the dinner hall and their separate tables. Once everyone stood at their seats, the Lion came in, followed by all the knights. Willow, the last one to enter, took her place at the far end of the head table. The Lion gave the blessing, and everybody sat down.

~

Wart said, "I don't think I could fight like she did. I'd be slaughtered. Whisperblade tried to take Willow's head off."

Grace said, "I could do it. I've seen worse. A little blood doesn't scare me—at least not my own blood. It's the examinations that scare me."

Everybody stared at her a few seconds before Wolf put in his two bits. "What scares me is being a fool in front of the teachers and then looking like one after the knights finish with me. Did you see that fist to her face? I bet she has a shiner tomorrow. They're all out to get a piece of you."

Harold said, "Willow's tough. I could do it. Well, at least I think I'll be able to when I reach that age."

"I could do it, too," George added. "The schoolwork is hard, but I'm managing. I don't mind all the bruises. It just makes me want more training so I can fight back. I hope Willow sticks around. She'd make a good teacher."

Chapter 39 ~ Preparations

Wolf forgot his birthday. Whisperblade gently reminded him one morning during self-defense class that he had turned fifteen. Then the word got around to all the other pages, and he received a lot of ribbing.

Whisperblade gave him a pair of large, leather saddlebags with hand-tooled flaps, suitable for Nudge for when he was grown. Raven gave him a book on poisonous and medicinal plants. Red gave him a pair of mittens made from rabbit skin. They were made with the fur on the inside and the leather on the outside and had been waterproofed. The mittens had long gauntlets so they covered the cuffs of his coat. His hands would be warm when on top of the snow-covered mountains at summer camp. A cake with his name on it was cut during lunch.

He had another surprise in the afternoon when he received a message to report to the Lion's office. He dreaded the summons, especially since he couldn't remember doing anything to get into trouble. He arrived to see Whisperblade, along with Raven and the Lion. The Lion motioned for everybody to sit down. "We're waiting for a couple of people. Wolf, do you know why you're here?"

Wolf looked at Whisperblade, but her face was blank. "No, sir."

At that moment, the door opened and Red entered escorting an old man. The Lion stood, and the other three adults did the same. The Lion moved out from the back of his desk and invited the man to sit in his chair, saying, "Welcome, Judge Stevens. I hope you bring good news."

"Indeed, I do. Is this the young man, Wolf?"

"Yes, sir," Wolf answered.

"Yes, Your Honor," the Lion prompted Wolf.

"Yes, Your Honor," Wolf repeated.

"Good, why don't we all sit down," Judge Stevens said.

Red turned to leave, but the Lion said, "Squire Amara, this involves you, too." Red grimaced but returned and sat down.

The judge started, "As a judge, I sometimes get to do something that's good and wholly satisfying. This is one of those times. I've interviewed Miss. Whisperblade, and I believe she's capable of adopting Wolf."

The judge turned to face Red. "Miss Amara, this is a great responsibility I'm going to ask of you. Do you desire to be a sister to Wolf? Will you guide him, as he grows up, to the best of your ability?"

"Yes, Your Honor."

"Good. I normally discourage single parent adoptions, but I see that Wolf has a father figure to help him grow into manhood. Now, young man, do you wish to have Whisperblade as your mother? You will have to love and obey her, as any son should do for his mother. This is for keeps. She will be your mother for life."

"Yes, Your Honor."

"Then I approve this adoption." Judge Stevens pulled a paper out of his briefcase and laid it on the desk. "This is the adoption paper. Miss Whisperblade, if you will sign here," he indicated a line on the paper.

Whisperblade signed her full name with a flourish. She turned the paper back to the judge.

Judge Stevens took it and turned it towards Wolf. "It is customary for the child to sign their name, if they are old enough to understand what is going on, and you are indeed old enough."

Wolf stood up and took the pen the judge offered him. "Your Honor, what name do I use?"

"Son, use the name you wish to be known as."

He looked at his mother and saw that she had a big smile. It almost unnerved him. He couldn't deny that he loved her. He felt everyone's eyes on him. He turned from his mother and faced the document. There was her signature, Aurora Walker Whisperblade. He sighed and signed the paper, Wolf Sureblade.

The judge took the paper and signed it. He offered the pen to Red, who signed as a witness, as did the Lion and Raven.

"Congratulations, Wolf. You now have a real mother. Miss Whisperblade, you now have a real son."

"I think a libation is in order," the Lion said. He produced a bottle of grape juice and glasses for everybody.

After they all had finished the drink, Judge Stevens shook Wolf's hand and then gave Whisperblade a kiss on her cheek. Raven reminded Wolf and Red that they had schoolwork and chores to attend to, so they left. When they were halfway down the hallway, Red whacked her fist into Wolf's shoulder.

"Ow! What was that for?"

"That's for being my brother."

~

Wolf had just finished an exam in history and felt good about it. He sat at lunch with his friends. Shadow had gone somewhere out in the fields surrounding the school. Wolf received a note to report to Mrs. Parker, his history teacher, in her classroom, so he left. There wasn't anybody in the hall since classes were over for the day. When he stepped into the classroom, the lights were out, so he would have to wait for Mrs. Parker. He felt sure she would be along in a minute, so he turned around to switch on the light.

Wayne stood there surrounded by his minions, Ralph and Edger. Wayne threw the first punch right into Wolf's belly. Wolf was prepared this time and tensed up hard, and the punch had no effect. He returned a punch to Wayne's chest, but it was blocked.

The other two pages grabbed Wolf's arms and held them back while Wayne rained punches into his belly. It started to get painful, and Wolf thought about crying for help when his roommates burst into the room and joined the fight. Harold tackled Edger, and George ran into Ralph, causing both to lose their grip on Wolf. Wart was a little slower, and Wayne swung his arm around to punch the younger page.

Wart dived out of the way, and Wayne fell on him, helped by Wolf's foot hooking his. Wolf dived on the squire and delivered two punches to the small of his back. Wayne rolled off Wart, and out from under Wolf, and managed to scramble to his feet. He barked, "Get out. It's not too late. Let's scram."

Wayne and his friends were gone, leaving the Secret Brotherhood of the Wolf to lick their wounds. There weren't any wounds that would show to get them in trouble. They picked up the classroom, and that's when Wolf discovered his belly muscles were beyond sore and were going to get worse as the adrenaline wore off. They retreated to the stables to check on Wolf's wounds.

"This has gone on too long," Harold declared. "Wolf is getting killed."

"How did you know they were going to ambush me?" Wolf asked between breaths.

"Well, when Mrs. Parker walked in for lunch right after you left, and Wayne wasn't there, we figured you might need help. What about you? It's going to be hard to hide those bruises," George said.

"I gave as good as I got. I'm sure he's going to be sore a long time."

"You're avoiding the subject," Wart said. "Whisperblade is going to know something tomorrow morning."

Wolf had a sudden idea, "Not if you deliver a couple of blows during self-defense. It'll cover up the bruising. You've got to hit me hard."

"Okay, but what do we do about Wayne and his buddies?" Wart asked.

"We get them at summer camp. We get them early."

"We'll make plans. It seems like nothing else will stop him."

~

The next morning at self-defense, Wart delivered a punch to Wolf's belly, and he doubled over. Whisperblade, seeing what happened, stopped the exercises and went over to face Wolf. "You didn't block that punch. You're better than that." She stepped back and assumed an attack position. Wolf assumed a defensive position.

Whisperblade's fist came at his belly, and Wolf flinched in anticipation of the blow that never came. "Wolf, kick my hand." She held her hand out shoulder high.

Wolf attempted to kick, but his belly muscles refused to cooperate, and his kick wasn't high enough. "Wolf, report to my office after you shower."

Wolf knocked on Whisperblade's door, and she beckoned him in and motioned for him to close the door. "Wolf, you're hurt. I don't know what happened yesterday." When Wolf started to tell her the standard story, she held up her hand to stop him. "Save it. You aren't a good liar. Now go to the nurse for a checkup."

Wolf left the knight's office, knowing that somehow he had crossed a line and he had to find a way to stop it.

~

It was only a week until mid-May, the end of the school year. Wagons left every morning to go to town and returned with new supplies. Wolf went on many of the trips. Mary and one of the other Percheron mares were teamed together to pull a wagon with Red as the driver. When they arrived at the rail depot in town, they had to load the wagon with heavy boxes of dried fruit that were piled up on the loading dock. Wolf and Red had to lift them together to place them in the wagon. On their return to the palace, they had to unload the boxes.

Fortunately, there were plenty of squires to help. In the dining room, pages opened the boxes, taking the dried fruit, which included apples, pears, mango, raisins, cranberries, and more. They placed them into small bags of waxed paper to use at summer camp. Then the fruit was packed back into the same boxes to go back to the train station. The purpose was to make the portion sizes manageable and the packaging more environmentally friendly.

The same routine was done for everything that would to be transported to camp: tents, sleep rolls, mess kits, and other supplies. Squires and pages went around with checklists verifying that everything was in order and that there would be enough to go around. To Wolf, it seemed like supplying an army. Wolf noticed when they returned to the train depot that supplies had disappeared, probably loaded onto a train car to be transported to the small village near the summer camp.

Then Wolf received a message telling him to report to the blacksmith who worked at the school part-time. The blacksmith showed him several bundles of bamboo and informed him it was the right kind for making arrows. Wolf couldn't be happier. There was more than he could use for the whole summer. The blacksmith informed him he wouldn't be the only one making arrows. Some squires and several other pages had expressed an interest in learning the craft. Wolf packaged the bamboo into manageable bundles and prepared them for shipping to camp. He also made sure he had enough thread and glue to manufacture the arrows.

The head chef had Wolf participate in the butchering of some geese and turkeys at a nearby ranch. For a few hours work on the ranch, he was given the opportunity to collect a large bag of white goose feathers and brown turkey feathers to use. He had enough feathers for the summer and some left over for trading. When he left the ranch, he had an appreciation of the hard work that went into raising large birds.

Wolf and Red had to attend to Raven's needs for all his camping supplies. Raven, as an instructor, had a lot to prepare. He had a large tent for himself with a table and other furnishings. There were school supplies for his outdoor classes, and his horses had to have all their gear ready.

~

Wolf knew Grace wasn't used to the work, and she struggled with it. Wolf and his friends helped her when they could, which wasn't very often. She told them it was a lot easier than living in the streets, not having to worry about her next meal. She didn't complain about the work and threw herself into it until she collapsed from exhaustion, and that earned her a trip to the nurse's office.

Wolf went to check in on her, "Grace, what were you trying to do?"

"I want to do my share of the work. It's the least I can do. Besides, I need to strengthen myself up."

"You're not supposed to kill yourself!" Wolf exclaimed. "We're supposed to help each other. The knights tell us that all the time."

"I've never had anybody help me. I always had to do all the work for them."

"And what did it get you?" the nurse asked.

Grace thought about this a moment and said, "Nothing."

"I think a little rest and some chicken soup will do wonders for you," the nurse said. "Wolf, I will send her to you when she is recovered."

Wolf went back to work. He had a lot to ponder about Grace. The first thing, she had to lose the title Scarecrow in body if not in words. He resolved that she had to build muscles on her bones, and he would help her to do it. He had noticed that she didn't eat much, and she avoided fruit and vegetables. That's where he would start on her. First, he had to consult with his roommates. He needed their help.

That evening during supper they were in line loading their trays, Wolf placed a banana on her tray and then he scooped a large spoonful of spinach onto her plate. She gave him a dirty look, but continued onto their table. When they sat down Wolf poured a generous amount of vinegar on his spinach and did the same to hers. Then he took a large forkful of his and ate it. She did the same. "This isn't so bad," she said.

"You've got to eat your vegetables if you want to keep up with us," Wolf said. "Whisperblade insists on it."

"Lady Jane says the same thing," Grace said.

"Maybe she's right," Wart said. "My mother always makes me stay at the table until I've finished mine."

"There you have it, we stay at the table until we finish our vegetables," Wolf pronounced.

Grace frowned and said, "I'm tired of men telling me what to do. You're no better than all the others." She stood up and stormed out of the dining hall.

Wart whispered to Wolf, "Go get her. Get her before she gets away. Apologize to her. Do whatever it takes. Run!"

Wolf caught up with Grace in the hallway as she headed for the stairway. "Wait, please, can we talk? I wasn't trying to hurt you. Please, I don't want you passing out again. I'm worried about you. I really, really, like you."

Grace stopped and turned around. "You like me?"

Wolf whispered, "Yes."

They stared at each other a moment then Grace threw her arms around him. "That is the nicest thing anybody has ever said to me." Then she added, "The others would tell me they love me, and then they'd hurt me."

"I won't do that. I swear."

"Don't swear. They did that too."

"Can we at least be friends? I'd like it."

"I'd like it too."

"Let's finish supper. I'm still hungry."

"Yeah, I am too."

Chapter 40 ~ Departure and Arrival

The end of the school year approached, and many students left to go home for the summer. Wart, Harold, and George went home for short visits, but returned before time to go to camp. Wolf used the quiet time to be with Grace and show her more about riding horses. Now that she knew the basics, he was able to talk her through the finer points. He knew Grace used the time to learn from Bear and the Lion how to work with Lady Gray, who was growing bigger. The puppy followed her wherever she went.

Wolf spent a lot more time with Nudge and had him mounted with a saddle and saddlebags. The saddle was very old and worn out. He found it in a forgotten storeroom in the basement of the stables, and no one claimed it. Nudge didn't seem happy about the saddle, but he finally accepted it. The school blacksmith informed Wolf that the saddletree, the wooden part of the saddle that gave it shape, had been broken. It could be used to get Nudge accustomed to the feel, but not for riding.

The visiting farrier informed Wolf it was time for Nudge to get his first set of shoes. Nudge, almost a year old, had grown very large. Wolf struggled to get the horse to hold still for the farrier while he trimmed the hooves and nailed on fitted shoes. Once the shoes were on, Nudge remained very unsettled for the rest of the day, trying to shake the shoes off. Wolf had to pay the farrier out of his personal account.

Before Wolf knew it, it was time to leave school and travel to the summer camp. All the wagons were brought out to the palace courtyard and loaded high. Since the trip to the train depot was on relatively flat ground, the horses had no trouble pulling them in teams of two. The wagons left the school for the train depot first. After a long, slow ride, they arrived at the depot. Wolf and Grace went to work partially unloading the wagons so they could be rolled onto the train's flatcars when it arrived. An hour later, the adults riding horses arrived with their squires.

Then the train arrived with loud blasts from its horns and stopped at the platform where the wagons could be rolled on to the flatcars and secured. The excess baggage was stuffed into another boxcar. Essential supplies were placed in the passenger cars. The train moved forward several hundred feet and stopped so the horses and school dogs could be walked into their boxcars. Once the train had been loaded, everyone lined up for a head count, after which all climbed aboard.

~

That evening the squires broke out a deck of cards, and Wolf, seeing an opportunity to make a few dollars, asked to join in. He just managed to hold his own when Grace whispered into his ear that she could do better. Wolf gave her five dollars in change and let her take his place. He regretted it when she lost on her first two hands. Then she won her money back on the next hand. She lost a hand then she started bidding big. The squires in the game kept matching her bid until it came time to lay down their cards. Grace won with a full house, three jacks and two fours. She collected her money and withdrew from the game over several objections from squires wanting to win their money back.

"How did you do that?" Wolf asked.

"I know a few tricks," Grace whispered.

"You cheated?"

"No, no. They would beat me if I did, or worse."

"I don't think that would happen. But you could probably be kicked out of school. What tricks were you talking about?"

"I watch their faces very carefully, their hands, too. I see if they squirm. People are funny like that. Anyway here is your money."

"Keep it. Just teach me some of those tricks."

That evening, all the girls were chased forward to the front passenger car with Whisperblade standing watch over them.

The rest of the long trip remained uneventful except for when they stopped and Raven and Red got off with their horses and headed for town to the forest service office. Wolf was disappointed when he wasn't allowed to go with them. The train arrived at the small village through which they had left the mountains nine months earlier. There, the long process of unloading the train began.

The wagons were loaded and sent on ahead while all the other supplies were stored in a nearby barn rented for the purpose. The wagons would return to fetch more supplies.

Wolf and Grace headed to camp riding in the first wagon. The majority of pages without horses rode in the first group of wagons, as did Bear and the quartermaster. They would supervise the initial erection of the tents and the stables.

Wolf rode shotgun with the driver, and Grace had to sit on the other side, holding her puppy. Henry, the senior squire, took time to show Wolf how to drive the wagon. The horses responded to the reins and verbal commands. The hard part was knowing how to control them to keep the wagon on the wheel track. A lot depended on the horses knowing how to follow the track.

When they came out of the pass into the valley, Grace gasped. "It's beautiful. Is this where we're going?"

"Just a little further up the valley, about three miles," Henry said. "It's not where we were last summer. We're letting the ground at the old campsite rest."

They arrived at the site after an hour, and the three of them unloaded the wagon on the top of a hill. Then Henry started back towards the hamlet leaving Wolf and Grace with Shadow, Nudge, and Lady. More wagons arrived, unloading their supplies and leaving pages and a few squires. Bear called everybody together and gave them assignments for the setup of the camp. He also issued leather work gloves to everyone.

The first order of business was to erect the quartermaster's tent. It had to be set up first to provide protection for the supplies. With a little help from the others, the pages were able to pull the tent into shape. Then they hauled all the supplies inside.

~

More wagons arrived every hour. More squires remained, and more tents were erected. The second tent erected was the Lion's. His would be at the center of all the other tents. Next to it stood the main tent. Wolf had a part in rolling out the canvas and rope and seeing that it was all in position. It would be erected once enough adults were present and some horses were available to pull the poles and canvas up. Bear had already moved on to organizing the construction of the stables. It would take a week to build sufficient covered space for all the horses, and they had priority over the students.

By nightfall, the camp looked livable. The horses had been put out to pasture. Darkness put a stop to all work, and the students built a large fire to roast hot dogs for supper. The weather remained nice, and bedrolls were laid out. The students and most adults slept in the open under the stars. Of course, Whisperblade and Lady Jane had established a separate area for all the women and girls to sleep in on the opposite side of the camp from the boys. The moonless night was dark, and Wolf fell asleep under the stars with Shadow lying by his bedroll.

~

After breakfast, the next morning, Grace told Wolf about a strange encounter she'd had during the night. "I was shaken awake by a hooded woman, who held a finger to her lips as a warning to be quiet. When I got up, she placed a cloak around my shoulders. Then I followed her into the woods.

"She reached up and lowered her hood. She was a large woman with a weathered, friendly face, and she said, 'Grace, I came here to talk to you.' I asked who she was and how she knew my name, and she said, 'My name is Maude. I saw you come into the valley with Wolf. He's a good boy isn't he?'"

Wolf wanted to say he'd also met Maude, but he didn't interrupt Grace. "When I agreed, she said, 'Good, trust him, he won't lead you wrong. Grace, what do you want?' I was surprised because nobody has ever asked me that before. I told her I wanted to get rid of my scars, and she touched my face with cool fingers.

"She said, 'I think they'll eventually get better. What do you want? What would you do if you could?' I told her I'd like to be like Willow or Whisperblade and save people. She said, 'And so you shall. You seek a hard life. What you've suffered is just a preparation for what is to come. I'll do what I can for you. Come to me when you're ready to decide on this way of life. It will be soon. You've lost so much of your life to darkness. It's now time for you to shine brightly.'

"I asked, 'How will I find you?' But she just smiled and said, 'When you're ready, you'll find me.' A while later, I woke up with the sun on my face, and I wasn't sure if it happened or was just a dream. Then I realized I was wearing the cloak she gave me."

Wolf looked at her a minute and said, "That's Maude for sure."

"How did she know my name?"

Wolf flapped his arms. "How does she know anything? She lives alone in these mountains. She's crazy. She sees things. She told me Shadow would be my friend. What else did she tell you?"

"It was a long night. I don't remember."

Wolf stared at Grace for a long time. Finally, Grace asked, "What?"

"Your face, it's changed."

Grace blushed and asked, "How?"

"Are you wearing makeup?"

"No. Not since leaving school. Why? What's wrong?"

"Your scars, they're gone."

Grace felt her face and shuddered. "It's not possible. She couldn't have."

"It can't be real. I don't believe it either. We've got to show somebody."

Grace and Wolf finished their breakfast and went to see Lady Jane. They showed her that Grace's scars had disappeared, and then Grace told her how it had happened.

Lady Jane said, "I think Maude has done more for you than any doctor could ever do. You are truly blessed."

"But who is she?" Grace asked.

"I would say she's just a mountain woman, a hermit, but everybody she touches is somehow changed."

"She didn't change me," Wolf said.

"I don't mean physically. I mean here and here," she said and tapping her heart and then her head.

"I don't feel different," Wolf said.

"When did you stop thinking about running away?"

Wolf thought for a moment and said, "Oh."

"When you stopped thinking of running away, you started to feel better about yourself."

"How did you know that?"

"We talk among ourselves, the knights and teachers. We need to know the students. Raven is very observant."

Chapter 41 ~ The Fall of Grace

Life in camp started to remind Wolf of the previous summer, and, after two full days, Red and Raven rode into camp. By that time, Wolf had managed, with Wart's help, to set up Raven's tent as well as their own. Raven then had a conference with Wolf and Red. He told them his plans for the summer and invited them to assist in the teaching. Wolf wanted to know why he was being asked. He thought it was just his duty as a page to help.

"Your responsibility will be greater than last summer. You don't have all the makeup work to do, and this responsibility has to be freely taken. It would be my pleasure to have you as a teaching assistant. Will you do it?"

Wolf said, "Oh yes, sir."

"Good. So what have you been doing with your free time?"

Wolf snorted, "What free time? All I've done is work on setting up camp."

"True, but you've also been spending a lot of time with Grace. It's good that you're helping her. She needs it. If she weren't under Lady Jane's care, I would take her on as a page."

"She was visited by Maude, just two nights ago."

Raven and Red exchanged glances. "We saw Maude yesterday morning at her cabin," Red said.

"That isn't possible," Wolf responded.

"Well, it is, if she had a horse," Raven said.

"Did Maude tell Grace anything?" Red asked.

"I don't know. Grace didn't say, but she made Grace's scars disappear."

The knight looked hard at Wolf, and then he sighed and said, "I always suspected Maude could do something like that. She once told me I would become a knight, but it would cost me most dearly."

Wolf and Red looked at him for a few seconds, and then Red asked, "How old were you?"

"Eighteen. She's very old if that's what you're asking."

"Who is she?" Wolf asked.

"She is one of the mysteries I haven't been able to solve. She supports herself by writing stories and other things, but I don't think she needs anybody's help. I think she's older than these mountains. Maybe she's a dream. She appears only to whom she wants to appear."

Raven changed the conversation to his lesson plans for the summer. It turned out Wolf would have a big role supporting Red. There were a lot more squires and pages this summer than the previous summer, students who had not been exposed to Raven's nature and survival courses.

~

Wolf and his roommates spent a lot of their free time planning pranks to play on squires. One of the most innovative pranks involved putting itching powder in their trousers; powder that Wolf had learned to extract from the dried seedpods of a weed bush he had located in a nearby glen. A few squires had an uncomfortable day in the saddle. Wolf made the powder weak so the squires would just be uncomfortable and not outright miserable. The plan had been not to invite retaliation.

The squires however were a clever bunch and used some distractions to lure Wolf and his friends away from their tent so they could powder the bedrolls. The pages ended up having to wash their rolls so they spent the night freezing. The stakes escalated until the knights had to warn them that their antics were getting out of hand. The pages knew that the squires had not ratted on them and wondered how the knights knew. Wart finally figured it out. The knights had once been squires and pages. Of course, they knew what was going on because they used to pull pranks themselves. When the pages ended up on the losing end, Raven chuckled and said, "Tisk, tisk."

Wolf approached Grace about helping with a prank, but she refused. "I can't do it. I can't get in trouble."

Wolf tried to make his case. "This won't get you in trouble. Nobody will rat on you. Besides it'll be fun."

Grace said, "You don't understand. I can't risk being kicked out, and I can't stay. I'm in enough trouble as it is. Please don't ask me."

"What's the matter? What trouble? Are you all right?"

"Yeah, it's just that I don't feel right. It's like I'm being watched."

Wolf, feeling sure about himself, said, "Nobody here would threaten you. Squire Wayne is the worst, but he can't mess with you."

Grace seemed exasperated, "It isn't anybody here."

"Have you told anyone?"

Grace snapped at him, "No ... and don't you dare say anything."

"You're really spooked. What is it?"

Grace looked down, "I keep having a dream ... I'm going to die."

"No way. It isn't going to happen. You're safe here."

"They're going to find me."

"Who?"

"The gang."

"What gang?"

"The gang that did this to me." Grace pointed to her face where the scars had been. "They won't stop hunting me. I've got to run."

"No! You're safe here. The knights will protect you."

"They can't. You don't know this gang. You just can't leave them. Nobody can help me. The school will kick me out if they find out about me. If the gang finds me, they'll hurt me or someone else."

"Why?"

Grace screamed, "Because I killed him! I killed Jacky! I'm a murderer!"

Wolf felt faint and his knees buckled.

"Please, please, don't tell anybody."

Wolf, still shaking, replied, "I won't, but who is Jacky?"

"Jacky Grimm; he runs drugs in Richmond. He made me carry them. I owed him a favor, but he kept demanding more and more. I killed him to escape. That's why his gang did my face."

~

They didn't talk for the rest of the day. Wolf had a lot to think about. He had promised not to tell anyone, and Whisperblade had told him not to betray her trust. But if what she said was true, she would be the target of revenge. She needed help, and he had to figure out how to get it for her.

~

Wolf awoke when Shadow pulled on the sleeve of his nightshirt. He sat up with a start, and Shadow growled at him and walked to the entrance of the tent. Wolf pulled on his trousers and shirt and followed Shadow to the stables. There he found Nellie missing and discovered a note Grace had left him, asking him to take care of her dog, Lady. It soon became apparent that Grace had taken her tent and bedroll, saddled Nellie, and left the camp.

He ran back to his tent and quietly put on his boots and tunic. Wart, who slept lightly, awoke and asked Wolf what was happening. Wolf handed him the note and mentioned the missing horse. He told Wart he had to find Grace and bring her back. Wart said he would help, but Wolf told him to tell Raven what was going on. He grabbed his knife and bow and headed back to the stables, where he saddled Pinto Bean. Shadow led the way, and they followed Grace's trail.

~

Wolf rode his horse through the dark forest, chasing his prey. It would be light soon, but the darkness still reminded him of his first night in the woods a short year before, a creepy night, with danger lurking behind every tree and up around every turn of the trail. The feelings raced back bringing a panic sweat.

Those days were long gone, he thought, not happy the same feelings reappeared at this time after all his training. He calmed himself by thinking of his new friends he had made, especially the gray wolf, Shadow.

Pinto Bean, the little horse with a big heart, maintained an easy pace. Shadow could easily outpace the horse, leaving him lost. Last year he saved the wolf from a vicious trap and had been paid back for that good deed many times. The wolf followed the tracks of the horse and rider in a way that the boy could not.

They arrived at a swift stream and Wolf pulled his horse to a stop to allow it to refresh itself. He could see the bottom of the rocky stream even in the twilight. Kneeling down to drink, he plunged his face in the freezing water.

What was I thinking, he lifted his numb face out of the water. refreshed and alert. The first time he encountered a mountain stream he had been thrown in and felt the freezing death. It's different this year, *now I am doing it on purpose*, he smiled to himself.

At midmorning Wolf and Shadow found the spent horse.

Wolf dismounted from Pinto Bean so he could check out Nellie and search for Grace's tracks. The exhausted horse could do nothing more than walk, she had been ridden too hard and not cooled down properly; any more work would cause the horse's muscles to cramp. Wolf unsaddled and hobbled Nellie; he couldn't do more for the mare. Hopefully the horse would recover by the time he found Grace.

Wolf searched for the tracks left by Grace and found something else, somebody big, following her.

The End

Special Preview

The author wishes to demonstrate his gratitude that you have read his work and certainly hopes you have enjoyed <u>Wolf Sureblade: American Knight</u>. He has been hard at work continuing the tale of Wolf Sureblade and those of his noble companions.

Please proceed on to this complimentary chapter from the next book in Wolf's story.   It is still in a rough form and may differ slightly from the way it will appear in the finished book, and so it is a peek inside the development process.

Courtesy of Kent Knowlton

Wolf Sureblade: Page Wolf
Chapter One - Decisions

Wolf rode his horse through the dark forest, chasing his prey. It would be light soon, but the darkness reminded him of his first night in the woods a short year before. Then, it had been an ominous feeling, with danger lurking behind every tree and around every turn of the trail. That feeling raced back bringing his breath up short. Those days should have been banished, he thought, not happy that he still had the same feeling after all his training. He calmed himself by thinking of the friends he had made, including Shadow.

Wolf maintained an easy canter to preserve his horse's endurance. Shadow, the large gray wolf who led him, could have outpaced the horse, leaving him lost. He had saved the wolf from a vicious trap the year before, and had been paid back for that good deed many times. The wolf could follow the tracks of the horse and it's rider in a way that the boy could not; the wolf's sense of smell followed the path that the Scarecrow had taken.

They arrived at a swift stream and Wolf pulled his horse to a stop so it could drink and refresh itself. He could see the bottom of the clear stream even in the twilight. As the boy knelt down to drink he plunged his face in the freezing water. "What was I thinking," he said aloud, as he lifted his numb face out of the water. Even still he thought it was refreshing and it would keep him alert. The first time he had encountered a mountain stream he had been thrown in and it felt like freezing death. A lot had changed in a year, "Now I am doing it on purpose," he smiled to himself.

The Scarecrow rode her horse at a gallop throughout the night. She couldn't see her path in the forest, so she kept her head down and trusted Nellie her horse to run a straight and safe course.

When the sun arose in the morning, her horse, slowed down, exhausted. It should have come as no surprise that when they came to a stream the horse balked and refused to go on. The Scarecrow almost fell off when the horse stopped. She tried to urge the horse on but the lathered mare ignored her commands. She dismounted and tried to pull the horse by its reins but again the horse refused to move.

The girl realized she had pushed the animal too hard. She

collapsed to the ground and started crying; she cried for the horse and she cried for herself. She had run away and taken the horse and now she had more trouble than ever. She knew there were gang members out there who would kill her. They had tried once and had almost succeeded except for the intervention of the mysterious man who called himself the Raven. Now she had become a runaway and a horse thief. Most of all she had betrayed the trust of the only friend she had ever known, the gentle boy named Wolf.

Wolf: who had saved the life of a real wolf, because it was the right thing to do.

Wolf: the adopted son of the fierce sword maiden known as the Wolverine.

Wolf: who listened to her and had never given away her secrets.

It shocked her that she told Wolf her biggest secret; that she had murdered a man. She had seen the reaction on his face and it surprised her that he had told no one.

Now she just wanted to escape from everything and in a way, she had. Lost in the middle of the forest, in the mountains, with a horse that could no longer run, she had nowhere to go. The Scarecrow felt lost, alone and very afraid; the ultimate escape would come soon.

"Grace, why are you crying?"

The Scarecrow jumped up shocked out of her skin. She spun around to confront Maud. "Where did you come from?"

Maud looked at Grace with a warm smile, "I've been here the whole time. Why are you crying?"

"I'm lost."

"You are lost but not the way you think." Maud reached out with her hand and rubbed Nellie's nose. The horse calmed down and started to breathe easy. Turning her attention back to Grace she said, "Why don't you come with me? I will show you your way." She took Grace's hand and they strolled through the trees leaving the horse to drink from the stream.

|

At midmorning Wolf and Shadow found the spent horse.

Wolf dismounted from Pinto Bean so he could check out Nellie and search for Grace's tracks. The exhausted horse could do nothing more than walk about. The horse had been ridden too hard and had not been cooled down; any more work would cause the horse's muscles to cramp.

Wolf unsaddled and hobbled Nellie; he couldn't do much for the mare. The horse should recover by the time he found Grace.

Wolf searched for the tracks left by Grace and what he found surprised him; there was somebody else, somebody big, the footprints were larger and deeper. Soon he determined the person walked besides Grace and not behind. A good sign, unless Grace had been captured and was being held against her will. But with the pace of the tracks being even and no sign of a struggle, Wolf relaxed.

Shadow urged Wolf to follow the trail Grace had left, so he remounted Pinto Bean and walked him in the direction indicated.

A short while later the Raven and his company, following the trail that Wolf had left, found Nellie. The knight, not surprised at the horse's condition, grimaced. Grace didn't know how to conserve her horse.

His reading of the signs left him less worried. He had confidence that Wolf would do the right thing, but he remained disturbed that the page would leave camp without talking to him.

Red, Wolf's sister, was angry at Grace for getting Wolf to run away with her, or so she thought. She had become convinced that the Scarecrow had played with his mind and that it was her job to protect him. Something about the Scarecrow rubbed her wrong. She acted different and didn't fit in with any of the other students; so Red wanted a piece of the page.

The Lady Knight Wolverine saw Red's dark mood and knew the cause of it. She couldn't do anything about it until the two girls met again. Then she would have to act fast to stop any hostilities.

Lady Jane knew Grace as well as anybody else at the school and guessed the dark nature of the girl's secret. She knew the terrible nature of it and she also knew it could come out in a way that could hurt her. She would do everything in her power to protect the girl.

|

Wolf followed Grace; he wanted to help her to come back to the school knowing it to be the only place she would be safe. He and Shadow followed her trail for a quarter hour until he came to a small clearing where he found Maud sitting on a log. She looked up at him as he came into view, and Shadow trotted over and sat down beside her.

Wolf dismounted and set his horse free. He walked up to the woman and saw several scars on her face, scars that had been on Grace's face until a few days ago. He could think of no reasonable explanation for how the disfiguring scars had been transferred from the girls face to the woman's face, but there they were.

He asked the mountain woman, "Just who are you? Where is Grace?"

"Don't you know me? No. It's not important. Grace is on a quest to find her way, to find out what she wants to be."

"What is that?" Wolf asked.

"She will be what she wants to be. She will find out soon."

"What about me?" Wolf asked.

"Do you know what you want to be?"

"Yes... no... I haven't decided," Wolf answered, not so sure of himself.

"You are still young. You shouldn't decide yet. Trust your heart; you will make the right decision. Wolf, there is something I must ask of you."

Wolf stared at the woman a minute. "What is it?"

"There is a trapper nearby. He kills animals. He almost killed Shadow once."

Wolf's eyes went wide, and then he turned red with anger, "He trapped Shadow last year? What do you want me to do?"

Maud said, "You must stop him."

"You want me? Why?

Maud's face and voice went hard, "Because of the murders he has committed against the peoples of the forest."

"Who? What people?"

"The wolves, the rabbits, the raccoons."

Wolf went slack jawed, "I've killed rabbit."

Maud took a deep breath, "You did not waste them. You did not kill for their skin and discard their bodies. You did not kill what you could not eat, you respected their souls." Maud paused to put her hands on Wolf's shoulders, "You must stop him."

Wolf seethed, "Where is he?"

Maude pointed down a dear path, "Hurry, he has been alerted and

315

is seeking to flee." Wolf hastened to follow the narrow path, and Maud shouted behind him, "Be wary."

Wolf and Shadow ran down the path, a regular deer run with lots of tracks. Shadow led the way. They went over and around two small hills before bursting into a clearing. The trapper dressed in camouflage, knelt, packing his bedroll into a knapsack. Next to him a pile of animal pelts lay on the ground. Wolf stopped short, while Shadow growled as he advanced toward the man.

The man had his back to them and without even looking reached for his rifle, which leaned against the pile of fur.

Wolf not even aware of when he had strung his bow now aimed a flint tipped arrow at the man. "Stop or I'll shoot." As soon as he had said it, Wolf realized his nervous teenage voice just didn't have the force for his brave words. He found out the truth of it as soon as the man turned to point his rifle at him.

"Why? You're just a boy!" exclaimed the man. He laughed and barked out, "Drop the bow, or I'll kill you."

Wolf didn't back off. He just stood there holding the bow at full draw. His arms started to shake, and the palms of his hands were getting sweaty. A drop of sweat rolled down his brow into his eye, making him blink.

"Call off your wolf," ordered the trapper. "Or I'll shoot it."

Still Wolf didn't move or speak.

"Well it seems we have a decision to make. You put your bow down or I decide whether to shoot you or the wolf. I'd rather shoot the wolf. He's worth something. I can get a pretty penny for his hide."

Wolf needed no more prompting, he moved to make himself less of a target and let loose at the same time. He didn't count on stepping on a trap. The jaws slammed hard against his ankle and he fell to the ground, the arrow flew off useless, and he screamed.

He tried to stop screaming and feel for the trap, he heard Shadow yelping in pain. He saw out of the corner of his eye the man swinging his rifle like a club. The wolf circled, looking for an opening, but stepped on a snare trap. At the first jerk of the wire on his rear leg, the wolf went into a violent snarling fit, helpless to attack the man.

The man took the opportunity to come and stand over the boy.

Pointing his rifle down at him, "Don't move, it makes the pain worse. The good thing about traps is they catch all kinds of prey, including nosey little boys. I ain't afraid of no wolf. They're my business. I'll take care of him soon enough. "

Wolf stopped thrashing and looked up at the man with hate and fright on his face. He gasped out, "Who are you?"

The trapper gave a toothy grin, "Just an honest hard working guy, I'd be doing a lot better with you gone, but I'm no murderer. I'll let you go, but the wolf stays here. Understand?"

"Go to hell!" growled out Wolf, as he struggled to keep from screaming.

"Which is where you'll be going, if you don't leave." The man reached down and jerked Wolf's hunting knife out of its sheath. He held it up, testing its edge with his thumb. "That's a pretty fearsome weapon you have. I think I'll use it to skin the wolf."

Before he could even think, Wolf reached over his shoulder, grabbed an arrow out of his quiver, and plunged it into the man's calf.

The man yelled, dropped the knife, and jerked down to grab the arrow, but Wolf stabbed him again, this time embedding the barbs of the arrow head into the calf. He could not pull the arrow back out. He kicked Wolf hard in the ribs and would have kicked again, but he was attacked by the flashing form of Grace, jumping onto his back. She wrapped her arms around his head blinding him.

The man had dropped his rifle to reach for the girl. She shifted her arms down to lock them in a choke hold around his neck. The man couldn't break her hold, so he reached for her head. She kept shifting her head around trying to avoid his fingers and he backed up until he smashed her back into a tree. Grace didn't let go, so the man smashed her again. Again she wouldn't let go. A third time he smashed her, but still she didn't let go.

The man started to slow down. He gasped for air his face turning gray.

A pair of hands grabbed Grace's shoulder and a woman's voice shouted for her to let go. Grace recognized Lady Jane's voice, she let go and fell off the back of the man and into the woman's arms.

The man's arms were being held by the Raven and the Wolverine.

They forced the man, face down, onto the ground. The Raven placed a knee in the trapper's back and pulled his hands together while the Wolverine tied them. She then tied his ankles together.

Squires Bob and Bill set to work on opening the trap on Wolf's leg. The springs on the trap were strong and it took both boys to squeeze them enough to let the jaws drop open.

Wolf felt immediate relief from the excruciating pain. As soon as he tried to move he again felt more sharp stabs of pain. He pushed himself to a sitting position and saw the blood soaked through his trousers. Sucking in a gasp of air he felt a sharp attack of pain in his side where he had been kicked. He felt weak and Bill lowered him back down. Looking over at Shadow he saw that Red had released him from the snare and he licked at his wounded leg. Shadow arose and walked over to Wolf and started licking his face. Wolf didn't complain. Grace shivered in the comforting arms of Lady Jane, her back sore from being smashed against the tree, and her face had been scratched by the trapper's rough hands.

With the trapper secured, the Raven went to Grace and asked her how she felt. She lied, telling the knight that she was alright, despite feeling like she had been pounded with sharpened sticks on her back. The knight looked at the back of her shirt and saw small amounts of blood. He placed a hand near one of the spots and Grace stiffened. "I suspect you will have some severe bruising. Report to the nurse when we return to camp. Let Lady Jane attend to the bleeding."

The knight walked over to Wolf and after a quick glance eased off his boot and took his knife to slit Wolf's trousers up to the knee. The page had heavy bruising on his shin with two cuts where the jaws of the trap had cut through the boot and dug into the skin. The man took the first aid kit from his horse's saddle bags, used some antiseptic to clean the wounds, and wrapped the shin with gauze. Satisfied he spoke, "Can you bear the pain?"

Wild eyed from the stinging of the antiseptic, Wolf whispered, "Yes, Sir." He coughed and winced from the pain from his ribs.

The Raven felt Wolf's ribs and found the tender spot. He pulled the boys shirt up and examined the wound. Satisfied the boy had no broken ribs. "Do you think you can stand?"

"Yes, Sir." The knight helped Wolf to his feet, and the boy put weight on the foot. When he tried to walk, stabs of pain shot up his leg. With a shaky voice he said, "I'll be all right, Sir."

The Raven mused out loud, "What is it about today's youth that you must bear pain by yourself?" The Raven said, "You have some explaining to do."

"Yes, Sir." Wolf took in a shallow breath. He faced the Raven and the Wolverine square on. "Sirs, I would have waited, but I had good reason to think Grace was in immediate danger, and she didn't have the experience to ride a horse that hard. I made sure you would follow, but I had to look after her; she's my responsibility because I keep her secrets."

The Raven thought a moment and seemed to accept Wolf's story. He turned to Grace and said, "And now how about you young lady?"

Grace looked around at the squires and said, "Do I have to tell everybody?"

The Raven glanced at the Wolverine and nodded to her. The Wolverine took Wolf by the arm, walked him over to the squires, and herded them all over to the other side of the clearing, leaving just Lady Jane to listen to the two of them.   "Lady Jane stays; she's your guardian."

"Sir, I'm afraid. If I stay at school, people will come to kill me. Students would get hurt. "

"Why do they want to kill you?"

Grace looked down, "I murdered one of them."

The Raven sucked in his breath and said, "I suspected something like that."

Grace looked back up in into the eyes of the knight, "How?"

"Since the day I saved you. I put the pieces together; the degree of violence they were doing to you had a reason. I found a picture of you in one of their pockets, marked with the cuts you were to receive. They weren't going to stop at cutting just your face. Mr. Rosencrantz helped me in finding out what they were doing."

"And you let me stay?"

"Yes, it is part of what I do, save lives. You are no less than myself; would you have been safe if you hadn't killed the man?"

Grace looked back down and mumbled, "No, they were going to kill me, I overheard them."

"Why would they do that?"

"Because I saw a drug deal that went bad. I would have been a witness."

"And your refusal to use pain killers?"

"They had tried to hook me on those drugs."

"We will get you help for that. You don't need to suffer."

"What about the creeps who want to kill me?"

"I will do my best to see they don't. I can be most persuasive. Will you stay with us?"

Grace stared at the knight a long time then nodded. "Yes, Sir."

"Good. It's going to be a long night and we have a lot to discuss."

The Raven attended to the trapper, extracting the small barbed flint arrow head from his calf. Wolf assisted in the removal by sponging the oozing blood and handing the Raven the needle and thread. "It is a good thing he hunts only rabbit, a full sized arrow would have cut your calf real bad."

"I'm going to get you, boy," seethed the trapper. "I always trap my prey."

"No," said the Raven. "You're going to face a judge first." The Raven and Wolf ignored the trapper and his threats for the rest of the night.

The squires built a large camp fire, fixed coffee, tea, and cooked some rabbit with vegetables. Red rode out to retrieve Nellie, since the horse now had time to refresh itself. The squires sang and told stories around the camp fire.

Red had to tell about Wolf's initial encounter with Shadow and how he had been afraid of being eaten. She seemed to enjoy telling that story to Grace.

Grace for her part told a story about how she had made a gang member look stupid in front of the whole gang. It got laughs from the squires, but Wolf knew she paid in pain for the prank.

After everybody else went to sleep Grace had a heart-to-heart talk with the Raven and Lady Jane. The Raven started, "Grace we can do a lot for you. We can protect you. We can teach you to protect yourself, but if you run away from us we cannot do very much. You can do whatever you want to do. You will have our support; we will not turn you away. Grace what do you want to do?"

"What do you mean?"

"What do you want to do with your life; do you want to stay in school, do you want to go to another school, are you going to return to the street? We can't stop you from running. Again, the question is what do you want?"

After a long silence Grace spoke, "Sir, if I thought I could, I would become a knight."

The Raven smiled then asked, "Why do you want to be a knight?"

"I had a dream; somebody I care for dies and I couldn't do anything about it. I want to be able to do something."

"You can. You've shown me several things today: you want the save lives, you are not afraid for your life, you are not out for revenge, and there are people you care about. You have what it takes to become a knight. It is a hard life; it is harder than anything you have ever dreamed about. It will be painful. Your back is a small taste of that pain. You have to want it very much."

"I do want it. I want it so much; I'll risk staying, even if it means they find me. I need this; there is no other place for me to go."

"Good. Lady Jane what do you think?"

"I think she is sincere." The lady faced the girl, "Grace, the life you would be embarking on is not for everybody, I did not choose it."

"But you are so good with weapons, I've seen you. You're perfect with a bow."

"I can defend myself. Being good with weapons is not the same as being a knight. It is a hard life, as a knight you will work on your own, but when it's necessary you must be a leader. I chose a different path."

"I couldn't be a lady."

"You will be. A female knight must be a lady just as a male knight must be a gentleman."

Grace looked down, shook her head, and looked up, "If that is what I have to be, I'll do it."

Lady Jane smiled, "Good, you'll have to talk to the Lion and if he agrees I will begin your training in the fine arts."

The Raven said, "You will have to remain a page for one year before you're eligible to be a squire. It is the same as any other older student must do. Lady Jane will be appointed as your foster mother."

Lady Jane added, "That is something you don't have a choice in. I've already acted as one for you, so you know what to expect."

"I'm not a very good kid."

Lady Jane smiled, "I consider that a challenge. You had better get some sleep; we have a long ride tomorrow."

Grace didn't dream.

The party of riders took their time returning to the camp. Grace had to ride Wolf's horse, Pinto Bean, with Wolf sitting behind her. He couldn't put his feet into the stirrups and had to balance, he couldn't place his arms around Grace. The trapper rode on Grace's horse, his hands tied to the saddle horn.

When the party of riders returned to camp in the late afternoon Wolf reported to the nurse's tent to have his leg treated with antibiotics and a stitch applied to the worst cut. His leg had been bruised, as well as his ego. He now understood what Shadow had gone through the year before.

|

Grace reported to the Lion. First she had a chance to refresh herself, than reunited with Lady, her wolf-dog, which had been watched by Wart.

Grace, now ready, reported to the main tent, where the Lion conducted camp business. The Lion expected her and moved his finished his work aside. He walked with her over to his tent where they sat down at the table.

"I hear you had quite an adventure."

"Yes, Sir, I was afraid I would bring trouble to the school. I felt I had to get away before anybody got hurt, but it seems I've just caused more trouble."

"You've been very little trouble, besides, we're used to trouble. I hope your back recovers well."

Grace mumbled, "I figure I'm dead."

"You look very much alive to me."

Grace grimaced. "I mean they are going to kill me."

He replied in a low voice, "I know what you mean. There isn't a knight here who doesn't have an enemy or two. The Raven has had death threats from several people who are capable of murder."

Grace said under her breath, "I've committed murder."

"I know." The Lion patted a thick folder on the table, "I have copies of the police reports about the man in question, and the recommendations from the district attorney. They say the man survived his wounds, and had later been murdered by other members of his gang, the same ones who attacked you to cover it up. You did not commit murder. You defended yourself, and you almost paid for it with your life.

What you did back in the woods was very brave. You didn't give up. You saved Wolf. The Raven has told me of your desire to protect others, that you would be a knight if you could. I'm going to give you the opportunity to not just graduate but to become a knight."

Grace's eyes went wide open then she furrowed her forehead. "You knew this all along. Why are you doing this for me?"

"Because you know what it means to be a victim. You, more than anybody I know, should understand what it will mean to be a knight, to save someone else.   You will of course have to stay in school longer."

Grace still couldn't believe it, "You're asking me to become a knight?"

"Yes."

"What does it take to become a knight?"

The Lion leaned back in his chair, paused a minute then said, "Remember the Ordeal that Willow underwent?"

"Yes, Sir."

"It represents the tip of what you must learn. It is both physical and mental. The real test is keeping your wits under the most extreme conditions. If you pass the Ordeal, you will have what it takes to be a knight."

"What if I fail the Ordeal? Willow almost lost her head."

"You will not be allowed to undergo the Ordeal if we don't think you will pass. I'm now going to ask you, do you want to become a knight?"

colophon

Brought to you by Wider Perspectives Publishing, care of James Wilson, with the mission of advancing the poetry and creative community of Hampton Roads, Virginia.
See our production of works from ...

Edith Blake
Tanya Cunningham-Jones
　　(Scientific Eve)
Terra Leigh
Ray Simmons
Samantha Borders-Shoemaker
Taz Waysweete'
Bobby K.
　　(The Poor Man's Poet)
J. Scott Wilson (TEECH!)
Charles Wilson
Gloria Darlene Mann
Neil Spirtas
Zach Crowe
Jorge Mendez & JT Williams
Sarah Eileen Williams
Stephanie Diana (Noftz)
the Hampton Roads
　　Artistic Collective
Jason Brown (Drk Mtr)
Martina Champion
Tony Broadway
Ken Sutton
Crickyt J. Expression
Lisa M. Kendrick
Cassandra IsFree
Nich (Nicholis Williams)
Samantha Geovjian Clarke
Natalie Morison-Uzzle
Gus Woodward II
Tanya Cunningham-Jones
Patsy Bickerstaff
Catherine TL Hodges

... and others to come soon.

We promote and support the artists of the 757
from the seats, from the stands,
from the snapping fingers and
　　　　　clapping hands
from the pages, and the stages
and now we pass them forth
　　　　　to the ages

Check for the above artists on FaceBook, the Virginia Poetry Online channel on YouTube, and other social media.

Hampton Roads Artistic Collective is the non-profit extension of WPP and strives to simultaneously support worthy causes in Hampton Roads and the creative artists.

www.ingramcontent.com/pod-product-compliance
Lightning Source LLC
Chambersburg PA
CBHW070044030726

47506CB00002B/333